SEPARATE CHECKS

MARIANNE WIGGINS

SEPARATE CHECKS · A NOVEL

RANDOM HOUSE · New York

"Millie and Hesh" first appeared in *Fiction International*
(St. Lawrence University, Canton, New York), Number 14 (1982).

Grateful acknowledgment is made to the following for permission to reprint material
from previously published works:
Little Brown and Company: Quotation from *New & Selected Things Taking Place*, by
May Swenson.
CBS Songs: Portion of the lyrics from "Try a Little Tenderness," by Harry Woods,
Jimmy Campbell and Reg Connelly © 1932 (renewed 1960) Campbell Connelly &
Co. Ltd., London, England. All Rights for U.S. & Canada Assigned to CBS
Catalogue Partnership. All Rights for U.S. & Canada Controlled by CBS Robbins
Catalog, Inc. All Rights Reserved. International Copyright Secured. Used by
Permission.

Library of Congress Cataloging in Publication Data
Wiggins, Marianne.
Separate checks.
I. Title.
PS3573.I385S4   1984   813'.54   83-17644
ISBN 0-394-53255-4
Manufactured in the United States of America

For the Daughters of
FANNIE KOKINOS
(1878–1976):

MARY ANTHONY KLONIS (1924–1981)

JOHANNE FRANCIS WIGGINS
MAHINDRA PRAKESH LYTTLE
LEEANNE COTTLE WALLACE

LARA COURTNEY PORZAK and
"SCOOTER"

"Morto un Papa, se ne fa un altro . . ."

—ITALIAN PROVERB

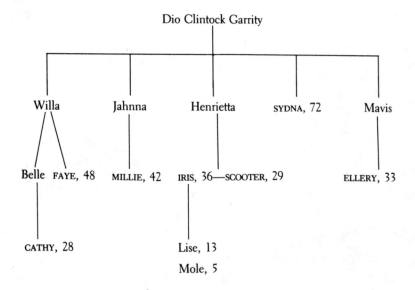

Dio Clintock Garrity

Willa Jahnna Henrietta SYDNA, 72 Mavis

Belle FAYE, 48 MILLIE, 42 IRIS, 36—SCOOTER, 29 ELLERY, 33

CATHY, 28 Lise, 13

Mole, 5

CONTENTS

SEPARATE CHECKS

1

MYSELF AND
OTHER MEMBERS
AT THE CELEBRATION

IN THE SUMMER OF 1955, when I was seven, Mavis and her male friend Uncle Alex decided between dry martinis on a cloudy day that they could teach me how to dive into a swimming pool. I remember this because I stood for hours w/ my toes clenched on the concrete ledge of a deep end, staring into blue-green water, and it was the first time that I knew exactly what it is to drown. I know what it is to drown a lot right now, but that first time stands out in my memory because Mavis was there, and her male friend Uncle Alex, and half the members of the Screenwriters' Guild, and (I think) Douglas Fairbanks, Jr. Also it was while Mavis and I were in California, and we went there only once. To Hollywood. I met David Niven and what I thought were some regular American kids, and everyone told Mavis she looked just like Norma Shearer. We ate in restaurants every night, and everywhere we went people asked Mavis if they could take her picture and they asked her to pose for them, sometimes w/ me but usually w/out. The kids I met turned out to be a bunch of little shits. One of them tried to have sex w/ me (I think). Anyway I saw a lot of things I'd never seen before in California. I learned to dive, too, but not right then. What I did right then was I stood for hours w/ my toes clenched and my arms arched overhead, and I stared into the blue-green water and I thought and thought about a moment when the water would come rushing up so happy in its greeting like a big old lapping dog, but the moment never came. Instead, I turned deep purple like the evening and I sort of faded into twilight where I stood, silent and empty, at the deep end, while Mavis and her friends and Uncle Alex fell into the water dead drunk and forgot about me. Much later in my life, in my freshman year at college, I compared learning how to dive w/ how I feel when I have to write something. Even now I feel a little sick like my air's been cut off. The prospect of real life did not present itself to me as a series of writing assignments. I thought I could get by on the spoken word and a few well-chosen quotes from other sources. Everybody thinks that as the daughter of a famous writer, I should just be able to sit down and write. People who don't have famous parents are really stupid on that subject. See, the story we have here is not the story of someone who just decides to take this writing business up because she needs a hobby. The story we have here is someone who is not in real good mental health being told that she should write things down so she'll get better. The people telling someone this are people on the staff here at a psychiatric clinic. I'm this someone that they're telling. My name is Ellery.

It wasn't as if I didn't want to write things down before—I did; just like I wanted to make that dive that afternoon in California. It's the depth that's so unholy scary, and the silence, and the solitude. Where *are* you under water, except all by yourself? I'd like to know how they think my writing these things down can help—I've *been* all by myself, been by myself all of my life except for Mavis and the household. Most people have a family, we had a *household*. I never understood about the servants. I thought because they lived w/ us, I was related to them. I thought we had a lasting kinship, but after Mavis died they never did anything to remember me. Toward Huan Hee our cook, especially, I felt a strong attachment, and I invited him to be my father when we had our Father's Day at the private school Mavis sent me to. I wanted him to be my father when we had our Father's Day when I was eight—and again each year until I was twelve. That's when I started having problems at the school, when I was twelve. Mavis nixed it every time, the thing about Huan Hee. *She* came. *She* came w/ the other fathers. Some fun, huh? Dressed up like a man, too, in a suit, and smoked a pipe for the occasion. Some balls, that Mavis, huh? Some balls.

The trouble at the school started in the sixth grade w/ the diving lessons. It wasn't even trouble w/ my grades or trouble w/ behavior, it was this eensy-weensy problem in Phys. Ed. w/ diving lessons. I did everything else real fine—kick turns, scissor kicks, treading water— but I refused to dive, and then I started making up stories why I couldn't so they wouldn't force it on me. I said I had one kidney and the impact of the water on my body in the dive might traumatize my sole surviving organ (I read that in a magazine). When that story didn't work, I said I couldn't dive because my father killed himself by jumping off a bridge and I got nauseous every time I looked into the water from the diving board. This happened to be true, but we had to have a meeting among me and Mavis and the Phys. Ed. teacher and the school psychiatrist anyway. This was a private school, so they always went the extra mile to iron out any problems. Mine was an overactive imagination, they decided, which needed chan-neling. I thought this meant they were going to give me something so I could switch from channel to channel in my imagination, which didn't make a lot of sense, because I did that anyway. What it meant was that I needed an "outlet," and when they suggested I write stories down instead of telling (little) lies, Mavis laughed. It sounded more like the sound somebody makes if they've just been hit between the shoulder blades w/ a blunt instrument, but her mouth was turned up at the corners, so we took it for a laugh. She told the school psychiatrist that Ellery (me) could never sit still long enough to write a story. Ellery (me) might *start* to write a story but she would never finish it. Ellery needed something more active, something that would burn off Ellery's nervous energy. *Lessons* of some sort is what she had in mind—mime, ballet, gymnastics . . . or a part in the school play. Well, as it happened, the school play was coming up, and I was told I should audition. I was never sure I got the part because I was the best one to try out for it or because Mavis pulled the strings. She was the raison d'être for everything in those days, you see? She and her sisters were these women who just knew how to do everything and left me bobbing in their wakes. Anyway, the part was Peter in the play *Peter Pan*. Even though I had to cut my hair off, I loved the part—especially the crowing. I guess I have a gift for playing boys and rough-edged girls, because when I grew up, my first important part at Yale was as Frankie in *The Member of the Wedding*. Frankie is a motherless, scrawny, unloved sort of girl just coming into puberty, and I played her in New Haven when I was twenty. I had to lose sixteen pounds and cut my hair for that part, too, and bind my breasts, but it got me noticed in the press. You want to know the funny thing about it, though? Mavis didn't come. Not to *Peter Pan* and not when I played Frankie. All my aunts came to my plays, though, and all my cousins, even way back when I was in the sixth grade—but not Mavis. Some mom, huh? I guess she didn't look upon my stage career as the kind of thing that she could show up for all decked out like a man.

The other thing about that diving business was it provided my first lessons as a patient of psychiatry. I mean, there I was in the sixth grade talking to a psychiatrist, and there was nothing awfully wrong w/ me and the whole time I thought there was. I was real concerned there was a normal way of being and I wasn't being it. I was concerned about people asking me all the time to tell the truth and my not really being able in all honesty to pin truth down. I was concerned about being unnaturally alone. When I did go crazy, these things didn't concern me one bit. I marched into my breakdown w/ exquisite certainty that I was finally being sane. I felt quite serene, for once, and in the company of great men, mostly poets. I heard things other people didn't hear and in a way that other people couldn't hear them. It was very sad and beautiful. I experienced the whole thing in a total void, a total absence and protection from all doubt. It was lovely in a clear and fragile way. Not that I miss psychosis; don't get me wrong. It's just that it existed w/ this one absolute Truth that sheltered me from other truths. Among the other truths it sheltered me from was that the man I was going to marry was shot and killed in New York City last September. The year before, in an almost parallel approach, a person had shot and killed John Lennon, uptown. Around the anniversary of Lennon's death, I started getting weird. Then, the week between Christmas and New Years, I had what is called a "woman's" breakdown, which is to say the kind that happens over love, not finances. Since then, my cousins have been great, the way they come to visit me. They look at me as if they think they got off easy, as if it might be written somewhere one of us was bound to break and it's their manifest good fortune it was me, instead of one of them. What is it like? they ask. What really happened? Will you ever be the same? Well, I tell them, it was like a trip on a Greyhound bus between Trenton and Los Angeles w/ no stops. What really happened? The bus was hijacked to Disney World, in Orlando. Will I ever be the same? Are you kidding? People who've imagined a lengthy philosophical discourse w/ Mickey Mouse are never really quite the *same*. Am I angry? Am I blue? Am I more hyperactive than before? Sure, you've got it, Jack. That's me. Fill me up w/ things to be, I'll be them. Don't misunderstand: the women in my family don't know why I'm angry w/ them yet. If one of them—Faye, for example—were to sit me down and say, "Ellery, what is your . . . *problem?*" how could I answer? History? How can you be angry at *history*, it's like being angry at a wall. A wall's a real dumb place to go w/ anger, or for understanding. A wall's a place that people are stood up against and shot. A wall's a place where suspects are led in and someone asks you to identify the one you think is guilty. Well, I think my mother's family are the guilty ones. I think the way they lived their lives and never told me anything is why I'm in this mess I'm in. Can I identify them? Sure. I've got them memorized by heart: first one is Grammar. Grammar was the Mother of Us All. Next come her children—Willa, Jahnna, Henrietta, Sydna and my mother, Mavis. They're all dead, except Aunt Sydna. Then next come all the other members who are still alive—the daughters of the first five daughters—my cousins: Faye, Millie, Iris, Scooter, Cathy.

I have two theories why there are no men in this.

The first theory is that males born into our family were exposed at birth; and the second theory is we ate them.

Grammar always said we ate them.

She said that's the only thing that men are good for and compared them to French pastries she called "petty-fors."

She was an awful bitch, that Grammar was.

She was my grand mah-ma, you know.

My mother's side.

I never met my father's side.

I never even met my father.

Grammar could have eaten anything—she had that look. Some people look like they could chew you raw, while other people look like they would have to cook you first.

Grammar looked like she would have to cook you first.

Mavis said Grammar always had bad trouble w/ her teeth.

Mavis said good teeth are a sign of money.

I always had grand, wonderful teeth, so Mavis also said good teeth are a sign of breeding.

I had a slight space between my two front teeth before I got my braces, and I could spit liquid through it, so I used to have spitting contests w/ my cousin Iris. Sometimes we used grape juice. Aunt Henrietta didn't want us spitting grape juice at the dining table, so we spat it sitting up on top of her Packard. Aunt Henrietta's Packard was a semiautomatic w/ hydraulic clutch and we decided that's what we were going to be when we grew up.

Semiautomatic.

Scooter was Iris's sister and she sucked her thumb, and so did Cathy. Both of them wore braces on their teeth.

I've always hated Scooter's teeth, the way she smiles.

Her teeth are small and even and they look like they were knit.

My other cousins, besides Scoot and Iris, are Millie and Faye.

All of us, all us cousins are what you'd call a close-knit family. We're what you'd call the perfect little baby teeth on the face of life.

Anyone reading this will wonder why there are no men:
We ate them.

I had another cousin, Belle, Aunt Willa's first daughter, whom I never met.

Belle was thirty years older than I am, and she shot and killed a man, and then she went to prison. After that she poisoned herself by eating great quantities of Queen Anne's lace. Everybody says I look like her.

The man she shot and killed was her daughter Cathy's father, and Cathy is my second cousin.

I like Cathy's teeth better than Scooter's, because even though she wore braces, they're still crooked.

All of Cathy is crooked.

All us cousins are expected to be vastly capable, and none of us is allowed to break. Everybody used to say that Cathy was the runt of the litter and if anyone of us were going to break, it would be her. That's a joke, because here I am, and Cathy has more men than any of the rest of us. . . .

My Aunt Sydna had a man once, Mr. Ingres.

He was in government, and they got married and then he had an accident and died. After that, Aunt Sydna turned into a lesbian, the way a frog prince turns into a frog. It happened almost overnight, I'm told, before any of us cousins were born. I have a picture of Sydna when she was young, and it didn't change the way she looked. In fact, she looks better now. Her birthday is in August, and this year she'll be seventy-three. I always send her orchids. She delights in getting orchids. She says she loves their colors, which remind her of the Gurkhas, and she says she loves their labia.

Sometimes I have to count to figure out how old Mavis would be if she were still alive, and it's sixty-nine. She was my mother but mostly she was a famous mystery writer. She'd taken her baccalaureate at Somerville College, Oxford, in '34 and thereafter she believed she was a native Briton. This is Mavis being a native Briton: "Pet and I put by at grotty pubs and steamy kaffes while on the Continent for Frog food." Pet was the name Mavis called my father.

In addition to Pet, Mavis had a set of Bedlington terriers she called Jarvis. Pet, to his credit, hated them. They never shat the way most dogs do. They just got sick in a shitty way. Whenever they were expected to be good and make *you know* Jarvis & Jarvis excreted Bedlington treacle on the rug. Pet was allergic to their treacle, so Mavis decided to divorce him. On the way to the Hôtel de Ville to obtain their divorce (they were living in France), her British Land-Rover broke down. Pet hated her Land-Rover. He was always having to push it downhill to Monsieur Pepin's to get it started. So Pet told Mavis she wasn't the only one who wanted a divorce. Between her Bedlingtons and her Rover, he said, he had had it. Everything she owned made messes. If the Rover were a dog, he shouted, it would be the kind that shits on the rug. Mavis thought that was pretty funny, so she put straight by a grotty caffe w/ him for Frog food and they ended up making love. They got their divorce, anyway, a few months later, but Mavis always told this story to explain to people how she ended up conceiving me: she was quite drunk at the time.

I don't think she ever told Pet she was pregnant or that I existed. He jumped off the Pont-Neuf into the Seine when I was ten.

You can imagine how I felt: the Pont-Neuf was my favorite bridge.

The summer I was in Paris w/ Iris in '65, and she was in her last year of Art History at Sarah Lawrence, and I was seventeen and *not* a virgin, we decided the Pont-Neuf was the best bridge, the most beautiful, especially at night, and we would linger on it and I would think that Pet might have stood *là* or *là* or *là* in the same place that I was standing. . . .

Swimmers never found him. Divers, really. *Divers* is the Frog word meaning "varietal," as in varietal meats: livers, kidneys, sweetbreads.

Mavis said that Grammar sucked her teeth and lived to be one hundred because she ate a lot of organ meats. I used to think organ meats were things that grew like mushrooms inside church organs and could make you holy. I used to think the sign FILL WANTED was put up by his family because Phil had run away.

I could never bring myself to run away from Mavis, because Mavis was not the sort of woman who deserved to be embarrassed. She was very thin, and all her crimes were bloodless. Once, I think it was in *Merry, Bloody Merry*, she actually exsanguinates a victim in a warm tub at the cocktail hour. Beyond that, she was bloodless in her writing. From my mother, nothing ever bled to paper as from Dostoevsky. Everything w/ her was safe and solved and easy. Life w/ her was always off to somewhere, like passing through a trellis or a wicket. She always smelled as if she'd just-come-in.

Everybody says that before 1949 she talked more to the two Jarvises than she talked to anyone. After 1949 she had a private secretary named Bother to whom she dictated her mystery novels. She had another private secretary named Dolores who came in twice a week and did the correspondence. She had a woman who kept house for us named Cooper and the cook, Huan Hee. She had tons of money, which she earned all by herself, and tens of "uncles" who visited w/ luggage. She wrote twenty-seven books. She had four older sisters and each of them was named after a man—Willa for President McKinley, Jahnna for General John A. Logan, Henrietta for Henry Ford, and Sydna for her Uncle Sydney.

Willa was the oldest, and she served as a lesson for the rest of us because she allowed herself to be carried off by a foreigner who made crazy love to her, then later beat her. We were not supposed to let that happen to us. We were supposed to be like Mavis, for whom life was vastly effortless, a series of exercises in enormous ease. Even when it came to having me, Mavis had no problem whatsoever. It was like "shelling peas," she said—an expression I later found out she borrowed from the play *The Women*. When it came to having me, she had Mr. Robert Lehman Alexander-*deah*, her obstetrician, simply put her out: he shelled her in the dark. They brought me around to her when she was conscious, and the first time I saw Mother, *both* of us had just-come-in: it was the first and last time she and I had any similarity in status.

All my life I was this very antsy girl, and Mavis was a substance of amazing grace. Put me near her and I toppled things. My cousin Iris claims she was the same way around Aunt Henrietta, who was her mother.

Aunt Henrietta was a vastly capable anthropologist.

My other aunt, Aunt Jahnna, was an aviatrix. She was w/ the WAFS in World War II. Vastly capable. You could smother in the folds of capability that billowed from these women. Aunt Sydna was in government w/ Roosevelt, and she did something undercover and courageous for which she was vastly paid.

Aunt Willa planned to study medicine but she ran off w/ the foreigner who beat her. He became a vastly famous artist and left her for a younger woman after fourteen years. After that, Aunt Willa married an insurance salesman and went to live w/ him in his house in Lake Forest, in the Midwest.

Aunt Willa and the Midwestern insurance salesman had a daughter, Faye. Faye is not vastly famous. She is an interior decorator in Manhattan, and people say her work is nice but uninspired.

Grammar never spoke to Aunt Willa or about her after she ran off w/ the foreigner who beat her. News reached the family house in Grand Rapids in the spring of 1921 that Aunt Willa had had an illegitimate daughter. My mother was eight years old and Aunt Sydna was twelve. Aunt Jahnna and Aunt Henrietta were both in their teens. Aunt Willa sent them a letter from the East Coast w/ the announcement, and it arrived around noon one day as they were taking their midday meal.

This is how Mavis would have written the scene, if it had been in one of her mystery novels:

> Grammar looked at the letter. She looked around the table. She picked up the heavy cleaver she used for dressing poultry and slammed it into the hard oak center of the table. It quivered, just a little.
>
> "Your sister is *dead*," Grammar said. A splinter from the table caught Sydna in the eye and she used it as an excuse to dare to cry. Grammar made them finish their noon meal. No one moved and no one moved the cleaver. It stayed where it was for days and weeks. In the mornings it cast an awful shadow and its reach into their lives was steely, cold and morbid. Once Jahnna said, "The blade will rust," and Grammar answered, "Let it." The symbol haunted every meal. No matter which way they turned to look at it, the angle of the blade was threatening. No one dared to touch it. One day, many months later, little Sydna found the letter when she was sent to turn the mattress in her mother's room. After she'd read it, she walked into the kitchen. With the calm that truth instills, she went to kill her mother with the chill, cold cleaver that was the very symbol of her sister's death.

After that Aunt Sydna was sent away to a Catholic girl's school in Ann Arbor, even though the family wasn't Catholic. She never really returned to the house in Grand Rapids—she went home w/ her school friends at the holidays, and in summers she took odd domestic jobs for money, much to Grammar's humiliation. She was probably very lonely—she sent Mavis letters and Mavis saved each one. The first letter includes pages torn from Sydna's copybook dated 23 September 1921, two weeks after she'd been sent away. Mavis saved letters she received and copies of letters that she wrote because she expected someone would come along and ask to do a volume of them someday. No one ever did.

This is Aunt Sydna's version of the story:

23 September 1921
Little Angels of the Light, Ann Arbor, Michigan

The assignment is *Describe the Event and Describe the Lesson Christ Has Helped Us Learn from It*:

I. *Describe the Event.*
The Event is very clear to me, in my memory. I believe the clarity of certain days is enhanced by solar particles that filter through the air and seem to grace the Inanimate with a Spirit, because on this certain day the sky was cloudless and blue like cornflowers growing in the rye fields where I come from. (I believe this is scientific, from the solar parts., and not religious.) "Mrs. Gritty" was in a Mood and sent me in to turn her mattress. She knew this was a full job for one person and I think she sent me to the task alone without Mave or Jahnny to help give me a pull because she had it in for me that day as I must have said something wayward sometime the week before. I threw the full force of my muscles at the featherbed, just to prove that I could do it. Wasn't I surprised, then, to discover something covert in between the linens? And in Willa's handwriting! Don't think it didn't give me such a turn I couldn't move for a full minute. It was as if I'd seen a ghost! I read it! What a thrill came over me, I could feel my blood in each part of its corporeal journey. Gritty had always been a vile and rigid woman, but I never thought her so perverse as to tell her daughters one of them was dead. I hated her! She was the one who should be dead! I walked into the kitchen; she was washing out some linens. She turned toward me from the tub. Her sleeves were rolled up and her arms were glistening with soap. I took one slow step toward the cleaver and I picked out just the place where I was going to put it—in that soft part at the base of Gritty's neck. Gritty saw what I was going to do and she looked at me like I was no good in the first place; then she turned away from me back to the scrubboard. She ignored me! She didn't think I had the strength to do it! The next thing I remember is Jahnny yelling Stop it! Stop! and Henny sending Mr. Hofstaeder in to pull me out. I do remember swimming, though, and I remember counting going back and forth from shore to shore 27 times and not wanting to stop until I reached 500. Everyone is lying when they say I tried to take my own life in the pond. I didn't try to take my own life. I was so angry I could have swum to China.

II. *Describe the Lesson Christ Has Helped Us Learn from It.*
The lesson Christ Has Helped Me Learn from It is that He and God and All the Angels must have been watching out for her that day, because it's a Holy Miracle I didn't kill my mother.

Aunt Willa's illegitimate daughter by the vastly famous artist who beat her was named Belle. Belle ran off when she was fifteen and a half w/ a man who was a writer and an alcoholic. They traveled together through the Southwest, and he began to become vastly famous as a writer of the beat generation. They had a daughter they named Cathy in 1953. Soon after Cathy was born, the vastly famous writer left Belle and ran off w/ a younger woman. In 1955 Belle shot and killed him in a motel room in Alamogordo, New Mexico, and she became instantly and vastly famous as a murderer.

In 1956 Belle poisoned herself in prison. Aunt Henrietta adopted Belle's orphan daughter, Cathy. She raised Cathy as well as two daughters of her own. All the while, Aunt Henrietta was a vastly capable anthropologist.

Aunt Henrietta's daughters are named Scooter and Iris. Iris is my favorite cousin. Iris married a signalman in the Coast Guard after she graduated from Sarah Lawrence and they have two daughters, Lise and Molly, and they live on Long Island. Iris is alone a lot when Hap is on tour, and sometimes she weaves bedspreads on a hand loom for local craft fairs.

Scooter and Cathy grew up as sort of twins. Scooter has her own decorating business w/ our cousin Faye, and Cathy works for the Museum of Modern Art in New York City.

Aunt Jahnna had a daughter, Millie.

Millie is my cousin and she's forty-two. She is a logician teaching on the staff at Marymount and she lives in Westchester. Her husband makes a lot of money, manufacturing.

All of us would like to know why everything seemed vastly easy for our mothers. Aunt Sydna says that everything they are or were they owed to Grammar. Well, what they are is dead.

People still read Mother, but the critics say she has no social value. She hasn't stood the test of time like Dorothy Sayers. She fashioned herself after Mrs. Christie, but she wasn't as good. She wrote about the upper class, and all her books take place in Britain. She was born in Grand Rapids, Michigan, and her real name was Mavis Garrity. She wrote under the pen name Mavis St. Clair.

I don't know how Grammar felt about the name-changing because Grammar didn't practice saying what she felt. I remember only one time when Grammar said anything at all about Mavis's career. We were in the drawing room of our apartment on Madison Avenue. Grammar had come east to visit, and I was still in school. Drinks were being served, and there were ten or a dozen people there. Mavis loved to entertain.

She was wearing one of those marvelous chiffon confections of hers that sort of floated and drifted on the light. Grammar was sitting on one of the two sofas in the center of the room and she looked like a mountain. She always wore black. I noticed in the course of the evening that Mavis was flitting about, more animated than usual, more intense, making smaller circles. She kept coming back like a mother bird to hover over Grammar's nest. Grammar ignored her. Mavis began talking too loudly and using her hands in a way that was strange to her. I noticed she knocked into things and stepped up too close to people. She leaned over too far, laughing, and spilled a double martini all over Grammar. Grammar never drank. She was a member of the WCTU, and the aroma of alcohol made her sick. Mavis made a big fuss about cleaning up the drink and drew the attention of the whole room. "You're acting like Regis Hallo-way," Grammar said. (Regis Halloway was a simpering nit in mother's latest book who mucks up a good piece of Moygashel linen trying to wipe out a bit of the evidence.) Mavis seemed pleased that Grammar had read the book. She got a look on her face that wanted to ask "Did you like it?" Almost at the same time, Grammar got a look on her face that wanted to answer, "It's trash." Luckily, Mavis and I were the only ones there who saw it.

I think if Grammar had been my mother I would have felt that I could kill her.

Maybe that's the power mothers have, knowing that they're safe.

Massive as she was in my life, Mavis shrank in the face of Grammar's power and I think she never meant for me to see her that way. I don't think we have the right as children to see our parents in a way that they don't want us to see, unless we hide it from them. It isn't fair to them for us to strip them clean, like bark. Especially when they're vulnerable; when they have shame. Unless they've stripped us. Unless they have attacked us. Unless they've marauded us. I'm speaking here of me and Mavis. I shouldn't speak for everyone. My thoughts on this are never clear. I have to tell another story:

Four years ago, during the summer of the '78 elections, I was featured in a double bill which we premiered in Washington. There was talk that if the plays ran well in D.C., we might be booked off-Broadway, so our energy was very high. The plays were brilliantly written, and although I'd never met him, I'd fallen in love w/ the playwright, from his words. I'd seen pictures of him and I'd seen him sitting in the back row at rehearsal, but we'd never spoken. I was crazy for him. His plays revealed intelligence, irreverence and sexiness. . . . I babble on. I get damp and limp. Mavis used to call the feeling "frowsty and subfusc." She got frowsty and subfusc over Louis, 1st Earl Mountbatten of Burma . . . well, over his *hardware*, actually—

We opened w/ the first of the two plays on a Friday night. In the first act I have to walk out into the audience in my bra and panties and try to sell off this bothersome ratty little Sicilian kid. The man who was playing the Sicilian kid was an old friend of mine and he kept goosing me and slipping his hand under the elastic thighbands of my underpants. It was very creative. Especially among the D.C. types.

So I'm out there in the center aisle shouting, "How much will you give me for the kid, eh?" and I feel a hand on my thigh and I fugure it's my friend. "His hair is free of lice and ticks!" I'm shouting: "He has all his teeth! What are you waiting for? How much will you pay?" And loud as day I hear this voice say, "Ellery, I have to have a word with you when this is over."

Everybody told me later no one in the house could hear it, but I heard it and I looked down and I lost a beat because sitting there was Mavis.

I lost the next line for a moment and I could feel my friend next to me tighten up the way someone you're working w/ or someone you love will do when he or she can feel you're in danger.

I remember I looked at her for a split second and she was looking right at me, and I never saw her look so frightened, and the light reflected from the stage made her eyes look yellow.

After the performance, I was going to kill her.

The playwright came backstage and I think he got down on his hands and knees and begged me to go to bed w/ him but I was too intent on strapping on my six-gun for a showdown w/ my mother.

That ought to say a lot right there about my sex life.

She didn't come backstage. She didn't show up in the lobby. She didn't come to dinner, either; but she'd left a note at my hotel that she was staying w/ Aunt Sydna so around one-thirty in the morning I got a cab to Georgetown to Aunt Sydna's townhouse.

"Where is she?"

"She's upstairs, Ellery. She's asleep."

"Sonofabitch. *Mavis!*"

I started for the stairs.

"I think you ought to know before you fricassee her that they've diagnosed a cancer."

"Oh really? What the fuck is this? A Bette Davis movie?"

"She won't know how to die."

"*Who does?*"

Sydna has great style because she didn't drop a beat and said, "*James Dean?*"

"She interrupted a performance to tell me she has cancer?"

"Well, my dear, where *else* was she supposed to tell you?"

"Is that supposed to mean I'm always in the middle of a performance?"

"No, that's supposed to mean *she* is."

"Fuck her."

"Good-o."

"I mean it."

"Of course you do, lamb."

"I really mean it this time."

"I know you do. You mean it *every* time."

I went upstairs, and the room she always stayed in when she was in this house was dark and she was sleeping. I called her name.

Mavis had always been a sound sleeper; nightly, she slept the sleep of death. . . . I called her name again and switched the bedside light on. A circle of yellow light fell across her pillow. I sat down.

She slept as a child would sleep, w/ one hand curled beneath her chin. She was breathing through her mouth. She was sleeping on her back, her right hand tucked beneath her chin, and her mouth was loose and slack; she had no teeth.

In a glass beside her on the bedside table, there were teeth.

I never knew she wore false teeth.

She might have told me, but I never imagined what it meant, what it would look like, how the vastly famous cheekbones would stand out, how the vastly famous profile would collapse to no great ending. . . .

She looked frail and mute.

All my life Mavis had been this large *field* that I was fenced inside—free to roam to the limit, but always kept inside. I was always kept in *her*. Now she was a small old woman breathing through her mouth, and she was dying. I wanted to caress her legs, to touch her; but we had never touched. I wanted to wake her up and tell her I would care for her; but she had never cared. How could I mother, who had never had a mother? How could the child become the parent, who had never been the child?

The next night I played the female lead in a play about a child's fatal place w/in its family. I played for Mavis, though I couldn't see her.

She came backstage when we were through. She was very large and charming and positively *floated* in a frock by Galanos. She said she didn't like the play. We posed for pictures. She was wearing too much rouge. She made some comments for the press about her dress designer.

She was dead w/in the month.

The people here have recommended that I write down these impressions.

They seem to think that if I make up lists of things and write them down, then I stand a chance of altering my perspective. I try to tell them Mavis was a vastly famous mystery writer, and I don't think she ever meant for me to see her any other way. I don't think she would allow it.

Grammar altered her perspective, by shrinking. I have the passport Sydna got for her when Sydna worked at State and it says Grammar's height is five foot four. I know when Grammar died she was only four foot eight because Aunt Sydna, Mavis, Aunt Henrietta and Aunt Jahnna measured her.

After she died, on the first day of the viewing, Mavis bought me a drink at the Hay-Adams down the street from the funeral parlor. When we sat down, Mavis said, "My God, Elly, did you hear the way Grammar started screaming at me as soon as I walked in?"

That night Aunt Sydna, Mavis, Aunt Henrietta and Aunt Jahnna got drunk and went to the funeral parlor and lifted Grammar from the casket and laid her out and measured her.

Aunt Henrietta said they did it because examination of a corpse satisfies a primal instinct.

Aunt Henrietta said a lot of things I should believe. She also said a lot of things I shouldn't. She made Iris drop things, and she wouldn't let us spit, but she once said we are a sex w/out a written history. And then she didn't write us one.

DIO CLINTOCK GARRITY (1865–1965)
"GRAMMAR"
Also called:
GRAMMA
GRITTY
TICK-TOCK
DY
THE OLD BITCH

THINGS I LIKED ABOUT HER
She gave me Life Savers.

She thought one potato was a good meal.

Although she wasn't educated herself, she worked hard to send each of her five daughters through college because she believed education, not marriage, was the only way a woman could raise herself up in the world.

She had a mustache.

THINGS I DIDN'T LIKE
They were spearmint.

She ate brains.

She never talked.

She never told us anything about herself.

I never saw her smile.

She was not tender.

She never kissed us and even if she had, she had a mustache.

I'm supposed to write a list of qualities or my impressions. But these aren't qualities. I suppose a quality is something like the quality of mercy or the quality of innocence in anything that shimmers.

Grammar did not own the quality of mercy. Mavis always shimmered. She was the most vastly famous of her sisters. It was she who started calling Grandma "Grammar," because of all the rules. Mavis, too, had rules: Ellery, hold still. Ellery, keep quiet.

She had roles, *a* role, *the* role of her life—St. Clair, *The Mystery Writer.*

I don't think Mavis ever thought about my life or that I'd ever have a life that might exist in any other way than as a satellite, a little moon, to hers because one of her first acts of motherhood was to come up w/ a name for me. Mavis must have thought of this as another chance to exercise invention. She named me "Ellery McQueen."

She must have been three sheets to the wind.

When she was three sheets to the wind she did bizarre things, like measuring Grammar's cadaver. Like having me. Like having screaming fights w/ Uncles, who, come morning, would be gone.

For years and years there had been slews and slews of Uncles— she once said, "Love is what one needs in the event one doesn't die. . . ." And then she died w/out it.

She died. I didn't. I fell in love. She didn't. He died. I didn't.

"Are you going to die, Berenice?" That's a line in Act Two of *The Member of the Wedding.* Berenice is a character in the play who's a big black woman who takes care of Frankie. There's a little boy named John Henry who is Frankie's best friend and he asks her, *"Are you going to die, Berenice?"* And Berenice says, *"Why, Candy, everybody has to die."* And John Henry says, *"Everybody?"* And John Henry turns to me and says, *"Are you going to die, Frankie?"* And I say, *"I doubt it. I honestly don't think I'll ever die."* And John Henry says, *"What is 'die'?"*

John Henry looks up w/ his face just beaming innocence each night and he says, "What is 'die'?" "What is 'die'?" each night, every night, as if he never saw a dried leaf in a gutter or an earthworm pale w/ water . . . .

"What is 'die'?" my ass, Jack:

"Die" is the last time you can claim your ignorance.

February 7, 1982
Lucy Hastings Clinic
Princeton, New Jersey

2

SCOOT AND IRIS

SCOOT AND IRIS came to visit me today because Iris knew if Scooter came alone someone here might hear her babbling on in one of her inane soliloquies and they'd toss her in w/ Florence, who is one of the weirder crazies we have in residence *chez nous*. Scooter isn't crazy, mind you, the way that Florence is (Florence talks w/ Jesus), but Scoot and Flo could pass a pleasant afternoon in conversation and it wouldn't make a bit of difference to either one that neither one made any sense. Scoot has three subjects that she's good at, conversationally: when and where and what she put in her little tummy; when and where she bought something and for how much; and what she watched on television and when. If it weren't for the fact that Scooter's getting married later this year and wanted me to try on bridesmaids' dresses and wanted to tell me that her fiancé, Raymond, had asked her to make sure that what was wrong w/ me wasn't something clinging to our family tree like an infestation of caterpillars w/ their teeny-weeny teeth, Scoot would never have driven all the way down here to visit me. "This guy Raymond sounds like a real champ," I couldn't keep myself from saying. She's so stupid she didn't pick up on my fine sardonic wit. Iris, on the other hand, hears everything. As soon as I was well enough to start to have visitors last month, Iris was the first to come. She comes every week to see me, and she calls me in between. She brings things I want to have around me—family pictures, family scrapbooks, some of my old stuff. Her two kids, Lise and Molly, draw me get-well cards. I think Iris is the kind of person who's a savior to everybody but herself. Scoot, forget it, never saved a thing. If you said, "Scoot, save your breath," she'd have no idea what you meant. She just prattles on. I listened for a while this afternoon because it's so hard not to, she's so animated. She talked about the wedding plans and about Raymond's difficulty finding a job and she talked about when and where and what she'd put into her little tummy. Then she started talking about a movie she'd seen two nights ago on cable television. The movie was called *The History of the World, Part One*, and Scooter started telling us the whole plot, all the jokes and who said what, and what each character was wearing. The movie was directed by Mel Brooks and Mel Brooks also acted in it and in this one scene, Scooter said, Mel Brooks plays a waiter waiting on the table where Jesus and the Twelve Disciples are sitting down to celebrate the Last Supper. Mel Brooks comes over to Jesus or St. Peter or Whomever, Scooter said, and he's got this clean cloth draped on his arm and a little tablet and a stylo like he's going to take their dinner order and he says something like "Are you all together, or is this going to be on separate checks?"

Scoot's so stupid she never noticed I stopped hearing after that.

3

SEPARATE CHECKS

THE #1 FIRST STORY EVER WRITTEN BY MYSELF,
ELLERY McQUEEN

IN THE HISTORY OF THE WORLD there have been 6,853,196,427 women; not counting Scooter.

Not counting Scoot, you could take the women in the history of the world and lay them end to end and they would be 5,451,027 miles long, or you could lay them the whole length of the Equator and they'd stack up 60 meters high, which is slightly higher than Niagara Falls.

The peculiar thing about the women in the history of the world is that there have been more women than there have been men, but when you go to look for clues of them they're hard to find.

Scoot herself is not concerned w/ this one way or the other. Scoot thinks the universe begins and ends w/ her. She thinks that history does not exist. Scoot could not care less about women disappearing in the history of the world. Whenever women as a topic sneak into the conversation, Scoot shrugs and wrinkles up her nose and says oh pooh just like a little bunny in an animated Disney film. Scoot is not just naturally stoopid: somewhere along the line she cultivated an addiction to the type of man who goes for big girls w/ wide shoulders and high waists and high wide satin breasts w/ dark brown nipples who play dumb.

If you think there aren't too many men like that who go for girls like that, then, boy, are you in for a surprise.

Also Scooter has these cascades and cascades of copper-colored hair and freckles in a matching color on her shoulders, down her neckline, in the summer; so much so that even I might wonder where they stop. She is not an ugly woman. This is important because sometimes women take up girlish ways when they think their looks are on the shy side of spectacular. Scoot's looks are far from being on the shy side of spectacular, but Scooter thinks she's too big for the way most clothes are cut and for most men which she probably is. So she acts flighty like a "little" girl even though she runs a business that supports herself and seven other people. If you have trouble picturing her, you might remember she is twenty-nine and the business she is in is called a "glamour" business. She does not, for instance, make rivets. What she makes are rooms, sort of, and she makes a lot of money. Her specialty is conference rooms. She makes more money than Raymond, I know that much, because Raymond right now is out of work. Not that it matters, but it does.

Have you ever seen two tiny people, for example, not exactly midgets but maybe people just about the same small size like four six, four eight, a little man and a little woman or two men or two women and they make you say out loud Oh gee isn't it just wonderful the way life lets two people who are just right find each other? You wouldn't say that about Scoot and Raymond, not at all.

Something is obviously not right about these two. I have no idea what Scooter's doing w/ this type, I really don't. After all these years of being everybody's favorite little flop-eared bunny, Scooter's turned around and bought herself a stuffed toy of her own.

Of course none of us knew any of this in September when she called up and invited each of us to lunch.

I was the first person she called. I remember that she called me on a Sunday and I was on my way out to meet Mark for lunch, and she made me late. This was before I had my nervous breakdown. This was before I started writing these things down.

After Scoot called me, she called her sister Iris.

I wish I had a way that would tell about Iris. Scoot's so easy to tell about. Scoot's not a woman anyone needs to invent; Iris is. Iris is iridescent w/ something aglimmer inside. Just being near her you feel her warmth spreading under your skin. Whereas Scoot gets her notions from people in crowds the same way some people develop a virus, Iris has knowledge of things before everyone else. She has a power she sees w/—a special gift. It seems so unlikely that they're sisters.

Faye is the person that Scooter called next. Faye is a woman locked up in herself, the saddest woman on earth that I know. She's forty-eight, but she looks like a Blackglama ad, the one w/ Myrna Loy. She wears her hair waved and close to her head and it's jet black w/ glints of blue. It's always perfect and it goes down in a V at the nape of Faye's neck and the V's have looked exactly the same for six years. She has her hair done every Saturday morning in the town where she lives all alone in New Jersey. Faye holds her sadness in. Something flutters in Faye, in her eyes when she speaks, and she speaks from a distance. She's *stern*, that's how she looks; when she drops the stern look, she looks frightened. Her son died; he was killed, accidentally, last year. He was twenty. His name was Davey. He was a sweet kid. I can't understand how Faye goes on living since then. She lives in the same house, and she gets her hair styled the same way every weekend. It seems to me one would collapse under all that. Faye is Aunt Willa's second daughter, the one Aunt Willa had late in life. Belle was Faye's half sister. Those two, Faye and Belle, must have been night and day as far as sisters go. Maybe more sisters are like that than I know; I mean, so unalike. I think having a half sister like Belle would have its effect on anyone. She was only my cousin and still there are times when I think about genes and whether or not I could kill. I have killed; well, I've had an abortion. This paragraph has gone on for too long.

This is the first story I've ever written.

After Davey died, after Davey was killed, Mitch, that's the man Faye is married to, Davey's father, took off. He disappeared. I liked Mitch. Everyone liked Mitch, except Millie. She didn't trust him. She said he was up to no good.

He took off, who could blame him? His son had died, had been killed. While he was around, Mitch had always been sexy and wiry and, I think, a bit dangerous. It was exciting to me the way he and Faye had been married for twenty-five years. It meant there was something sexy and wiry and dangerous just a little in Faye. Millie was right about one thing she said about Mitch: he wasn't safe.

When Scooter called Faye, Faye was startled. She and Scooter were partners. They worked together. They never went out for lunch w/ each other, unless it was business.

"Is this business?" Faye asked.

"Not business, just lunch," Scooter giggled.

Patiently, w/ a hint of fatigue in her voice, Faye said, "Scooter, I know better than that."

"Well, okay," Scooter admitted. "I want to talk to you outside the office. I have something to say."

Faye closed her eyes and resigned herself to the idea. Faye was the only one of us to guess Scooter's plan from the start. Faye's isn't the same kind of knowing as Iris's. Iris has powers. Faye's kind of knowing comes at the back of a torment, of night after night after night of real sitting and smoking French cigarettes, seeing how all of life wavers like parachute tissue after the jump.

If I were my cousin Faye, I would kill myself.

After Scooter called Faye, she called Millie. Millie's our sexiest cousin. She's so smart, really, but there's a part of her always asking for trouble. I guess she looks like Maggie Smith and Elizabeth Ashley, but mostly she's like Hedda Gabler in the second act. Very bright woman, acid-tongued, very quick-witted and ready, like a cat. No one survives Millie's shitlist very long. In her bitch goddess mode she's exactly like Mavis, which is why, I suppose, she and I get along. She thinks Scooter's a twit. I can tell she thinks of Faye the same way. She has trouble w/ Faye, and it may be about Mitch.

Millie may have tried to solicit Mitch a long time ago. This is just rumor. And common sense. All you'd have to do is see Millie and Mitch in the same room, and you'd know something had happened between them. Nothing has ever been said. It's the suggestion that's there.

When Scooter called Millie to ask her to lunch, Millie was washing dried milk from a drinking glass at her kitchen sink and daydreaming. When Millie answered the phone her voice sounded anxious, and Scooter, not usually right about things, even Scooter could tell that Millie was hoping it was a call from somebody else.

Scooter so rarely called any of us that the first thing Millie asked was, "Is there trouble, kiddo?"

"Oh golly no," Scooter said.

"What's the deal?"

"Lunch." Scooter giggled.

Millie talked like a gun moll, in Scooter's opinion. Scooter thought it was funny.

"Just lunch." Scooter giggled again.

"Not if Faye will be tagging along. *Will* Faye be tagging along?"

"Well . . . I . . . you know, what difference does it make . . . I mean, no, if it would make a difference, gee, no, Faye isn't coming . . . I mean, I'm not going to ask her, you know, to make a point of being there, but if . . . I mean, gosh, well, she and I work together and, gee, we sort of go to this one place all the time with clients for lunch, so . . . I mean, if Faye's there, you know . . . well, at this one place, if she happens to be there . . . I mean, gosh, you know, I don't see how you could say, well, it's my fault or anything."

Millie waited a moment before saying, "Scoot, I want you to listen to something. Are you ready?"

Scooter giggled.

"Okay," Millie said. "Listen carefully. The next sound you are going to hear will be the sound of Truth. It will be entirely new to you. Listen to it anyway. Are you ready?"

"Yeah, gee, sure, go ahead."

Millie hung up. Scooter stayed on the line and she listened. After a while she said, "Mill, this is Zen, isn't it? Millie?"

The next person Scooter called was Aunt Sydna. Scooter is scared to death of Aunt Sydna. Bears, too, I suppose, and lions would have to stop dead in their tracks faced w/ Sydna, so forget waiters and shop clerks. Just forget them. Sydna's attitude is that individuals born into waiting and clerking are not really human. She is seventy-two and, I should add, unforgiving White-Anglo-Saxon-Pissand-vinegar God. She is the family historian, our oldest living member and relic. She remembers what everyone looked like, what they said and what they were wearing. She will say, for example, "You remember, dear, that was the time Millie was wearing those ill-fitting pants and Cathy had on a hand-me-down Schiaparelli."

Sydna's conversations are spiked w/ surprises that never connect. Millie once said that sitting w/ Sydna and trying to hold a conversation w/ her was like trying to hold the sense of a landscape from the lights one sees from a train in the dark.

Every now and then Millie says something I will remember just about forever because it is something very fitting, very right. In that regard, in coining aphorisms-on-the-wing, she is all that Mavis ever tried to be. One time, it was at Davey's funeral, Cathy had had too much to drink beforehand, and as we were walking to the grave site from the cars her legs gave out and she just thupped down on her knees and began to sway in a precarious manner like something that's unhinged and not going to be upright for too long. Sydna said sharply, "Stand up, child! One should have learned how to walk by your age!" Millie turned around to Sydna and said, "For your information, she was trying to *fly*." There was a grave-site decoration nearby, an urn made out of papier-mâché, and Millie held it up for Cathy to be sick in as we all moved on. I remember about twenty minutes later Cathy's face appeared in the crowd beyond Faye's shoulder as they lowered Davey's coffin in, and her face was white as death. Cathy's face is pale all of the time. She's blond and she has dark-brown eyes w/ dark-brown eyebrows and she looks intent, the way a prophet looks. She's very skinny. Not everybody in our family likes Cathy the way Millie does—there's something slightly off about her. She looked spooky to me that day at Davey's funeral, in her baggy black dress and her torn stockings where she'd fallen to the gravel on her knees and her pale blond hair and white, white face and dark expression.

That's the last time I saw Cathy, before I had my breakdown. I'm not close to Cathy, not close the way that Scooter was. Scoot and

Cathy were so close when they were growing up, they'd been like twins. They dressed alike and did everything together, but Cathy was more shy, more fearful of the world than Scooter was. They'd even gone to the same college and roomed together. Scoot had been a year ahead of Cathy, and when Scooter left w/ her B.A., so did Cathy, w/out. Everybody expected Scooter would set Cathy up in business w/ her, but Scoot took off and went to California. Cathy hung around New York, around the East Village and SoHo, where she picked up jobs in art galleries and she picked up a drug habit. After a while Scooter came back to New York and settled uptown, and Cathy got her act together a little better and got herself a job at the Museum of Modern Art as assistant to the person in charge of raising all the money for expansion. She still lived south of Houston Street and wore secondhand clothing and roller-skated to work, and she hadn't seen Scooter in four months, so when Scooter called her up that Sunday in September and invited her to lunch, it made Cathy feel better than she had felt in weeks. She missed Scoot's friendship the way she thought the world had missed James Dean when he was killed. The world, in her opinion, would be a whole lot nicer if it didn't wait until you died to say it missed you.

On the day that Cathy thought she was going to have lunch w/ Scooter, just the two of them, Millie drove her Fiat in from Mamaroneck and parked it in the Kinney lot in the Hilton on Sixth Avenue. On her way out through the lobby a man came up to her and asked if she was looking for some company. Millie looked at him a brief moment. He was young, in his early thirties, tall and expensively turned out. He smelled of citron and had a winning smile, except that around his eyes his skin looked tight. He wore a gold chain, and she turned her eyes away. She had no sympathy for men who wore jewelry anywhere but on their hands. Well, she thought, smiling to herself, the truth was she was not averse to the idea of a man w/ a gold earring, now and then. . . .

"*Momentito*," the young man admonished her. "What's your hurry?" He stepped in front of her and tried to stop her. "Little mother," he cajoled, "*momentito* . . ." Millie closed her eyes and hurried by him. I look *that* old? she wondered. She caught an image of herself reflected in the plate glass as she passed through the main door, and she looked terrific. She still had a great tan from the summer. She was wearing her knit dress in teal blue that had a scoop neck and showed her collarbones, and her bones were great. She had flat, narrow hips and a flat stomach and high tight tits that looked as if she ran a lot, even though she didn't, so fuck him. He hadn't even looked her over, he just zeroed in. God's fucking gift, she marveled, smiling to herself.

The sound of her high heels against the Tarmac echoed in the hotel portico outside, and she crossed the avenue and walked the short block to the museum at a fast pace. There was a sign on the street amid construction that read SIDEWALK OFFICIALLY CLOSED. Officially, but not in fact, she thought, stepping gingerly across the rubble to the entrance. Inside, she asked the woman seated at the small desk just left of the entrance to ring Cathy in the executive offices, then she stood to one side and waited near a man in a brown suit w/ a walkie-talkie on his hip. She watched the people, mostly elderly, seated on the banquette by the cloak room. Against her will her mind ranged to a poem by May Swenson that she didn't even like. The poem, she remembered, starts like this, "At the Museum of Modern Art you can sit in the lobby on the foam-rubber couch" and the first stanza ends, "You don't have to go into the galleries at all." Millie remembered all the words in between because that's the way her mind works. She looked around at all the people, and she thought, This place doesn't look like a museum; it looks like a family clinic for the wealthy in Milan. What was lacking was a sense of humor.

The next thing that happened was that Cathy appeared, looking stoned and crazy and forlorn, as usual.

"Hi." Cathy frowned. Her hair was trimmed to the bone, little wisps of it fluttered at the crown and nape, but the rest was too minimal to stand. Her eyes were smudged w/ charcoal or w/ soot, and there was a miniature tarot card stenciled on her cheekbone. She was wearing a gold-plated safety pin through one ear and Day-Glo green plastic sandals w/ striped socks.

"Jesus Christ," Millie murmured. "What the fuck do you call this?"

Cathy lifted her arms slightly from where they hung at her sides, as if she were attempting to fly, then she let them fall again. "Punk," she answered gamely.

Millie was transfixed. There were other details—a sort of general tatteredness about the cloth from which her clothes were made, an aroma of dusty cloves—that lent to the effect. Millie wondered if Cathy actually put planning into what she wore, rehearsed it before the bedroom mirror, or if the whole thing was potluck. "Don't they fire people who look like you?" Millie asked.

Cathy shrugged. She seemed almost confused, and Millie was about to ask her if she was doing heroin again, but she didn't. Cathy's disorientation came from a central source. Not the bloodstream but the heart, Millie thought. Then she congratulated herself. Every once in a while she was convinced she had a poet's sense. "You look like a fucking dyke," she said, reaching to touch Cathy's hair.

"Maybe I am," Cathy answered quietly.

Her eyes looked round and flat, and Millie was suddenly frightened for her. "You put out for too many men," Millie said, "so we can drop the subject, right? It's just your hair looks like shit, that's all."

"It *is* shit." Cathy reached up and plucked a tuft of hair from her scalp w/ her fingers.

Millie was appalled. "You're losing your hair," she said. Cathy nodded. "Jesus Christ," Millie said.

She took Cathy's hands. They were thin, the skin on them looked transparent. She'd painted her fingernails purple and green. They were chewed.

"What the hell's the matter with you?" Millie whispered. "Cath, you're fucking up all over again, aren't you? Tell me the truth. Are you messing with that shit again? Huh? What's the story?"

Cathy blinked. "Can we go somewhere else to have this conversation?" she requested.

"Sure," Millie said.

She pulled Cathy past the information desk through the ticket taker w/out paying and headed for the back wall. She stood Cathy against the window.

"So?" she asked.

Cathy stared at her. "You're really pretty, Millie, you know that?" She had been touched by the play of light on Millie's hair. She saw things like that, always asked when visiting a strange place where the sun came up and figured in herself where it set and how it struck a room at noontime. She had an artist's eye, the way she saw light, the way she knew by instinct that a surface takes the light it needs, no less, no more, to define it. Her grandfather had been a famous artist. She had a bit of that. Not enough for anything too great. Just enough to make her crazy. "Iris is really pretty, too," she added. "And Scoot. Don't you love the way Scoot looks? I do. I love the way Scoot looks. I love the way Scoot puts herself together. I wish I could put myself together that way. . . ."

"Cathy, Jesus Christ, what's the point?"

Cathy picked her lip. "I'm a little weird," she said. "I'm the weird one, that's all. I'm the squeaky wheel. Some people are born that way. You know, born black-and-blue." She touched the cloth of Millie's dress, the weave of the expensive knit. She worked her fingers over it. "I'm not doing drugs," she said evenly. She lifted her chin and managed half a smile. "I'm doing Real Life in the Eighties."

"Oh, like *up*town," Millie mocked.

"No, like up *yours*," Cathy answered.

Millie smiled. "I want to buy a pen," she said.

Cathy blinked.

Millie relaxed against the wall and said, "I think you look like hell and I think your wardrobe is alarming and your diet's probably deficient, but I want to buy a pen and a couple of other things in the Museum Shop and I want to use your discount and then I want to take you to lunch so I can learn all the disgusting details of your life. You look like shit, really, like you have the clap or black lung or something. . . ."

"I can't," Cathy said sadly. "I can't come to lunch." She smiled a little, and it made her look somehow less intent. It made her look fleetingly pretty.

"C'mon," Millie cajoled. "It's me and Scoot. You'll love it."

Cathy's eyes started to dart around as if they were tracking the flight of something very small and erratic. She began to breathe hard. "Scoot?" she said.

Millie laughed. "C'mon," she repeated. "We'll make it a party. We'll get drunk and talk about our mothers and some guys will send drinks over to our table and we'll get one of them to drive me home, and you can have the rest. . . ."

Cathy had begun to cry. By the time Millie had sorted out the details and understood that Cathy thought Scoot had asked her to lunch *exclusively* and had ignored the consideration of why in God's name anyone would want to lunch w/ Scoot *exclusively*, she was standing at the phone booths on the little landing on the way downstairs and dialing Faye's and Scooter's office.

"Hello, Faye?" she was saying. "It's Millie, darling, you remember. Cousin Millie." (She must be *dying*! Millie joked w/ Cathy, but Cathy didn't smile.) "I'm in town, darling, and just thought we might get together over lunch. . . ."

Cathy listened intently, dabbing at her eyes. "Oh?" Millie said. "Really? What a coincidence, so am I! You don't say! Why, me, too, on Sunday! I'll be damned. Well, I'll see you in a little while, right, dearie? Right. Same to you."

"She fucked us," Millie announced, hanging up. "The whole fucking family's showing up."

They stared at each other in silence for a moment.

"Oh for Christ's sake stop crying," Millie said. She threw her head back and took a deep sigh. "Christ. Listen, do you have any vodka on you?"

Cathy nodded, and they went down the short flight of steps to the ladies' lounge and ducked in together.

"I'll take care of you," Millie promised.

Cathy asked, "Then who'll take care of *you*?"

Millie fixed her mouth before the mirror and told herself she should have worn the ugly piece of jewelry Aunt Sydna had given her. "Damn," she said. "What the hell does Scooter think she's up to, anyway?" she asked no one in particular. She took another pull on Cathy's pint and held the little bottle to her chest. "Do drugs feel like this?" she asked. "I mean, in your limbs this way?"

"Always." Cathy nodded.

Millie sighed. "Oh shit, why is everything we like tied to sex?" she asked.

A woman w/ a small child and a B. Altman's shopping bag moved her body between her child and Millie on the way out and told her daughter, "Don't stare at the strangers, Rachel. It's not nice."

I wish I had the kind of power that could jump ahead ten years and let me rap on Rachel's window on a summer's night and ask her what she thought about the two strange ladies in the ladies' lounge drinking vodka halfway through the morning and talking about sex right there in front of their own reflections. And I wish (me, Ellery) that little circumstantial Rachel would respond to my query that her encounter w/ them in the restroom was an event in womanhood that shaped her life—I'd like that very much. I think Cathy and Millie would like it, too, if they found out. Maybe if I had that kind of power, I could give Rachel their addresses and she could write them notes saying how the chance encounter had done more to provoke her to thinking about the kind of woman she could be than her entire adolescent lifetime of advice from Mum. That's the thing I'd really like, probably because I'm crazy. Rachel, if you're reading this, I hope you understand that when you write something, life passes through a process called the human mind and it comes out w/ its edges trimmed and it sounds tinny. Mabye it wasn't a B. Altman's bag your mother carried and maybe the woman w/ you wasn't your real Mum. If not, if it wasn't, then forgive me. That's the way I see it being true and this is my first story. I hope somewhere in your memory the women in my family have a special place and that you think about them as quite different and as wonderful and strange and it's okay w/ me if you don't like them, just please don't look so frightened when I see you in that scene.

Every little girl has memories of a ladies' lounge.

I wish (me, Ellery) I had the power to make a jump in time and speak to people in a story once they've left. I wish that I could follow them along and find out that knowing me or seeing me or seeing other members of my family made a difference in their lives. I don't think this is just because I'm crazy. I don't think it has anything to do w/ being a woman. I think it has to do w/ spilling over from the vessel of one's life. One's life becomes too full, and one needs pouring out. I wish I had the kind of power that would let me be like Emma or Jane Eyre, whose lives are captioned in a volume and are ineradicable. I think I wish I didn't have to write my own life. I wish I had the kind of power that could make a jump in time and see how it (me, Ellery) will end; that I could trust the author to know what she (me, Ellery) is doing while I'm doing it.

I need to say I never understood before the unrelenting rush of things it seems important to include, like water all around you in a dive. I'm so afraid I'll miss something too obvious and fall to telling details that miss the point. I shouldn't think about it. I should just get on and tell the story in a chatty way, but I keep thinking Mavis cheated. At the end of all her stories, at the very end, just like Mrs. Christie, she would assemble all her characters in one gigantic scene between her Hero and the Suspects, and her Hero would review the facts in what was almost always an eight- or nine-page monologue, and if something very obvious had slipped through in the telling that's where she could catch herself and right the situation.

I can't seem to come up w/ a way to right the situation.

I guess it's important, for example, that Sydna took the train in from Darien that morning and arrived at Grand Central Station and took a cab to Saks (seven blocks).

And it's important not to forget the young man in the Hilton pleading *"Momentito,* little mother," because he turns up again, much later.

And, let's see, what else: I'm thirty-three. I know I sound much younger. And I have brown hair, a nice color brown, and the texture of my hair is silky. My hair is very long. I have green eyes and thin, thin wrists, and the texture of my skin is silky. I have size 8 hips and I have what I call ordinary breasts but I'm told by men they're grand and wonderful and Mavis hadn't any. She was flat-chested, literally. She had the body of an aging boy. I look very good in clothes, and I have a fine long neck that lets me wear a hat w/ great style. I remember on the day this story is about back in September some man came up to me while I was in a hurry to cross Seventh Avenue and he said, "Hey, aren't you a model?" and I said, "No, I'm full-scale."

I have a pretty healthy sense of humor.

I think it comes from having lived w/ a Chinese cook and Mavis and slews of Uncles all my life who showed up in silk robes at the breakfast table different mornings and always seemed surprised to see me and invariably ended up assuring me that they loved my mother very much. I think the record was four Uncles in a single week. Maybe it was Huan Hee's breakfasts that made them come and go that way. Hot and sour soup w/ seafood moo shi. I didn't know until I was nine or ten that most people came down to breakfast every morning to a set of friendly and familiar faces that ate eggs and toast and whole grain cereals and talked about the new day in terms of weather and anticipated fun. I learned this by accidentally seeing *Father Knows Best* on television one afternoon in the appliance department at Macy's. Father (his name was Jim) was reading the newspaper and talking to his son (his name was Bud) about the chores Bud was supposed to do that afternoon when he came home from school, and everyone looked happy (Betty, Mother, Kathy) and they were drinking juice and milk and eating toast w/ jam and sausage patties. After that for about a week I read breakfast menus in hotels and wherever else I could, and none of them ever featured hot and sour soup. When I mentioned this to Mavis she said, "What exactly is it you are saying, Elly, dear—that you wish to eat like every other bland insipid mollop in New York, or that suddenly out of nowhere after all these years you've decided you no longer like our hot and sour soup?" I think it was about that time that Huan Hee started fixing egg foo yong for me on Saturdays. And it was about that time that I took to responding to an Uncle's saying "Allow me to assure you that I love your mother very much" by stating that I'd like to have the kind of conversation they have on *Father Knows Best*. Also it must have been about that time my father killed himself in Paris.

Another thing Huan Hee's cooking must have done for me was give me a cast-iron digestive system. For years and years nothing could upset my stomach. But before I came here I had an abortion. Before that, when I was pregnant, I threw up a lot. Then I had an abortion. And I came here. And I still throw up a lot. It's one of the things I do. They say that it's a sign of my hysteria. And I can't menstruate. Sometimes I have so much pain on the surface of my breasts that I think I'm going to die, and they feel full and heavy all the time and I scream in pain if anyone ever tries to touch them.

I hope I haven't said too much. I want you very much to like me and to like this story. I think I'm trying awfully hard to impress you w/ my cheerfulness.

I think if you could see me you would cry. I'm the kind of person children stare at in a crowd.

Around noon on that Tuesday in September all the hearts of all my cousins quickened, and their paces picked up.

Cathy had borrowed twenty dollars from Millie to take a taxi home to SoHo so she could change her clothes. Millie told her this was silly and Cathy said what I have always said, "They're going to look at me and judge." Besides, she added, didn't Millie think the whole thing, what Scooter was doing, didn't Millie think that it was sort of strange, that it must mean something important? "Like what?" Millie had asked. Cathy looked mournful and chewed the inside of her mouth and said, "I bet Scooter's getting married."

"No one gets married these days, for Christ's sake," Millie said, but in her heart she knew if anyone were dumb enough actually to get married, it was Scooter.

Millie walked around the first floor of the museum for a while, and then she went next door to the Museum Shop and bought a thirteen-inch-blade, high-carbon-steel cooking knife w/ beechwood handle on Cathy's employee discount and a pen. She was a little buzzed by vodka w/out breakfast. She walked to Bendel's on Fifty-seventh Street and bought herself a ridiculously expensive pair of pure silk underpants. She walked through the cosmetics department downstairs and sprayed herself w/ a ridiculously expensive perfume from a tester bottle. The male transvestite who was selling eyeliner to a trio of wealthy but very ugly women saw Millie load herself w/ free perfume and scolded, "Naughty, naughty!" Millie stopped and looked at him. "Excuse me," she said through the dim, expensive light. "Are you a *man*?" She said it somewhat loudly, and it was obvious the women he was waiting on thought the question was in bad taste.

The transvestite brought his finger to his lips and rolled his eyes. "Ssh," he vamped, "I don't want to let it *out* . . ."

"Believe me"—Millie smiled—"I don't want to *see* it." She was entirely buzzed.

As the designated time drew near (Scooter had said twelve-thirty), Sydna looked at her watch and said softly, "I must go." This happened on the fourth floor of Saks Fifth Avenue, about eight blocks away. Sydna's companion sniffed. She dabbed a time-grayed silk scarf to her eyes. Years and years ago, about four decades, Sydna and this woman (a White Russian named Irina) had been lovers. Their love affair had lasted several years, and then Irina's head had

been turned by a very wealthy Polish émigré living on the West Side
looking for a young companion. Sydna had been hurt, it was supposed, although no one ever knew, because no one ever spoke of
Sydna's attachments of the heart as if they were real. Homosexuals,
it was supposed, did not really love the way other women love and,
besides, the women in our family (except Willa and her daughter
Belle) had never made a big fuss over love. Sydna's companions sort
of came and went like so many Uncles, though it must be said of
Sydna that she was not nearly so voracious in her appetite as Mavis.
I remember once when I was in high school I finally asked Huan
Hee if he thought Mavis actually slept w/ all the different Uncles
and he said, "What difflent uncle, Miss, same uncle alwa time."
All Caucasians looked alike to him.

Anyway, Sydna's lovers (I recall three) did not look alike, and
they always seemed wonderful to me because they were so very
individual in their ways and never fawning. I never saw a picture
of Irina, but apparently she was the most beautiful physically, and
Sydna remained celibate for several years after Irina left her. Five
or ten years later Sydna "married" Mrs. Betts, and they lived together
in Mrs. Betts's house in Darien until she died in 1973. About three
years after that, Sydna was in Saks looking for a new evening dress
because Ella Grasso had invited her to the inaugural ball. At Saks,
they still call Sydna "Mrs. Ingres" owing to her brief and mournful
marriage to Mr. Ingres, who was a cousin in the Gimbel family and
related somehow to the store. Anyway Sydna was up there in Formals
standing in her new emerald-green crepe de Chine chiffon, and the
matron clapped her hands and said, "Send a seamstress here for
Mrs. Ingres," and soon thereafter—bent a little, plump and sad and
sorrowfully obsequious—in walked Irina w/ her pins.

Irina, it seems, recognized Aunt Sydna right off and her hands
began to shake. Sydna, too, recognized Irina and expressed to the
matron a desire to refresh herself w/ a glass of chilled wine. This
was in the days when one could still command a glass of chilled
wine in the Formals dressing rooms at Saks. Left alone w/ her former
lover, whom she had not seen for forty years, Sydna said, *"Eta
zadacha ne trudnee chem predydushchaia,"* which was a joke, in
Russian, just between them, that means, "This problem is not more
difficult than the preceding one."

It had been a standard phrase of Irina's when Irina was teaching
Sydna how to construct sentences in her native language. They had
used the phrase together whenever they encountered new things that
required degrees of concentration in a series, including the time a
Pakistani friend of Sydna's in the State Department had sent them
a handbook on lesbian lovemaking positions. Irina, it should be said,
was much relieved at Sydna's joking, and she didn't cry, although
she wanted to; but Sydna couldn't restrain herself from noticing how
badly her former love had aged. Near the end of their first conversation that afternoon, Irina confided to Sydna that sometimes she
was so tired she felt she could not go on any longer in her work.
Sydna remembered that Irina was the kind of plaintiff who makes
confessions of malaise and of personal fatigue to grocers or to people
who sit down beside her in the park or on a bus, but the soft guttural
intonations of the wondrous, lush language, allowed her to forget
Irina's shortcomings and say, "I'll take care of you, Irina; you can
always trust yourself to me."
    Since that day, whenever Sydna comes to New York City, which
is once a month or so, she goes around to Saks w/ some bit of minor
mending, a loose button, for example, and takes it to Irina on the
fourth floor. They sit and have a sherry, and Sydna lets Irina talk
and (more and more, now) cry, and then she leaves. In the pocket
of the silk blouse or the linen jacket Sydna's left, there are always
several hundred-dollar bills. Irina never mentions it, and Sydna
never brings it up, and sometimes at home in the fragrant hush of
her walk-in closet Sydna will lift the sleeve of a silk blouse and touch
the tiny, tiny, almost invisible stitches, almost invisibly mended like
time mends the heart; and Sydna's heart is happy.
    On the Tuesday noon, Sydna cut her visit w/ Irina short and went
to stalk about Saks to see if she could find a suitable present to take
to her niece. It was atrocious what they'd done to Saks. There
were . . . gizmos . . . all around; it was worse than Marrakesh. She
became quite disoriented and lost a sense of where she was and
wandered into some boutique or other—Burberrys it was, thank
God, on the ground floor—and bought Scooter a pith helmet
in what seemed an appropriate dimension for a girl w/ so much
hair. Then she had a Mr. Collins, a man from the Shoppers'
Service, accompany her out to Fifty-first Street, where she found

a taxi that would take her the full distance to the restaurant (six blocks).

Iris, meanwhile, never suited to the city, was struggling up Sixth Avenue from Pennsylvania Station in her peach-colored straw hat. She looked like a picture of Victoriana, w/ her little straw hat and her clean, wonderfully open face, her white blouse w/ its white high collar and little brooch, a lightweight knit shawl in sort of heather colors that kept changing in intensity, and a dusty-rose wool skirt that caught the breeze and billowed out and up over the subway gratings. She was carrying a yellow rose for Scooter from her garden and a sprig of fresh peppermint, which had wilted on the train. On her straw hat she'd pinned a bunch of dried sea lavender her husband, Hap, had given her. She looked around a lot at the people as she walked, and she alone of hundreds, maybe thousands, on the street seemed to be aware that there was weather, that the sun was shining in a faultless, clear September sky. At Fifty-fourth Street, two blocks before the restaurant, she stopped and drew her change purse from her shoulder bag. She took out two quarters, then three, then put them back and took out the newest dollar bill that she could find and gave it to a man in a wheelchair who was begging. He was a middle-aged man w/ short gray hair and hard eyes, and he was quite clean-cut. He had tattoos on both arms beneath a short-sleeved light-blue shirt. Both his legs were clamped onto the wheelchair, and he had a sign that read DISABLED VET. When Iris handed him the dollar, he took it, looking her right in the eye, and nodded. Iris nodded back. There was a fraction of a moment when neither spoke, and then Iris turned and walked up the avenue. Hap had left her two Sundays before. She had twenty-seven dollars in her wallet and two hundred dollars more in a drawer back home. There was a full tank of oil in the ground near the house, which, if the weather held, might be enough until the first or second week of December. She had a B.A. from Sarah Lawrence in Art History, and she hadn't had a paying job in fifteen years. She had six hundred dollars in the checking account, but half of that was Hap's, even though he'd said he wouldn't need it. She had two daughters and some of Aunt Henrietta's gold jewelry and advice from a well-meaning friend to watch the gold market, and that's all Iris had. She had a sister who had called up and had said she'd buy her lunch, a crazy sister. Iris was embarrassed to find her eyes filling up w/ tears at Fifty-fifth Street. For heaven's sake, she thought, people will think I'm lost or I've been weaned too soon. She took a deep breath and her senses filled w/ the aroma of roast lamb and fried onions from the street. If Scooter was going to tell her she was getting married, Iris wasn't sure that she could say, "Oh, wonderful," the way she should. "That's wonderful," she rehearsed out loud to no one in particular. The guy on the corner selling souvlaki heard her and answered, "Hey, chickibaby . . . hey."

Faye had it easy. All Faye had to do that day was leave the office (one flight up, two down from Bendel's) at 12:25 and walk around the corner to the restaurant on Fifty-sixth Street. She was ready. Scooter hadn't shown up for work at all that morning, so Faye was cool as talc. She was prepared. She was prepared for Scoot to tell them all (paying her, Faye, no special courtesy as her partner) that she was going to get married. That was all right. Then, Faye thought, sometime next week, Scoot will say that we should have a talk, just she and I, and then she'll give me an opportunity to buy her out or else she'll point out how w/ Mitch and Davey gone I don't really need to be in business. Faye closed her eyes a little and resigned herself to what she knew was going to happen. She felt helpless but, as usual, dead certain that she'd survive.

She almost died when she ran straight into Cathy getting out of a cab right there at curbside. The two of them collided. I bet Faye had never before been close enough to Cathy to catch Cathy's smell. I think Faye had always been scared of Cathy because Cathy was her half sister's daughter. I think Faye was always afraid of what she'd learn about Belle if she got too close to Belle's daughter. Maybe those things, those kinds of fears, happen only in novels. Whatever it was, Faye noticed Cathy smelled as if she'd already been drinking and that she (this was the really awful part) seemed to be wearing an old, old dress of navy-blue crepe de Chine w/ tiny ivory polka dots and a lace collar that had belonged to Willa, Faye's mother. Furthermore, Cathy was wearing a little scrungy pillbox hat w/ two moth holes in it and white ankle socks w/ a little lace trim, and red-patent-leather tap shoes w/ real taps that went *click* when she walked on the sidewalk. More alarming than that, Cathy's face was scrubbed clean, and Faye saw for the first time in her life how much Cathy resembled her own son, Davey, who was dead, and it made her feel weak like a little trapped thing, pinned in panic in a foreign place.

"Oh it's you, Aunt Faye," Cathy said. "Hiya." She was smiling at the coincidence of their timing. She didn't often smile.

Faye didn't know what to say. In a way, she wished Cathy wouldn't smile, because when she smiled, she didn't look like Davey, and Faye searched her face, trying to fit pieces together, trying to see something again out of fear, wanting to see it again to get used to the fear.

"I knew I'd bump into you today," Cathy said as a joke. Then she got serious. "See, I was with Millie when she called."

Faye realized she was standing there staring, the sort of thing one realizes only out of the other person's discomfort.

"I was . . . just . . . noticing . . . your dress," Faye said calmly, recovering herself. "It's Mother's dress."

Cathy's right hand came up to her throat, and Faye saw how her fingernails were all chewed. They were smudgy w/ traces of color, as if their polish had just been removed.

"Moth-er's?" Cathy said.

"Willa's. My mother's."

Cathy frowned; Faye watched her closely.

"I bought this dress down on Canal Street," Cathy said. "There's a flea market there where I buy all my clothes. . . ."

"No, I'm sure it's Mother's. . . ."

"Really. Look." Cathy reached around and her little tap shoes tapped on the sidewalk as she hobbled a bit to pull out the neckline from the back to show Faye the label.

Faye glanced at it, but mostly she saw for the first time how terribly thin Cathy was.

"It's circa, all right," Cathy said. "Believe me, they sell only used items."

"I'm sure they do," Faye agreed out of politeness, stepping back. "I could have sworn it was Mother's dress," she commented.

"Well, it's factory-made," Cathy said.

They nodded, both together.

"Maybe Grandma had one just like it."

"Grandma?" Faye repeated.

"Willa," Cathy reminded her. "She was my grandmother. I call her Grandma even though we never met. Maybe she had one like it. Since it's factory-made."

"Yes. Maybe she did. It gave me quite a start. She had one just like it."

Faye touched Cathy's collar.

"I remember her scolding me in it," Faye said.

"Oh well," Cathy said. She stuck out her chin, just a little. Faye's heart stopped dead in her chest as she watched. That was it. It was the chin. "I never knew her," Cathy said.

Faye felt the sting of tears in her eyes. "No," she said. "Neither did Davey. She . . . never knew . . . either of you."

Faye turned sharply toward the restaurant. "Shall we go in?" It was more a command than a question.

Cathy blinked a couple of times and followed Faye into the restaurant because it seemed to be the thing to do. All the same, she couldn't help believing she had said something that had made Faye turn away. She believed her hair was falling out because just when people started to pay attention to her, she always said something that made them turn away. The sound of her tap shoes went tap tap past the bar; then there was Scooter, big and bountiful w/ her hair flying out around her filling up the room w/ light, and she was waving. "Here we are! We're over here! Yoo-hooo!"

Some people make a lot of loud disruptive noise and people think they are disgusting, and other people make a lot of loud disruptive noise and people think they are the honest-to-God true-blue embodiment of the American spirit, and Scoot was one of those. No matter where you go w/ Scoot she makes a show-off of herself, and people think it's vastly entertaining.

"This is my cousin," Millie was explaining to a man at the next table, "Miss Nevada."

"Oh." He seemed really pleased. "I'm from Vegas, myself," he confessed.

"Yeah. It shows," Millie told him.

She used her sexuality and her verbal acuity like a weapon sometimes, and she knew it. It wasn't good to do, she told herself. She could end up sounding shrill and being a shrew, her claws out all the time, but life was boring, oh shit, here comes Faye. Smile, Millie. Stand up. Good. Smile more realistically; that's good. Take her hand. Don't kiss. Women shouldn't kiss in restaurants, it looks asinine. Keep smiling and say, Faye how good to see you. She was really buzzed: "Faye . . . Jesus Christ, your hand is freezing. What the fuck's the matter with you?"

"I . . . just . . . I . . . Millie, really . . ."

"Here, sit down, move over for Christ's sake, Scoot. You want some water? Drink some water. Waiter, bring a Cutty straight up, no ice, Cutty neat; right, Faye? You still drink Cutty, don't you—?"

"Yes," Faye murmured.

Millie noticed Cathy frowning at her. She made a mental note to tell Cathy sometime in the future she, Millie, was not herself around her cousin Faye.

"Nice dress, kiddo." Millie winked at Cathy.

"Gosh yes," Scooter agreed. "You look really funky. Is it Perry Ellis?"

Cathy turned a blank face toward Scooter and blinked. She licked her lips. "It's factory-made," she sort of whispered.

Oh dear Christ, Millie lamented. What a bunch of ziprods we turn into. She wished she'd sober up a fraction and then she thought, oh fuck it. She had no idea what a ziprod was. Somebody's last name. She began to laugh.

The waiter who brought Faye's scotch leaned his lips up close to Millie's ear and said, "The gentleman at the next table requests permission to send Madam a drink." Millie looked across the waiter at Faye. Faye was staring at her scotch and listening. "Yeah, sure," Millie said. What is Madam's pleasure, she was asked. She watched his stubby little pencil quiver on the pad. "Um, Madam's pleasure is to see the wine list." She saw the corner of Faye's mouth pull back a little, and Faye shot her a quick look from the corner of her eye. Millie smiled up at the waiter. "Um," she said, "my cousin comes here all the time, so maybe she'll suggest a little something?" Millie leaned toward Faye.

Faye turned toward her and commented, "There's a Grand-Puy-Lacoste, a Pauillac, in the '61 which is . . . really special."

"Okay, sure, that sounds great," Millie said. "The Médoc, '61. And bring a couple glasses, will you?"

Even the waiter couldn't keep from smiling.

Faye lit a cigarette as he walked away. "Eighty-six dollars," she murmured, exhaling. "He'll never go for it. . . ."

"Yes, he will," Millie said. She motioned w/ her head for Faye to check-him-out. Faye glanced over her shoulder at Mr. Las Vegas at the next table, and the two women fell to giggling like two adolescents over fart jokes.

"What's so funny, hey, come on, gee whiz, what's so funny, it's not funny, you guys ruined my surprise and I don't think it's funny—"

"Surprise? What surprise?"

"The lunch, don't kid around. The lunch is my surprise—"

"Oh you mean like *tuna* surprise . . ."

"Millie, cut it out . . ."

"I mean like everyone getting together for a nice lunch and just sitting down together for a change and talking."

"That's really nice, Scoot," Cathy said, meaning it.

"I think I'm going to puke."

"Millie, come on, stop acting like a wet petootie."

"Oh my Christ."

"I think you're not . . . fooling us . . . quite as much as you think, Scooter."

"What do you mean?"

"I mean . . . no one in our family ever gets together except for an . . . occasion."

"Well, maybe now we do, maybe I wanted to change all that, maybe, you know, it wouldn't be such a bad idea to give me a little credit once in a while for trying to do something that's really, you know, well, Cathy said it, nice."

"Bullshit."

"I agree."

"Two bullshits."

"No, I mean with Scooter. I agree with Scooter."

"My goodness, isn't that . . . Iris?"

"Jesus, look at that, it's Mary Poppins. . . ."

"Yoo-hooo! Here we are! EYE-ris! Over here!"

"She looks like she's . . . about to faint."

"She looks terrible."

"Uh-oh," Scooter said.

"Help her over, will ya, Faye? Jesus. She looks like her cat died. . . ."

"Uh-oh," Scooter said again.

"Uh-oh *what*, for Christ's sake?"

"Never mind, it doesn't matter," Scooter whispered in a hurry. "Just be *nice* to her, will you, Millie? Hi! Surprise! Oh! Cissy, oh! You look so nice!"

Iris stood there tugging on her little wilted sprig of peppermint, looking like the kid in a children's play, the one who wanders on off-cue and can't contrive an exit. "What's all this?" she whispered breathlessly. "What's going on? Scoot?"

"It's Scoot's surprise," Cathy attempted to explain.

Iris steadied herself by reaching out and taking hold of Cathy's chair. "You shouldn't have done this," she said to Scoot. She seemed very shaky. She gave Scoot a look that was at once reproachful, pleading, full of warning. Her eyes were working some kind of older-sister thing the other women recognized, even though they'd never had an older sister.

"Oh no," Scooter said in a great flurry, "it's not what you think, hey, it's not that at all, please, come on, really, Iris, I didn't even tell them . . ."

Iris sank in dread into the empty chair between Faye and Cathy. It was a big round table, set for seven. Iris stared at it in shock and thought the whole thing felt a lot like charity.

"Cissy, really, this doesn't have anything to do with you, I had this planned before you even told me, I mean, please believe me, they don't even *know* . . ."

Iris touched her fingers to her forehead and stared in total disbelief at Scooter. Her face had gone completely white, as white as her white blouse, but now she felt a fierce heat rising from the skin along her neck and she thought her pulse would burst her collar. She reached up to take her straw hat off and found her fingers were shaking too much to be trusted to the effort.

Cathy stood and helped her w/ the hatpin, from above.

"Well, whatever it was we didn't know before, we sure don't know it now in spades, you shithead," Millie said.

Cathy smoothed Iris's hair.

"Hey, come on," Scooter pleaded. She looked extremely flustered.

She hated Cathy smoothing Iris's hair. Iris was her sister. Cathy was always nosing in like that, between them. "You guys aren't being fair. . . ."

Iris sighed and squeezed Cathy's hand. Scoot was beginning to feel very angry. Every time she tried to do something nice, the family turned on her and made her feel real dumb. "It's not your fault, Scoot." Iris sighed. She managed a little smile. "I overreacted."

Scooter pouted.

"Really," Iris assured her.

No one said anything.

"I'm sorry," Iris said.

The table was dead quiet.

"Please accept my apology," Iris offered.

"Okay," Scooter acknowledged grudgingly.

Iris looked around. No one was going to help her out, she knew. Everyone expected her to tell them what was going on.

"Hap and I have separated," she announced.

Millie felt the gooseflesh on her arms beneath her knit dress and Faye shivered. Hap and Iris had been married fifteen years. No one had believed this could happen. Not to Hap and Iris. They were everybody's favorite couple.

"I have no idea if it's permanent, or not. We don't know. The girls are"—she took a deep breath—"the girls are taking it, I guess, pretty badly, at least Lise is. . . ."

A waiter appeared w/ the bottle of Médoc and made a big show about displaying the label, and no one at the table moved or said a word until he'd left.

Iris shrugged and folded her hands in her lap and pasted on a little grin. "I don't want a lot of people to know. I would have told you in good time, I mean if Hap, if he, if he doesn't come back. . . ." She cleared her throat and shrugged. "I didn't want to tell you all, just yet, because I'm so . . ." She looked down at her hands and seemed to see them for the first time; then she looked up, distantly, staring off beyond the table. "I think the word for what I'm feeling is . . . it's all confused . . . I think I feel . . . humiliated." She began to cry.

Cathy laid her head on Iris and whispered, "I'm so sorry."

Faye had the chance to say, "I understand," and didn't. I, Ellery, must try not to judge her for that. Still, she had the chance to reach across the small distance between them and say, "Well, cousin, fate has dealt us the same hand"; but she didn't.

Millie sat and stared. She'd sobered up a while back, when she'd first seen Iris. She was so sober, in fact, she was immobile w/ anguish. And woe. She sat and stared.

Mr. Las Vegas came up to the table right behind Cathy and said, "You all are one fine-looking bunch of women, good God! Are you sisters?"

They all just sat there as if they'd been drugged, and finally Cathy answered, "Yeah."

As she spoke, he put one hand on her shoulder and leaned across the center of the table toward Millie. "This is for you." He placed a business card by her plate. "You all enjoy your wine now, hear? You have as many bottles as your little hearts desire. . . ." He stepped backwards and made a ridiculous gesture w/ his hand. He made his hand look like a gun w/ the barrel pointed right at Millie, and he popped the safety w/ his thumb as he said, "I'll see you later, sugar."

Millie closed her eyes.

"What an . . . asshole," Faye murmured.

"Are we supposed to know that person?" Iris asked quietly.

Millie turned the business card over in her hand and read it.

"What does it say, Mill?"

She handed it to Faye, who, after reading it, passed it to Cathy, who reached for it. Cathy read it and looked up at Millie.

"I'll go," she volunteered.

"Don't be ridiculous," Millie forced herself to say.

"No, really, I'll go." She looked around. "Come on, drink up, everybody. Drinks are on me. Waiter! Come on, everybody, this is Scooter's party, let's drink up! Waiter!"

"Cathy . . . really. This is . . . inappropriate."

"Cathy, holy Jesus."

"Another bottle of this, whatever it is, Château Médoc whatever. . . ."

"Look, kiddo, believe me, you're not being funny, so just knock it off, okay?"

"Oh, no, I'm going. I'm going to go."

"Hey, guys, really what's going on, you know?"

"This is what I *do*, Mill, no sweat; I can make myself a few bucks."

"I don't believe this—Faye, say something to her, you're her aunt—"

"Cathy, we were having . . . fun. It was all . . . a joke."

"What kind of joke was it? I don't think it's funny. How much does this stuff cost? Don't tell me it was a *joke*. The guy thought you were serious. Free enterprise. The man is spending money here, and he should get a little something in return. . . ."

"The man . . . is *not* spending money, *we* . . . are paying for the wine and that . . . is *that*."

"The child is really fucking crazy—"

"Will somebody please tell me what's going on?"

Cathy showed Scoot the business card and Scoot read: "Statler Hilton (across from the Felt Forum), Room 1107, four o'clock." Then she looked at Cathy and said, "I don't get it."

"Jesus."

Millie poured a glass of wine and handed it to Iris and poured a glass of wine for Faye and one for herself and then she stood up and said, "I would like to make a toast to my cousin Iris. . . ."

"Oh, now I get it! Geez, you mean that guy thought he could pick us up just by buying a bottle of stupid wine?"

"Guys try it with less than that and get it all the time," Cathy told her.

"To Iris—"

"Well, only if you let them," Scooter sniffed.

"So, let them."

"Well, if that's what you want to do, if that's the way you want to meet guys, great, you can go ahead."

"What difference does it make to you how I meet guys?"

"It doesn't make any difference to me, just forget it—"

"TO IRIS!"

Suddenly the whole restaurant looked around, and there was Millie standing all by herself w/ a glass of wine held in her hand and suddenly she couldn't think of anything to say, so she started singing "Happy Birthday." Millie has an absolutely dreadful singing voice, so Faye stood up beside her, and then the waiters joined in and people at the other tables, and when they got down to the end there was this really loud chorus of "DEAR I-RIS . . ." so Iris stood up and raised her glass and toasted everyone and the whole room cheered and what you have to understand is every time there's a chance for someone in my family to say something rich and just a little bit sustaining to another member of my family, she makes a joke of it and scenes like this happen all the time whenever members of my family are together, like a circus, like an entertainment, outrageous scenes, I mean really extraordinary things and just as an example right when the entire restaurant was applauding Iris, Sydna made an entrance w/ the goddam pith helmet.

What I hope you understand is things go on like this all the time. Just on and on.

Life among us is and has been one big everlasting joke.

Let me try to explain what happened next:

Sydna, you must understand, looks like the Queen Mother, the one who sat in on Prince Charles's wedding and suffered all those British balconies through the Duke of Windsor thing and World War II and Princess Margaret's adolescence. You can't be in Aunt Sydna's presence very long w/out feeling what she's been through and she's been through hell, historically. She knew Franklin Roosevelt and managed to be friends w/ both him and Eleanor. She went to the same school as Eleanor, and it was w/ a letter of advisement from the headmistress that she presented herself to the First Lady in 1933, at the age of twenty-four. Immediately she was hired and put to work for government. She was in the field w/ darkies during the liberal campaign. She opposed McCarthy, and he tried to run her out of State because of it. Over the years she knew Churchill and Robert Oppenheimer, Hemingway and Gandhi. Jack Kennedy called on her in 1961 to try to coax her back to State after she'd left Washington, but she was settled in w/ Mrs. Betts and much too happy. She knew Gloria Swanson and Anaïs Nin and Edith Sitwell. Recently it seems she wants to know us.

Sydna w/drew her lorgnette and peered around the table. She noticed Iris had been crying. She noticed Cathy's hair was falling out. She noticed Faye looked immaculately preserved and that Millie might have had a bit too much to drink. She hardly looked at Scooter, but when she did, she shivered.

"*Tiens, enfants,*" she sighed. She heaved her breasts. "Who's going to brief me?"

She focused her inquiry across the table at Iris. Before anyone could speak, she said: "I know very well it's not your birthday, Iris, because your dear departed mother handed you over to me for four months when you were six weeks old so she could go off on the Stanford expedition to the ruined Nagasaki, and we all know that was in late summer of 1945. . . . Now there are far too many of you," she intoned, surveying us, "for me to remember all your birthdays, but I do know for a fact that the fifteenth of September does not figure as a date in any of your genealogies or I would remember it. You see, lambs, I am not so far gone as all of that. . . ."

"No one thinks of you as far gone, Sydna," Iris said.

"That does not address the point, my dear," Sydna rejoined.

"Sure it does," Millie argued. "Why the hell would Scooter get us all together on a Tuesday afternoon if she didn't think we needed to talk over what to do with the old lady? Just look at her," Millie gestured. "Really, Sydna, I think Scooter's after all your jewelry. I think she has her eye on your garnets. . . ."

Scooter turned a shade of red. It wasn't fair that she should only get attention as the brunt of someone's joke. What she had to say was serious. What she had to say was just as serious as anything Iris had said plus what she had to say was news that wouldn't make them all feel so unhappy.

"Well?" Sydna demanded of her.

"Tell us, Scoot," Cathy encouraged.

Scooter looked around. This wasn't quite the thing that she had planned. For a minute she couldn't even think why it had seemed like such a good idea to invite them. Millie started to say something, but Faye gently touched her hand. Scooter leaned back and took a deep breath. She tossed her head and put on her very best expression. Millie calls Scoot's very best expression the Sandra-Dee-Has-Moved-Her-Little-Bowels look:

"Well, okay, here it is." Scoot beamed. "I'm getting married!"

There was a real big silence. Finally someone said, "Wow, great." Then someone else said, "Great." Then somebody said, "Wonderful."

Then Sydna said, "To whom, if I may ask, or does one do it by oneself these days?"

Scoot blinked a couple times. It occurred to her just briefly that she might have passed out during their congratulations. "Next June," she said.

Iris stood and went around the table to embrace her. Everybody else just watched, dumbfounded. Faye thought that Iris looked like marble where she stood, her arms around her sister. She thought that Iris might have gone behind her so her sister couldn't see her face.

"The second Sunday in June, actually," Scoot rattled on. "I really just, gosh, I really love that time of year. Of course it's going to be a *big* ceremony, you know me! I want all of you as bridesmaids! I think I want, you know, antique lace and that kind of lavender that's always been my favorite. . . . But I guess we have plenty of time for all that! And of course, Aunt Sydna, you have to give me away. And I think we'll do that lawn canopy thing, Faye, that's so popular; I mean for the reception. I've already gone over and registered at Tiffany's and— Did you know they have this new thing, a wedding service at the Metropolitan Museum? I went there, too. . . ."

This last part gave Millie a whole lot of trouble. "The Metropolitan Museum of *Art*?" she said. "You mean the one right here in *New York City*?"

"Oh, they have great stuff!" Scooter gushed. "Glass bowls and great-looking reproductions and all kinds of silver—" Suddenly she began to sense the shock that had set in. The silence stopped her, and she blinked. Cathy was weeping. Sydna gave her one of her lace-trimmed linen hankies.

"Scoot," Iris said softly. She knelt down next to her and looked up into her face. "Darling?" she asked kindly. She touched Scooter's cheek. "We're all waiting to hear who's the lucky guy, sweetheart."

"Oh!" Scoot laughed.

She thought this was especially hilarious.

"Oh, gosh!" she giggled. "I forgot! Good grief! How could I forget? I'm sorry! Gee! It's Raymond. . . ."

No one knew who Raymond was. Well, Faye did: a new name on the Rolodex. White cashmere scarf. Tall. Holds his leather gloves in one hand.

"Raymond," Sydna repeated. "Does he have a last name, dear, or do we call him as one calls a pup?"

"I'm sorry, yes. I'm so excited. Here—"

She handed around a glossy 8 × 10, the kind a casting agent would send out.

Faye looked at it. That's him all right, she thought. She lit a cigarette.

The other women huddled over the picture. Sydna said he looked aristocratic. Cathy excused herself and took off for the ladies' room. Iris asked sweet, loving questions of her sister and called for some champagne. Millie sat still and put her head into her hands. She looked once more at the photograph to make sure there was no mistake, then she put the whole thing from her mind. This was not her problem, she consoled herself. The world was full of things, she told herself, more tragic than her cousin and her cousin's brand-new fiancé.

"So how'd it go?" he asked. He didn't seem too interested. He seemed more interested in looking at the other people's tables.

"Raymond, you could look at me, you know, when we're having conversation," Scoot reminded him.

She hated it when he got jumpy. Why the heck was he so jumpy? She was the one who'd had the hard day.

"Did you have a nice day?" she asked politely.

"It was okay," he said.

There was a long silence while Scooter sipped her glass of water. It tasted chemical. She thought she could remember reading somewhere, maybe in *Good Housekeeping*, that when you're feeling emotional, it affects the taste of things. She was feeling emotional. She'd like to tell him a few things, she really would.

"Tell me about it," she said, setting down her glass.

Her motto was, Let the guy do all the talking. It was pretty good, so far as mottoes go. It meant what she had to say was saved for last.

"You know," he said distractedly. "A couple of my deals fell through, that's all. I don't want to talk about it."

"Which deals?" she asked.

"A couple. You know."

"Which ones?"

"I said I don't want to talk about it!"

She saw him catch himself. She saw him draw himself in and physically command his face to look at her, look pleasant. She hoped she wasn't making all this up.

"Listen," he said, "let's eat. Okay? We better eat so we can catch that movie. What time is it, anyway?"

She said she didn't know.

He looked down at the plastic-covered menu. "God, this place sucks it, doesn't it?" he said. "It would be nice for once to go to someplace decent."

He stood up, to draw attention from a waitress. "Miss?" he called. "Hey, honey?"

Scooter looked away. She wished he wouldn't call them "honey" all the time. She hated that. Sometimes he called them "little mother." She hated that one even more.

"God, the cunts they hire here," he said.

She felt the anger rise in her.

A woman smelling of sweat and cheap perfume appeared beside their table. "Okay. What'll it be?" she said.

She did a double take at Raymond. Her whole manner changed. Scooter acted as if she didn't notice. She was used to women going ga-ga over him. It didn't bother her. Usually, it didn't bother her, and she was used to it.

"I'm not ready yet," she said.

She tried to capture Raymond's sympathy, but he had disappeared into his menu. The waitress turned from her, smiling to herself. She brushed her hip on Raymond, Scooter noticed, and smiled at him.

"I'll have the New York cut," he said, oblivious. "Make it medium rare. And no potatoes."

The waitress practically drooled on him.

"And see if you can get them to really char the outside for me, will you, honey?"

Scooter felt sick.

"Can I bring you anything to drink with that, doll?" the waitress asked.

Scooter thought, Why doesn't she just throw herself across the table and let him have a go at her? It was amazing what a go-around w/ Millie could produce. Millie had had no right to say what she had said, Scooter thought. It made Scoot crazy, that was all. She'd planted a little seed of doubt, and Scoot should know better than to fall for that.

"Bring me a vodka martini," Raymond answered. "And make it nice and strong for me, will you, luv?"

The waitress turned a final time toward Scoot the way you'd turn toward the condemned.

"I'll have a glass of wine, I guess," she murmured weakly. "And the chef's salad."

"White or red?" the waitress said.

Scoot looked at her.

"The wine," she prompted.

"White . . ."

"French, Russian, blue cheese, Italian, garlic or the lemon vinaigrette?"

"Oh, lemon vinaigrette, I guess," Scoot muttered.

"Salad with yours, hon?" she turned toward Raymond.

"Sure."

"French, Russian, blue cheese—"

"Blue cheese for me, sweetheart."

"Separate checks?"

There was a very long, very real dead silence during which Scoot felt the waitress scoring points.

"Why not?" Raymond answered cheerfully.

Scooter looked at him as if he were from another planet.

"So how'd it go?" he asked again when the waitress left.

"Fine."

"Where'd you take them?"

"The Orangerie," she answered tightly. "I told you that."

Raymond was so stupid he didn't hear the warning in her voice. "I hear the food is great there," he commented. "What'd you eat?"

"Crow," Scooter answered softly.

He looked surprised and a bit disgusted. "God, no wonder you don't have an appetite. . . ."

During the meal he chatted on about the wedding, asking twice if she was sure she'd gotten their approval. "Did you show them all the picture?" Raymond asked. "How'd they like it?"

Scooter lied and said they all thought he was handsome.

"What did the old lady think?"

Scooter watched him.

"Who?" she asked.

"The old one. The one with all the money. You know, the dyke. Uncle Sydney," Raymond said.

"Sydna," Scooter prompted. Anger came now like a constant, not in waves. Her stomach tightened.

The waitress brought the separate checks and laid them on the table face down next to Scooter. Raymond wiped his lips on his paper napkin and said, "Let's go. We better hurry."

He slid the checks w/ him and took them w/out looking at them toward the register. Scooter rose and struggled w/ her jacket. Millie had been wrong.

There had been a lot of scenes as usual what w/ Iris coming in and spoiling things and Cathy crying in the ladies' room. Millie had had too much to drink, and she'd been wrong taking Scoot aside to speak to her that way. The truth was, Scoot decided, Millie was afraid of getting old. Millie was jealous.

Scooter watched as Raymond popped a sweet mint in his mouth, across the room, standing by the cash register. She watched as other women looked at him. The woman who was serving as cashier was flattered to be seen w/ him. She hesitated.

"*Momentito*," she thought she heard her lover say.

She stopped.

"*Momentito*, little mother," Scooter heard him say.

She watched him turn from the cashier toward her. She watched him pat his pockets, boyishly, in mock surprise. If Millie had been wrong, how come she knew that Raymond said "*Momentito*, little mother," like this, now and then?

She'd said to Millie, standing there on the sidewalk after everyone had left, she'd said, "Millie, you're a shit."

It had been a big deal for Scoot to say that. It had made her feel grown-up. It had given her a power over Millie she had never had before because she saw Millie get tears in her eyes. She felt her power leach away, seeing Raymond's pantomime across the room. He patted at his pockets, smiling, unaware. He held his palms flat, feeling like a blind man, and he pleaded w/ her, "Honey, have you got—"

Scooter, big and bountiful, the all-American girl, stepped up to the cashier. If you think this is a happy ending, boy are you in for a surprise.

February 17, 1982
Lucy Hastings Clinic
Princeton, New Jersey

4

MILLIE

WHEN I WAS YOUNG, before Assassination was a word, all stories had a Happy Ending. If Death came, if Death was included, She played the part of Leveler, and all the Dead were swept away into a common, pleasant Mist. There were no saints. There were no ghosts. There were no demons. There was Death for some, like dragons and old men; and for the rest there were Happy Endings.

Little girls had Happy Endings; so did little boys, if they were very good.

I was growing up w/ Mavis in America, so Death the Great, Death the common pleasant Leveler, existed on a distant shore. Suddenness, the Rapier, was Death's quick Knight. I first knew Death and Suddenness the week the President was shot. Up till then, the losses suffered had been Pets:

1 father
3 goldfish
2 hamsters
an Easter chicken

Until the week the President was shot, contemplation about Death had been restricted to vague wondering how the goldfish could drown UP; and to doubts surrounding Huan Hee's alibi the day the chicken disappeared. Then in 1963, the week the President was shot, we watched Jack Ruby murder Lee Harvey Oswald in the kitchen. We were having lunch. Mavis was wearing a peignoir. She was slicing a green melon w/ a slender knife. That was the day Death's dread color guard, Simultaneity, swept in. I was fifteen, but it took Mavis slicing a green melon on Thirty-sixth and Madison while Jack Ruby shot Lee Harvey Oswald in a Dallas jail for me to start to understand that no one Truth, no one Reality exists.

She ate the melon.

After that there was the war, Our War, the war that wasn't nice; and in the evening on the tube in kitchens Death tried hard to speak a local language and Assassination was the Word.

Then there was Richard Nixon. W/ Pat and Trish and Julie. Someone writing about daughters in America should take a look at Julie.

Then there was the Apotheosis of the Questionable Profession, and an Actor became President and an Actress was First Lady. Suddenly Equity Membership was reference for a car loan. Suddenly things were looking up. Steven Spielberg was the same age as Yrs Trly: Look at him. Suddenly entertainment was the hallmark of achievement. Not service. Not the doing of good deeds. Not great art. Entertainment.

Mavis was so smart she knew it all the time, and as her daughter I'm so smart I gravitated to it from an early age, like drowning UP: defying gravity, I kept afloat, defying Truth w/ little truths and happy endings.

What is Truth?

This is: Death is no Great Leveler the way they say it is. It raises some to myths. He shot and killed John Lennon. He tried to kill the Pope. They shot Anwar Sadat. He shot at Ronald Reagan. They shot at each other and killed Mark.

Death is no Great Leveler because no two people can be mourned the same way by the same survivor all the time. And it's no ending, either. Death is not the end of life for the survivor.

"When are you going back to work?" my cousin Millie's husband, Sy, kept asking me.

My cousins come, and they're concerned w/ what's the matter w/ me. They can't understand.

When are you getting out, when are you going back to work, when are you coming back to join the living? Am I dead now? Aren't I living?

"I've, uh, joined the unemployed, Sy. As a statement."

Sy's so white, he looks like he's been rolled in flour.

"Save it, Ellery," I'm told. "Sy gave to Reagan."

"Gave what? Blood?"

"No, money."

"Oh, thank God. No threat of hepatitis, then."

"Millie, for God's sake. Who I vote for is a private matter."

"*Whom*, for God's sake."

"Like what you tell a lawyer."

"I don't have a lawyer."

"Is that a fact," he says, the venom dripping from him. "Poor Mill. Maybe we should get you one. . . ."

I (me, Ellery) know Suddenness and I know Death and I know the Factors that precede them: tension, calm, slow motion, intense colors, a dry mouth. Tonight I felt them all.

"When are you going back to work?" Sy asks. "Work will take your mind off all of this. . . ." (He thinks my mental illness is an indulgence, something I went out and got myself, like a Mercedes.)

"I couldn't entertain the thought," I say, "of going back to work until I'm better."

"Why not?" he asks. "Look at Patricia Neal."

"I'm sorry?"

"She has that speech impediment. She gets work."

Millie gives me a look that seems to say, "Don't argue with him." Millie *always* used to argue w/ him. What's going on here?

"That comment was in pretty bad taste, Sy. Besides, Patricia Neal had a stroke, and I had a nervous breakdown. I've lost all ability to control emotion. That's what acting is—a masterful control over one's emotions."

"Do you want me to believe you couldn't go on the tube and hold up a box of Excedrin or whatever like she does?"

"Sy, that's not acting."

"Well, she won an Academy Award. Do you want me to believe that since she won the Academy Award, everything she does shouldn't be considered acting?"

"I don't understand the question."

"Don't get so upset."

"I never did that kind of work, movies and TV. It's not what I do. I'm a stage actress."

"Well, pretend it's like the war, then. There you're trained for something, and you do it. When the war ends, you do something else. Life goes on. Maybe TV work's an answer. You were always good. I can't believe you don't have offers rolling in. What would it pay? Are the wages any good?"

"It's not what I *do*, Sy."

"Well, you've got to do something, doll, or you'll be in here till you die. Positive Action. Keeps you young. Just look at Millie. Doesn't she look great? Positive action. She keeps working. Look at me. Look at these biceps. Tennis. I'll be fifty in four weeks. Not a line. Not a wrinkle. How's that other problem, by the way?"

"Which one?"

"The ovarial, ah, problem."

"Sorry?"

"The one with your, ah, menstruating."

"It's still the same."

"The same?"

"The same."

"Can't they cure these things with hormones these days?"

"I don't know."

"Testosterone?"

"Beats me."

"Estrogen. Estrogen's the one. They feed it now to chickens. That's the way they plump 'em up. Isn't that the one, sweetie? You have it in your night cream. Estrogen."

Millie sits like ice upon a frozen pond. She gives me chills.

Sy says, "How's the food here, by the way?"

"I'm sorry?"

"The food. How's the food here?"

"In the clinic?"

"Yes."

"A one-star place, Sy.

"How's the service?"

"The . . . service?"

"Nice and efficient, are they?"

"I guess so. . . ."

"You know another thing that might do just the trick, might snap you out of this? A new man. A new love interest. Right, sweetheart? Wouldn't that be just the thing for Ellery? A little *sex?*"

Oh *ho*, I think. Oh *ho* ho ho.

Real quick Millie rustles from her coma and says, "What the fuck is this décor, anyway? They used to bury Pharaohs with less shit than you have here."

"Did you hear what I said, Millie? Press Harris is a nice guy for her. . . ."

"It's depressing, all this shit. Jahnna in her flyboy outfit over there. Aunt Sydna. A hooked rug. *All* this shit. Whatever happened to green walls and rickety I.V. stands?"

"Press Harris is a real nice guy. A nice young man. Divorced. I think he has a little kid. Doesn't Press have a little daughter, sweetie? He's looking for a woman. I see him all the time there at the health club. I could speak to him. We could set them up together, how 'bout it, honey? Wouldn't you get a kick seeing all the gals in your family happy like we are? Scooter first. Then Ellery. Then Cath. We'll get you all wrapped up. Of course, Scooter we don't need to help. Scooter's quite a gal. . . ."

"Tell me about Raymond," I say, staring hard at Millie. "You met him, didn't you?" I bait her.

"Well, you know," Sy butts in, "Scooter asked us in one night for drinks to meet him, but the city doesn't do it for me any more. That Koch is some real arrogant kind of guy and I just feel that attitude these days and I resent it. I'm a suburban guy. Millie goes in all the time but by the time you park, where are you? So I said no. I think it was a weekday night or something when I had to work the next day, so we said we'd do it some other time and then she never called. Maybe we should call them, sweetie. Have them out. Me, I like to go out to the Meadowlands. Have you been out there, Ellery? Have you ever seen that place? That guy Brendan Byrne knew what he was doing when he put his name on that arena out there. People will remember him for that. . . ."

"You've met him, Millie. Haven't you? I know you have."

"Byrne? Neither of us met Byrne yet, did we, sweetie? He's not that guy we went to that fund-raiser for down in Ocean City, was he?"

Millie looks at me. "Yes. I met him. I sat next to him on an airplane, once."

"An *airplane*?" I repeat.

"You sat next to Brendan Byrne?" Sy asks.

"For God's sake, Sy, to *Raymond*," Millie says.

"And when was this?" Sy asks.

"What did he say to you?"

"Nothing," Millie says. "We didn't speak."

"When *was* this, Millie?" Sy repeats.

"Did he come on to you?" I ask.

"Not at all."

"Millie!"

"I don't remember, Sy!"

"You take so many plane rides that you don't remember?"

"Okay, it was last year. Happy, Sy?"

"*When* last year? What *month*? The only plane ride we took last year was in December when we went to Mexico and the Bahamas—"

"It must have been December, then."

"You're lying to me again, Millie—"

"How was he dressed?" I ask.

"I don't remember, Elly."

"Was he wearing a cologne?"

She thinks about it, fingering her pearls. "Yes," she finally whispers.

"I hate it when you lie to me," Sy says.

"All right, then: it was March. It was when I went to San Francisco for the seminar."

"Don't think I don't know right away when you're lying to me."

"Millie, was the fragrance citron?"

She frowns.

"No, I'm sure it wasn't."

Her fingers stop around a single pearl and she closes her eyes.

"Elly, it was sandalwood."

When she looks at me again she lets me see the Truth: she never spoke to Raymond, and he never spoke to her. He saw her coming back from somewhere. He saw her coming home from someplace no one even knew she'd been.

"You have a lover," I conclude.

She's very still.

Sy has gone to get the Fiat, and we're waiting by the door. I see the headlights in the distance. Millie takes a breath.

"Yeah. Hesh. He's a lawyer, in Chicago. He's married. He has kids." She looks away from me. "God." She shivers. "I have to ride in the goddam car with him for two whole hours, and I don't even have a *drug.* . . ."

"Mill, have you got anyone to talk to about this?"

"Oh Christ—tons of people."

"Please, Mill, I think you ought to be real careful. I think Sy's suspicious."

She turns to me. "What the fuck's the matter with you, Ellery? What do you mean you *think* Sy's suspicious? Sy already knows! Sy's already told the *kids* about it, baby—"

"Oh, my God, that's terrible."

"No shit."

"You have to get away from him."

"What?"

"He's an awful man. What an awful man! You have to get away! Just get away! He'll try to kill you—"

"Come on, stop acting like a wacko, El. . . ."

"Promise me you'll call me in the morning. Please, promise me. I won't sleep unless you do. I'm so afraid for you!"

"Sure. Just take it easy. Calm down, will you?"

"Millie?"

"Okay, okay, I'll call you, kid. . . ."

I study her: Mill is one stunning woman, no argument on that. A "knockout,"if you'll let me borrow from ol' Sy. We're all shame-lessly blessed w/ interesting looks in this one family—and health. We're the people other people write Letters to the Editor about, which read: "How dare you be concerned w/ So-and-so's divorce (breakdown, bankruptcy) while 30 million (billion, trillion) people starve each year in India (Wisconsin, Africa)?" A person's *life*, I want

to say, a person's *life* will suffer many ills. Of these, there are Major
Ills and Minor ones. What is today's criterion, I ask myself, which
dictates differences between a Major Ill and a Minor one? Survival?
If one cannot decide the color of one's bridesmaids' dresses, *will one
live?* If one finds no animal to kill by sunset, *will one survive?* Suppose
a being is so sated by the wealth of one's society that the color of a
fabric has the same survival value to the psyche as a protein? Should
we all go crazy; or should I alone? Look at Millie—it doesn't seem
to cause her any hesitation if the local Lord & Taylor runs a window
featuring the same bath mat in sixty different colors, because she
knows no shade of doubt. She holds Reality together—a lover here,
a family there: a mistress of the art of living simultaneously. She
looks so cool. Why can't I look like her? Maybe what I need to do
is study Logic, which she teaches. Maybe then I'll look like her,
intact. I'll ask if I can go to Princeton in the morning to the Co-op
for some books. She's just so goddam smart. So cool. She's just so
beautiful.

"I love you," I say.

"Oh, fucking Christ," she answers. "Let go of me, for Christ's
sake. Jesus, El. You're like fucking dealing with a goddam retarded
child. . . ."

5

MILLIE AND HESH

A STORY BY ELLERY MCQUEEN

HESH HAD CALLED LONG DISTANCE. Millie had been thinking he might call, and by the morning of the next day she had
booked a flight. Flying out, she had had a window seat, and from
the window of the plane she had seen ice on Lake Erie. She had
seen a naked man lying on his belly on a floe of ice, drinking from
the lake. She had thought:

If Lake Erie is dead, then the naked man is suicidal;
if the naked man is suicidal, I wish him peace;
if the naked man is not suicidal, he is fantasy.

The Lake is not dead;
Therefore,
the man is fantasy.

She had drawn her notebook from her briefcase and made the following notations:

1. if dead, then suicidal	$(D \supset S)$
2. if suicidal, peace	$(S \supset P)$
3. if not suicidal, fantasy	$(\backsim S \supset F)$
4. Not dead.	$(\backsim D) \, /$
5. . . . therefore: Fantasy	$\therefore F$

From the notation she had drawn her proof:

$\backsim S \vee D$	(Material Implication)
$D \vee \backsim S$	(Commutation)
$\backsim S$	(Disjunctive Syllogism)
F	(*Modus Ponens*)

Elegant.

Millie is the queen of elegant proofs.

She had capped the perfect pen she had gotten at discount through her cousin at the MOMA and had sat back to consider if the geodesic dome is womb fantasy or trinity made spheroid. Specifically, she had not thought what she would say to Hesh. Hesh would have rehearsed it all already; Hesh is always dear to detail. Details abound. Children, for example. She and Hesh have seven of them. It is convenient to remember the parentage of each. They have:

two boys w/ two fathers
three boys w/ one father
two girls w/ one mother each
two bedrooms seven hundred miles apart
no analysts
guts
money
sex

They are married, not to each other. Married lovers, Millie and Hesh.

It has been said of Millie that she is both beautiful and brainy.

1. She is not beautiful.

Think her not beautiful
Think her face a closed mask upon a pillow
Think her body closed and cold

2. Coffin Millie.
3. Film Millie through gauze; watch her. Watch what Millie's mind can do: her eyes open like sprung locks on the lids of boxes. She sets her mind to work its morning exercise; she sets her mind to make her face before rising, make her buttocks smooth as glass, sublime as mathematics; make her nipples cognac on a tongue, make her belly white and narrow as an underwater shelf, make her face a vellum invitation, make two eyes that take one past wanting.

Millie makes it clear there is nothing she cannot do when she sets her mind to do it; she sets Hesh arush. It has been said of Hesh that he's the Young Turk of the Illinois bar. Corporate law. Buy/ sell. Afternoons of racquetball at the club. Parties w/ hash and Lady. Always a woman or two on the side. Models. The kick of fucking public women. The kick of Carol coming into his home on a television commercial right there in front of the kids and his having fucked her upside down just Tuesday afternoon. He is the king of the model fuck. Takes pleasure in the way models keep themselves. Clean. Long and hairless. Wordless and smiling on a three-color page.

The most exquisite mental exercise Millie has ever devised is to allow Hesh to believe that at any preorgasmic moment her concentration can be threatened by consideration of Russell's Paradox.

The most exquisite physical exercise Hesh has ever devised is to try to fuck Millie's brains out.

They tend to congratulate each other a great deal on the success of their relationship. Hesh says: Karen got me into coke. Millie discourses on the odds of simultaneous climax. Hesh says: Carol got me into Corvettes.

Once Hesh told Millie she was very beautiful. Once he told her she was gorgeous. Once Millie told Hesh he was the gentlest man. Once she told him he was tender.

Not until the most recent time did they cling one to another come morning. Never do they speak endearments. Never do they speak hello, good-bye, what news. Always: time, it's time, the upward spiral, life w/in a life where neither changes, nine days, six nights, five cities, four rooms, three countries, two years.

Hesh says: Other women keep score.

Millie says: We are not the Great Loves of our lives.

Once, in ecstasy, she called him baby. Once, in a bar, a woman wanted to take their picture. They said: Uh-uh, no-no, thank-you.

Hesh says: Congratulations, Millie.

Millie says: Congratulations, Hesh.

Hesh had been half an hour late meeting her plane and had lit their first joint on the road from the airport. Millie had gulped it and had coughed and had begged off the last half because she had started to feel marooned in her body while reason slid to the horizon like a distant, silent ship. She had thought, Remain calm, help will arrive in time. They had stopped before a liquor store, and Millie had realized the conversation she had been overhearing had been theirs. Hesh had said, "Need some wine." He had been standing outside the car on the other side of the passenger window trying to open her door saying, "Want to come w/ me?"

"No, no, staying here."

She had thought she had been trying to unbutton her jacket for some time. She had seen Hesh inside the liquor store, and then she had noticed her jacket was open. She had thought she would stare at the clock on the dash and recite Zen:

if one tries to hold up the door of a falling house, then

She would stare at the clock on the dash and recite Zen, but Hesh had handed her a brown paper bag through the window, and they had been passing along a road of shopping centers, and the directional signal had gone on, and she had carried her own luggage, and Hesh had said, "Close your eyes." She had put the luggage on the floor and walked around the room, and then they had been making love on the water bed, and she had been marooned w/ Hesh in her body, and her goddam mind was on a tour, and she had gone dry, and Hesh had said, "I don't want to hurt you."

Once, in Washington, she had been on her way to meet him and a moving van had run into her car and she had broken two ribs and a thumb.

Hesh had rolled away but had kept his arm beneath her and had lit another joint and had turned on the video looking for a porno-graphic movie, and Millie had said, "I don't like what this grass is doing to me." Hesh had said, "You can control it if you want." He had gotten up and had dressed and had gone to the office to ask the clerk to run a movie, and Millie had seen herself distorted in the mirrored glass above the bed. Millie had seen herself spread along the white fake fur throw of the water bed, had seen herself laid back in Hesh's detailed purple fantasy room loaned for the occasion by a client of his, and she had started to laugh, and the white hope of reason had approached hard by starboard like a Coast Guard cutter, and she had laughed until tears had come to her eyes and the whole goddam room had begun to swim in riotous detail. "Oh, Hesh."

Details: Once Millie had pressed her thigh against Hesh under a table while his wife had eaten pastry w/ her fingers. Once Millie had wanted to fall in love w/ Hesh. Once she had wanted to kill him. Once she had tried to convert sexual energy to a passion for routine.

But Hesh had called long distance. And the women she knew stared across restaurant tables on Saturday nights at their husbands drinking vodka straight, and they had never left their children notes taped to the kitchen cabinets w/ instructions for dinner.

Once, she had returned to the room too soon, and Hesh had been in the midst of The Call, and she had heard him say, "Love you, love the kids." And she had searched herself for emotion and she had felt nothing.

Once, Hesh had asked if she'd like to learn how to roll a joint, and Millie had said, "Why on earth . . ." and Hesh had said, "A passing of the mantle . . ." And she had felt an exquisite sadness that even though she is older than most of his women, she's still younger than he, his student in sex.

It is not unforeseen in the ways of such things that he would have her teach his son all that he had taught her.

He had introduced her to cocaine, to what she called Euclidean intercourse: new highs, amyl nitrite, every source of sexual stimu-lation known among the species, mirrors, massage, fantasy.

Throughout the night and into the following day, they had played at frenzy, they had worked to perfect their act the way an attorney draws a contract, the way a logician works a proof. Hesh had worked to make everything perfect for her; his gift, he had called it. He had approached her sideways and backwards, talked dirty, talked too much, asked how she liked it, didn't talk, nibbled, sucked, caressed, cupped his hands like a mask to her face as she had swooned w/ nitrite, and she had thought, oh! if this is drowning, then . . .

Hesh had cried out w/ his mouth pressed in her ear. Hesh had cried out w/ his head between her breasts. Hesh had cried out w/ his body in her body. And Millie had almost lost her mind. Almost.

By the evening of the second day they had used up all but the inferior grass; they had cracked the last popper, exhausted the coke, run out of wine; and had moved to the Holiday Inn. Millie would be catching the shuttle come morning. Breakfast on the plane. Two-hour flight. Breezy parting. Simply done. Do it again sometime. Maybe.

And Hesh had said: "We have good sex."

And Millie had run her hand along his body.

She had thought: The Holiday Inn, the bed vibrates for a quarter, people from Kansas outside in the hall, half of America. She had placed her head against the pillow, and Hesh had turned out the light and told one of his long, twisting stories while Millie had traced circles w/ the back of her hand upon his chest, and later Hesh had asked if she experienced different kinds of orgasms w/ different partners, and Millie had said that for years there had been only Hesh and her husband, and Hesh had wrapped his arms about her and Millie had asked, "How 'bout you?"

And Hesh had nodded in the darkness, and Millie had asked, "Because of bodies?" And Hesh had brushed the hair from her forehead w/ the tips of his fingers and had tapped gently on the side of her head, and Millie had seen through to the sweetness of Hesh's passion for detail, and right there in the Holiday Inn where the marquee welcomes the nation and the beds are all the same and couples and conventions sleep as one Millie had said, "Watch me."

And she had made her mind up in an instant and had wrapped her mouth around him and had made him move to the rhythm of her mind, and Hesh had whispered, "Millie, what . . ." and she had led him through her body until he had hit upon her mind, a perfect detail, they, a perfect Hesh and Millie once, then twice. They couldn't come apart.

And then they had talked and danced and giggled, gay as children, which is why grown people take lovers, and they had slept w/ bodies touching, and in the morning they had dressed and Hesh had turned on the *Today* show and he had stood behind her as she had brushed her hair, and she had said, "Flying out, there was ice on Lake Erie," and Hesh had said, "Well, that will soon be gone," meaning, spring would come. And he had carried Millie's luggage to the car, and she had left the key at the desk, and she had watched the road signs on the way to the airport, and she had watched the planes taking off, and she had left him sitting in the car w/ no good-bye.

Flying home, she had not had a window seat, and six days later she had been standing at the kitchen sink washing dried milk from a glass, and through the kitchen window she had seen a man and a woman playing like two children in the morning light across her yard.

She had thought:

> If fantasy is fact, then the man and woman are real.
> If the man and woman are real, then they are lovers.
> If they are lovers, they are perfect at it.
> If they are perfect at it, they cannot be real.
> Therefore . . .

Millie had closed her eyes and leaned her weight, the weight of logic, against the kitchen sink. All of life, she knew, she could explain if she could set her mind to do it. All of life, she knew, including love, she could explain, therefore . . .

Millie set her mind to do it. She set her mind to making lovers real, her lovers. She set her mind to doing what she'd done for years until a time when Hesh would call to her, long distance.

.

February 22, 1982
Lucy Hastings Clinic
Princeton, New Jersey

6

ASH WEDNESDAY

MILLIE CALLED TODAY, just like I asked her to—a good thing, too, because Some Person here is getting on my nerves, and Millie calmed me down. How the hell was I supposed to know it was Ash Wednesday? What the hell does that mean when you're not religious? There's this Person here named Florence and she's real fat and a Jesus Freak. Every night she stays up past the curfew eating sour cream and onion chips, watching something called the "700 Club" on the TV in the Dayroom. Sometimes she turns the volume up real loud and the rest of us complain. "Why's it called the '700 Club,' Florence?" I once asked her. Her answer was, "Jesus came to me last night and said you'll never menstruate again until you beg forgiveness for the murders of the unborn children of the earth, and even then you'll never ever have a child that's yours, and if you do its nose will look like a pig's snout and it will have a tail and it will have the devil's curse on it, so there."

I'm disgusted w/ her. She has rolls of fat and waxy stuff and lint collects along her seam lines. Today she had this soot smudge in the middle of her forehead.

I said, "Florence, what's that soot smudge in the middle of your forehead?" and she said, "Jesus came to me last night and said the Law is after you and you're a fugitive from justice and the only sanctuary for you is in His temple."

She Walks w/ Christ and Talks w/ Christ more often than the Pope, and there's no telling her the vast volume of communion wafers she wolfs down are really sour cream and onion chips. She's so hostile toward me. Why me? She leaves the others pretty much alone. After we had had that little go-around about the soot smudge on her forehead, she walked up to me in Free Time and spat on me. It didn't touch my skin exactly, but I had to change my clothing. She makes the steel bands tighten in my throat so I can't breathe.

Later someone else, a nonbeliever, had the grace to tell me it's Ash Wednesday. This was a relief, because I thought the soot smudge on her forehead marked the spot where Florence's brain must have imploded.

I hope the next time Jesus comes to her He takes her.

A CONVERSATION ABOUT FAYE W/ MILLIE ON A DAY
OF RELIGIOUS SIGNIFICANCE

"Hey, kid. Hozit goin'?"

"Not good."

"What's the matter?"

"Some Fat Follower of Jesus spat on me."

"Oh. Miss Manners doesn't cover that one. What'd you do? I mean aside from taking it very personally and getting extremely depressed. . . ."

"I changed my clothes."

"Good girl. You want the news?"

"I wrote a story about you."

"Great, you want the news?"

"I got a day pass and went to the Princeton Co-op and got books—"

"Would you feel better if we limited our conversation to talking about *shapes*? How 'bout *colors*? Are you up for *colors* this A.M.?"

"I read through all the books, and then I wrote a story."

"And I bet it has a lot of baby animals in it, doesn't it?"

"It's just got you and Hesh. And some naked man you see from an airplane in Lake Erie on an ice floe."

"Oh fuck, they went ahead and put you on an opiate without asking me—"

"I've been writing stories about everyone in our family, not just you, so don't get so upset."

"What you hear's the sound of wonderment, dear heart: I have to wonder what you think you know about my life. . . ."

"What you tell me. What I make up. The Truth or falseness of my conclusions don't matter so long as the method of my proving them is valid."

"Here's *spit* on your method of proving them, genius."

"Well, don't get mad."

"Then don't get lily-white with me. . . ."

"Sorry, it comes and goes."

" 'It' does?"

"Me, Ellery. Tell me the news."

"I called Scooter this morning."

"That's the news?"

"Shut up and listen: On the ride home last night, all Sy talked about was when had I seen Raymond and why was Ellery making such a big deal about my seeing him—"

"Uh-oh . . ."

"So I said, 'Ellery's had a *breakdown*, for Christ's sake, who the fuck knows what's going on with Ellery?'"

"Thanks, Mill."

"So just to get him off the subject, I said I'd call Scooter in the morning and make some kind of date among the four of us so Sy could cross-examine Raymond for himself, for God's sake."

"You're a peach."

"Hey, don't I know it. So I called Scoot this morning at her office and guess what she told me? The shit has hit the fan with Faye and Mitch. Scoot told me Faye hired a detective to help her find him.

The detective traced him to a job in Sante Fe. She flew out there
late last night to see him. . . ."

"To Santa Fe? New Mexico?"

"No, Santa Fe, Bohemia, you douche . . ."

"Oh my God, she's going to kill him!"

"Oh for Christ's sake, here we go again—"

"Oh my God, no, Millie! Can't you see she's going to kill him?"

"Ellery, will you get off it—"

"She's going to shoot him! Why else would she go out there?"

"Just put a lid on it, pissbrain—"

"Just like Belle did! They're sisters! Oh my God! It's just like Belle
did, it's the same state—!"

"Will you *shut up*—"

"We have to find out where he is and warn him! Millie, find out
where he is! Call the state police! Millie, don't just let another thing
like this happen to us again!"

"*Shut* up or I'm *hanging* up and calling back and telling them
to throw you in a padded cell. I'm counting, listen—one-two-three—
by ten you better be a bowl of cherries, baby, right? Seven-eight-
nine-ten. Are you still there, or did it self-destruct? It doesn't talk?
Where did it go? I hear it breathing. Now, listen, Faye's the most
nonviolent person that you'll ever meet. That's not hyperbole. That's
not 'made up.' You want to write about the family? Fine. But then
you'll have to learn. You can 'make up' to your heart's content, but
then why write about your family? Why not write about someone
else's family? There is all this information about lives, about the
way we go about our living that's right in front of you. I saw it in
your room. I saw what you are doing. Right now, though, you're
treading water so fast you're capsizing everything. Faye. Let me tell
you about Faye. You have a lot to learn from her. Do you know
why? She lost Davey the same way you lost Mark. Listen to me.
I'm talking like a walking Euphemism: Davey was *killed*, and so was
Mark. Are you still with me?"

"Yes."

"Is this too heavy for you?"

"Yes."

"Tough shit. Faye doesn't even get *angry* anymore. She preserves
a balance. Her life is a tableau. She treats that fucking house as if
it were a mausoleum. She's entombed in it. It's a fucking dried

arrangement, like her hair. This is not a woman who can contemplate a small disturbance anymore. It would be a big thing in her life to move a fucking piece of *furniture*, for Christ's sake, like a *vase* or something, from one room to another in that fucking house. . . ."

"Is that why you don't like her?"

"Who says?"

"Because you think she's a coward?"

"For Christ's sake, kid, Faye has never been a coward. Never. Shit. She has more courage than the two of us together. . . ."

"Faye? Our cousin Faye?"

"She stole Mitch away from the girl he was engaged to marry. I mean walked away with him. She slept with him the week before the wedding. I was supposed to be the maid of honor, too. In fact, I still have the bridesmaid's dress, isn't that pathetic? I should take it out for Scooter's wedding. It's yellow. That was Mitch's favorite color. In fact, it's because of me the whole thing hit the fucking fan, because I'm the one who introduced them. Mitch was going to marry my best friend. Ultra-pulpy so far, don't you think?"

"Ultra. When was this?"

"Sixty-two, before folks started making love, not war."

"You're carrying a twenty-year-old grudge?"

"It's not a grudge exactly, puddin'. It's more like an Ancient Taboo. I like Truth in advertising, understand? Mitch and Trudy were childhood sweeties. Lived next door to each other. *Dressed* alike when they started going out. Fucking too adorable. Trudy and I are living in New York in this asshole apartment with our first jobs, and Faye drops in one afternoon and I introduce her to Mitch. They were engaged already, Trudy and Mitch; they were fucking *born* engaged. Anyway we all four hung around together during what Trudy later called the months of winter's torment. No one knew that anything was going on. The week before the wedding, the first week in April, we were all going to take a couple of cars, a whole gang of us, and go down to Bucks County to find enough cheap furniture to furnish their new apartment. Some weird fucking disease happened to everyone except Guess Whos. So Saturday morning Trudy calls Mitch and says, 'Take Faye with you,' because Faye knew furniture already from her job in the design showroom. I'm telling you, Innocent, not one of us, nobody, knew from *shit*.

So they took off. Around nine that night Mitch calls the apartment. Trudy's sleeping, so I take the message. 'Hey, Mill,' Mitch says, real cheery, 'we only bought one thing, so we're going to give it one more day.' 'Great,' I say. 'Where are you?' 'Outside Philadelphia,' he says. 'Great. Good luck. I'll give your love to Trudy.' 'Great.' This is April sixth or seventh. We didn't see the two of them again till after May Day. . . ."

"How come you never told me this?"

"It's real hot copy, ain't it?"

"No kidding, how come I never knew?"

"Well, no offense, Miz Scarlett, but part of it's because you never asked. . . ."

"What did they buy?"

"What?"

"What's the one thing that they bought, like Mitch said?"

"Jesus, baby, you ask the damnedest questions. . . ."

"Can you remember?"

"Sure I can remember. Christ. They'd blown all their money shacking up in that motel for three weeks. Plus, Mitch had lost his job. I mean, three weeks in a motel is a *lot* of fucking. . . . Faye had been boarding at the Barbizon, so when they got back to New York they moved into the place that Mitch had rented for himself and Trudy, and believe me I went straight over as soon as they got back to give them a whatfor. There was nothing *in* that place. They'd gotten married, they didn't have a bed, there was no rug, there were no curtains, there were no pots and pans, and right in the middle of the floor was this piece of furniture like a fucking monument, and I remember walking down those crummy stairs from their apartment thinking, 'What the fuck can two people possibly be doing on a fucking *desk?*' "

7

DESK

A STORY BY ELLERY MCQUEEN

SO SPRING CAME LIKE AN INSULT at the tail of winter's torment.

At first it seemed he'd gone away a little, and she kept his things as he had left them. But weeks went by, and Mitch's clothes went shabby on their hangers, looking worse than if he'd worn them, and the next thing Faye knew she was calling the police to report a missing person.

Don't think these things can happen overnight: Mitch had planned on becoming missing for some time. He never bothered telling Faye because she would have stopped him. She would have stopped him w/ her common sense and seasoned caution. Sometimes all Mitch had to do was look at her and courage drained right out of him. She wasn't the ol' Faye, risky, playful, any more, and he blamed himself for that. Something deep and mournful like trapped water

underground resounded through them no matter how he tried to
tap bright running past; oh! in the old days they'd had fun. Sure,
people say it's wrong to think about the old days in the face of such
a tragedy, but how could he forget that Faye had worn bright colors?
She'd had snap, like campus mornings. She'd kept him keen, away
from sadness. Once she had been to the bone good health, clean
living, lively, crisp. Now what gaiety she had seemed like a wash
of artificial light across a ghost town, a stark version of a failed effect.
He blamed himself.

The blame itself grew restless as a specter on a parapet. He knew
he loved her, yet he didn't know, for instance, how she'd mourn.
She never used to show her mourning. He had in mind that he'd
take off, and she'd be spiky like before. He hadn't thought too much
of where he'd go; he thought he'd pull a little time. He took to
sunny climes. He took to wearing funny shirts in too-bright colors,
flimsy shirts whose dyes left rings in motel sinks in places such as
Indiana. He lost a lot of weight. When he hit Santa Fe, New Mexico,
he knew he had slowed down. He took the job as night desk clerk
at the Sands of Time Motel, right there on the corner of Don Gaspar
and Alameda.

Faye tracked him down; it wasn't easy.

Nights she'd sit before their desk at home and figure scenes between them, staring at the wall. So many scenes played through the
wall it wore thin like the wall of a vital organ, until Faye, no mystic,
could see its webs and granules like wet reaches of a thirsty life in
sand. For God's sake, why the desert? she would wonder. If Mitch
had needed to take off to anywhere, why for God's sake to the desert?
Even if it was the U.S.A., it seemed foreign and religious. She
thought he must have sought a sultry climate just to punish her.
She thought he must have gone to prove that certainty ranged in
him as easily as space defined by four walls and because being young
and carefree was a dimension he fulfilled. He was trying her, tempt-
ing her to take up the uncertain and not to cling to sadness. He had
always been her better for adventure. Even after they had built the
house and decided to have Davey, Mitch lived out of his suitcase.
It wasn't until Davey almost died the first time that he settled down.
Even then he spent the weeks surrounding Davey's illness in the
hallway by the nurses' station. He always liked the rhythm in a room

of strangers. He was never good at making small talk w/ the ones he loved. More than once Faye had to tell him that the chambers of his heart resembled motel lobbies. She couldn't see Mitch in the desert, she just couldn't picture it at all, so one night early on in spring while she was sitting at the desk she booked a flight to Santa Fe on impulse.

She imagined there'd be music when they met; there wasn't. And it was dark, hours after sunset, when her plane touched down. She had the sense of mountains in the purple sky. The taxi driver asked if she was one of those who'd like to drive out to the Opera House to see it, and she motioned no. When he delivered her downtown, he looked at her and asked, "You sure you have the right place?" She tipped him, but she didn't speak. She carried her own suitcase to the door. She could see someone w/ Mitch's back behind the motel desk, and she looked away. She almost lost her courage. The flight had given her a headache, and she'd never been out West before. The lobby smelled of disinfectant. She held her breath and counted her own footsteps as she walked across the floor.

"Surprised?" she heard a strange voice asking. It was hers. Facial muscles near her mouth pulled back in dread of it. She should have practiced speaking on the plane, she thought. She'd counted on there being music, but instead a bent man pushed a vacuum cleaner near the door.

"Nothing surprises me," Mitch said w/out emotion.

He was sorting motel registration forms, his fingers moving, hidden, on the desk. He hadn't looked up when she entered.

She sensed the rhythm of his fingers falter, so she said, "I hired a detective." She wished there was a bell, the kind they have at large hotels. She would have rung for his attention. "It took a lot of courage," she said. It was as if she was arguing a case. She tried to smile and couldn't. She thought the lobby reeked of a delousing. It was worse than all the hospitals they'd ever waited in together.

Mitch looked up and took her in. He had a way of surveying the baggage when he looked at her that some men have. Faye knew at once from his expression that she'd put herself together wrong. She'd worn a tailored suit to travel in. It was a dark gray fabric that wouldn't show the dirt and never wrinkled. Her hair had grayed in the last five months.

Mitch had trouble keeping her in focus. What w/ all the heat and working w/ the transients, there were times he thought he had a fever. Many things he looked at seemed a bit unreal.

"If this is over money, just forget it," he said levelly.

"It's not," she answered, and her voice trailed off.

She noticed he looked younger. Someone had cut his hair all wrong, but on the whole his face seemed smoother and his eyes showed much less pain. He'd lost a lot of weight.

Suddenly she felt filled w/ shame that she had come, as if she'd interrupted something of great moment.

"Beat it, will ya?" he requested.

She sucked in a tiny bit of air, it had a foul taste.

"I'm sorry, Mitch," she whispered.

"Faye, just beat it."

He was wearing a new shirt, flimsy, yellow, nylon, short-sleeved, the kind one sees in snapshots of vacationers in Yugoslavia. The police had asked what he'd been wearing the day of his departure, and Faye had known in detail. So many wives and husbands never know, they told her. But she and Mitch had been close that way, close a lot of ways. Their marriage had never been heroic. It had been the result of a just habituation of conditions, like the green growth on an outdoor wall. It was never meant to be heroic.

Faye was tightening a hand around her suitcase handle and starting to back up when she heard someone enter from the street behind her. She felt cool air from the mountains on the backs of both her knees, and it revived her.

She watched the blood drain from Mitch's lips. His hand froze in an uncompleted gesture.

"Brought you coffee, sugar daddy," someone said.

A woman less than half Faye's age walked across the carpet in her bare feet and hitched her rear end up onto the desk. Faye could see she wasn't wearing underwear beneath her high-cut shorts. Her feet were clean. She had an open, honest, pasty sort of face, the kind that central casting would have sent out for a woman in a crowd scene. She was wearing a flimsy yellow shirt identical to Mitch's. She had wrapped and tied it flop-eared at her midriff. She handed Mitch a thermos and the kind of paper bag a kid would take to school for lunch.

Faye leaned against the lobby wall. No wonder he looks younger, she thought. Then w/ mercy she hoped maybe it would kill him.

"Sam and Kate are outside in the van," the girl said. "We're riding out to Pincha's to listen to the new band. Pick me up when you get off here, will you, Daddy?"

She kissed him on his neck, her mouth open.

"Sure will," Mitch said.

He leaned against her, and his hand slid round to just beneath her breast.

"Miss me?" she giggled.

"Like how," he promised.

All this, Faye watched. She stood near the stamp machine clutching her suitcase in the lobby w/ its bright orange carpet. She was about to disappear, and she turned, a little blinded, toward the street. She stopped. There seemed to be an awful lot that he should know.

"Mitch—" she began.

The two of them turned blank faces toward her like two halves of a hymnal.

"The desk," she said.

Mitch stared at her.

The woman leaned away from him just slightly, out across the carpet toward the stranger.

"The desk upstairs . . . the one we bought that afternoon . . . outside Philadelphia." Faye was speaking slowly. She was measuring her words. "That time . . . we pulled off . . . from the Pennsylvania Turnpike on that impulse . . . Do you remember?"

The woman frowned and fondled Mitch's hand.

"What about it?" Mitch finally asked.

"I moved it," Faye said.

Her husband narrowed his eyes.

"I pulled it away from the wall so it faces on the meadow from the bedroom window." She watched Mitch as he closed his eyes. The woman in the yellow shirt tapped her heels against the desk.

"It opens up the whole room," Faye said.

Mitch paused.

"It looks much better there," she went on.

Mitch paused, as if before a mirror on his way out.

"Yes." He nodded.

Faye could see that he had pictured it.

"Yes, it's better there," he said.

He opened his eyes. When he looked at her, there was a little kindness in them. "That was some afternoon we spent there, wasn't it?" he said.

"Sure was," Faye agreed. She felt a warm tear chill her cheek.

"October, right?"

"April," Faye prompted.

"April sixth," he said.

She saw the cruelty in both of them remembering too much.

That night Mitch hitchhiked out of town, thinking he should see Vancouver. For a few weeks after that and then again at unexpected times during the next winter, the woman in the yellow shirt wondered why he'd taken off like that. It wasn't hard to figure out that Faye was his old lady. Still, when she told the story to her friends, she always wondered right out loud what the big deal was about some purchase they had made on impulse outside Philadelphia. It wasn't till much later that it dawned on her that the whole thing w/ the desk had been a cover-up, and Faye and Mitch were really fugitives from justice.

February 27, 1982
Lucy Hastings Clinic
Princeton, New Jersey

◆━◆

8

THERE OUGHT TO BE A LAW

"THERE OUGHT TO BE A LAW against *heartbreak*," Sylvie said this afternoon.

I guess that started the whole thing, what you'd have to call the "Get Ellery" session. Once a week we have these sessions w/ the people from the Red Barn. The Red Barn is our psychiatric ghetto, where all the *really* crazies are. The rules around the Red Barn are real strict—they don't accept just anyone, you have to be *real* crazy. A lot of people from the Red Barn leave and graduate up to the Big House. *I* am in the Big House—w/ a bunch of other minor crazies. So far, I've told you about Florence. Florence is at one end of the scale of the kind of person we get here. We have one woman here for a little rest because she's depressed about being forty, and then we have Florence, who's never depressed about anything because she talks to God. The Big House is like a clinic upstairs; but downstairs it has three big rooms w/ fireplaces and a big old kitchen where we eat, so it's called the Big House. I was never in the Red Barn, but a lot of people in the Big House used to be, so we have a session w/ the Red Barn people once a week.

They have a rule at the Red Barn that you can only stay three months. After three months if you're not well enough to move up to the Big House, they refuse to treat you any more. This is a private clinic, so they can do that. In the eight weeks I've been here, I've gone to only five sessions w/ the Red Barn people because in my first weeks here I was still too "sick." The first two times I went I didn't say anything, and I sat next to someone called The Wet Brain. His name was Ed, but everybody called him The Wet Brain. He was in real bad shape, one of the people that we get here over whom you'd have to toss a coin to figure out which part of him was in worse shape—his body or his spirit. The Wet Brain couldn't keep himself from shaking. Even Thorazine, he confided to me, didn't stop his shaking. He was rattling for a drink, he said. He was very thin, thinner than the addicts are. He was from some place on the Outer Banks in North Carolina, and all he talked about were storms. "Yep, that was a big 'un," he would say.

"What was, Ed?" I'd ask him.

"That blow," he'd say. "September '35. Jee-sus!"

Every once in a while he'd focus on me and ask, "You wouldn't have a drink on ya by any chance, Miss?" and I'd say no. Then he'd nod and roll his tongue around his mouth, and then a few minutes later he'd say, "You wouldn't happen to have a *pint* with ya, would ya, Miss?"

There were several alcoholics in the Big House, and Ed and a guy named Dev in the Red Barn, but none of the others was half as bad as Ed was. His perception of what was going on around him never intersected w/ what was *really* going on. I don't know how they got him dressed every morning, how they got him to eat—he was always riding out a storm. It was hard for me to concentrate those first few times on what was being said because Ed kept whipping his arms around, fighting off the wind and sand and shouting at some other sailors now and then to do things w/ their lines. He scared me half to death. I felt like someone w/ poison ivy being treated right along w/ someone w/ a case of leprosy. And you can't complain behind somebody's back here, either—you have to say whatever it is you have to say right out in the open, in Group Session, as if Democracy, for Christ's sake, were a tenet of mental health. I couldn't go, for instance, to my own therapist and say, "Hey, The Wet Brain's really creepy, and I don't want to sit beside him any more"—I'd have to bring it up at Group. Almost the first thing that I learned in Group is that whenever somebody brought up something that they didn't like about another person, the whole Group immediately took against the complainant. Or so I thought. Until today. So I kept quiet. And anyway I hated Group. I think it is designed to make us want to get well just to get the hell away from all these people. . . .

At the third session w/ the Red Barn people that I went to, The Wet Brain wasn't there. Philbin (he's the therapist) said The Wet Brain had been transferred.

"Where?" I said.

Everybody stared at me, including Philbin, because I'd never spoken out in Group before. Dev, especially, he's the other alcoholic from the Red Barn, started looking at me in this certain way and doing Humphrey Bogart things w/ his eyebrows and his cigarette.

Philbin said The Wet Brain had been transferred to the Veteran's Hospital in South Orange.

"Why?" I said.

Because the time allotted in his recovery contract had elapsed, said Philbin.

"Well, why'd you ever let him come here in the first place?" I asked. "Anyone could see he'd never get any better in three months. Why'd you limit him to three months? Why couldn't you just let him stay here in the Big House?"

"Where people stay forever?" Philbin asked me pointedly.

I felt my face get hot.

"He'll get boozed up in the V.A.," Dev said.

"You don't know that for a fact, Dev," Philbin said.

"Oh, yes, I do."

"They run a very stringent program."

"Well let me tell you something about stringent programs, doctor," Dev said. He rolled his cigarette between his thumb and index finger. "When you're an alkie, there are no 'programs.' There are no rules. There's just you and thirst. If there's booze, you find it. Or it finds you. You find each other. Aren't I right, sweetheart?"

Everybody turned to look at me. Dev was staring at me w/ this macho Robert Mitchum the-kindest-thing-that-I-could-do-for-you-is-fuck-you look, and I turned to look behind me just to be real certain he meant me, and then I said, "How the hell should *I* know?" and he just smiled.

"He wants to *do* it with you," this woman Paula told me later.

"I can't wait."

"No, no, he really does. There's a way you can do it, too. Outside."

"Hey, sorry, Jack."

"I'd give my right arm for some of him. When he looks at me I just *feel* it. All he'd ever have to do each night is *look* at me . . ."

"And what would *you* have to do, I wonder?"

"Honey—*with pleasure*, whatever it was!"

"I don't think Dev holds women too high in his esteem. . . ."

"Oh, he's not *queer*, I'll tell you that much!"

"I mean, I get a feeling from him that it could turn a little nasty, now and then."

"Oh, that's a certain kind of drinker, that's all. I can handle them," she told me w/ a little smile. She moved her shoulders, too, as if adjusting for a fight.

I guess a lot of mental patients start to act like trained psychiatrists in time, we all get real good w/ the lingo—"latent," especially, gets used a lot. Jell-O latent pudding. Latent cream pie. Potatoes *latent*. For a while I figured Paula was a latent alcoholic because she had the hots for Dev, but then she told me a week later that she also had the hots for Buzz, The Four-Times-Attempted-Suicide, and I changed my diagnosis of her to latent self-destructive. Florence, my old favorite, didn't need a diagnosis because she is just plain schizophrenic. We have about forty schizophrenics *chez nous*, and their disease is not schizophreni*a*, but the schizophreni*as*, because there are about eighty different types. Florence is just mildly weird, but still, you wouldn't want to be alone w/ her in any unguarded place much after midnight. Teabury, on the other hand, is *very* weird. He's in the Red Barn. He and Sylvie. Sylvie is a schizophrenic from the Red Barn who started coming to the Big House weekly sessions the first week after Ed, The Wet Brain, left. She looks so much like my cousin Cathy I couldn't stop staring at her. She has Cathy's same pale scraggly hair, except Sylvie's is longer. Her skin is real pale, too; and she has Cathy's build and dark brown eyebrows grown real close above her nose and dark brown eyes and eyelashes. She bites her lip, too, and chews her fingernails. "Hey, tell that bitch to stop staring at me!" she stood up and yelled. The bitch she meant was me. "What are you, *queer* or something?!"

"No . . . I'm sorry," I said. "You look a lot like someone in my family—"

"Tell us about who that might be," said Philbin.

I *hate* Group: "Just someone. My cousin. Her name is Cathy."

"Don't you want to tell us more about her than her name?"

"No."

"*Why* don't you want to tell us more about her than her name?"

I *hate hate hate* Group: "She's my second cousin, actually. She lives by herself in a loft in SoHo, in New York City. Except . . . she has this pet canary she calls Angie. See, she was born the night *Marty* was first on TV, and her mother was watching it when she went into labor and Angie is the name of this character who's always asking Marty, 'What do you want to do tonight, Marty?' and Marty's always saying, 'I don't know, Angie . . . what do *you* want to do?' So Cathy named her bird after him. To keep her company. . . ."

This is why I don't like Group: the mind, a healthy mind, declares itself too subtly for soliloquy. I was thinking of a way to express Cathy—not to them, out loud; to *me*, internally. And that involved a picture of her coming home from work alone, same as I used to, and there being nothing in the place to eat, and Cathy walking over to the birdcage and opening the little door and coaxing Angie to step out on her finger, saying, "Hey, Angie. Hiya, Angie. So what d'you want to do tonight, huh, Angie?"

And right while I was thinking this, Teabury said, "I know somebody *else* who's in your fam-i-ly. . . ." He sort of sang it. He's such a weirdo. Up to that point the only thing Teabury ever said was, "I lived on Main Street in Wellesley, Massachusetts, all my life and nothing ever happened, till *it* happened." Nobody asked him what *it* was but presumably *it* is why he's here.

Paula says she thinks he is a latent child molester.

"Do you have something you want to say, Albert?" Philbin asked him.

"No," Teabury said.

"Are you sure, Albert?"

"Yes. I'll talk to her about it later."

"Why don't you talk to her about it now?"

"I want to talk to her about it later."

"That's against the rules, Albert, to interrupt that way and then not share your thoughts with us," Philbin said.

"I lived on Main Street in Wellesley, Massachusetts, all my life and nothing ever happened, till *it* did," Albert answered.

After Group, he came over to me and after staring at me for about two minutes he asked me to subscribe to *Romantic Times*. If he could get four new subscribers to *Romantic Times*, he said, he'd get his own subscription, free.

"What's *Romantic Times*?" I said.

"You've never heard of *Romantic Times*?"

"I'm afraid not."

"Haven't you read . . . don't you read romances?"

"Romances?"

"*Black Tomorrow. The Last Kiss. The Primrose at the Window?*"

"Gothics, you mean."

"*Not* gothics! *Ro*-mance!"

"I'm sorry, no, I don't."

"You won't buy a subscription?"

"I'm sorry, no, I won't."

"I know who you are."

"I know who *you* are, too, Mr. Teabury."

"I recognized you the first time I saw you. You look exactly like her."

Who? I wondered.

"Belle," he said.

He actually got all choked up. "I loved her," he explained. "We *all* did."

Before I could consider who we "*all*" were, he handed me an old rolled-up copy of *Life* magazine dated February 16, 1956.

"Perhaps you'll autograph it for me on the *inside*," he whined.

He didn't have to tell me *where*—"*we all*" had grown up around this issue of *Life*. It was one of the more painful little episodes of dog-and-pony drama in our family: "Hey, *fuck this, Jack!*" I told him. I gave him a little push—I mean, I'm not a big woman, so how big a push could I have given him? "Where do you get off, bringing this to me? What are you, crazy? What are you trying to do? Who the hell are you to say I look like her? Are you insane? Do I look like I'm going to shoot somebody? Like I'm going to kill myself? You're looking at someone who's her own woman here, asshole! You think I have a problem knowing who I am? Are you suggesting I have some kind of half-assed problem knowing who I am? Fuck *your* noise, Jack, I'm walking out of here! I've had *it* w/ all you cheesebombs, believe *me!*" . . . And like that, etc., for what must be construed as an unreasonable length of time for a little show of temper; I mean five days.

So today it was "Get Ellery" time.

Paula had already told me since my fit two weeks ago she thinks I am a latent manic-depressive. I am also, according to my peers, a latent goddam everything else. It all started when Sylvie said, "There ought to be a law against *heartbreak,*" and I started to laugh.

"Is there something funny about that?" Philbin asked.

"Well, I'm sorry, but that sounds like a country-and-Western song. . . ."

As I looked around, I saw no one else was smiling.

"Sometimes country-and-Western songs address topics that come straight from the heart," Philbin informed me.

"'Bring the Bear-Fat w/ You, Mama—Let's Grease Up the Pole Tonight'?" I joked.

I saw I was the only person laughing.

I looked over at Sylvie, and I wondered why I ever thought she looked like Cathy. Cathy is too special to look like anyone.

It started to occur to me *it* might be happening again. I started to feel very frightened, and for a reason that I didn't understand I said, "There ought to be a law against *handguns,* for Christ's sake."

"What makes you say that just now, Ellery?"

"Because. That's what . . . there ought to be a law against."

"But why does that come to your mind just now?"

"Because. There ought to be."

"But *why?*"

"Don't *trip* over yourself to get at me, Philbin. You're not dealing w/ a wet brain here—"

"What *am* I dealing with here, Ellery?"

"You better be real careful, Jack," I warned him.

"Or *what?*" somebody shouted. "You'll hit on him the way you hit on Albert?"

Well, that started what goes down in history as the Let-the-bitch-have-hers Sweepstakes right here, folks, in the Big House, U.S.A.

Among the more engrossing comments of the day was this, from *Florence*: "I think she calls everybody Jack when she gets mad, the same way infidels invoke the name of Christ Our Lord. It's called invoking the idealized father figure. . . ."

I told her to go invoke a latent catatonia.

"You sound *humble*," Iris said when I called her tonight. "Are you all right?"

"I want to give Cathy a call, and I don't have her number."

"She doesn't have a phone, remember? She's going to try to get one now because she wants to put up posters, but she still owes them money on an old bill and has to use a made-up name, or something like that. . . . She gave me the number of that restaurant downstairs, do you want it? If they're not busy, they go upstairs and get her, then she calls you back. . . ."

"Sure . . . what do you mean, she wants to put up *posters?*"

"For Angie."

"What about Angie?"

"I thought you knew."

"Knew what?"

"I thought that's why you wanted to give her a call—"

"I-ris!"

"Angie flew away."

"*Angie?*"

"The *canary*, El."

"I know who *Angie* is, for Christ's sake!"

"She's real upset. Angie was her best friend, you know."

"Christ, when did this happen?"

"Two days ago."

"And she doesn't have a phone?"

"No. She owes them money."

"For Christ's sake, tell her to go over and use mine. Tell her she can stay at my apartment—"

"Why don't you tell her? Here's the number; the restaurant's name is 'Tamala Design w/ Bagel'—"

"Oh, for Christ's sake—"

"That's the name of it. You want the number?"

"Can I tell you something?"

"Of course you can."

"I'm not going to kill myself."

"Why, Ellery, nobody ever thought . . . oh. *Oh*. Does this mean you can come home?"

"Soon . . . two weeks ago I lost control and put a little wimp in traction. He wanted me to autograph that picture in *Life* magazine."

"You never had your picture in *Life* magazine—"

"The one of Belle."

"*Which* one?"

"The awful one. That one that gave Cathy those nightmares—"

"Why you?"

"Why Jodie Foster? The guy's a looney in the first place. . . ."

"But you don't have the *criminally* insane there, do you?"

"You mean *murderers*, Iris? People like Belle? No."

"She wasn't a *murderer*, Elly, like you're saying. Not like . . . not like . . . well, that man who climbed that tower with a gun in Texas. She didn't kill against society—or for money, either. Or for self-promotion or material gain, the way the murderer always did in your mother's books. . . . You know, love never figures as a motive for a killing in those books? I could always figure out it *wasn't* the jealous wife. . . . No, Belle was more like Romeo. You don't re-member Romeo for being a murderer, but he definitely was. . . ."

"What do you remember Belle for, then, if not the murder?"

"Her tragedy. That final picture."

"What should I call it, do you think, since you're playing Book Critic?"

"Call what?"

"The story I'm going to write about her."

"I don't know. How about 'The Truth about Belle'?"

"You're a nice person, but you have a tin ear, Iris."

Tonight, talking about Angie, Cathy said grief is a process in our family like going off booze is for an alcoholic: it gets better in time, but it's a lifelong preoccupation. . . . The only other thing she said that someone should write down is when she asked me where the clinic is so she can come to visit me and I said Princeton, New Jersey, and she said, "New Jersey—is that somewhere I can *hitchhike* to?"

9

GOING OFF BOOZE

A STORY BY ELLERY McQUEEN

"The war changed him. The war gave him balls. The war made him a man in a man's world, where a piece of ass and a fuck weren't credentials. He was over his cuntlust, the war gave him that. The war made him a man."
> Kit Tikhmenov, *The Conflagration of Round-Eyed Boys*, 1946

"A cunt and a drunk were all he needed. Just a cunt and a drunk and a dark hole to dig as his grave."
> Kit Tikhmenov, *The Emergence from Kuskurza into Tuwaqachi*
> *—the Fourth World, World Complete*, 1951

JUDGE WEMBLEY SCOTT [Judge, Third Judicial District Court of New Mexico]: Miss Benû, is there anything you wish to say before I pass sentence?

BELLE BENÛ: *(inaudibly)* No.

SCOTT: I'm sorry—what?

BENÛ: *(louder)* I have nothing to say.

SCOTT: This is your last chance. The press are still here.

BENÛ: Please don't taunt me.

SCOTT: What?

BENÛ: I ask you don't taunt me.

SCOTT: Of course you do. Of course. I'm sorry for my lapse of restraint. The rigors of this trial, of these events, have been hard, they've been real hard, I'm afraid. On myself, on all

of us. On Skip [David "Skip" Douglass, Assistant District
Attorney for the District of Alamogordo] . . . Certainly it's
been the hardest in my career on the bench, I know that—

BENÛ: (*breaking in*) I want to say I'm not a bad person. I haven't
been a bad mother.

(*This remark distresses* SCOTT. *He regards her a moment; then he
lowers his head to pronounce sentence.*)

SCOTT: Belle Benû, I'm charged by the state of New Mexico to
impose sentence on you as mandated by law. I wish personally that the events of July 16 had never taken place and
that you had never left Flagstaff, Arizona. It's unhappy for
me that I must sentence you. Miss Benû, I remand you to
the care and custody of the Department of Corrections to
be confined for life at the New Mexico State Penitentiary
in Santa Fe. This court stands in recess. I'm sorry. Good
luck to you.

DEFENSE ATTORNEY JAMES MCMURTY: Sir?

SCOTT: (*repeating*) Court stands in recess.

MCMURTY: Sir, her right to appeal?

SCOTT: I'm sorry?

MCMURTY: An appeal?

SCOTT: Didn't I say that?

MCMURTY: No, I'm sorry, sir, you didn't.

SCOTT: You have the right to appeal these findings, Miss Benû.

BENÛ: Thank you.

SCOTT: In a higher court.

BENÛ: Thank you.

SCOTT: That's the law. Everybody is the same under the law. Nobody's doing anything special here for you. Is that it? Have
I covered everything, Mr. McMurty?

MCMURTY: I believe you have, sir, yes.

SCOTT: (*looking around*) Anybody got anything else to say? No? Okay,
boys. That's it. Court's adjourned. Show's over. Praise the
Lord, huh? What do you say? Everybody gets to go back
home.

—From the transcript of Belle's trial,
as printed in *Life* magazine

I

SOMEONE HAD LEFT the radio on in the truck, she could hear it scratching and squawking outside in the yard w/ the chickens. It was a sound, like the sound of the hens, one gets used to. Kit and Sanchez must have come in after midnight, after the station had signed off, and left it on. The station is always the same, KFLG, out of Flagstaff, the only one they can get. KFLG has the nearest broadcasting tower, about twelve miles away, and it drowns out the rest of the signals down on their side of the canyon.

Belle and Kit rode out most clear nights w/ a six-pack of Mexican beer and Kit's fifth of Jack Daniel's and two pairs of binocs that Kit had stolen from the army, and they scouted for UFOs. Kit was sure they were coming, whoever they were. He was sure they were coming, and he wasn't going to miss out on a chance to evacuate planet Earth. Biggest fucking recon action since the devil stuck his dick in Eve, is what Kit called it. Clear nights he and Belle would sit out in the pickup truck, and Kit would switch on his harangue of why he wanted to evacuate the planet Earth, and Belle would argue, "Honey, but I've heard all this before," and she would switch on the radio, dialing the knob round and round in the search of far-off stations. After KFLG left the air at midnight, she could pick up KEVT, the Spanish station out of Tucson. Once or twice when they were way up around Humphreys Peak she got Chicago, WGN. The signal from Chicago would go in and out, and in the lapses Belle would think about how she had met Kit there, in Chicago, at the fair in '33—the Chicago World's Fair—Sally Rand and the Hall of Science. Before Hitler. Before Hitler and the war. Before the war and all the sadness. Far off.

It was still early. She knew it must be: Sanchez hadn't come to fill their thermoses or she'd have smelled the coffee brewing and the bitter reek of the tobacco he chewed. She'd hear his boots, those fancy boots Kit had bought him in Laredo, the ones w/ gaudy rowel spurs big as Ferris wheels. What a sight he was in those boots out back, his little figure hobbled by the rangy physics of a life spent in the saddle, his hips too loose for solid ground from years of waltzing w/ a horse's spine—he couldn't walk; no rider can; and Kit had bought him boots the size of Texas. Sanchez loved those boots. He lived in them. He'd die in them, no doubt, as sure as Kit would die someplace inside a blacked-out room.

Ever since the war Kit wouldn't sleep inside a room w/ windows that showed morning light. Northwest side is what he asked for in a motel room, or a hotel suite, whenever he booked in somewhere for a night. They'd built this house; it was adobe. Belle had built it w/ Sanchez and her friends from Oraibi, where the Hopi reservation is. West/northwest was what he wanted, w/ no windows in the bedroom. The Hopis seemed to think this was a given, like their kivas—windowless w/ a hatch on top. Belle told Sanchez she would suffocate w/out night air. She didn't mention light. The truth was Belle respected light, the desert sky, the desert morning, more than she respected desert air.

Sanchez said he'd talk to Kit about the windows. It would be "O.K." Sanchez always said "O.K." like the Hopis, as if "O" existed as one sex, and "K" another, and the two, spoken together, were a sacred, smiling given in the universe. Hopis speak a lot of "givens." What many peoples take as blessings, Hopis take as givens. So they built the windows. Two, in fact. One west, one northwest, and Kit hung his army blankets over them. He slept soundly, like a dead man, in the darkened room. Sometimes he'd sleep till noon. Belle liked mornings, so she bought a rooster. His crowing got her up. Then she bought a dozen hens to keep him happy. Pullets. Fatties, Sanchez called them. They were fat for Western hens because she overfed them. She overfed them because she couldn't stand to hear the noise they made inside their throats when they were hungry. After she bought the hens they got raccoons and skunks and coyotes. Sanchez said it was only time until they got the big cats, too.

The first one came in February, and he looked as if he was starving. It was lucky Belle had baby Cathy safe in tow because she froze right where she was the instant he looked up at her and she saw into his eyes. Cougar, Sanchez said it was, from the prints the cat had left in the light snow. Kit made her learn to shoot the rifle after that. Put the shell in, pull back, keep the barrel low, raise it steady, sight, and fire. That was in March, three months ago. They'd had cats, a bobcat once, and Belle had shot the rifle off into the air. It made an awfull smell, just from the shot, like burnt human hair. They had never had these troubles when they lived up on the mesa. No cats or people dropping in or Kit staying out all hours in the truck. She liked living on the mesa, she liked higher ground. But since the war—since 1945—Kit had said he wanted flat ground near a flat road running into town.

The war. Everything these last ten years seemed to come in headlines like the broadcast news. The war. The bomb. The UFOs. The Senate Hearings. Willie Shoemaker on Swaps, Duke Snider's lead in RBIs. Everybody's laying odds on Brooklyn and New York—w/ Campanella playing like he did last night a Yankee-Dodgers Series is a sure bet—now this from John Cameron Swayze for Timex.

Belle rolled over on her side of the bed. She realized she was hearing KFLG's sports broadcast w/ Ted Devane. Devane didn't have too much to talk about this time of year, so now he was asking her to write in her favorite sport joke and if he read it on the air she'd get a free game at Tom Thumb Tees two miles from the center of Flagstaff on Route 6. The noise from the radio seemed to be coming in much louder now, and Belle knew she should get up and turn it off before it woke baby Cathy. She rolled the sheet back and sat up. She'd been right to think it was still early—Ted Devane went on the air at seven-twenty every morning, except Sunday. Sundays Brother Prescott and the Sunrise Singers started in just after the National Anthem and went all morning in their exhilaration over Christ. All of Arizona, in fact, was crazy about Christ. His figure in the local churches was gaunt and tan and blue-eyed. All he needed was a denim jacket and he'd look just like the man on billboards who says he'll walk a mile for a Camel. Camels were Kit's cigarettes. Twice he'd set their mattresses on fire, smoking late in bed, and once he burned baby Cathy by mistake, bending over her to make her smile. When he was out of doors he stripped his butts as if an ememy were still behind him. He wouldn't walk a mile for anything, Belle was sure. But she would. She'd walk a mile for him.

She could hear Ted Devane signing off and she knew the weather report would be next and then a Halo commercial and then "Don McNeill's Breakfast Club." She knew all about the radio because during the war she had lived by it; it seemed a part of government. News was delivered as it happened, and she used to listen for some news of Kit or for a place name he had mentioned in a letter or someone's story who'd been there of what was going on and what the war was really like. She knew that when he came back, there would be no catching up. She tried to keep a diary in those years

so Kit could know what she'd been doing, but no sane person can
sit down and write about the daily work on a reservation, about
putting brown eggs from the henhouse in a yucca basket, when at
the close of every day Edward R. Murrow's voice is going to come
into the house and fill it w/ a sense of urgency as authentic as the
smell of smoke or the dry sound on the tail end of a rattlesnake.

Her sense of duty throughout the war was to preserve for Kit the
life he knew before he left for England. Why else were they fighting
if not to preserve a way of life? Not a single thing that had happened
in her life since the first attack on Britain had been Belle's idea, but
she held out like a fortress, like the outcroppings of earth north of
Oraibi on the Navajo land people call Monument Valley. Everything
had changed, was changing. Last week she had gone out w/ Sanchez
to drive his sheep to higher ground, and they had come across a
herd of pronghorn taking water up at Reilly's Creek about sixteen
miles north of the house. Belle loved to watch the pronghorn, fastest
mammal in America, and finding a whole herd of them at rest had
been a special treat, but w/in moments of their sighting she and
Sanchez had the sense something was wrong. The deer seemed
uncoordinated. They didn't skitter at the sound of Belle's and Sanchez's horses, and when they raised their heads and looked across
the water at the two on horseback their gaze was milky, their eyes
were white-blue like human milk, w/ the iridescence of an internal
organ. It appeared their retinas had been burned.

"*Tengo pesadillas,*" Sanchez said. It was one of his expressions.
It means, I'm having nightmares. "*Es la irradiación,*" he said. "It
can't be," Belle told him. "*Es la irradiación,*" Sanchez insisted. He
had been finding the effects of radiation on small animals for ten
years, first along the flats of the Sacramento Mountains when he
used to live w/ his woman in Las Cruces, and later all along the
Pancake and the Silver Peak ranges when he was managing a ranch
outside Beatty, in Nevada. Sanchez had gone many times to the
Department of the Interior, but no one believed him. Belle knew
there was a test site in Nevada three hundred miles away, somewhere
around Nellis Air Force Base. It seemed impossible that these deer
might have looked up all at once into the glare of an atomic deto-
nation and then stumbled, blindly, several hundred miles. She refused to think of it even as a possibility, as if radiation sickness were

another threat right here in her own backyard along w/ communism and the niggers.

Everyone in Flagstaff hated communism, somehow equating it w/ Jews and foreigners. Kit was foreign, from Cardigan in Wales, but he had a Russian-sounding name. He and Belle were real bohemians, what w/ Kit's strange fiction and their not ever being married even after twenty years, and Belle could feel the people in Flagstaff, the God-fearers, talk behind her back whenever she went into town. They never used to snub her this way, but recently the news was full of innuendo and suggestion that engendered doubt about one's neighbors. For Belle the news engendered nonspecific dread. So did the radio commercials and the new rock-and-roll music. She didn't know what she might hear, but she knew she didn't want to hear it.

When she'd gone to visit friends up on Oraibi yesterday, when she was taking paper and colored pencils to Bessie Chööchökam on the reservation, she'd heard the children playing from far off. Hopi children always chant while playing, and the sound of ancient chants in children's voices always thrilled her. There was an endless incantation of six syllables, as they hopped on one foot and then the other, and involuntarily the chant became her way of walking, and she began to sing w/ them, smiling as she sang: "Hélo shampú helö . . . Hélo shampú helö . . . Hélo shampú . . ." Belle stopped. It was the Halo jingle. She realized w/ a jolt it was the Halo jingle from the radio, and it made her sick. Sometimes, in the mornings, she was sick. Sometimes she felt that while she'd stayed at home these years, the world had gone off and seen something it was never meant to see; and whatever that something was, it had the force of evil to make her feel the world and everything in it, excepting her, had gone insane.

The chill, the dread, the tightness in her throat, the light-headedness did not develop every morning. It had not developed at all until last winter, and the first few times it happened she was afraid it was a pregnancy again. Her fear intensified the sickness—Kit would never let her have another baby, there'd been too much controversy over this one. And now Kit refused to use precautions—something else he'd picked up in the army, a Trojan disregard for rubbers. The guys he knew in Italy, he said, always carried rubbers on them because Dago women weren't that clean. And he said Kraut women were clean all right, but you had to do it from behind because they stare at you. He said you have no idea what it's like to fuck a woman while she's staring at you. He called Oriental women "titless snakes." He said the only reason he could think of for fucking one was out of hatred for their race.

He said these things and talked like this when he was drunk. When he was drinking the stories he told were never nice, they were roiling w/ sexual rage that masked a deeper sorrow. It was almost as if he were afraid to mourn or unwilling to admit despair. The men that Kit knew, the ones he talked about, seemed to have adapted to male company by scrapping distaff aspects of their temperaments in exchange for bluff. W/out women everything became a test of bullshit—who could piss the farthest, who could drink the most, who could go in and come back out of combat w/out crapping on himself, who could fart the loudest, who could hold a stiff dick longest, who could take a bullet manliest, who could take out the most Krauts, who could fuck the most Kraut women, who could come up w/ the most equitable alternative to justifiable homicide and dub it justifiable rape.

Somehow Kit's angry stories of the war, his vision of it, didn't square w/ Belle's assessment of Dwight D. Eisenhower and George Catlett Marshall and the shy one, Omar Bradley. These three all seemed decent-looking men. She couldn't imagine Ike and George and Omar gangbanging local pussy the way Kit described it. You could look at them in photographs and tell they weren't excessive men, they weren't extremists, if they thought of sex at all it seemed likely that they thought of it theoretically, as they thought of war, on a higher plane, in the context of love and marriage.

Kit had never been like Generals Eisenhower and Marshall—Kit was a sensualist. His sensuality had tempted him from Wales into America, into the American Southwest. Everything on the desert was sensual to him—the pulpiness of cactus flowers, the pulsations of a blue mirage on dry, hot sand, the purple rocks, the reds, the pinks—but what the war turned out to be for Kit was sensual over-load, a stimulation that, once triggered, could not be sustained, like walking w/ a stiff dick all your life. He tried very hard to reassemble elements outside the war that could excite him in that way, that nervous way when everything's at risk, everything is heightened—

color, sound, sight, touch, aroma, kinship. Bourbon did it for him
pretty well every now and then. Or cocaine. Or peyote. But bourbon
was his first love, and it pissed him off the way it wasn't putting out
now as it used to. Any man who doesn't think of alcohol as sex
doesn't know what he's missing, Kit said. Bliss. Warm liquid bliss,
but she gets harder, cunt, you have to work her harder, start a little
sooner in the day and chase her half the night through different bars
w/ different music, different lights.

He stayed out a lot at nights. Sometimes Belle went w/ him, but
when she did Kit forgot that she was there. His mind held a single
locus for her and that was home. So Sanchez went along w/ him
and did the driving. Sanchez wouldn't drink. Sanchez was a saint,
Belle thought; Sanchez took a lot of shit from Kit. Theirs was the
perfect kinship, like the termite and its fungus. If it weren't for
Sanchez, Belle would have had to spend her mornings searching
through the county dives for Kit. As it was, Sanchez always managed
to get Kit back home somehow. Sometimes it was not until mid-
morning of the next day, and Belle would wake those mornings and
a chill would start along the hollow of her lower back and she would
realize Kit was not beside her. She'd feel alone in their blacked-out
room, and it would take a minute or so to distinguish day from night
or day from day, what day it was—and then she'd start to gather
details.

She was a good girl, a wholesome, decent product of her nation
except in choosing the one man whom she should love. Her sickness
came w/ the suspicion that she loved someone whose love for her
had twisted to a cruel disdain. Her purpose every morning that she
woke w/out him in their bed was to convince herself that everything—the world, the day, his love—was fine, just fine, and everything would be O.K.

She dressed hurriedly w/out ceremony, slipping into the same
shirt and pants she'd worn the day before. She moved quickly,
soundlessly in her bare feet past the room where Cathy slept. There
was never any knowing where she might find Kit. If he'd been on
a talking jag the night before, Sanchez would unload him in a
kitchen chair and let him talk and drink until he passed out. Sometimes Sanchez brought him all the way to bed and then went out
the back across the playa up the steep arroyo half a mile to the small
adobe where he kept his bed. Halfway through the night Kit might

wake and take it in his head to go get Sanchez, and Sanchez and Belle would find him lying in the dust or sprawled against the chaparral, his mouth caked w/ vomit and his garments reeking of his nightmares. Once Belle stumbled on him in the kitchen. He was sitting upright on the floor, his back propped against the Frigidaire. W/ his mouth open, his eyes rolled back, his face blue, Belle was certain he was dead. She was sick right there at the sink before she even went to him. When she did, Kit came round mid-sentence, riding the same train of thought he'd been on when he blacked out. He was no more aware of her as a witness to his dereliction than history is of its observer. She was very careful where she stepped.

Outside the house, the light was harsh, the stones already hot. The hens were out and ran toward her, expecting to be fed. The western hills were still the many shades of blue of morning, but behind the house the sun had lighted up the snow-capped summit on Humphreys Peak. It seemed, as she squinted out across the waves of heat dancing on the gravel, that no one was inside the truck. The radio was blaring, but the truck was parked as if it had been airlifted in and dropped downwind from its mark.

Sanchez was gone, and the door on the driver's side was still ajar. Belle could see his tracks, the draggle of his fancy spurs leading off toward the arroyo. The tracks showed he had been alone, and Belle cocked her head, squinted and frowned as if seeing his hobbled figure in retreat. It made no sense. Sanchez wouldn't leave Kit. If they'd run into some trouble, Sanchez would have come for her. So Belle squinted fiercely at the low sun after Sanchez's tracks. She was a true believer in the bonds between Samaritans. She felt that she and Sanchez were angels of mercy in Kit's life. They were a team. His first allegiance, as well as hers, was to Kit's health, and they trusted each other. He would never do, as she would never do, a thing that went against their peace and Kit's well-being. So this was strange.

She was certain when she found Sanchez, when he came around to make the coffee in the kitchen very soon, he'd have a fine O.K. excuse for all of this, he'd have one fine O.K. adventure story they could laugh at and remember fondly, later.

Belle turned from his tracks to the truck to turn the radio off. A lizard skittered in her path. Suddenly the sound from the truck radio snapped and went dead, as it so often does, to no one's sensory

enjoyment, proof that Communists controlled the broadcast media—
and in the sudden shock of silence Belle discerned two tiny sounds.
The first was Cathy's sound coming from the house, the sound she
made when she was waking, a sort of whimper-cackling cry. The
second was the sound of breathing rising from the flatbed of the
truck.

"Kit?" she asked.

She went immediately around the truck and saw the outline of
his sleeping form beneath the layers of his army blankets. Her heart
skittered in its path—at least Sanchez had remembered to shelter
him securely from the light. The truck had obviously broken down;
she should have thought of that. Broken down too far from the
house, too far for Sanchez to carry him all that way and so he'd
tucked him in and covered him up . . . the sight and transport of
this miracle endured for one brief breathless moment until, just as
the radio snapped on again, blaring out an advertising jingle, Belle
saw a second body next to his and tore the blankets back to reveal
a young girl, naked, very young, perhaps fifteen years old, w/ Kit's
war-hardened hand inside her thigh, her legs grotesquely blotchy w/
her blood and bruises and Kit's blue-gray shriveled penis exposed in
this harsh light as something that no creature w/ a memory who
loves him should ever be allowed to see. She turned and ran, then
circled back, half wheeling like a bird of prey, to rip the radio antenna
off the metal hood w/ her bare hands. She kicked at it and kicked
the truck. She heard Cathy crying from the house, a fearful cry.
She ran. About ten yards from the back door of the house, near a
spot where she often stood to feed the chickens, she was finally sick.

The hens pecked along her body expecting to be fed.

II

IN 1933 THE PEOPLE IN AMERICA stopped begging w/ their
hands and words and sat instead on door stoops where they pleaded
w/ their eyes. To look into these eyes was to see something stripped
of its pretensions. What was so unsavory for most to see was how
completely hunger humbles history. Years and years of greed and
affectation, sophistry and cant, dissolved as poverty restored its vic-

tims to the primal elements of a religion: death and dust and apples up for sale on the streets of Eden. Not everyone was poor—that was a fact explained to Belle by her mother, Willa, as something equal to the phenomenon that "Not everyone is stricken down with polio, either—that's just life." There was nothing pretty or romantic about life in the Depression. Belle was confused in later years by people's recollections of a so-called spirit in the land, of sharing. If there was anything, she thought, there was the sort of quiet among people, the resignation that exists in wards where victims of disease are sent to die. The dying watch each other die w/ childlike understanding that they are many, they are next. The poor that Belle saw, on the streets and living off the coal along the train tracks in the winter of '33 when she and Willa took the train from New York to Chicago, were childlike, waiting out the hard time as a child would wait. By this time, Belle thought of the homeless and the dispossessed as kin. She knew the sorrow of their lives, she understood their deprivation. She was fifteen years old that year, fifteen and a half. She was miserable and living in a ten-room house in Lake Forest, Illinois, and she was stealing money systematically from her stepfather's chiffonnière so she would have enough to buy herself a family when she ran away.

The family that she'd had from birth—herself and Max and Willa—had broken up two years before. Max had left both Belle and Willa, but Belle knew it was all a big mistake: Max had meant to leave just Willa. Willa in her crafty way had interposed herself between Max and Belle, preventing him from taking Belle along, and now he was in exile somewhere probably, she thought, mourning, mournful, all alone. She loved her father. It was Max who filled out life, who chased it out of corners, who attacked it night and day w/ all the violent passion of a gypsy dispossessed of motherland. Belle could never quite decide if gypsies are the way they are because they have no country or if they have no country owing to the way they are. If the Benûs had to stake allegiance to a country, Max would sometimes claim Rumania. He claimed the blue mists in the mornings of his youth spent in the town Babadag were left by angels come to bathe in the Black Sea beneath a silver Balkan moon, and Belle believed him, even though his passport showed that he was French and he had given away two paintings worth $5,000 each to the Basque Nationals, claiming he was one of them, an orphan son of

Spain. He was plain crazy. He would dance around the rooms of their apartment on the Promenade in Brooklyn, shaking his cocktail shaker to the rhythm of the march from *Carmen*, and Belle would think his blood must be as *agité* as his famous margaritas. Max was always *agité*, except when he was painting. When he was painting he was like a priest. Not only was he silent, he was scrubbed, and he had that white skin priests have that seems unsullied. He looked holy when a picture was going on. The storms came only when a picture was just coming. They were terrible, and Max would try to kill himself, because he was bored or because he was mischievous or because he was frightened of the picture coming on and that maybe this time his genius would fail. Max tried to kill himself in stupid ways, in ways that made Willa seem his accomplice. Once he tried to kill himself by threatening to jump into the Promenade from sixty feet unless Willa went at once to Secaucus, New Jersey, where there were famous pig farms, for fresh tripe. Once he threatened to eat a light bulb unless she immediately made an item called "Pesteana Jiù," his favorite, which called for not only fresh tripe but squid, a certain sort of plum tomato, truffles, and "sfintû." Nowhere in Brooklyn, nor anywhere else in America, can one find the equivalent of "sfintû,"and when Willa tried to tell him this, Max struck her. To his credit, Belle remembers that in his guilt Max ate the light bulb. She forgets that later he would not eat light bulbs. Later he would not even pretend that he felt guilt. Later he would strike his wife for dust or for loud noise or for a pint of spoiled cream in the icebox—but that was so far along in his daughter's adoration of him and in her natural disaffection from her mother that such offenses in her eyes were justified. She would have dealt her mother the same blows, given the same chance. These are awful feelings to admit. Mothers do not set out to make their children hate them. The fault can't be w/ mothers. The fault must be w/ awful children.

First, Max had been in love w/ Willa, and he painted her. He painted her w/ full round brush strokes and the burnished palette reminiscent of Renoir's. He loved her; and he lavished on her his great gift. The critics scorn these pictures. They're tender and erotic and full of callow pining over parting that haunts a love when it is new, and they impart nothing of the vehemence that Max is famous for. Willa as he painted her these early years looks proud and shy and like a new recruit, a fresh enthusiast, to sex. Her face is very round w/ square jaw and her eyes are hooded; her neck is short and thick. Her mouth is opulent. One goes away w/ thoughts about the things a mouth like that can do, because that's what Max evoked by painting her that way.

For years Belle reasoned that Willa's mouth was why he married her. They were an unlikely pair. She couldn't see a man's desiring a thing banal as kindness in a woman. Solicitude. Or charity. These were weak and passive virtues in Belle's eyes, fit, sometimes, for nuns. She was nothing like her mother. She was thin, thin-lipped, a scrawny child, a taut tight boyish adolescent and a tomboy. A *soldat.* Max was drawn to painting her the moment she was born while she was still on Willa's breast. He painted her on mornings and in evenings before and after he had turned to his real work. He named her *belle, "la belle,"* the beauty, and he always wrote her name w/ a small "b." He gave her colors he thought suited her, blues and yellows, lemon yellow and sea blue, the colors of the house fronts on the Calle Compostela where he lived one year in Old Havana. Sometimes he painted Belle as a *soldat,* sometimes as a clown, sometimes as a little Bedouin. Sometimes when he dressed her up he painted in only her face and tiny little hands. She had an angel's face, he said, an angel who's been very bad in life here down below.

She had Max's face, is what she had, and he painted her as he must have looked himself as a child. These paintings lined the walls in the front room, the one room on the Promenade w/ good light, stacked along the floor like souls waiting at the Gate, half-finished. They are known as his *"la belle"* paintings, and they're universally gossiped about and overblown, made silly w/ pretensions. An artist couldn't piss against a wall, Max was fond of saying, w/out some idiot somewhere claiming the stain as a great work of art. Max himself was chiefest claimant of such idiocy. Everything he drew was up for sale, including paper cutouts torn from menus during meals, including sketches for kitchen improvements never carried out in the apartment on the Promenade in Brooklyn, including the whole sorry lot of the *"la belle"* paintings, which are stiff and sentimental and a form that he reverted to w/ repetition, lacking all progression, that believers take up in Hail Marys in the interstices of their daily lives. He never painted Belle as looking any older than she had at six, although she posed for him in her teens. To critics this is the stuff of meaning. To Belle, it was the stuff of loss. Her father by not seeing her was painting someone she no longer was. Some critics say Max painted Belle as she had been in 1922 or '23 because those were his last happy years w/ Willa, the last years of their love. First, Max had loved her, and then—by 1924—he had not.

In 1924 Max began to paint his *"Ma Femme"* portraits. They are his evocations of Woman—of one woman, Willa—and they're horrific. Critics say Max never painted Belle as a young woman because his view of Woman in this period, his "ideal" of her, as painted, was part banshee, part rag and bone, part lizard. The woman's mouth in all these paintings is wide open, exposing square blunt teeth w/ bloated tongue, and she is screeching, nagging, raving, a contortion of insane demands. Her neck is elongated and bent as if it were broken. The words "It would be so nice to have a country house" and "Not good enough" are painted on the throat of one of them. The words "Will" and "Wilhelm," "ill" and "willful," "villa," "vile," "vilaine," "vielleux" appear on all of them in one form or another. It was supposed in the beginning that the viewing public wouldn't know and wouldn't care that these were wordplay on a woman's name and that that woman was his wife; but word got out, as such words do, and so it was supposed at the beginning of his fame that he was married to a harridan, a witch, and after 1925 one can't find a photograph of them together where they're touching or where Willa doesn't have a gloved hand held against her face to hide her mouth. And during this time Max painted other women. He was, in person, a most charming man, and women were attracted to him. He was in love w/ women, w/ their form, w/ their demeanor of submission, w/ their breasts and thighs, especially—those parts of women that can't speak. He drew his women as smooth gourds and vessels—great, round things—and in his life he used them as repositories for all the things he didn't like about himself.

He blamed his fame on Willa. He lamented that the fame would bring him compromise. He made her out to be demanding and insatiable, but it was Max who craved the pleasures and excitements of popular celebrity and an American type of wealth. He stopped loving her. He could not stop needing her as part of him outside himself that could receive his loathing, so they carried on in her debasement until the spring of 1931, when Belle was thirteen, when Max said he had finally had enough. Willa would have stayed w/

him. She would have stayed w/ him even though he beat her and they fought. She would have stayed w/ him because their passion was a pitched incline—their passion was sheer, exhilarating, deadly. Max married right away in Mexico, as soon as the divorce went through; and three times after that. He made films, designed stage sets, sculpted, lived in Corsica, threw terra-cotta figurines, welded, threw commemorative plates in porcelain, dabbled in photography and always painted. Willa married a man named Vern Rinehart who owned a house in Lake Forest, Illinois, and later, w/ him, her great dormant passion was undammed for good. She turned to God.

Belle was sitting w/ her in Dr. Colmar's anteroom in Lake Forest the week of April 9, 1933, because Willa had been feeling dizzy. Dr. Colmar might give Willa tests, and if he did, the tests might make Willa feel too dizzy to drive home by herself, so Belle was w/ her. Vern was working late that afternoon. While Belle waited, she looked at magazines. She looked through an NRA bulletin and then she read *Time*. She wasn't comfortable in Illinois. The young people were jejune compared to her old friends in Brooklyn, and they were cruel. They didn't know a thing about her father or about the well-known people who used to visit him at the apartment or about dressing up like a Bedouin before dinner and posing until midnight while the opera records blared on Max's Gramophone, or even anything about the kind of life a Bedouin must live, out on the desert. Dr. Colmar's anteroom smelled of patent medicine, and he wore alligator shoes. She could hear her mother breathing deeply and coughing on his cue high in her chest. She could taste medicine at the back of her throat, and even as Dr. Colmar's nurse sat watching her Belle tore a page out of *Time* and folded it and slid it in her pocket. "That isn't nice, you know." "I know." "It isn't fair to people who'll want to read it after you." "I guess not." "The doctor isn't going to like this when I speak about it." "So don't speak about it." The nurse looked down and wrote a bad thing into Willa's chart. She had the slippery hands of an anointer. She had to grip the pen w/ purpose so it wouldn't slip away. Belle had come to notice the way people held things. Her stepfather, Vern, when he spoke to her held his pipe w/ his side teeth while he was talking. Willa held her skirt, as if she were afraid a gust of wind would sneak up on her and expose the tops of her cotton stockings. She took Belle's arm as they went out and, apropos of nothing as they noticed Dr. Colmar's crocuses, she said, "I've always liked Faye as a name, haven't you?" "Is that the nurse's name?" Willa laughed and held onto her skirt. "For a little girl, you silly."

Willa didn't come right out and tell Belle she was pregnant until June, but Belle had pledged herself to run away that day in Dr. Colmar's anteroom, so the news could hardly matter less to her. Willa w/ a baby would make it easier for Belle to get away, that's all. She was due that fall, the third week in October, and it seemed like an interminable wait. By August, Belle had accumulated almost a hundred dollars, a huge sum. She kept the page from *Time* she'd torn out that day in Dr. Colmar's office inside the same tin box w/ the money. It was a message written by the son of Thomas Alva Edison to the employees of Thomas Alva Edison, Inc., in West Orange, New Jersey. Belle liked the sound of it, it sounded like the benediction that they say before a battle. "President Roosevelt has done his part," the message said: "now you do something. Buy something—buy anything, anywhere; paint your kitchen, send a telegram, give a party, get a car, pay a bill, rent a flat, fix your roof, get a haircut, see a show, build a house, take a trip, sing a song, get married. It does not matter what you do—but get going." Willa went into labor eight weeks early and the first week in September delivered a five-pound baby girl that she named Faye. Belle waited until Vern brought word that Willa and the baby were doing swell, then she took her money and her message and her cardboard suitcase and lit out for Chicago and the World's Fair and the world, and to find Max.

Five hundred thousand people came to Chicago that same weekend. It was Labor Day. Belle lit out Friday afternoon on the local into Union Station. It was jammed. That weekend the Pennsylvania line had added forty extra trains to their scheduled runs from cities in the South and East. New York Central brought in twenty thousand people Thursday night alone. There were no vacant hotel rooms for miles around, and outside Union Station people, mostly women, were lined up w/ their signs advertising rooms for rent. Even people w/ money couldn't get a place to stay. Belle kept stopping just to catch her breath. Roads were like long parking lots, and families had to leave their cars miles away in people's yards and alleys, and there were people holding signs advertising yards to park in. There was so much light and so many people and such gaiety on State

Street by midnight Friday that it felt like a Sunday afternoon. The lamps along the Midway cast copper orbs onto the night sky, which seemed very near. It was always light as day, which was good for anyone w/out a place to sleep. Belle stayed awake, mostly on her feet, for two days w/out rest, but nothing bothered her. She lost her sweater, but she held onto her suitcase, switching it from hand to hand when one arm got a little stiff. It wasn't heavy, but she had to hold twice as tight as she would have if there hadn't been a crowd. Her money was in a pouch fashioned from a scarf inside her shirt under her arm. She'd worn a cap, too, and overalls, and she tucked her hair up underneath the cap so at first glance she almost passed for a boy. She didn't make a show of anything, she even watched the way she walked and never lingered long, and people were so busy w/ the mood of things they never gave her any trouble.

The fair was called officially "Century of Progress." The main theme was the new inventions, new since 1833, and that included mostly cars and the Sky Ride, but the thing people talked the most about was Sally Rand, the fan dancer. Next to her the biggest attraction was George Washington's authentic wooden teeth. Belle went to the Hall of Science to see them. They were stained and hanging on two silver rods in a display case. They made her wonder what his voice was like. The guard said the display case was bulletproof. "Well, who would want to shoot them?" Belle had asked. When she talked, you could tell she was a girl. "You never know with Dillinger around," the guard had said. He was dressed in a blue velvet coat like a Colonial, and he needed a shave. "Yeah, and what about Baby Face?" someone else brought up. They looked at her as if she'd been real dumb to ask. She couldn't wait to tell Max about all the fuss over George Washington's teeth and the bulletproof glass and the people peering in. It was the kind of image of America that gratified him. But maybe he was there. Maybe he'd walked by. She had that feeling sometimes, in big crowds, of expecting to look up and see him there. She knew even after two years it was still her way of missing him. She didn't miss her mother, not at all. She didn't think once about Willa and Vern, or if she did it was only to congratulate herself she wasn't thinking of them. She stopped once to peer into a perambulator a woman was rocking near a bench, and the baby she saw inside was what she always saw in her mind's

eye years later if she ever thought about having a half sister named
Faye. Other than that, she didn't think about them.

Sunday night real late while she was holing up inside the comfort
station she got to talking w/ some other runaways, but really it was
vice versa, and one other runaway told her she had come to think
of her parents as if they were dead. Belle didn't think of Willa as if
she were dead, but she didn't mention it. She thought of Willa the
way somebody doesn't think about a thing that hasn't been. And
she was never wistful. She was glad and not glad there were other
runaways. She was glad because they told her things she hadn't
thought of—and she was not glad because some of them had tried
to steal her suitcase when she almost fell asleep.

Right after noon on Labor Day she started for those parking lots
on the farthest edge of town, as the kids had told her to. She didn't
want to go too far, because they had told her that Chicago was so
tough. Capone was there out in that suburb that had that Roman
name, and there were white slave traders all around looking for
young girls. Her breasts hurt when she thought of that, so did her
feet and legs, and her arms were very tired. She started looking for
a couple w/ a kid or a single man or woman w/ two, three children
looking tired so she could volunteer to entertain the little darlings
while the adults drove them home. She started looking for lots w/
ten maybe a dozen cars w/ plates that said Ohio, Indiana, New York,
places East. She found one near the lake about fifteen blocks from
Lincoln Park, and she put her suitcase down and sat on it and waited.
The other runaways had said the bad part would come Monday
night real late w/ people panicky to leave. When people want to
leave, they said, they won't pick up any cargo. The bad part comes
real late, they said, so start out while it's early. So she did. The sun
was hot. A fly was buzzing. A barge dozed inches off the lake on
the horizon. Everything was working out. The bad parts were all
good. The only bad part was the scarf that held the money was a
little itchy and the rest of her was hot. The only bad part was she
fell asleep.

When she woke up a man in white wool pleated pants and white
suede-leather shoes and an off-white tennis sweater w/ one stripe
navy blue and a second stripe the deep clear color of a gypsy wine
was leaning over her. He was the most beautiful man she'd ever

seen, and the sky behind him was deep blue, and she was sure she was still dreaming until he jumped up and ran after someone and she realized her head was bleeding. Blood was falling down before her eyes, but she didn't feel that anything hurt. She sat up. The man in white was running, there were bright rhapsodic lights, and someone said, "Another drifter." That meant her. A dog was barking. "Look, Roy, she's cut," she heard. The moon was coming down. And then, the way things happen, the grass was a good thing to know. She knew that she was sitting on it. There were people all around. They were staring at her, and that was okay, just like the paintings she had posed for, so she sat very still. The blood was bright red falling on her sleeve, and still she didn't feel a thing that hurt. A woman bent down saying, "It's all right kid." There were fireworks. In a minute there were fireworks all over the sky, and all at once she knew that the trouble was a cut above her eye and her suitcase was missing. The people standing around lost interest once they saw she had survived. They left. A lady left a handkerchief on her eye. The grass was very worn where they'd been standing, very stiff where she sat down. She felt the grass, she felt the pouch that held her money. It was very late, and stars came out between the fireworks. After a while it dawned on her to check her teeth, and they were fine. She checked her cap, and it was fine. She checked her face, and she was crying. Still, she didn't want to think of Willa. She didn't want to think of her at all. She didn't want to think the way a child would think. She wanted to think as an adult, as a woman of experience, as a woman of some means, as Bette Davis would.

The man in white returned. Belle thought he looked like someone in a movie, too. Everything seemed to be occurring on a movie's shallow plane. The man in white had chased away whoever had attacked her. Now the man in white was here. And here her suitcase was. The man in white was offering the cardboard suitcase to her, and the part of her that thought she had the wherewithal to carry on like Bette Davis thought she said, "Thanks, really: you're too kind—"; but words came out, "I gotta thank you, Mister." She knew nothing about men. They shaved. They wore elastic garters on their lower legs that looked like slingshots when they took them off. All of them had parts she knew she'd recognize if she saw one, but she couldn't tell you how to build one from scratch or what they looked like in the daylight. She didn't know what men do when they kiss you. She didn't know until just now, at least she never knew she knew, that plain skin has aroma. She could smell him like a bun or pie or something good that draws you closer. She had a sudden great increasing curiosity about him and it made her conscious of the things she didn't know. She didn't know if men could read your mind or had some other kind of power, so she said, "These days people have to be real careful with their baggage, what with Dillinger and all."

She watched as his lips parted and he said, "Bloody, you're a girl—!"

She nodded. She hoped this wouldn't change his interest in her.

"But you're done up like a boy—"

"Oh, that." She shrugged. "You know. Coming to the fair and all. Alone. And men. You know. They'll try and oh, you know . . ."

He smiled. "Who told you that, your mum?"

"Yes." The thought of Willa made her wary.

"What's your name?" he asked.

"Belle."

"Well, Belle, you tell your mother she was right."

This seemed to mark an end to conversation. He looked off, as if to say good-bye.

"I can't tell her," Belle said. She could hear her own voice rising. "I'm a runaway."

He looked at her w/ no new interest.

"I know," he said. "If you'll excuse me, I must find the car. And Jack. I'm sure I left them hereabouts. . . ."

"Hey, wait." She touched him. "You have a car?"

He looked at her hand on his arm, at her nails trimmed too short and her fingers and shirt cuff like a boy's. Something crossed his expression that she couldn't read. She said, "I need a ride to New York." Before he could answer, she told him, "I'll pay you." She let go of him, reached up and took off her cap. Her blond hair fell to her shoulders. She unbuttoned her shirt. She undid the scarf around her chest that held the money, and he watched her. She noticed a moist line of sweat appear along the bottom of his throat, and she knew it must run all the way around his neck and down the middle of his back. She held the money out to him in her fist.

"A hundred bucks," she said. She sounded almost tough.

She watched his self-possession falter. "Please," she urged. She thrust the money toward him.

"How old are you?" he asked.

"Eighteen."

"Don't lie."

"I'm seventeen. . . . Fifteen and a half."

He closed his eyes. "I've had too much to drink," he said, finally. He touched his head. "Put your money away. For God's sake. Button up your shirt."

She looked down. The tops of her breasts were showing. They looked pearly in the light.

"Then you'll take me?"

He watched as she buttoned her shirt.

"We'll see how it stands, when I'm sober. . . ."

She misbuttoned her shirt.

He reached w/ his right hand and undid the third button down and slid his two fingers under the placket where her breast curved around, and he rubbed her there, twice, while his thumb and his forefinger buttoned her right.

"Can you read?" His voice sounded thick. "Are you a good reader, Belle?"

Surely he must feel her heart. His hand was on top of it. "Uh-huh," she answered. Her heart was pounding.

"I'll like you to read to me," he said.

He moved his hand away from her and his expression changed as if he'd had some bad and urgent news. "Put your cap back on," he said.

As she did, her hands shook, and he watched her as one watches an event.

She knew he'd take her w/ him, so she grew more brave. "Do you like me as a boy or what?" she asked.

"What makes you think I like you?"

All she did was look at him.

"It's Jack I'm thinking of," he said.

"Who's Jack?"

"Oh, Jack."

He picked up the cardboard suitcase and began to walk. Belle fell in behind him.

"Jack's a scabby whoreson of a bitch who takes up after little girls. He'll try to fuck you."

"Don't talk like that," she said in Willa's tone of voice.

He laughed. "Well, he will. It's only proper I alert you. I mean, come on. It's the same as posting railroad signals at a freighted junction."

"You wouldn't have to say it like you did. You could just say he's not nice."

"He *is* nice. He hands out lollys with his dick. Do you think you'll like that?"

"Don't talk this way."

"Why not?"

"I don't like it."

"What do you like?" His gaze was searching rows of cars parked in the narrow field. "I like . . ." She thrust her chin out. She'd lost his attention. "I like men who don't talk rough, who smell like limes and taste like piecrust when they kiss me."

He turned to look at her, and she saw him start to laugh.

"Oh, bloody Christ, aren't you the limit!" He clapped his arm across her shoulder. "I ought to do a book on you—"

"Stop teasing me," she said.

"An American best seller. *Teenage Runaway in the Depression.* My Christ. My Christ, Belle . . ."

Something happened when they accidentally touched. Belle felt it mostly as a heartbeat in her body so severe she couldn't stand it, like being on the pavement near a jackhammer. She had no idea how he felt it, but she knew he did. She felt him flicker.

"I want to call you something," she said, dumbly.

"Kit."

He kissed her.

He didn't taste like piecrust. His lips were cool, and he had a bitter taste because he had been drinking, and he showed her how to leave her mouth a little open where his tongue slipped in.

"You're a very pretty girl," he whispered.

"I'm not."

"You're very pretty, and I'm very drunk. . . ."

He swayed a bit. His hand slipped to her hip. "Otherwise I wouldn't lay a hand on you. But you're a natural, do you know that? You're the sort they warn about in horny classics. Do you understand? Like Cleopatra. Do you know that story? She was younger than you are, and Caesar started doing this. And this. You like this, don't you? I can tell. No one ever did this for you. No one ever kissed you, did they? No one put his hand here, did he, and told you that you're pretty and that he'd like to pamper you and bathe you and press fresh flower petals to your flesh and to your breasts and to your nipples. . . ."

As he passed out, he slumped over. She went down w/ him. He lay dead still, and she thought it was a joke. She rolled him over, and his eyes were closed. She shook him gently and said, "Kit," but he just lay there. She had never seen a person who'd passed out, and this condition scared her. She made a pillow for his head from the jacket in her suitcase, and she tried to bring him round by shaking him again.

There was hardly any movement in the car park, and it made her jump when someone said, "Oh, Lord, no, now what's this?"

A Catholic priest bent over her. The night was full of miracles.

"Oh, Father, geez, you're just the person."

"Well, Kit, I might have known," he said slowly, sadly. "I tried to part him from that last pint, but he got away. And who are you?"

"I'm Belle."

"Well, Belle, lad, let's see if we can get him to the car, shall we? It's just down there. You take his feet and I'll bring up the heavy part. Here, is this your suitcase?"

"Yes."

"You're not out here on your own, now, are you, lad?"

"Well, yes."

"Well, you're a fine clean sort to care about this drunken wretch. Here, lift. That's it. We'll have him loaded up in no time, it's that Bentley over there. Good boy. Now prop him steady there. That's it. All right. My God. Well done."

They hunched Kit in the tonneau of the Bentley w/ a golf bag as a pillow and a plaid throw tucked around his legs.

"Well," the priest said, smoothing his black jacket. He was bald and pink and corpulent above his collar. "Lovely cars, these, don't you think? This is the four-and-a-half-liter. . . ."

"Yes," Belle acknowledged.

There was an odd, mute lapse while she studied car tracks on the ground.

"I don't believe in changing money for such favors, but if you're quite hard up—" He reached into his pocket, and Belle heard the kind of small change rattle that reminded her of Vern.

"Kit promised me a ride to New York City," she said.

"That's strange," the priest said, frowning. "I don't believe he has that as his destination. . . ."

"But he promised and—" She turned away and slipped her hand inside her scarf and drew out half her money: "I said I'd pay him. He must have been afraid he might pass out, because he said for me to keep the money, but a deal's a deal. He kept saying he was drunk."

The priest frowned and hooked his left thumb up beneath his chin and placed his index finger on his nose. His eyes were twinkling.

"What else did Kit say?"

"Nothing."

The priest cocked his head.

"He told me to watch out for Jack."

The priest raised his eyebrows.

"Well, Belle, lad," he said, smiling, "I guess we're both Kit's guests for the time being, though I only go as far as South Bend. If you'll go round over there and climb in, you and me will see if I can get this started, and maybe if we're lucky our good friend will come round before we reach my place in Indiana. . . ."

Belle went to the left side of the green convertible and climbed in. The seat was made of smooth black leather and it was large and comfortable. There were a dozen gauges on the chrome dashboard before her and more knobs and gadgets than she'd ever seen. She and the priest both sighed and shrugged at one another.

"Vern had a Ford," Belle said.

He didn't know who Vern was, but he nodded. "So do I."

He pressed a button and let out a latch. All the gauges danced. The engine rumbled.

"That was good!" Belle shouted.

The engine was too loud, but it got less loud as they started.

"That's the supercharger!" he yelled back.

They looked happy.

Belle turned around and tucked the plaid throw around Kit when the wind got stronger. "How long have you known Kit?" she shouted.

"Oh, a good many years. I read at Cambridge a while back. Philosophy. And he was there. Well, in England, that is. You?"

"Someone ran off with my suitcase, and he took after them and brought it back."

"Oh, well, he's very valiant, that's the truth. When he's sober, that is. Which is less and less. But he's between books, so it's to be expected, I suppose. He's a writer, don't you know."

"I didn't."

"And a liar!" he yelled, smiling. "And a drunk! But a stout heart, Belle, lad, so far. A good stout heart."

Belle watched the gauges on the Bentley's dash. Their pointers leveled and held steady as they passed through city lights and streets that were less lighted. Then they drove along in darkness, near the water. She rolled her head back on the leather seat and looked up at the night sky. She could see the glow of factories ahead on the horizon. She could see the city rise, a black shadow w/ pinpoints of light like fireflies behind her.

Once Kit stirred, and she and the priest both turned to look at him in a shared moment of conspiracy. She almost said that she felt lucky, but she was hesitant to speak. She'd never known a priest. She'd known the Reverend Ordway, who was Willa's chief confessor, and she'd hated him. He smelled sour. She liked this priest because he fell in like a friend and didn't ask a lot of questions.

"Can I ask you something, Belle, lad?" he said, finally.

"Sure."

The wind had died down somewhat.

"Would it be all right with you if I gave up pretending to believe in your disguise?"

"I guess." She smiled.

"That way you can curl up there and sleep awhile and not be bothered with your cap, and I'll just drive."

"Okay."

"You're a runaway?"

She nodded, and he frowned. "I won't ask you any questions," he said.

In a while she saw the signs for East Chicago and for Gary,

Indiana. Beside the road along this stretch of highway ran a deep ditch, and beyond that she could see the bonfires glowing and the embers of the barrel fires throwing sparks into the night and the dark hunched shadows of the hobos and the homeless and the people on the move.

"Are you a priest in a big church?" she asked him.

"The biggest." He smiled.

"I mean, is your church big, the one where they pay you for your preaching."

He laughed. "I don't have a congregation in that way. I teach. I'm a teacher at the university."

"But you're still a priest, right?"

"Yes."

"A real priest?"

"Yes."

"I thought priests were . . . oh, you know . . ."

"Different?"

"Yeah."

"We are."

"Well, maybe. But I like you."

They drove in silence as the steely yellow glow of factories grew nearer, to their left. "I was born in Gary," he shouted, when they crossed the river. He pointed w/ his chin. "This was one big sand dune back in '05. That's the year that U.S. Steel discovered Gary. Look at it now, Belle. A hellfire. I owe my priesthood to it. . . ."

She watched the mills spill orange-and-yellow smoke into the night.

"What's wrong with U.S. Steel?" she asked.

"What's wrong with sand dunes?"

That seemed like a stupid question. It would have given Vern a laugh.

"Sand dunes don't make jobs," she said, "for those that don't have work. They don't make railroads, either, that deliver goods. They don't make girders for tall buildings. . . ."

There were lots of things sand dunes didn't do.

"That's true," he said.

He made it sound as if it weren't.

"Do people call you Father?"

"Oh, sure. Some do. Some call me Father Reardon."

"Can I call you Father Reardon, even though I'm not a Catholic?"

"Well, my heaven, yes. You can call me what you like, for goodness' sake. Kit's not Catholic, heaven knows. You can call me what Kit calls me. . . ."

Belle waited.

"What?"

He looked at her. "He calls me Jack."

The blood drained from her face, her mouth fell open. She felt a cold wind run all through her. Father Jack tossed his head back and laughed and laughed until the tears rolled from his eyes.

"I'm sorry, Belle, lad. There, now. Don't be frightened. I can well imagine what he's said. I know Kit the way a conscience knows transgression. I'm his angel, one of them. Kit has many. He's the devil in me. Once he broke into my classroom at Cambridge. It was Ethics, I remember, a tutorial. Kit had with him his three cronies from those days, all drunk, and they got themselves some white lab coats. Well, don't you know they burst in, and Kit has this stethoscope and these glasses, and he cries out, 'Lo! we have you now, you devil!' and before my upperclassmen don't they clap me in a strait jacket and haul me out, declaring I'm escaped from the asylum!" He broke out laughing again and wiped his tears away. "Ah, God, Belle. God takes care of widows, kids, and alcoholics, so they say. And who am I, if not God's servant. . . ."

The steel mills churned and rumbled where the dunes of Father Reardon's youth had been.

"I'll see you on a train from South Bend in the morning, Belle, lad. To New York, if you insist, so long as I can see you've got a friend or family there. But not with Kit."

He looked at her in the firelight thrown by the mills and she saw he was frowning. "Not with him," he repeated. "He'll part you from your youth too quick."

He nodded toward the mills as if they'd parted him from something, and he scanned them as a man in exile would survey a line of hills along a distant shore.

She didn't think she was that fond of youth. She didn't see the point in it.

"I like the way the steel mills look," she said defiantly.

"Oh, sure. There's always those who will," he reasoned sadly.

She woke the next morning on a faded horsehair davenport in the front room of Father Jack's house on a paved road across from a cornfield that stretched as far as she could see till it stopped at the town w/ three white church spires and a banner proclaiming the Tri-County Fair. It took her a moment to think where she was and to know that the low *schush-ing* she heard was hot wind through dry cornstalks over cracked, brittle ground. She felt the heat of the day just beginning—dry heat, the dry heat of ovens, of dry Christian women and dry jokes; not the moist heat of cities, Chicago and Brooklyn, the moist heat that beads on the skin; and she counted one, two, three, four . . . this is my fifth day from home.

She sat up on the davenport; its horsehair was starchy as straw, and it smelled slightly of camphor. A thin blanket was bunched at her feet, and she saw a damp spot on the pillow where she'd slept. She was dressed in her blue cotton shirt and the same overalls she'd been wearing for days. She longed for some water. She was hot.

She followed the logical sense of the house to the kitchen— through the parlor, down the hallway, past the front stairs, through the dining room, to the back. In a good house, Willa had taught her, you can follow your nose to the kitchen. In a good house a woman is there, always cooking—not *always*, of course, but most of the time; or something is baking or just-baked, or something is setting atop of the stove. Under Willa's training, a good house, a kitchen, a woman were all of one thing. But this was a priest's house, a bachelor's—the first of its kind she was to explore. She expected a neat, barren waste, like an ice field. Instead she found coffee and berries and sweet cream and sausage and the big table set w/ a red-and-white cloth and a glass vase of butterfly weed and snapdragons and asters, and white plates w/ blue borders and big linen napkins laid out for two.

She felt a catch in her throat, and she blinked back her tears, and had he seen her, he would have thought she was homesick.

The kitchen was large, very large, the full width of the house, and it was bright, too bright for African violets, she would have thought, but they flourished under Father Jack's care and covered the sills of all the six windows. The curtains were made of white muslin w/ tiny mock flowers cross-stitched in blue at the hem. There were books in the kitchen, a whole wall of them banked near the table, suggesting he read in this room while he was eating, alone.

There were pictures, as well, on the walls—sketches in ink and in pencil of landscapes, and drawings of churches, and cutouts of cartoons from newspapers, the kind that are drawn in one box, the political kind. There were photographs, too, framed and mounted, some of them over the sink and above the gas stove—Willa would have a conniption fit if she ever saw anything hanging above a gas stove. It was a hazard. It wouldn't be *clean* . . . yet, these were. Everything was. Water glasses were shining, pots and pans were wiped clean and stored, of all places, on hooks from the ceiling near the stove. Willa would die. There was a rug on the floor in one corner, a rag rug, and a rocking chair. There was a small table beside it, along w/ a lamp and more books and journals, a music stand, some sheet music, a violin and a bow, a harmonica, some screens on which seeds of all sizes were drying, some baskets of remnants and yarn and a green-and-white neck scarf half-knitted, suspended on two wooden needles. It seemed Father Jack did most of his living in this large room—it was crammed w/ his interests, his projects; w/ life. She had felt in an instant swept up in its force as one is a victim of surf. She had felt in an instant not homesick for *her* home, but homesick for this one—she had felt lift or start to lift the weight of austerity, the burden of living that cheerless *Protestanten-Moralisten* existence that Vern and Willa had been so eager to pass off as Life.

Vern, Vern especially, had a way—he gave Belle the creeps. For one thing, he walked on his tippy-toes, because of weak feet. He couldn't lift. He was a thin man, very slight, like an invalid; and his hands shook most of the time. He was dry-looking, as dry as talc—dry as a moth is; or a ghost. His hair was thin. She thought if she touched it, she'd see it crumble to dust. His skin was that of a pebble—a perfect white thing that can't blush, or blanch w/ panic, or go quick-pink in the cold. He looked dead, actually. "Jesus came to me last night and said I ought to speak to you about your conduct" was something he could say as they were sitting down to supper. It was the sort of thing he *liked* to say as they were sitting down to supper. As he ate, he would intone the lessons of his Life in Jesus, balancing his fork against his middle finger while the light reflected off its tines; and Belle would watch as he chewed every mouthful seven times, for his digestion. He had a delicate stomach, a near-death condition of the stomach lining that Jesus, Christ Our Lord, alone, had saved him from. Vern believed this. Vern believed this when he met Willa, and Belle had watched suspiciously as his persuasiveness and his persistence had worked inroads through her mother's passive nature. "Tell me what you think of Vern," Willa had pressed. "Isn't he the sweetest?"

"I don't like him."

"No!"

"I don't."

"I won't allow you saying that."

"I already said it."

"He's done nothing bad to you—"

"I don't like him hanging round that much."

"Shesh up. You shesh up. You just think for once what's good for me. You just think what I should do, for once. That Mister who's your father, I don't hear him givin' an opinion what we ought to do. I don't ever hear you saying, 'Life is hard for Mama,' while it is. I don't see you worried what I have to do to make ends meet—"

"Max sends money."

"Money. Sure. 'Max sends money.' Money's easy for that man. Money doesn't ever change a thing for any woman. A wealthy woman can't get anything she wants just like a wealthy man. What could money buy for me? Could it buy up everything in sight before they saw those things about me? Where am I supposed to go? You tell me, Miss Smartypants. What am I supposed to do? Turn my back on one nice man who treats me nice? You wait. You'll see. You'll see in your own day. I hope you'll see. I hope you'll get it good. . . ."

It's funny about niceness, how it does what lime will do in certain soil: So Vern would say, "Our Lord Jesus Christ told me to say to you you hadn't ought to talk back to your mother."

"What language does he talk to you in, Vern, plain English?"

"Hesh, Belle, and let Vern say his piece. Vern, some carrots?"

"Jesus says you're careless in your ways."

"Some limas, Vern? They're boiled."

"He says He misses you. You're on His mind. He says He wants you, Belle."

"Some beef? Some more potatoes?"

"He hungers after all His wayward flock. He's willin' to forgive you."

"I ain't done nothin' yet."

"Vern, try this boiled dressing on your lettuce."

"What about that report we had from Mr. Fleischer over to the school?"

"What about it?"

"He said you refused to come in after."

"He was flirting with me."

"Shesh, Belle, and let Vern finish—"

"He flirts with all the girls. He's silly. He's a silly man."

The fork would waver, up and down; the fork would waver and beneath the table Vern would tap his foot.

"The flesh is too much on your mind."

"Is that another thing that Jesus said to tell me?"

"No, that's a fact."

"Well, you just prove it. . . ."

"We haven't said the grace yet, Vern, and look, you've started in already. We haven't had our evening meditation. . . ."

"Are you denying that the flesh is not the foremost in your mind?"

"The foremost in my mind is being rid of you."

"I know the time you spend alone in front of mirrors, putting on. I know what kind of things go on. . . ."

"I don't believe a minute Jesus talks to you. I don't believe it, so leave me alone."

"He does. He does. He talks to him."

"Oh, shesh it, Mama."

"But He does."

"You won't be speaking to your mama that way, Belle, in the now on. The Lord says, 'He that curseth his mother shall surely be put to death.' And the Lord says, 'Children, obey your parents in the Lord; for this is right. Honour thy father and mother; (which is the first commandment with promise;) That it may be well with thee, and thou mayest live long on the earth'—"

"Are you threatening me? Are you saying you're going to kill me, is that what you're doing?"

" 'Only take heed to thyself,' child, 'and keep thy soul diligently, lest thou forget the things which thine eyes have seen, and lest they depart from thy heart all the days of thy life. . . .' And the Lord says, 'Gather Me the people together, and I will make them hear my words, that they may learn to fear me all the days that they shall live upon the earth, and *that* they may teach their children.' That's the Word of God. That's Deuteronomy. Four: nine and ten. . . ."

"*God* didn't write that, you know. Mama, tell him. God never wrote all that down. Max says men wrote it. A lot of men. Max says it was written at all different times, because of politics. Plus, he says, some of the men were lunatics. Tell him what Max says, Mama. You can't believe God wrote *a book*! Also, how come none of these chapters are written by girls? And also, none of these people back then could speak in English, so Max says—"

"You won't talk of that Mister in the now on," she was told.

"He's my father."

"We won't talk of him inside this house in the now on," she was informed.

"You're saying I'm not supposed to talk about my father?"

"He's saying—"

"He's my father! You just told me I should honor him!"

"He's saying *he's* your father now, Belle. . . ."

"And Jesus is."

"I'm sorry, Vern. Of course."

"We all are children in the eyes of Christ the Lord, Our Father, Willa."

"I know. Yes, Vern."

"We don't forget the Father, Willa."

"I know, Vern. Never," Willa would submit.

You can't believe in this, Belle would try to say to her.

"I asked Jesus to show me what to do, and He said It would be revealed to me, and then before I had a chance to bring it up with Vern, he told me he had bought this house for us along the North Shore of Chicago. Imagine that! It sounds real ritzy, don't you think?"

"Mama, please don't marry up with him."

"Go on."

"He's had a change on you already."

"Hasn't he? Go on. It's just the extra henna rinse I'm using. . . ."

Then: "Mama, how'd you ever run away?"

"What?"

"When you ran away."

"Back then?"

"Yes. Then."

"Oh, it was easy."

"How?"

"I hated her. 'Ol' Gritty'—that's my mother. And Max took me away."

"But what about if Papa hadn't taken you away?"

"If Max hadn't? Oh . . . I guess somebody else had would."

And then: "Mama, you don't believe all that. You don't believe it, really, do you?"

"You know, we get word back you're too smart-alecky. You know that, don't you?"

"I'm not talking anything about all that."

"These are people Vern and I must see in church. Vern sees these people. Menfolks."

"Listen to you . . ."

"People that he sees—"

"You just said 'menfolks.' Listen to you. Listen to the way you talk."

"And then I have to go to Christian Women's Meeting and they say, 'That *Belle*' . . . But it's the way they say it. They say, 'That *child*.' You can hear, 'That *mother*,' in it—"

"People would like you better if it weren't for me. . . ."

"That's not the subject in discussion. The subject isn't people liking *me* . . ." She was confused. She placed her fingers at the corner of her mouth as she always did when she was confused, and a deep line developed on her brow. Sometimes it seemed to Belle that Willa had lost her way. There was a look in Willa's eyes sometimes that signaled she was afraid she wasn't being understood. "It's *you* I mean to talk about," she said. "These things people have been saying. Can't you try to be a little lady? All we ask is that you try. We don't feel you're trying. It's as if you throw it in our face—good home, a Christian family, friends and neighbors. It's as if you're saying it's not good enough for you. Couldn't you be more polite? Couldn't you just hold your tongue? No one else but you wants your opinion. Trust to God a little. Not a lot. Go easy. Take a simple thing; say, a decision on something in school, or what not. Instead of you just getting all upset and giving over to frustration

and smart talk, just ease up, give in to God, relax a little. Close
your eyes and think, 'I'm blesséd in His sight.' You see? Close your
eyes and say, 'I'm blesséd; Lord God loves me. It is *I* that Lord God
loves. The Lord God is the One who knows me.' You can send
your thoughts to Him. You can trust Him with your misery. He
knows. He will provide. He takes care of those who—"

"Mama, I don't *have* a misery."

"Oh, but you *will*, Belle . . ."

"Do you want me to?"

"It's nothing you can help."

"But do you *want* me to?"

"It's nothing you can choose, is all. It's something chooses you."

Like living, in the first place, she would think. Like parents. Or
one's sex.

"What made you hate 'Ol' Gritty' so much that you ran away?"

"She was . . . well . . . let's see. Making a family with five and
all is hard work . . . she . . ."

"She . . . what?"

"She . . ."

It seemed a year would rotate on that axis: *she.*

"She would never talk the way you and I do. She wouldn't let
nobody close. You're lucky, Belle. We're close. The two of us can
talk. We couldn't none of us say two words to Gritty. Oh, she was
cold. There wasn't any talking to her. There wasn't any getting
close. . . ."

Belle had a thousand questions: Did you miss her? Did you miss
your sisters? Did Papa know he loved you right off? How does someone know she loves another person? What does love feel like? Where
does someone go to learn about it?

THE LORD WILL PROVIDE was the sole wall ornament in the kitchen
in Lake Forest; Willa set the words in needlepoint herself. There
was a church calendar that had a spiritual depiction for each month
thumbtacked to the swinging door that went into the dining room.
There were no mirrors in the house, except the one that Belle had
carted home from a sheriff's sale one afternoon when she had stopped
to watch a family's household items moved onto the sidewalk after
school and auctioned off to meet the mortgage. She hadn't known
the family, or else she would have walked right on. They had a
mirror, about three feet by two, that she bid up from ten cents to a

quarter. They had two little girls, who looked about four and nine, who stood together, watching. It seemed like a game to the younger one; she kept calling numbers to the auctioneer when he said, "Six, that's six, now who will give me seven . . . ?" To the older girl, Belle heard a thin, worn-out-looking woman, who may have been their mother, saying, "They're thangs. Thangs is easy for a soul to come by. We can always get more thangs. . . ."

Belle watched the crowd of passers-by pecking over the disorder of a family's life, disporting on the scraggly lawn and cobbly pavement of a decent neighborhood; and she wondered what had happened to precipitate the tragedy. "First off, it's not so tragic," Willa told her, "because it only happens when a person hasn't paid his bills, and that's brought on by pure sloth and extravagance nine times out of ten. Why, look at us! Times are hard is all you hear, and Vern saved back a thousand dollars just last year—"

"Did you marry him because he's wealthy?"

"Oh, Vern's not wealthy, so to speak—"

"But is that why you married him?"

"No. Of course not. Watch your mouth."

"I never see you kissing him."

"Why should I? There's a place for that."

"Does he kiss you then? I never hear a thing. Sometimes I listen. I could hear the bedsprings if he was really kissing, but I never hear a thing but just him snoring—"

"Watch your mouth. You watch that fresh talk in this house, Miss Smart Aleck—"

In this house, soon after that, for a never questioned reason, Vern altered a lifelong habit of emptying a day's small change into a chipped, discarded shaving mug, once belonging to his father. All his life he had saved up pennies in the mug, rolling them in stiff brown paper at the end of every three months for deposit in the bank just before the day the interest for the quarter would be tallied. The mug was kept next to the jar of blackstrap molasses on the lower shelf of the kitchen cabinet next to the sink. When Vern came home each evening, he'd hang his hat inside the door and leave his jacket folded on the banister of the front stairs. Then he'd go into the kitchen to say hello to Willa and to take a spoonful of blackstrap molasses, for his digestion. Then he'd empty the small change from his pockets and put it in the mug and wash his hands. Then he'd unfurl the evening paper and sit down at the kitchen table and comment to his wife about some bit of unsettling news as she fixed supper. But late in winter for a never questioned reason Vern altered his habit and at first Belle had not noticed why. He started coming right upstairs, where Belle was usually alone, reading in her room. He hung his jacket in his closet, left his change out loose on top of his chiffonnière, washed his hands in his and Willa's bathroom; and then went back downstairs to take his dose of blackstrap for his digestion and to read the paper while his wife made evening supper. It was Belle's job to set the table, and she did this every night at five o'clock. One evening Belle came down at five o'clock and walked into the kitchen for the plates and Vern said absent-mindedly, "What day is this; it's Friday, isn't it?"

Both Belle and Willa stopped and looked at him. He kept on pretending he was looking at the news.

"I guess Gus Welch will be around tonight for the paper money."

He looked up at the wall clock.

"Belle," he said. "Go upstairs and get the thirty cents from off the top of that there chiffonnière so I won't have to be disturbed halfway through my supper—"

"Now wait," said Willa, rooting through her apron pocket, "I think I've got the thirty cents right here. . . ."

Belle saw Vern's face turn yellow and waxy as a candle, and when Willa saw it, her hand shook and groped its feeble way back to her apron pocket. The pocket had white eyelet trim, and it wavered like a candle flame where her hand was shaking. Still, Belle wasn't too quick to catch on, and it took several calls on her over the next few days to go up to the chiffonnère and bring him back some change before it dawned on her one night that it wasn't like him to leave a dollar bill lying about. Or a half dollar. Or three quarters. Or a stack of dimes. So she took one. She took a dime to see if anything would happen. She hid it in her room and nothing happened. She woke up in the middle of the night and moved it to what seemed a better hiding place, but nothing happened. Vern didn't say a word. A few days later she was sent to get some change to take to Mrs. Whitcomb for the eggs, and she took another dime. A few days after that she was on her way downstairs to set the table and instead of walking past their room she went in and took a quarter. The next week she took sixty cents. Some evenings Vern would stop by her bedroom and he would say, "You had a good day, did you, Belle, today in school?"

"Oh, yes, Vern, I had a fine day today, thank you."

"Dinner sure smells good."

"Yes, it does, doesn't it?"

"Your mother sure is a fine cook."

"She sure is."

"Boiled beef. M-mmm! My favorite."

"Uh-huh. With those little new potatoes."

"And limas . . ."

"Ummm. Well. I guess I'll be down soon."

"Oh, no. You take your time up here. You go ahead and do whatever you'd be doin'. Longer that boiled beef cooks, the better anyway. . . ."

Belle behaved in that house as if Lord Jesus had in fact delivered His own message to her. And Vern—Vern, who had hoarded pennies from the cradle; Vern, who had put back a thousand dollars in the worst year of the Depression; Vern lined the silver dollars up as if they were votive candles on a silver salver on an altar, and Belle would come in minutes later and would take a minted coin and read, "In God We Trust"; and it was the closest they could come to shared religion.

"So you think he left the money there on purpose, do you?" Father Jack has asked her.

"Yes."

"But is that in his nature, do you think?"

She had come to like this man a lot in a short time.

"Well, yes, I guess so," she stammered.

She wasn't as keen an observer of human temperament as he was. She noticed different things—the texture of skin, an aroma, light. He probed for reasons; he pressed one to explain. Faith, he said, must be seized inside the cusp—faith excites in suspension of one's reason.

"I mean," she continued, because he was frowning intently, "*anything* can be in *everyone's* nature. . . ."

She watched his eyes light w/ amusement, and he smiled.

She felt he liked her, too, the way she liked him—they liked each other as compatible parts of their quixotic opposites. . . .

He had been outside gathering eggs in the henhouse when she had come into the kitchen. She was glad of that—it had given her a chance to snoop. After a while she'd heard his voice gently exhorting the hens against their slovenliness and she'd gone out through the screen door to the backyard in search of him.

She'd never been inside a henhouse before. She didn't like it. There wasn't much air; what air there was required cleaning. Father Jack was engaged in scolding a large biddy w/ white feathers and a chipped beak. He was wearing a straw hat, work pants and a white cotton shirt w/out his clerical collar. The hen he was scolding seemed haughty and he seemed disheartened. She hadn't laid. "And after only four months," he lamented to Belle. "She should have another good year of laying in her. . . ."

It was dusty as a dirt road in mid-August in there.

She could hardly breathe.

"Mrs. Whitcomb sings to hers to get them started when they've stopped," Belle suggested.

"Ah. Mrs. Whitcomb." he said.

"She's our neighbor, down the street. The egg lady."

"Ah-huh."

"In Lake Forest."

"Oh, Lake Forest! I said Mass there once. It was a funeral Mass; but nevertheless . . ."

Belle was surprised to find the eggs so warm.

"Did you know these birds are direct descendants of the lizards? Look here. . . ."

He lifted one leg of the recalcitrant biddy.

"A similar skin type and structure, see?"

She didn't see, but she nodded.

"You like chickens?" he asked.

"Chicken pie," she confessed.

"You hear that?" he warned the hen. "They're stupid animals," he whispered to Belle. "Plus, they're cannibals." He raised his eyebrows. "Still, they're heartier than the thrushes and the hummingbirds they ate back in Rome. Sure! You didn't know that? They ate dormice, too. Bones and all. Sometimes raw. Do you know the *Satyricon?* No? The first known novel. So-called. By Petronius. 'Trimalchio's Dinner'? No? Ah, there's a description in there of a roasted dormouse seasoned with honey and poppyseed. I find that most attractive. That seasoning sounds splendid, don't you think? Oh, not the mouse, of course. Still, if we eat *frogs*, what's so reprehensible about a *mouse*? . . . No, I mean the seasoning. Of course, I'm a honey-user, anyway: convinced that bees are more efficient fabricators of a basic sugar than human beings with machetes in the cane fields. . . . Do *you* eat sugar? Have you ever seen it harvested? No? Go to Cuba. Anyway, that honey with the poppyseed—it still appeals to a man's senses after nineteen hundred years. I'll never forget the awakening to history I felt when I first read that. Do you read the classics? No? Remind me that I have a volume that I give all my beginners. . . . It frightens me that man—that *we*, excuse me—men and girls have changed so little over all these years. . . ."

While he'd been talking, he had led her outside—now he studied her beneath bright sun:

"So it's Lake Forest, is it? Let me see: I can't recall anything worth running from in that town. Let me think: No, it was a nice little town. . . ."

Belle noticed his face didn't look so pink this morning. And he seemed slimmer. His eyes appeared a darker blue.

"I didn't like it there."

He raised his eyebrows and his hat slid down.

"Like it? What's not to like?"

"It's not where I'm from. . . ."

"Oh, well, my goodness. Now, let's see. You let me talk about my growing up in Gary last night, didn't you? And then I said I wouldn't ask you any questions. But you see this opens up an avenue, don't you? This thing about 'like' or 'not like.' . . . And it's hard for me to understand that—don't you see?—unless we get to know each other: that is, until I get to, so to speak, ask questions. Where are you from?"

He'd stopped her halfway between the house and the chicken yard.

It was no good place for Belle to ask for shelter from a question.

"Brooklyn."

"Oh, the Dodgers!"

"Well, I guess . . ."

"Why did the family come west?"

She looked at him.

The thing about the land in the Midwest that she was used to is

it's flat; but she could see some hills behind him and she thought—
I'm facing east:

"We got divorced."

"I'm sorry. You're not Catholic?"

"No."

She spotted Kit's green Bentley parked along the house.

"And how long ago was this?"

"What?"

"The divorce."

She hadn't noticed last night what a flashy car it was—it looked flashy and vagrant next to Father Jack's two-story house.

"Oh . . . two years ago."

"And so now you're going back, between two parents?"

She nodded.

"Well, that's common enough. Your father, is it?"

She nodded, again.

"Well, that explains a great deal." He took a step forward, moving them along, and said, "Why don't you take your time and go wash up while I make biscuits? Then we'll have breakfast. Then we'll talk. That's a fine plan, don't you think?"

"Where's Kit?"

Father Jack looked at his egg basket and seemed to count his eggs.

"He's gone."

It was a stupid lie: They both looked at Kit's car.

"Can you imagine," he said, blushing, "even as a child, not being able to tell an honest fib? I never could. Well, that dictated something, didn't it?" His gaze lifted swiftly upward, glancing off the corner window on the second floor. "He's still asleep, I would imagine . . . still sleeping it off. You'll leave him be, Belle, I would ask. . . ."

"Oh, sure," she answered; *she* could lie.

She'd stolen into his room the same way she'd stolen into Vern's to take his money. She had no thought of being caught or of being held accountable for her behavior—it was something that she had to do and so she did it. The only voice she had to answer to was the one that voiced her instincts, the one that prompted her to act outside her reason, on the cusp.

Once inside the room, she stopped; his stillness stopped her. The room was square—it was painted the orange-pink of a cameo, and it had two dormer windows fronting on the road. Through the windows came the same dry corn breeze she had awakened to. Now and then, in its shifting, the breeze sucked thin white curtains to the screens, flat and still. There was an aroma in the room that she recognized as Kit's—but it was sour, like something made w/ baking soda that had been sitting out too long. He was asleep, and he was naked. The sun was coming to that side of the house so everything, especially the sheets and the bottoms of his feet, looked pearly, like carved cameos. She couldn't hear him breathing. She was afraid that if she took a step it would wake him, and she didn't want to talk to him as much as just investigate him.

He was a sight—the way a sunset is. He was dark-haired, but he had fair skin, and the cheeks of his buttocks were white. They were round, and she wanted to touch them. It surprised her. She'd never before thought of a body as something perfect in its nature, as a shell is. Kit was perfect. He slept on his stomach w/ his right leg drawn up, and along the inside of his legs there was dark curly hair. His back was well muscled. It looked smooth. The skin on his hands was stretched and tight, and his fingers were long and thin. He wore a signet ring on his right hand the color of dried blood, the detail of which she couldn't see. His face was half-hidden from her by his outstretched arm. She watched him a long time, or what seemed like a long time; and then, as w/ watching a sunset, there was a shift, and it was time to go. She'd followed the line that swept up from his waist across his shoulders back down the narrow hollow of his spine to the curve of his hip and the plane of his thigh. She had memorized it. She'd committed it to her store of remembrances. She tested herself as she drew a cool bath in Father Jack's tub; she could recall the sweep of Kit's body the way other people recall simple shapes. If she closed her eyes, she could recall every detail, including its color. She could imagine its feel.

In the cool bath, she floated in reverie in slightly green water; she made her breasts float. She had almost no hair on her body, she noted. She was so pale. Who could want her? Her body was flat and perverse. Who could want her except in perversity, as a freak. She was knock-kneed. The fat of her knees floated up. Her toes were too long. No one would love her. They'd been right. No one would love her but Jesus. "Dear Heavenly Father," she prayed. She made little waves in the water. She closed her eyes, and she summoned the image of Kit, of his body. "Dear Heavenly Father . . ." Her nipples got hard. When she put her finger in herself she was wet, but not like the water. It happened. She did it again. This time while she did it, she let him watch. She pretended she had asked him to watch. It was better that way. It was much better that way. He said something. She pretended he said something. He said, Go in a circle. He said, Like this. His fingers were long. With his other hand he held her nipple between his thumb and his finger. And he pulled. He gently pulled, and then it was his lips, pulling there, and he went in a circle, up and down, and his hair smelled like piecrust where his head lay on her breast, and he went in a circle, in and out, and he said, No one ever put his hand here, did he? No one ever did this for you. . . . I did, she thought, knowing it was she, but knowing it was he, too; knowing and not knowing, but pretending not to know and yet suspending reason and just giving in. What control she lost was hers to lose. It was not the slightest thing like prayer, this dialogue. It was not the slightest thing like anything, except fainting. What control she lost was hers to lose— and she lost it to herself.

"How pretty you look," Father Jack remarked.
"You think so?"
"Oh, my, yes."
"My dress is mussed from being in the suitcase and . . . it's . . . it smells a little musty. . . ."
"I mean your hair: the whole *roundness* to you."
He really seemed to find her pretty, she could tell.
"I used some of that cologne."
"Oh, fine. I keep getting it at Christmas, and I never use it. Coffee? I made biscuits. I confess I am too temporal. Can you make an omelette? No? Well, watch. Seeing a thing done is one good way to learn—my omelettes are my *specialité de la maison*—I thought we'd have them sweet this morning, with the cream and berries. . . . Tell me: What are you reading?" He looked at her expectantly.
"Right now?"
"Well, you know: this week."
She lifted her skirt a little in a funny, helpless gesture—Willa's. "Nothing."

"Ah. Well, you were busy leaving home, I guess. That's a little joke."

He peered at her. "You *do* read?"

"Oh, sure."

"Tell me what you've read just recently that you especially liked."

"Um, I read the serials in magazines."

"Ah, magazines! Good! What do you make of this latest bit from the *Fascista* there in Spain?"

She stared at him blankly.

They both had blue eyes—his were the color of cornflowers; hers were damson.

"This disestablishment of the Church," he prompted.

His eyelashes were silver, like hers. She could pass for his daughter.

"Have you been following that? You have? Well, good. Then you know. I'll tell you, Belle, lad, the Church has no fine history for steering clear of State, but this latest détente with Mussolini and his kind—oh, I throw Franco in there, too—this hand-to-mouth cooperation with these popinjays makes my blood boil. Did I tell you I met him? Sure. Sat right beside Benito at the signing of the Concordat in '29. My God. The man's appalling. I know human nature. Priests tend to know a little something when it comes to human nature, and there we all were—Achille Ratti and Gasparri—fawning and making pleasant conversation about weather with a man whose evil any *child* would sense. . . . Watch here, this is my little trick: you add cold water to the eggs here, and it stiffens them right up. . . . Where was I? Oh, Achille Ratti. So there's Achille Ratti sitting on his ancient derrière and sipping *anisetto* with Il Duce while the Spanish seize two thousand Catholic churches and turn them into armories or, God knows, *las casas de correos*—and what does Achille Ratti do? *De nada. De cero.*"

"Who's Achille Ratti?"

He pursed his lips. "Belle, lad. Have you ever heard of something called a *Pope*?"

She made a gesture that meant, go on. She wasn't used to being w/ people who knew as much as she thought she did.

"Well, Achille Ratti is the *Pope*. Pope Pius the Eleventh. Prince of the Apostles. Hero of the Holy See."

"How come you make fun of him like that?"

"To provoke reaction."

"I didn't know you were allowed to be so disrespectful about . . . things."

" 'Things'?"

"The Pope."

"The Pope is not a Thing. The Pope is a tenet of my faith. You're not following one bit of this, are you?"

"Well, a little . . . I mean, it doesn't come as a surprise. I'm used to it."

She meant to show him she wasn't so stupid: "Everybody that I know who's Catholic talks that way—you know, like a big shot. Or they talk about, well, their families a lot; about not wanting to disappoint their parents. . . ."

He smiled. He took a brown nut shaped like an almond and grated some of it into the cream. It occurred to her this would be the first time in a year that she'd be eating a whole meal that didn't have a single *boiled* thing in it, except water.

"You know a lot of Catholics, do you?" he inquired.

"Three or four my age. But we used to know a lot of Europeans because Max is European, so we always had these strangers in the house and all of them were . . . what's a *lapsed* Catholic? All of them said they were that. None of them seemed to know too well what they ought to do. I mean, when it ever came to a religion. Even Max. He always went to Mass at Christmas and at Easter even though I don't think he believed one word of it. Easter always used to hit him very hard. He wouldn't eat. He used to go to synagogue with Jules, too. Jules was his best friend. If Jules came over Friday night for dinner, Max would cook, like you're doing, and then Jules would light the candles. I remember that. I think Max just liked the parts about religion that included lighting the candles. When I was little, I would blow them out right away and beg Max and Jules to do it over, and they would. Secretly I was doing it because I knew Max liked the lighting of the candles—"

"Max is your father?"

Belle nodded her head. She hadn't thought of him that way, in the flesh-and-blood, in a long time. It frightened her. It frightened her to think of him as something other than a destination.

"Tell me about him," he said casually.

"Oh . . . well . . ." She looked around. "He's not *tidy* or anything, the way you are. And he's shorter than you. He's real short. And he wears a hat all the time, different hats . . ."

She tried hard to *remember* Max, remember the particulars; the biscuit tins w/ brushes soaking in them, the cotton shirts soaked through w/ solvents, oils and wine . . . "I think you and he would hit it off just fine because he treats some things that happen in the world so seriously, I mean, the way you do, I guess—he treats the whole world the way some people treat a neighborhood. If something happens halfway around the world, he treats it like it's happening to him."

"It is."

She shrugged. "I don't know if I agree with that so much. . . ."

"And your mother? Tell me about her. Where does she stand in the world?"

"My mother?" Belle flipped the fabric of her skirt again. "Willa's impressed by what people think . . . *of her.*"

The way he looked at her she knew she had impressed him w/ that answer. . . .

"Where are they from? Not Brooklyn, I take it. . . ." He tilted the pan the eggs were cooking in and lifted the edge of the omelette w/ a spatula.

"Willa's from some place up in Michigan, and Max's passport says he's French. But he's Rumanian, I think. He talks about this one town, Babadag, on the Black Sea, as the place where he was born, but whenever I try to look it up, I can't find it. I don't know where he's really from. Whatever kind of place where he could get the name 'Benû,' I guess. . . ."

He looked up sharply. "Your father's name is Max Benû?"

She shook her head.

"B-E-N-U with the circumflex?" He made a little steeple w/ his hand and the spatula.

"Yes."

"I know that name. . . ."

"He's a painter."

"Oh, dear God! Here, take this—"

Everything came off the stove in a great hurry.

"Oh, dear God—"

Everything went slapdash to the table.

"What a day!" he exclaimed.

He rummaged through a stack of journals by the rocking chair. "What a day, dear God—" He discarded circulars and magazines, sorting through them w/ great relish. "Look at this! This is it! Look at this, lad!" He thrust a magazine in front of her.

One half of one whole page was a timid reproduction of a painting of a blond girl in a Pierrot costume.

"That's me," she said.

"I *see* it is! Dear God! Read it."

The text was written in a foreign language.

"I can't."

"He's joined up!"

"I don't understand."

"He joined up with the Abraham Lincoln Brigade. He's in Spain! How could you not know?"

"I still don't."

"Your father went to Spain."

"My father?"

"Max!"

"My father is in Spain?"

"Yes! Fighting! Isn't that the limit?"

"*Spain?*"

She looked at him. How was she supposed to get to Spain? All she had was just about a hundred dollars. . . . She began to cry. Not little by little: all at once.

"Oh dear, oh dear," he murmured. "I guess I'm not as tidy as you thought. Oh, my. I'm sorry, Belle. Here, here. I shouldn't let myself get so transported by enthusiasm. Come, come. Of course this would upset you. Please. Don't cry. Here, have a biscuit."

"You don't understand. . . ."

"Well, no, I—"

"I can't go back, they'll murder me."

"I hardly think—"

"I'll kill myself."

"That's quite enough! What good does it do you to threaten that to me?"

"I'll kill myself," she promised.

She grew suddenly, preposterously, *calm*: it chilled him. Her eyes grew round, their color turned deep purple. Her face grew masklike, and she looked straight at him, into him. Her expression was almost trancelike, he felt—but, no, it was asking too much of him. It was asking his involvement, the way a work of art will ask, the way a painting asks. . . .

He held the portrait of the Pierrot-costumed little girl in the magazine in his hand and studied it: The loose blouson costume was checkered blue-and-yellow. The little face was whitened, and the cheeks had been rouged in. The little hands were folded, as if waiting to receive—the damson eyes stared out at all the world, beseeched the trusted artist, *"Pay attention to me; love me"*—*that* was Belle's expression, that was the quality she possessed: *lovelessness*, like a phosphorescence. He'd seen it in a few young girls before— one of them had been a Carmelite. Another one became an alcoholic. One was Isadora Duncan, and another married a nice young man and bore four sturdy children. . . . So, he reflected equitably, who can tell? Why should he wish something at all special, dispensational, for this young woman? What was at all special about her?

He placed the magazine back on the table. From that angle he could see the portrait in a different way—he could see it was a picture of a young girl who was posing for her *father*, not an artist, who had rendered it as if he'd seen a *subject*, not his daughter.

"Suppose you tell me," Jack began in even tones, "suppose you tell me everything, so I can help. . . ."

By the time they'd finished breakfast and he'd heard her story, he'd decided absolutely she should not go back. Something really terrified her there. Even if the things she said were untrue or exaggerated, she had real fear that something in her that she guarded, something *that she loved* about herself would perish there. But she must go somewhere, and he wasn't sure that Max would have her, even if he weren't in Spain. Max, it seemed to him, had no desire to renew his parenthood. He hadn't been in touch w/ Belle for two years, except for major holidays and her birthday. He seemed to feel toward Belle the same way that he felt about religion—she was there and she was beautiful and so, because he loved all beauty, he was obligated. . . .

The sun had come to the far corner of the kitchen by the rocking chair, and Jack moved her there, near his baskets of yarn, where the sunlight picked out random colors in the rug.

"Do you knit?"

She said she didn't

"Oh. I'd hoped you did. I'm way behind in this. . . ." He lifted one corner of his half-knitted scarf and looked at it w/ something like nostalgia. "Well, we'll set you up with a good book instead. Here's two, just out. I get them sent to me. . . ."

He handed her two books—one thin, the other one too thick. Her preference was the thin one.

"Virginia Woolf. A dear book, I would suspect. I haven't read it yet. About the dog called Flush who was Elizabeth Barrett Browning's. . . ."

Belle wrinkled her nose. She lifted the larger of the two books.

"*Anthony Adverse.*" He advised: "Probably the better of the two. . . ."

She hefted it in her hand. She liked the title. "Where are you going?"

"To telephone."

She watched him. "Willa?"

"First; yes."

"What are you going to say?"

"Something . . . professional." He made himself look priestly and remote. He smiled. "Trust me. . . ." She did. He knew she trusted much too easily. He knew she was likely to trust anyone who was kind to her. He knew that was the thing that put her in such awful danger. . . .

She started to read *Anthony Adverse,* but she couldn't concentrate. It was a long book—1,224 pages—so it took its own time and moved slowly. She found that she could read and think of other things at the same time. She could hear Father Jack's voice, faintly, from his study down the hall. She could tell from the sound of it that he had engaged her mother in a conversation, long distance, and suddenly out of nowhere Belle felt a dreadful weight on her, an invisible force pulling her down, from inside. Her hand shook and she felt condemnable, the way she would have felt if they had caught her stealing money. She had run away from home. She had run away from *that house*—and suddenly she wanted *in*. She wanted them to *let* her in, to let her know it was a place to come to, instead of a receding galaxy, a spiral valve locked at the center. She wanted back, wanted a second chance w/ Willa as she now seemed, from a distance, warm and unassuming. If only Willa could be warm and unassuming; if only she could be a different way a little, then Belle could be a little different, too. It seemed so simple. It seemed so bad a thing that she had done. Willa must be half-dead w/ anguish, awake nights, not eating. Willa must be full of pain. Willa must be feeling this most dreadful loss. They were a *mother and her daughter*. She wanted to know what Willa was feeling. She wanted to be told. Willa must be feeling something: she was surprised when he came in.

She had been crying softly to herself and now her nose was running but she held quite still, again, posing, so he wouldn't see her. His movements were slow. He poured himself a cup of coffee, then he rubbed his head. His back was more or less to her, in three-quarter profile. He was barefoot. There was a line along his instep where the color of his foot went from pale to dark. He was wearing his white pants, unbelted—she could tell that he had slipped them on w/ nothing underneath. He was naked from the hips up, and his waist was slimmer standing than it had been in repose. His jaw was strong and taut, but she could see the skin around his eye was puffy. His hand shook when he took a sip of coffee. He seemed unsteady, sick. He tilted slightly toward the sink, then turned the water on and splashed his face. There was a linen towel on an extension rod above the sink beside the window. He reached for it and began to dry his face. He started visibly when, at last, turning from the sink, he saw her. She must have shocked him, because he leaned against the stove top for support. He tilted, as a deck passenger would tilt, and squinted at her from a distance. It seemed hard for him to focus. He seemed staggered by the light—the sun behind her was unbroken, strong. He blinked repeatedly and squinted. She was backlighted, she knew—the sun behind her hair would make her seem afire. Without intending to, she moved slightly forward, and the chair began to rock. He dropped the towel and held his right hand up to shield his eyes.

"Kit?" she said.

He parted his lips, as if to speak; then squinted. Finally he pushed off from the stove top like a leaky dory pushing from shallow shore. He left the kitchen. He left her w/ the feeling that she wasn't real. Then, a little later, she got the feeling neither one of them was real.

"What did Willa say?" Belle asked.

Father Jack had just announced that he had made a plan for Belle to go to New York. They had to hurry—the "Zephyr" would be stopping in South Bend at two o'clock, and he'd agreed to put her on it.

"Did she say she missed me?"

She could tell he didn't like the question.

"Did she send a message to me? Did she say my *name?*"

He seemed pained by all this and a little tired. "No." He sighed.

Belle blinked a few times. She'd thought she'd been ready, but she wasn't ready. She'd held out, as always, for the unexpected, the improbable. . . .

"She didn't ask a thing about you. Ordinarily, I wouldn't be so cruel as to tell a person that," he admitted softly, "but I think it's something that you have to know. I think it's something you should recognize completely, in case—"

"In case I think I might go back?"

"Yes."

"Well, I already know all that, and I don't let myself have thoughts like that. . . ."

She felt the center of that spiral feeling, that reeling sense, tighten like a turned bolt in her. Something closed. It banged shut. Something shuttered in her, a high door bolted in a killing wind. She tossed her head.

Jack saw it as the tough little gesture orphaned children often make.

"So, who gets me now?"

"Well—Max."

"You told me Max had gone to Spain."

"He has a new wife."

His conversation kept arriving like pronouncements and he tried to draw it out. "Her name's Lucy. Lucy Ten Eyck—she's from an old Dutch family, so she said. She sounds quite young. I believe she's probably been brought up in some wealth. . . ."

Belle tossed her head, again. "Does she have kids?"

It was a necessary inquiry, the sort a child would need to ask, for territory. It touched him.

"No."

He tried again to soften what to him seemed hammer blows instead of words. "She sounded very sweet. She said she's fixed a room for you. She said she hoped the two of you would get along as friends. . . ."

Belle stared at him, unblinkingly.

He wondered where she found the strength to stare at him that way.

"I'm going up to say good-bye to Kit."

"Well, I—"

"Then we can go."

"Belle—"

"It's the same as if I'd been adopted. I'm not the first kid in the world who's going to think about her mother as if she's dead. Don't think so much about it. It's not half as bad as you imagine. . . ."

She walked w/ steady grace down the hall and up the stairs into the corner room, where Kit was writing, propped against the pillow, on the bed. She didn't knock. He turned his head toward her when she came in, assessed her, then turned away.

"You don't remember me," she prompted.

She sat down at the foot of the big double bed. He looked over at her languidly. "Sure. Catherine the Great. Right?"

"No: *Cleopatra*—"

Almost as she said it, she realized he'd been poking fun at her, and she had fallen for it. "What are you writing?"

"A letter to my wife."

She colored deeply, and he smiled.

"Father Jack says you're a writer, so I just thought—" She felt increasingly shamefaced and stupid.

"You just thought?"

"I'd ask."

"Um-hum."

She studied him a moment. She watched his eyes move over her, taking her all in. "*Do* you remember me?" she dared to ask.

He stared a moment at her breasts. "Well, actually, here's what happens: One consumes a lot of gin in a great hurry, see? Say, a pint or so every half hour for two hours. During this consumption, see, one remembers everything in sequence, evenings strung like rosaries, moments strung like beads. . . . Can you follow this? Then one is told one has been, well, *present* at the party, but the last thing one remembers is the last drink, then the morning. One last drink and then the morning: *Nothing* in between. Time sandwich.

Sometimes in a blackout I say and do most clever things. Things distinctly to my credit. Other times I'm not so fortunate. Sometimes I wake up the next morning and I think, 'Kit, old boy, you could have *died* last night, you could have Met Your Maker and you'd have *never known it*—' Frightening, don't you think? I mean, to think I could end up absent at my death. . . ." He watched her. "You don't drink, I take it."

"No."

"You're much too young. . . ."

"Well, yes, I guess."

"What *do* you do?"

"For what?"

"For fun."

"Nothing."

"*Nothing?*"

"I sneak around. I look at people. I think about what they do inside their houses, while they're sleeping. . . ."

Kit looked down at the nearly blank page he'd been writing, then he looked back up at her. The expression in his eyes had changed. "Actually the reason that I drink is boredom; and yes, I *do* remember. And—*that* awakens a brand-new desire for another drink: I don't usually make conversation quite so early in the morning."

"It's afternoon."

"Exactly. And I almost never make conversation, afternoon or otherwise, *in bed.*"

"We're not *in* bed. We're *on* it."

"And *never* with a prepubescent. . . ." He stood up. He walked over to the chest of drawers and tried to find a shirt among its contents that would fit him. "What do you think of my friend Jack? He's a right-fine fellow, isn't he?"

"He's fixed it so I'm going to New York. . . ."

"Well, he's a fixer, that's for sure."

"Yes. He fixed everything. I like him very much."

"The Frowning Priest . . ."

Belle stood up, too, and wandered toward the nightstand. It seemed their mutual intention to put as safe a distance between them as they could. "I just came up to say good-bye and thank you for last night." She blushed. "I mean, about the suitcase—"

He turned toward her. "Don't mention it."

He'd found a cotton work shirt several sizes too large, and he slipped into it. The collar was contrary and stayed turned up.

Belle picked up the book that lay on the nightstand. "Are you reading this?"

"I finished it this morning. Take it with you, why don't you?"

"*Death in the Afternoon* . . . Well, I don't know. What's it about? I get real tired with these books about young boys—"

Kit smiled. He took a few steps nearer. "It's about bullfighting."

"Oh, I won't like that. . . ."

She put the book down, but he urged it on her. "Read it for the writing, for the way it's told—"

She picked it up and flipped through the pages. There were pictures. She could feel his body next to her, even though they weren't touching.

"I don't think I'm going to like it. . . . I mean, what happens to the men on horses and that stuff."

"He'll make you."

"What?"

"The author. Hemingway. He'll make you like it."

"I don't think so. . . ."

"Yes, he will. He has enormous powers. He's a great writer. A brilliant writer."

They were standing very close.

"He'll make you *love* it."

"No . . ."

"You read enough and long enough, he'll make you love it, he's relentless—"

"He will not. . . ."

"He will. He'll make you love. He'll make you love despite yourself. The way all love should be."

She looked up at him. He seemed surprised at what he'd said. It seemed a natural gesture that she turned his collar down, not touching him. He seemed surprised to find they'd made a pact somehow, and that he, of all people, seemed to be keeping it.

Every week over the next fourteen months, a letter would arrive at Lucy Ten Eyck's flat in mid-Manhattan addressed to Belle from Father Jack. He never had dull news. He would report that while cleaning his kitchen cabinet he had discovered some oddity—a dead yellow jacket or a Vatican library card—and from that he would launch a flight of inquiry into the nature of Life w/ as much startled enthusiasm as a flock of grackles heading off into the wind from an unsheltered field. He wrote w/ a florid, impossible hand that knew no punctuation and hacked across the grain of standard paragraphing. He wrote first horizontally from left to right (although not always) and then gave the page a quarter turn and attacked it perpendicularly. It sometimes took a week for Belle to transcribe a single page. Once, he set about to teach her how to knit by mail w/ diagrams. He sent her recipes. He wrote her about books he'd read and the natural phenomena he'd seen, comparing the emergence of Luigi Pirandello's works in English since his Nobel Prize that spring to the way he (Jack) had seen thin ice chuck up on Indiana ponds like beaver huts in a false thaw. Always he would write to ask, "What are you *reading*?" In her turn, Belle composed grave, tepid little notes on formal paper. She didn't have a gift for letters, the gift of animated monologue—the questions posed would look so stiff and stupid: How are you? How's the weather out there? For her, writing letters was addressing something that you weren't too sure was really there, like praying; and she wasn't good at praying, either.

"Dear Father Reardon," she would write, "The weather here has been real cold, but not so cold as Indiana. Lucy bought me a new coat. I didn't really need one except Lucy doesn't buy things so much for warmth and wear as she does for fashion and last year's was too short, because I've grown. Lucy is swell. We're reading Hemingway (the one about the man whose ——— is shot off in the war). Sorry to hear about the President of Germany who died. Yes, I guess if I were a Country I would join the League of Nations. Lucy says it's like a private club. She joins a lot of clubs. Do you ever hear from Kit?"

What she didn't write was that she'd bobbed her hair. That, at Lucy's urging, she had given it a platinum rinse. That she wore outrageous clothes for the attention they would get her, and she never wore a stitch of underwear. She smoked cigarettes. She was sixteen and a half, and she had accomplished in the last year an effect on her personage less related to the transformation of a teenage chrysalis than to the sandblasting of a dun-colored monument. She was a new girl. Under the new skin, one forgot what the old girl had been. This one shone all crystal-flecked and glisteny as ice formed in a quickly freezing rain. The result would have given anyone who had known her pain, perhaps; perhaps not. She had a swagger and a smart way that was a big hit in New York, in Lucy's crowd. Surprisingly, for reasons that she didn't fully understand, the men that came around adored her and they loved to bring her clothes and see her dress, they loved to tell her where to place a brooch and how to wave her hair, but these men never tried to put their hands on her, they never touched her on her skin. The women friends of Lucy's who were always in the house seemed very caught up w/ themselves and w/ the others and were equally as distant from her as the men. Theodora, who often stayed on in the bedroom next to Lucy's, always wore men's clothes, and Belle thought she was smashing. She had tiny little feet, size five, and wore satin slippers w/ different-colored clip-on bows, and she worked in the theater w/ Le Gallienne and La Cornell. Belle thought Theo was as swell as Lucy, but in a different way; and she tried to copy both of them. Lucy had a nonstop disturbance in the air around her that one couldn't copy, though, like a hive, even when she was standing still. Theo, on the other hand, was cunning as a lizard. One, or two, quick words from Theo, like a lashing, could quell even the most stalwart. She was a bitter pen, Theo was, a poison quill, as someone once described her, and since her venom never touched on Belle, Belle thought her whole act was smashing. She thought the whole lot of them was smashing.

When she wrote Father Jack that Lucy entertained a lot of theater people, he wrote back about Pirandello which, to tell the truth, put his knowledge of the theater in a sort of provincial light, owing to the fact that Belle was pretty sure that anyone named Luigi wasn't part of Lucy's group. But when Belle mentioned in a note that Theodora had done some sets for one of Le Gallienne's little plays, Father Jack wrote back w/ enthusiasm about the work Le Gallienne was doing down at the Civic Repertory, and Belle was much impressed. "I remember," Jack wrote, "an evening at the Civic in what had been the old Théâtre Français on West 14th Street, and being so moved by this little stretch of a girl (that's all she was!) that when I walked out of the theater in a stupor I traveled east on 14th to the desolate sadness of the el on Sixth and (to avoid its black and weighty shadow) west again on 15th until, within a short half block,

I came across the colorful awning of an Italian restaurant called Casa Johnny and so went in there to sit awhile and, of course, to eat. Next to me, at an adjoining table (the meal, by the way, was a thick soup, pasta, *finocchio al forno*, some squid, some veal, a salad, and a sweet) was a single lady with whom I had a lively conversation. I remember after coffee I inquired if she'd care to take a walk. 'A *walk?*' she said. 'A walk,' I answered, referring to the kind of evening stroll we have in Indiana. 'To *where?*' she asked. 'Why, anywhere,' I said. 'What do you mean?' she asked. 'You mean walk somewhere for a drink? Walk to another restaurant?' Well, Belle, I was taken aback by this and so replied, 'I thought we might take a walk just for the pleasure of it.' I'll not forget the manner in which she looked at me. 'I walk *to work,*' she said. 'I walk *to lunch.* I walk *to the subway.* I walk *back home.* Are *you* crazy?' Then she caught herself—she realized I wasn't flirting with her, and at the same time I realized something about her daily life as having set points on a geometric grid. We both laughed—and did we walk! Did we ever! We walked down Seventh Avenue past poor Tom Paine's death house. Then we walked through the Italian neighborhoods where the men on cane-bottomed chairs sit outside the social clubs drinking espresso. We walked west to the River and then south along the docks. It was a clear late summer night with just a sliver of a moon. I remember all those boats, those countless cargos—they say four thousand boats come through New York Harbor on a given day. I remember standing there with that small and lovely dark-haired woman thinking to myself, Here passes wine from Lombardy, olive oil from Attica, figs and dates from Marrakech, cotton and tobacco from Savannah, Vermont wool—the children, refugees, the going *to*, and coming *from*, the living lyric of man's eternal need to make a destination. . . . I think if ever in my life I came near to what's so often called 'being in love,' it was on that night. My fondness for New York is since bound up in that fond memory and living there, you must know the quality of real excitement that I mean. Do write me, won't you, and give me the 'true gen' on all the small surprising miracles you've found on streets in all those lovely neighborhoods. . . ."

The truth was, Belle saw little of New York. She saw the doorman, whose name was Henry Tompkins. She saw Park Avenue, and Lex, and Madison and Fifth. She'd never been to Harlem, and she'd never gone to Greenwich Village. She didn't ride the subway, or the el. Her life, outside of private school, from which she was more or less permanently truant, revolved around Lucy's social life at the apartment, shopping, dressing up and going out w/ Lucy and her friends, and sleeping. Everywhere she went, though, people said she looked a lot like Harlow. She had a way about her, that same unconscious way Jean Harlow had of seeming to suggest she'd be a great deal more comfortable talking to you while the two of you were making love—and being that *way* seemed to take up most of her time. She was quite a draw at Lucy's parties, quite a freak among the male and female homosexuals. She thought she understood their innuendos, she thought she understood what was going on. It didn't really matter to her if one man kissed another or if Lucy and Theo danced real close . . . what disturbed her was that everybody left her so alone. They were always talking, they were always having fun, and Belle was happy, sure; but nothing, no thing, no one ever really touched her, made her feel outside herself, or part of any other. She looked like Harlow, and she tried to act like other women, while she coasted.

Then, the first week of December, 1934, Lucy gave a party to commemorate the one-year anniversary of the repeal of Prohibition. The anniversary fell on a Wednesday, but the fact that some folks might be working midweek didn't for a minute impede Lucy's plans— gin, the real stuff, was a priority; champagne, of course, and caviar were both pedestrian, so she opted for a gin party w/ crabs and Creole cooking and a jazz quintet from the Cotton Club for entertainment. Anybody who was anyone could come, and after the first hour (from eight o'clock to nine), nobody would care much who you were, anyway. Open House at Lucy's seemed to be the invitation, and the invitation was by word of mouth. To say it was a zoo would be an insult to God's lower animals: it ended up w/ people standing in the bathrooms, drinking; standing in the halls, in open closets. People opening the kitchen cabinets to find something to eat because they couldn't reach the tables in the other rooms. People throwing crabs and ice cubes out the window onto traffic on Park Avenue. People starting to undress, or dressing up. One man Belle knew, a really ugly man w/ large ears and acne scars, took a satin gown and feather boa from Lucy's dressing closet and put it on over his sleeveless undershirt. People started petting in twos and threes, like puppies,

and Belle had too much to drink. She was drinking whatever people
handed her, and now she felt a little sick. A little toast, she thought,
would be a good idea. Something dry and bland. The smells of
things began to sicken her. Cologne. Someone was wearing too
much cologne. She thought she'd better go sit down. If she could
loosen a few buttons or the buckles of her stocking garters. Someone
put a crab leg in his mouth. Someone put a cigarette butt in a drink.
She was seeing two. Two things. One there, one over there, and
when she blinked they came together and had halos, then they came
apart. It was really hot. A button undone would really help, or a
place to go lie down. She ran into someone, and he caught her.
"Sorry," she murmured.

"A little sickie, are we?"

"No. Fine. What makes you say that?"

"Well you're falling *down*, lover. . . ."

He had four eyebrows and a halo of pink light.

"That's René," he said, and pointed.

Belle moved her head in the direction that he pointed. Her head
was heavy, like a hard rubber toy one plays w/ at the end of an
elastic band. It bounced back. A boy was swaying back and forth
before a group of men. "He came with me," the man said. It made
no sense. Someone else came up to her and said, "Hi, sweetheart."
She turned her head, it bobbed, and she said, "Hiya." She could
see him smiling. He had two halves of a face that didn't meet in
the middle. "You should tweeze your eyebrows a bit more, you
know that, honey?" he told her. "You could have Jean dead to rights
if you'd thin your eyebrows out a bit." "Okay," Belle said. The man
on the other side of her said, "Do you like him?" "Who?" Belle
said. She leaned a little on one leg. "René," the man said, pointing
once more to the swaying boy. Belle looked at him. She tried to
concentrate. "Sure," she said distractedly. The boy had drawn a
crowd. The boy was dancing. Now the boy was taking off his clothes.
"He came with me," the man said. His voice sounded a little cold.
Belle was staring at the boy's nipples. There were four or six of them.
"You like him?" the man next to her asked. People were hooting
and they began to clap. "Sure," Belle said. The boy had started to
wriggle from his belt, and then he pulled it back and forth between
his legs and Belle noticed that her breasts were getting hard. He was
just about her age, or older. "Would you like to suck his cock?" the

man w/ the cold voice asked her. "What?" Belle said. "His cock.
René's gorgeous cock. Would you like to suck it?" Belle blinked.
The room came together. Then it drifted apart. The man w/ the
cold voice took her by the wrist and led her into the center of the
crowd and said, "Kiss her, René." The crowd got quiet. Belle could
see some drops of moisture on René's chest. Belle could see fine
golden hairs down the middle of his torso. "Kiss her, you little shit,"
the man w/ the cold voice said. He was hurting Belle's wrist. René
stared at Belle, and she could see his lip curl. The man hurled them
together. "Kiss her!" he shouted. Belle felt the boy's body tense as
he pulled back from her. "Kiss me," she whispered. She put her
hands on his chest and looked up at him. "Please," she said softly.
He pulled away, and she gripped him. His eyes showed her his
disgust. She held him. She pressed her body against him. She held
his head in her hands. She offered her mouth to him, and he turned
away, but she held him. "Kiss me," she breathed, brushing her lips
over his face. She caressed him, fondled his head w/ her arms, kissed
his eyes, his temples, his forehead, light loving kisses, baby kisses
across the bridge of his nose, on his eyes, rapidly, eagerly, lovingly.
He smelled so good. She wanted to lick him. His skin felt so good.
She held on to him. People had started to laugh. She held him,
forcing his mouth onto hers. Her whole body shook as she clung
to him. He was a stone. It was like kissing a stone; she fell away.
People were clapping and laughing. People were laughing at her;
they were having their joke. People were milling around, laughing
at her while the boy called René lifted his forearm and wiped off
his mouth. Over his shoulder, Belle saw the face of a man in the
crowd. A calm face, staring at her in his anger.

Someone said, "Darling, where did you find it?"

"It's so authentic! Look, Theo!" someone said. "This bitch has
come dressed as a priest!"

Belle turned toward the voices.

"Honey, wherever . . . wherever did you find it? Oh, you have
the little pins and everything. What does this one say? 'Knights of
Saint John of Jerusalem'. Oh, they're great. What does this little
one say?"

"Hi, Jack," Belle said.

"Hello, lad," he said sadly.

"Oh, you two *know* each other! Isn't his get-up a terror? Belle,

honey, really, you look undone. Fix your strap. So tell me, where
did you get it? Priests don't frequent pawnshops, that much I
know. . . ."

"How've you been?" Belle said.

"Well, lad. Very well. Very fit," he replied.

"So I guess you're in town, huh?" she said.

"It seems so. . . ."

"Excuse me. Excuse me. Is this section *closed?*"

"He's a priest, Joseph," Belle tried to explain.

"Sure, and *I'm* Dolores Del Rio. . . ."

"He *is* a priest, Joseph."

"Oh, go *play* somewhere, Belle."

"I *am* a priest."

"Go on—"

"I am."

"You are, really?"

"Yes."

"Say something."

"*O quam tristis et afflicta / Fuit illa benedicta / Mater Unige-
niti,*" Jack recited, "*Quas moerebat et dolebat / Pia Mater, dum
videbat / Nati poenas incliti.*"

As he finished, Kit came up.

"Cristofer!" someone shouted.

"Was that dirty?" Joseph asked.

"Holy, rather," Jack replied.

"Cristofer, *darling!*" someone said, again. It was Lucy.

"I thought I heard the word 'penis' in there, in that last part,"
Joseph persisted.

"Look he really *is* a priest, so bug off." Belle said.

She didn't like the way that Kit was staring at her, w/ so much
anger. It *had* been him she'd seen before, across the room. She
thought she'd drunk too much, that she'd imagined it.

"Kit, darling!" Lucy said. Lucy was there. She draped herself
around him. "Everyone," she said. "Everyone, this is my darling
Cristofer!" She bowed and swept and dipped and motioned w/ her
arm all at a single time, presenting him. She was, as usual, quite
flushed w/ a well-being from her cocaine; and she'd had a lot of gin
to furl the powder's ragged edges. "This most *edible* of men," she
said, "this *stunning* man and I and, let me see, *five* other women

shared a bed one dawn—where was it, darling?—oh yes, in *Peoria!* That's Illinois," she added. A crowd of people laughed. Belle looked at Kit. She felt herself get sober. "Of course," Lucy went on, "Kit came only *three times* for the *six* of us and so I had to do . . . some . . . *missionary* work. . . ." Belle felt a firm hand on her shoulder. She turned a quarter turn to catch a whisper in her ear: "You'll want to get a good warm coat, Belle, lad." Jack urged.

"What for?"

"The cold."

She squinted, her face close to his.

"I'd think you'd want to do it quickly, lad," he urged. "And change into some clothes."

"Did you hear what Lucy said?"

"Go on, now, Belle."

"They slept together—"

"I would think some woolens and a sweater and a coat and a warm woolen hat would do. . . ."

"Hey!" she said.

He had started to guide her toward her room.

"I think about two minutes ought to do it," he said firmly. "Before things take a *very* nasty turn. . . ."

She heard a glass crash, breaking, on a wall behind her.

"Kit and I will meet you in the foyer. By the elevator," Jack said.

"Hey, what are you doing here anyway?" Belle asked, suddenly a little sober.

"I always come to town in winter when I can to see the opera. And I knew Kit was going to be here. And there's the Poultry Show over at the Port Authority. And you?" he said.

"No, I mean *here* here. In my apartment."

"Kit heard there was a party."

"He wanted to see *her*, didn't he?"

"No, actually, he was hoping he'd see you. . . ."

"They *slept* together."

Jack looked at her the way somebody looks who knows a lot of real bad news.

"Belle, Kit has slept with everyone."

"He hasn't slept with *me*," she said. "He hasn't slept with *you* . . ."

"He's slept with both of us, Belle lad."

"Not *me* . . ." she repeated.

She was drunk.

Fifteen minutes later she stepped into the hall, and there was Henry Tompkins the doorman and some policemen and the neighbors who lived two flights down, and there was Father Jack, and there was Kit. She and Kit and Jack got in the elevator. She looked at the narrow rubber matting where the door pushed in, and she thought she felt like that, and out loud she said, "Lucy is a whore. I don't know why my father married her. She's a bitch. I'm going to write and tell him. I'm going to run away from here and never see her face again in my entire life—"

About then, as the door came shut and as the little metal cab that they were in gave a sudden lurch, Belle turned, smiling, toward Kit and Jack, and Kit, in all his anger, threw his arm out, like an awful bird, threw his arm across her throat and hurtled her against the far wall of the cab, and the whole thing rocked on its thin tether.

Jack said, "Kit!"

Kit was on her, and his eyes were full of anger: "What did you think you were doing to yourself?" he demanded. He held her chin and pushed her face against the wall.

"Kit, Holy Jesus, man!" Jack said, tugging at him.

"You look like a little prostitute!" Kit said.

Jack pulled Kit away from her.

"Bastard!" Belle kicked. She caught Jack w/ her shoe. "What the fuck do you care what I do?!" she shouted.

Between them, Jack urged, "Kit!" and, "Belle!" The elevator rocked.

"What is the matter with you, man?" Jack demanded. "Have you gone insane? He's probably been drinking since the morning," Jack attempted to explain to Belle.

"I know plenty of people who can drink since morning, and they don't punch women," Belle said.

"You dyed your hair," Kit said. "She dyed her hair, Jack," he complained.

"For God's sake, man . . ."

"She made herself into a tramp," he said. He looked at Jack w/ round grieving eyes as if he were a small boy wrestling w/ his first experience of pain. "Why do they all turn into tramps?"

"Oh God, Kit, but you're boiled," Jack said. He turned to Belle. "He cries on you when he gets boiled. He gets all potty for the Virgin Mary. . . ."

Belle began to weep.

"Oh, Jesus," Jack sighed. "The two of them. Two bloats. As if just one weren't good enough. . . ."

He led them out into the chill sharp air. Kit turned his collar up against the cold and stayed close to the building. Belle leaned against a parking sign. "Well," Jack said cheerfully, swinging his arms: "I say we go once around the block for good measure, then hop a cab downtown to Mott Street for some bird's-nest soup. How does that sound? What do you say to that, eh, Kit?"

"I say, 'Stuff it, Jack.' "

"Good, then," Jack said. "Let's go."

He led off down the block, swinging his arms and whistling. Along the way he greeted passers-by and entertained no one in particular w/ a running commentary on the local architecture. Kit and Belle straggled silently along. At the corner of Lexington Avenue, he hailed a cab and, w/ Kit and Belle installed in the back seat, he sat w/ the driver. Every once in a while, on the pretext of pointing out sights, he would steal a look at them, Belle in her corner of the seat, Kit in his. Jack learned the driver's wife's name was Berthe, and they were newly emigrated to Manhattan from Mannheim. His wife taught at the "University in Exile," the New School on West Twelfth Street—Abnormal Psychology. Heinz-Gerhardt, the taxi driver, was a Herr Professor himself, of Musicology. Jack was hearing *Faust* at the Metropolitan the next night, and so he asked Heinz-Gerhardt for his opinion. Heinz-Gerhardt said, "Gounod is what you say in German *Ein Blätterkuchen*, you understand?"

"Where are we going?" Kit asked.

"Uh, a *pâte à choux*, they say in French," Jack said.

"Yes. How do you say this in the English?"

"Puff pastry," Jack said.

"Where are we going?" Kit repeated.

"Puff, oh, yes. Ha ha. *Puff.* Who is singing Marguerite tomorrow night? It will depend on that. . . ."

"Uh, Ponselle. Downtown, Kit. Yat Bun Sing's, I thought. On Mott Street, isn't it?"

"Let's go to Hang Low's. Yat Sing's won't serve liquor."

"Ah . . . no, they won't. But the soup is good."

"Let's make it Hang Low's."

"Ah . . . no. I think we'll stick with Yat Bun Sing's. An unfortunate choice, I agree, so far as liquor is concerned, but the bird's nest will make up for it, I'm sure."

"You think too much about food."

"Possibly . . ."

"You think too damn much about food, Jack. Economic Depression fucking everywhere, and you get creamy over bird's-nest soup. We'll have to stop. Tell the Kraut to stop at the next liquor store. . . ."

"Tell the Kraut yourself."

"*Halten Sie . . .* uh . . . He's not going to listen to me, Jack."

"I wonder why?"

"I want to go to Café Latino. Let's go there. Take us to Café Latino. Spare us no expense. On Barrow Street."

"You forgot to call him Kraut, Kit."

"*Kraut.*"

"I think we'll find some peace and quiet at Yat Sing's," Jack mused. "Some jasmine tea. Some steaming bowls of soup. Help us rest awhile to work out some solution for the lad. . . ."

"She'd like Café Latino. We could rhumba there. A little rhumba. *Sopa de camarones por el Padre, eh?* Belle would like that. . . ."

"Belle's asleep, Kit."

"Café Latino . . ."

"*Ich habe überall Schmerzen,*" Jack confided to Heinz-Gerhardt.

"*Es ist spät,*" Heinz-Gerhardt said. "*Sie sund über müdet.*"

"*Nein. Ich kann nicht essen . . . schlafen. Ich habe Angstträume.* Drive around awhile. Tell me all about Johann Sebastian Bach. . . ."

Three hours later Jack could tell that Kit had gained a foothold on sobriety because his eyes took on a certain warmth and he asked good-naturedly, "What's this stuff I'm eating anyway?"

"Dim sum."

"It's great. It's like boiled sacs, you know? Balls. How's yours, kiddo?"

"I don't have any, remember?" Belle smiled. "I could have had. But I said, 'Naww, I'd rather be *intelligent*, instead. . . .' "

"She's very funny," Jack pointed out.

"I run with a fast crowd," she bragged.

"Too fast, perhaps, lad?"

"That a question?"

"No. A provocation, I would hope."

"You know, you make a big deal about words too much. Defining. Why don't you just say what's on your mind?"

"I think I will, thank you." He smiled. The broth was excellent. The Chinese did something w/ their soups, he'd just been saying, that no Western cooking paralleled—they floated crisp raw vegetables in a clear rich broth that added *tooth* to the experience. . . .

"I think," he cautioned, "I think you've recently come under an extreme influence. It's not a healthy one. I feel you ought to find some other home."

"I *ought?*" she mocked.

"I didn't mean to make it sound that way." Jack quickly apologized.

"*You* put me there," she reminded him.

"Oh, well. That encapsulates my guilt for me, doesn't it?"

He turned to Kit.

"Look, what difference does it make?" Kit said aimlessly. He hated drinking jasmine tea. He once wrote that it tasted like a dry desire: "She's already *made*. She's seventeen, almost. She was made when she ran into us. What the hell's this rancid preoccupation you've got with changing her?"

"Rancid?" Jack repeated doubtfully.

"Have you got the hots for her or what?"

"Certainly *not!*"

"Then what's the deal? You playing Let's Pretend? You pretending that celibacy can breed you a quick daughter?"

Jack knit his brows. "I care for her," he said.

"Just you alone? Maybe I care for her, too. . . ."

Belle felt her face grow hot.

"That's different," Jack said. He looked away from Kit and glowered at a spot of liquid on the table.

"Maybe you should just let nature take its course," Kit said casually.

Belle held her breath.

"Is that what I should do, Kit?" Jack asked evenly.

"Yeah."

"Whose nature—yours or mine?"

"You've always said they are the same."

"But *are* they?"

"Sure. Why not? All men are brothers, right? Under the *cloth* . . ."

Jack looked at him a long time. It seemed to Belle his look, his silence, his expression were sorrowing over many things. She was aware for the first time of Jack's age, of how old he suddenly seemed. When he looked at her, he appeared to be very tired.

"Back to Lucy's, then?" he asked.

"Where else?" she answered. "I've been everywhere else. . . ."

"Your father?" he offered.

"That's a joke," Belle scoffed. "Max could be dead for all that I know. . . ."

"I'll take her," Kit volunteered.

"You'll take her *where*, Kit?" Jack seemed peeved.

"Back uptown."

"No trouble, thank you, don't disarrange yourself. I'm going up, myself. You're at the Breevort downtown anyway—don't trouble yourself. . . ."

He called for the check and allowed Kit to pay.

He seemed distant and troubled.

"Where would you have *gone*, Belle?" he finally asked. "What would you have done, do you think, if I . . . if I hadn't interfered?"

"I don't know," Belle answered.

"Have you ever wondered?"

"Not really."

"You don't find it seductive to wonder?"

"Not about things you can't change."

"I see. But, consider: *once*, at one time, at one given instant, what is now the past was open to change. . . ."

"Let's get off it, okay?" Kit said.

"What would have happened to you?" Jack asked mildly.

Belle didn't know what to say. She felt Kit shift on the bench seat next to her.

"Sometimes you just do something and you don't bother much about how it will come out," she tried to explain. "You just . . . trust." She shrugged

She felt Kit's leg against hers.

"But what I'm asking is, was my involvement the reason *for* the blind trust, or was my involvement just an interference in some grander scheme? Did I *help* you?"

"Oh, yes, definitely," she answered, in a kind of rush.

"And if I hadn't put you on a train to New York?"

The question hung in the air.

"She'd be dead, or knocked up, or in Des Moines," Kit answered. "You seem tired, Padre. Or your cosmology does. *Vaminos* . . ."

"*Vayamos*," Jack consented. "To God, or to the devil, Kit?"

"To *bed*," Kit said.

They walked a few blocks south, searching for a cab, three abreast down Mott Street.

"Are you tired, Belle?" Jack asked her.

"No. Not so much."

"Do you think Lucy will be angry when I bring you home so late?"

"She probably won't know the difference." She caught Kit's eye a moment, before he looked away. "Besides, I've stayed out late before," she said.

"It's *very* late," Jack said. "It's after two in the morning."

"Oh, I've been out this late before," Belle bragged. "I go to all-night movies with the 'boys.' "

Kit suggested they head up to Broadway and Canal Street, where, if they didn't catch a cab, at least they could take the Blue Line uptown.

"You have some friends, then, do you, Belle?" Jack asked her as they walked.

"Oh, yeah."

"Boy friends, are they?"

"What?"

"Boys, are they?"

"Oh, you mean the 'boys' . . . No. You know. They're 'boys.' You know. They take me around. . . ."

"What do you mean, around?"

"She means they're faggots, Jack-o." Kit smiled. "I think the Blue Line is definitely our best bet for the night," he added, surveying the empty street when they reached Broadway.

"You're coming with us, Kit?"

"Yeah, I think I'll travel with you uptown to Eighth Street, if you don't mind."

"Why should I mind?"

"A lot of reasons."

"Name me one."

They had stopped beneath the blue lamp at the IRT.

"You're more pissed with me tonight than you've ever been."

"Am I?" Jack asked evenly.

The blue lamp made the puffs of warm air when they spoke look eerie.

A man w/ cotton rags around his feet and a tattered balaclava on his head was slumped over on the top step. Belle felt like telling him that he'd be warmer farther down.

"Tell me something, Kit," Jack said, "is it likely I'll be even angrier with you before the night is over?"

Kit nodded. Jack looked him over. "I thought so," he said.

He gave Belle and Kit a nickel each, and then he went before them down the steps.

The air inside the tunnel was thick w/ condensation and smelled of burned fuel and urine. Men huddled in groups against the walls, silent men, w/ a week or two's growth of beard, in dark coats stained w/ grime. It was warm in the tunnel, and so long as they were peaceful no one came to move them out at night.

Jack stood a little apart on the wooden platform and waited. At one point he took Belle's hand and squeezed it, and she smiled at him.

"I've never ridden on a subway," she confessed.

"A little bumpy," he told her.

She noticed that his eyes were tearing.

Soon there was a rumbling noise from down the tracks on Belle's left. Kit came and stood very near her. She smiled up at him. Jack put his arm on Kit's. Belle thought she heard him say, "When will I see you again?" but w/ all the noise she wasn't sure. Jack was holding onto Kit's arm. Kit smiled and looked over Jack's shoulder at the approaching train. "Tomorrow," he said. "It *is* tomorrow, Kit," Belle heard Jack tell him. The train arrived and the doors slid open and a motorman called, "Canal! White Plains Road Express! Lafayette, Fourth Avenue, Lexington Uptown, Mott Haven, Morrisania, Crotona Park and Bronx Park East!"

Jack had shouldered past the motorman and disappeared into the coach. Belle stepped forward, and Kit touched her arm. She turned to him. The motorman clanged a bell and pulled a cable switch above him. Belle was afraid the doors were going to close. "Kit, hey," she said, and took a little step toward the train. "Belle," he said, "Belle." She stepped closer to him, and he placed his hands very lightly on her shoulders. The train doors closed; she heard the train pull out. They walked along the platform, up the stairs into the sharp and silent air. Outside, in the custody of darkness, he finally kissed her.

Kit wrote his book *Hot Tickets* in three months during the winter of 1935. He wrote it w/ great speed and w/ an intensity Belle wouldn't see in him again for years. He'd wake late, drink some coffee and, w/out shaving, sit down at a makeshift table in front of an old Royal. Hours later Belle would know he'd finished for the day when the typewriter was silent. Then he'd come to her, wherever she was sitting, and undress her. He'd make love to her, his face still unshaven, and fall asleep for ten or fifteen minutes. He'd wake, bathe, shave, and Belle would fix him something to eat. Then he would work some more, often through the night. More often, though, he'd finish around midnight, and he and Belle would take a walk. They'd find some deserted place, and Kit would want to make love to her again, outside. The risk of being seen or being found seemed to excite him, and Belle did whatever seemed to make him happy.

They were living in a rented clapboard house that stood on stilts on a spit of land looking out across Pamlico Sound toward the town of Sealevel, North Carolina. Sealevel had a population of about three hundred, and the town nearest them, Yaupon, was about one-fifth that size. It was an island town—not a town so much as a place that arose from necessity: there was a general store, a cemetery, seven houses and a hall. The hall was both a church and a veterinary's office, and in very bad times, it was a boathouse. Yaupon was named for the holly tree that grew in the region. It was a Catawba Indian name, meaning "bush." "Catawba" itself was the Choctaw Indian word for "people apart," and that's what they were. Everyone living on the Outer Banks seemed strange and "apart." Kit said it was an island mentality, a psychological state of being surrounded on all sides by water and fierce winds. Even around Chicago, Belle had never known such winds. The men and women living on the Banks—the Bankers—were more or less preoccupied w/ wind.

Kit had a way w/ all the Bankers that made it seem he was one of them, but Belle felt very shy. She felt guilty, too, and embarrassed because she knew the only reason they had come here in the first place was to hide and sleep together—no really respectable place would ever rent Kit a room once they got a look at Belle, at how young she was. For Kit to be w/ her was still against the law in most states, especially down South. One night when they'd first started out, the owner of a motor court in Elkton, Maryland, came pounding on the door at 3:00 A.M. and Kit had almost killed him, he was so mad. He knocked the poor man out, and Belle had had to plead w/ him to get dressed quickly and get out of there before the people in the cabin next to theirs called the local cops. She tried dressing up and looking older, but traveling long hours in a car in silk stockings proved to be impractical, and Kit had thrown away her make-up. Without make-up, she looked young. To get around the problem, at least temporarily, Kit bought her a wedding ring at Talheimer's department store on Broad Street in Richmond, Virginia. All that day and the next, Belle could not stop looking at it.

She was in love w/ Kit the way an infant loves: she depended on him to fill her life. Stretches of time she had to spend alone passed slowly. She wasn't used to waking late, so she woke hours ahead of him and lay very still and watched him, watched the shadows on the wall, the way the light changed. It was very quiet where they were, the only sounds being sea and sea birds. She was conscious that she didn't know the names of things around her—she didn't know the names of the wild flowers that grew outside the window, and she didn't know the names of the different kinds of birds she heard. Kit had brought a lot of books along for her to read, and though she spent a lot of time w/ them, at heart she was afraid she was too simple or too stupid, because she found herself longing for a glossy magazine. Kit encouraged her to go to town, such as it was; and of course she had to, now and then, for their supplies, but she didn't like it. The sand was loose and deep on both sides of the road and the winds were such that sometimes the narrow road was blown away, leaving an expanse that looked just like a desert valley. She was afraid of getting stuck, she told him; and he laughed.

"You?" he teased her. "You—afraid of *anything*?" Sometimes she wanted to ask him what he was doing w/ her, anyway, because she felt so low. Every now and then he'd give her a small clue by saying something nice, but most of the time she was painfully aware that she didn't know how to cook or how to buy drygoods or how to sew or how to talk about religion, or politics or books; and besides, he'd never said he loved her.

The days she had to make the trips to town were awful, because she felt exposed and came home angry, thinking if only Kit would say he loved her, then she'd have some armor for the way people stared at her. Grocery buying was the worst. She knew old Mr. Harris Beebe who owned the store must be laughing at her behind her back ever since he'd asked her how much flour she wanted and she'd answered, "Some." "Five pounds? Seven?" he asked, and since that sounded sort of small she'd said, "Oh, I reckon I could do with twenty." She had no idea how many potatoes made up a pound or what kind of sugar was called "10 X." Milk went bad on her, and lard burned in the pan. She could make a decent cup of coffee, thank God for that, and that would start Kit on his day, but then she'd have to face planning a day's meal, and she'd grow anxious. Fish were plentiful—mullet, whiting, tarpon, sea bass, blues—but they required cleaning, and how was she supposed to know you had to cut their bellies open and take the insides out? She cooked a whole bluefish one night, and it came out just right, until they cut it open.

"Holy shit, you didn't clean it, holy Christ!" Kit laughed. He poked his knife into the green mess she was responsible for, and she began to cry. "What the fuck is this?" Kit asked, looking at her.

"I can't cook. . . ."

"So what? Anyone can cook."

"Not me."

"Who cares?"

"I want to *cook* for you," she sobbed.

"Why? What's the big deal? We can hire someone."

"I want to, 'cause I *want* to—"

"Well, that's sound reasoning, Sapphire. . . ."

"Because I love you."

"Well, I love you, too, but that doesn't make me want to go out and clean a fucking fish for you or hang the rugs out on the goddam line and beat the shit out of them or whatever half-assed piss-brained domestic bullshit you think you're accomplishing—*fucking* is what counts, my dear beloved. Fucking. And you're an Ace at that. The best."

"I guess you've fucked enough so you should know," she accused him.

"I guess I have." He smiled.

He stood up and walked outside the cabin, leaving Belle sitting at the table w/ the fish. He was gone a long time, and when he came back, he entered through the porch door at the front and she could hear him in the bedroom. After a while, he called to her.

"What do you want?" she answered.

"Come here."

"No," she said, but she got up anyway and wandered to the bedroom door. He was standing in the corner, by the bed. He'd lighted a candle in a glass jar, and a golden light wavered on the bed.

"Lie down," he requested.

"I don't want to."

"I'll rub your back," he offered. He stood very still as she approached the bed. "Turn it back," he suggested.

"I don't want to, Kit," she repeated.

He turned back a corner of the faded quilt, and as he did so she could see he'd filled the bed w/ blossoms of the wild flowers that grew outside. Some of them were brown-edged and bruised by winter, but most of them, especially the blue and yellow asters and the oxeye daisies, seemed fresh and innocent and other-worldly in the dusky room. "Come on," he said. His eyes were aqueous and sad, like water reflected in a dying light. "Buck up," he said. "Let's have a smile."

Later, as they lay together, he said, "It's a long life, kid," and she took that as an expression of celebration instead of hearing in his words any meaning of fatality. He never did say that he loved her in the way that she wanted him to. He never said that he loved anything. Instead, he'd make a gesture, or create a grand effect. Sometimes he would buy her an expensive gift she neither wanted nor expected nor could use. Belle came to accept these expressions as his way of showing love. Should anyone have suggested that they were hollow, even sad, she would not have understood. She saw him as a man in possession of emotions charged to a heroic dimension, too big for an ordinary life. If anyone had asked her to define an "ordinary" life, she wouldn't have known how to. She had not discovered the enjoyments of an examined life yet, nor the fact that one must stand still sometimes, in order to examine it. But when there's nothing else to do—as there was not, that winter on the island—the human eye will focus on small things and notice subtle changes: while Kit wrote his book, Belle began to notice shades of difference in the Carolina winds.

She began to notice birds and where they nested. Instead of sitting in the house, trying to read, she started taking walks. Short walks, at first, across the mud flats at low tide; then longer walks along the ocean shore when she learned that it wasn't likely Kit would stop his work midday and miss her. At first she gathered seashells, then sea oats and lavender and bouquets of dusty miller that she set in the broken cream pitcher on the window sill in the kitchen. She found a basket in the crawl space underneath the porch and started taking it w/ her. She collected round sea stones and laid them in a pattern on the porch. She liked their smoothness.

For a long time, until the end of February, she never saw another person on her walks. The coast was wide and wind-swept and deserted. Occasionally, she'd see some pitted foot tracks in the sand or spot a hooded figure w/ a rake working in the shallows far off in the distance; but her chief company was birds. She longed to learn their names. She knew the quick-stepping nervous birds that rushed the water line were sandpipers and plovers, because Kit had told her, but she didn't know which ones were which. There was a terrible-looking bird that swam in the brackish water on the flats w/ its whole body under water and its long coiling head and neck exposed, and Belle called it the snakebird to herself. There was a small, hawklike bird that had a cry that sounded "killy-killy-killy." There were a few large birds, about two feet high, w/ long, curved beaks that seemed to plow the water. There were vultures. There was no mistaking what *they* were. She hated them. Wherever they were circling, she knew that there was death; and when they came to circle over her, she ran.

She was walking on the high dunes along the shore one day in spring when she spotted one, high above her. Suddenly it dove, sweeping down w/ its awful wings splayed out until she saw each feather; and in a panic, Belle darted back across the dune. The little black-and-white birds who were stopping there must have been alerted to the vulture, too, for suddenly they swarmed into the air, calling "tee-ARR, tee-ARR!" She didn't realize they were terns and that she'd trespassed on their breeding ground until one after another hovered around her and attacked her. They aimed for her hair, diving in and striking at her w/ their beaks. The vulture, sensing a diversion, struck. There was a great confusion of sand and white feathers and noise until Belle very clearly heard the words, "Run toward the water!" As she did, a few terns followed her, but most swarmed after the vulture, and soon she found she had escaped beyond their range.

A tiny woman in all-weather clothes came toward her, dragging a large basket and a rake.

"Are you badly hurt?" she asked.

"I don't think so," Belle said.

"You got to stay away from terns," the woman told her, " 'less you want your brains pecked out."

"It was the vulture I was scared of," Belle confessed.

"Oh, they're good for nothing," she was told. "Work from smell. Prob'ly got a whiff up there of broken egg. Don't bother humans none, until they're carrion. . . ." She squinted close at Belle's eyes and said, "Well, you look okay to me. You take care now," she added, "and watch your step with them damned terns." She patted Belle on the shoulder, and walked away.

"Hey!" Belle called after her. "What're you doing?" She pointed to the heavy basket and the woman's rake.

"Kelpin'."

"Need some help?"

She felt the woman size her up. "Why not?" the woman said.

"My name's Belle," Belle said, as they started walking toward an inlet down the shore.

"I know who you are."

"We live on the—"

"I know where you live."

After a while, the woman asked, "How old are you?"

"Seventeen."

"I was married, too, when I was that."

"Oh, we're not married," Belle said.

"Well, you're living with your man, aren't you?"

"Yes."

"That's what it means."

Before the woman showed Belle how to take the kelp, she told her that her name was Grace Beebe and she was sixty-four. "Are you related to old Harris Beebe up at the store?" Belle asked.

"He's my man. My husband."

"He's from around here, isn't he?" Belle asked.

"Hatteras," Grace said.

"How about you?"

"What?"

"Are you from these parts?"

"No, siree. I'm from over to the Reservation."

"What's that?"

"The Reservation. For Cherokee."

When the basket was full, Belle asked, "What're you going to do with this?"

"Everything. Eat it."

Grace said she'd be taking kelp at low tide again tomorrow if Belle thought she'd like the company. Belle said she thought she would. "You bring your own rake next time, then," Grace told her. "You'll do good."

From Grace, Belle learned the arts of clamming, kelping, oystering, "predictering," and rolling dough. "Predictering" was understanding weather, in and out, on sea and land and of an individual's body. Grace was a medic, the healer thereabouts; the midwife. What Grace owned, the quality that Grace possessed, or that possessed her, was something Belle had never seen before in any woman—a quality of gravity, of standing firm, of being planted both feet at the same time at any given moment. Grace was a certain entity, as kelp is, as the tide is, as is the continental shelf. She knew who she was and how she fit in a larger expanse; and it was perhaps this that gave her gait its steady lateral roll, as if because of her the earth turned. Her hands, especially, were subjects of Belle's respect: they looked as gray and blistered as weathered siding, but they were cool and silken to the touch. Her eyes were little flames w/in her face, very tiny, like the light one catches through the pinhole in a paper. When she spoke, she barely moved her lips, and when she laughed she made the girlish gesture of doing so behind her hand. Some teeth were missing in her smile, which lent her jaw a forward thrust. She'd lost the upper half of the little finger on her right hand to a snapping turtle. She stood about four feet ten inches high, and through the months Belle shared her company, Belle's most tender wish on seeing her stocky little figure come toward her every morning was to rush to her and lift Grace up.

Belle learned to cook from Grace. One day Grace gave her a

funnelful of dried peas rolled up in an old newspaper, for her garden.
"I don't have a garden," Belle admitted.
"I know you don't."
"I don't know how."
"I know."
"I don't know how to cook exactly, either."
"Well do you know about the cuckoo in the sparrow's nest?"
"No."
"It's what you'll be until you learn," Grace said. So Grace taught
her. There were no miracles in Belle's conversion—cream still cur-
dled in the chowders, gravy stuck to the bottom of the pan, and
water biscuits had atomic weights of undiscovered elements; but
small, stray things began to come under her control. "Who made
this?" Kit asked one night at dinner.
"I did."
"It's damn good."
"Yeah. It is, kinda."
"What is it?"
"I call it Pisces Chowder, for the Pisces. That's the constellation,
the one we were looking at the other night next to the Big Dipper.
Pisces means fish," she told him. He was watching her w/ ill-dis-
guised amusement, and she felt embarrassed.

She became more childlike as her capabilities increased, and it
entranced him. She seemed gayer w/ the warm weather, more spir-
ited, more prone to fun. She would set his meals before him w/ a
little flourish, a "Ta-*da*," and she made up funny names for her
dishes. He could hear her singing songs out in the garden, and she
shook her head from side to side, giving lyrics their expression. He
watched her, now and then, from the bedroom window. He'd stand
and smoke and watch her, and she'd never notice that the sound of
the typewriter had stopped.

By the beginning of April, Kit was done w/ the book, and he
needed some outsized entertainment. He took the car by ferry to
Morehead City on the mainland, to have his manuscript typed. He
was gone five and a half days, and when he came home Belle could
tell the restraint from alcohol that he'd practiced while writing had
come to The End, along w/ the book. He had written a masterpiece.
The world was his oyster. He was feeling expansive. He'd brought
her a crystal vase for her flowers. He'd bought a boat. "A boat?"

Belle echoed incredulously. They'd never sailed, and Kit had never talked, as Bankers do, of a deep-seated fascination w/ the sea.

"What kind of boat?"

"You'll see. She's being fitted out in Morehead City. You'll see. She's a beaut. She'll be here in a week, or so."

"She" turned out to be a diesel-powered twenty-seven-foot motorcraft w/ twin screws, double rudders, two auxiliaries and enough space below to sleep the Brooklyn Dodgers. She was called, appropriately, the *Belle* and she was out of Cape Hatteras. She was also, incidentally, the sleekest craft Belle or Kit or any of the people gathered at the dock had ever seen.

"Do we own her?" Belle marveled.

"We sure do."

"How could we have had the money?"

"Ah . . . we didn't."

"Then how'd we buy her?"

"Ah, we didn't."

"Is she stolen?"

"Let's just say she found us, right?"

"She found us?"

"Yes. . . ."

Things were always going to find them that way, or lose them, or remain beyond the pale of explanation—like Kit's wife, for example. Kit would never speak of her, even when Belle pressed him; but Belle knew he wrote to her because he had her post the letters. "Marion Tikhmenov. That your sister?" Belle had asked. "My wife," he'd said. Belle had a fantasy that Marion was a fragile creature, living as a shut-in. It made her feel robust and somehow vulgar. Marion never wrote him back, as far as she could tell. But Kit went on writing her for years at the same address in Massachusetts, always asking Belle to post the letters. Many times, she was sorely tempted to read one before she sent it. Once, years later when they were staying w/ some movie people on the West Coast, he handed her a letter publicly, saying, "Oh, I forgot this. It's for Marion. Mail it for me when you get the chance." He hadn't sealed it, and she carried it for days, intending once and for all to find out what he had to write her about. But each time she thought of reading it, she'd lose her courage, and the letter stayed as he'd given it to her in her purse. A week later, in a taxicab, he opened the purse to look for money and found the letter. "I'm sorry, Kit," Belle protested, "I just forgot about it. . . ."

"You read it, didn't you?"

"Of course not. I wouldn't do a thing like that. . . ."

"You *didn't* read it?"

"I said I'm sorry. I forgot."

"Don't you want to read it?"

"No."

"You're never curious?"

"It's not my business."

"Can't be tempted?"

"I said it's not any of my business—"

"My God, you're a disgusting middle-class *Hausfrau* sometimes, my darling. It makes me want to vomit."

During the war, when Kit was following the 90th Division through Luxembourg, and the reports of casualties from there were very grim, Belle broke down and wrote to Marion out of despair for Kit's survival. Two weeks later a very kind reply came from a gentleman named Mr. Teabury, living at Marion's address. His letter stated that since 1934 he had been receiving letters addressed to a Marion Tikhmenov w/ no return address. He did not know anyone by that name, nor did his postman, nor did any of his neighbors on Main Street in Wellesley. He'd asked around, of course, as being thorough was his habit, since he was an accounting clerk, retired, he explained. The first few, he wrote, he'd thrown away, and he was very sorry for their loss and begged Belle to understand that he'd no foreknowledge to expect the letters to continue at the rate of two or three a month for what was now nine years. He had, after the third one, saved them all, unopened, hoping one day one would arrive w/ a return address. He waited on her kindness to instruct him what to do w/ them, or if she wouldn't mind, to send him money for the postage and he would seal them in a paper box and send them on to her in Arizona, and he signed himself "Your respectful servant, Albert Teabury."

It was not until February of 1945 that a packet came to her containing all the letters, two hundred and fifty-seven of them. By then, Belle had had word from Kit that he was going back to Paris to work on a piece about the Battle of the Bulge; but seeing his handwriting on all those envelopes gave her a most awful heartache.

There were letters postmarked from New York City in '36, '37 and again in 1939. There were letters written from their idyllic island on the Outer Banks, dated 1935—letters from San Francisco in 1939 and '40, letters from Phoenix and from Albuquerque, Key West, Reno . . . she was shocked at the clarity of detail they evoked, shaken that she could remember mailing every one, struck by the fact that there were none from Kit's post in Great Britain or in France—none, in fact, since he'd left for the war. It was that fact, that single observation, that led her to open the first one, a letter dated December 12, 1934, mailed from Petersburg, Virginia, where they'd stopped for the night after Kit had bought the wedding ring in Richmond.

The letter read, "Dear Bazooms" (Kit's nickname for her), "Caught you this time, didn't I?" The next letter was dated January 17, 1935, and she'd mailed it herself from the general store in Yaupon. It read: "Dear Bazooms, Caught you this time, didn't I?" The one dated February 8 read the same. And the one after that. And the next one, and the next: the same "Caught you this time, didn't I?" two hundred and fifty-seven times—an obsession so calm, so unerring, so singular that it had never been meant as a joke. It came from the black spot on his heart, the one that attracted the love of innocents the way that leaf markings draw prey to the carnivorous plants. A man who would write "Caught you this time" for nine years, never catching her, *needed* to catch her, she thought.

He did *not*, as a matter of fact, have a wife, though he allowed everyone to believe that he did. The press made a splash w/ it later, when it came up at her trial. "The deceased never asked you to marry him?" she was asked.

BENÛ: No.

DOUGLASS: Why not?

BENÛ: It never came up.

DOUGLASS: After twenty years?

BENÛ: He was married already.

DOUGLASS: No, ma'am, he was not.

BENÛ: Well, he told me he was.

DOUGLASS: Do you ask me to believe, Miss Benû, that *anyone* could be that stupid?

McMURTY: Objection!

SCOTT: Sustained.

BENÛ: He told *everyone* he was married.

DOUGLASS: *Everyone* didn't shoot him, though, honey.

McMURTY: Objection!

BENÛ: He told Jack. He told Sanchez.

SCOTT: Sustained.

BENÛ: We *all* thought he had a wife that he couldn't divorce. . . .
    I don't see what difference it makes!

SCOTT: Your attorney will instruct: A common-law wife doesn't have
    the same rights a wife does. Not in New Mexico.

BENÛ: He's better off dead.

SCOTT: I have to ask you to restrain your client, please, Mr.
    McMurty. . . .

McMURTY: Belle, please—

BENÛ: He broke my heart.

SCOTT: Well, there's no law against *heartbreak*, Miss Benû. . . .

    Hot Tickets was a grand success. Parts of it appeared in the July
issue of *Collier's*, and Kit's book publisher wrote to say the magazine
was selling out on newstands all over New York City. *Collier's* cabled
for a second installment; and the publisher decided to move the
publication date from January to the preceding fall. All this news
arrived while Kit sat in the bo's'n's chair aboard the *Belle* and watched
brown pelicans compete for chum he tossed into the water. He'd
never had success before, and he was thirty-two years old. He wanted
it. He wanted it so badly he would lie and cheat for it. For ten years
he'd been writing pieces in terse reportorial style about the upper-
class indifference to the labor force, and he had had the shits of it.
He wanted money. He wanted a 200-piece sterling silver place setting
for Belle, all matching. He wanted to be looked upon as someone
a publisher could not afford to insult. He'd eaten rejection for too
long from people who were at best ignorant of the real world and
at worst pretentious, and now he felt his hour for revenge had come.
Ulysses had paved the way in '33—not that Kit pretended his genius
approached Joyce's; but the ruling by Judge Woolsey in Manhattan's
Federal Court made clear the modern view toward pornography: "In

spite of its unusual frankness, I do not detect anywhere *the leer of the sensualist*—I hold therefore that it is not pornographic," the Judge had written: and the words *"leer of the sensualist"* were words Kit took to heart. He knew he would write the big book—the big dirty one, as he called it; and he knew that if he restrained himself to the reportorial style, restrained a Peeping Tom view, he'd get away w/ it—and he knew what he'd write about: a teen-age American girl indoctrinated into sex, into becoming the sex symbol for a whole nation of men generations older than she. And he knew, even then, on whom he would base the story. He knew he was writing about something so hot it couldn't miss—because it had nailed even Jack, incorruptible Jack. And the whole time he was using her, she had no idea that he'd had this in mind. She remained innocent, un-inhibited. Take your clothes off, sweetheart, he might think. Get over here. Join me. Join a nation, he might think. Let me see you. Stay there. Let me look at you. Let everybody look. Let everybody see.

He was drinking that summer—there was really no time when he wasn't drinking from early morning through the summer—but he had it under control. He could pace himself. He handled the *Belle* as if she were pure gold, and he took care of her. In a wind, he was very prudent. He was scared to death in water, and fear had a sobering effect. He didn't want to drown—maybe die at high speed, but not drown. And writing had been pure hell. One can't drink and write at the same time, so he'd been good, and now he deserved both a vacation *and* a drink. He'd earned it. "We'll go up the Waterway, take the *Belle* and a crew, in September," he informed her.

"The Waterway?"

"Through the Chesapeake. They're throwing a little party for us in New York."

"Who is?"

"The book people. Want to meet you."

"Me?"

"You, baby."

"Why me?"

"Because you're the ticket."

"The ticket? The ticket to what?"

"To whatever we want."

She didn't want to leave North Carolina. Her garden was in bloom; she had beans and broccoli yet to harvest and late-season melons. Besides, the summer had been glorious. Sometimes Kit had been silent and remote at night, or moody from his liquor, but most of the time he was loving and attentive, lying long hours w/ her in the sun, or fishing late at night from aboard the *Belle*. It was a fine, enriching way to pass a life, she thought. She hadn't read *Hot Tickets*, and she didn't know what it was about. It was Kit's, and he had written it, and she did not imagine that she figured in that process. She was surprised, then, when the *Belle* was met at the marina one evening in late August in Hampton Roads, Virginia, by a half dozen men in lightweight suits, a few w/ cameras. "Hey, Belle!" they called to her. They whistled, and Kit told her to climb up on the texas deck and wave at them. She was wearing white sharkskin shorts and two red bandannas tied together across her breasts. Her hair was loose and bleached bright by the sun, and she was tanned. "Are you Belle?" a man in a light tan fedora and a gray suit called to her. "Sure!" she called back. "Pose for them," Kit said. "They want to take your picture."

"Hey, Belle!" another man called out. "Give us something, honey! Give us something for the Prince of Wales!"

"Sure!" She laughed. She thought they were friends of Kit's, or that they were put up to this by him as a joke—he was a *Welsh*man, after all.

She leaned over and her shorts rode up and her breasts fell forward, and the men on the dock cheered and whistled.

"Can we say you wouldn't mind being Queen of England?"

"Sure!" She laughed. "Why not?"

"Can we say you wouldn't mind spending a night in Buckingham Palace?"

"Sure! Go ahead!" They thanked her and they whistled; then they left. "Well, they seemed like a cheerful bunch," she commented to Kit.

In New York, the publisher put them up at the Algonquin Hotel in midtown, and Belle didn't like it one bit. The lobby was dark and crowded w/ little tables where people sat drinking all day long, and the elevator was too small for more than two average-sized people and their bags. The rooms were nice, but Belle felt cramped w/out fresh air, and the street noise bothered her. "I hope we won't be staying here too long," she said.

"Why not?" Kit asked casually.

"Oh, I don't know," she said, a little frightened. "I guess I'm just not used to it. . . ."

"Hey, honey," he requested, "take your stockings off tonight when we go out to dinner. . . ."

"Why? All the girls in New York City wear silk stockings."

"They don't have your tan."

"But all the girls wear silk stockings. It's indecent."

"Take them off. Your legs look great."

"Well, don't blame me if all the women look."

"Women?"

"You know."

"*Men*, you mean."

"Oh, sure, them, too. But women look at you to let you know they think you look real trashy."

"You don't have too high a regard for other women, do you?"

"Who says?"

"Listen to yourself."

"I just meant, you know—that certain *kind* of woman . . ." She felt her face grow hot—he made her feel embarrassed. She had a perfect right to say what she had said, she had a right to her opinions. She meant there was a kind of woman who would always disapprove of her. He didn't have to try to make her feel more separate from her sex. . . .

Kit closed the window shades and led her to the bed, and they made love under the stiff, starched sheets. Street noises wafted in w/ city heat, mixed w/ the aroma of Kit's bourbon. She wondered how many times a day they came to make the beds up in a place like this.

While they were getting dressed to go to dinner, a soft-spoken man in a wine-colored vest came to their door and said reporters and photographers had lined up in the street outside, waiting to see Belle. He asked if they would like the manager's assistance to effect an exit through a service door.

"What do photographers want with me?" Belle asked.

"Well, madam, you are very popular," she was informed.

"*Me?*"

"Yes, madam."

"Why?"

The man's diplomacy could not extend to such ignorance, so Kit took him by the elbow and the two of them stepped into the hall to speak in whispered, gentlemanly tones. Belle was afraid something awful must have happened to Max. Or to Vern or Willa. Or to Lucy, or to Lucy's lover Theodora. She was afraid some element of her past was pointing toward her, singling her out—she had inherited a fortune, or a rare disease, or she was the last living relic of a royal line. . . .

"What's going on?" she said to Kit, and he said, "Nothing."

At dinner that night a couple of the men from the publisher's were familiar w/ her in a way she found alarming. They looked at her too much, as though they had a license to. They watched her breasts. They set their gray, translucent teeth against their fat lips or licked the thick ends of their cigars and looked at her. Finally, just before dessert, a busboy said, "Excuse me," and he took a rolled-up copy of *Collier's* from his jacket and set it down before her and said, "You're the one, aren't you?" He pointed to a printed story. It was the excerpt from *Hot Tickets.* "You're the one, you're Belle, aren't you?" the busboy asked excitedly. "Will you sign it for me? Right there by the title, will you sign it, 'Love, Belle'? I save autographs." He handed her a pen.

For a moment Belle felt as if she were traveling through a tunnel—her sight of things along the edges of the room got darker and the things in front of her appeared much brighter. She saw a silver salt shaker and a crystal drinking glass and some bread crumbs on the eggshell-colored tablecloth. She saw a gleaming drop of water on a pat of butter. She saw lines and textures in the china and in the linens and in the skin of her own hands, and she saw the first line of a story called "Hot Tickets" from the novel of the same name by the man who claimed to love her. She would never breathe again, she felt, in the same way—or move, or wink, or smile, or sigh that someone would not be watching. Each gesture was executed as if the crew of tradesmen were on hand: the cameraman, scriptwriter, portraitist, light technician, dress designer, publicist, spectator, viewer, listener, follower, audience, respondent, fan. She could not make love w/ him w/out the certain knowledge he was watching. So she began to watch. She began to do everything she did less for the doing of it than for the drama she imagined it created on a field of vision: every moment came to count w/out regard to history. It was slow, this process; no epiphany. Love deepens, or it grows, or it dissolves, in drams.

She drank a lot that night, and so did Kit, and in the morning they allowed the tapping at their door to go unanswered until a clear boys' choirmaster's voice called, "They'll think I'm here to administer last rites, should you keep me standing here much longer!"

Belle opened the door w/ just her yellow silk kimono pulled around her, a bleak headache overtaking any sense of daylight, while Kit struggled, soundlessly, to pull the bedclothes up, over his head. "How did you know where to find us?" she started to inquire, but the pressure in her head was so great, she almost swooned and Jack had to catch her, holding her in his arms. She could smell his soap and pipe tobacco, and she could feel his heartbeat pounding in his body. Even standing w/ him in her bare feet, he seemed smaller than he had been. His neck was thin where she put her hand above his collarbone to caress him. He let go of her more roughly, she thought, than was really necessary.

"Kit, man!" he shouted, slapping the sheet-wrapped figure on what was approximately his back: "Day breaks. The day is broken!"

"Fuck off, Roscoe," Kit said.

Jack laughed and sat down on the bed. Belle could see his hands were shaking. "It's the museum today for us, lad," he pronounced. "The Metropolitan. Then a stroll through Central Park. Then dinner. Where should we have our dinner, Kit?"

"I am not . . ." Kit said painfully, from beneath the sheets, "passing the . . . day . . . in anybody's fucking *park*."

"Well, fine, the lad and I will have a fine time, won't we, lad? Where shall we meet for dinner?"

"The *lad*," Kit said, lying still, "reeks of come and gin, in case you haven't noticed. . . ."

Across the room, Belle tried to smile, but she felt sick. "It's good to see you, Jack," she murmured.

"How about Café Latino?" Jack pursued. "You always liked Café Latino," he said to Kit.

Belle said, "Excuse me," and disappeared into the bathroom. She sat down on the tile floor and leaned her cheek against the toilet seat. She wrapped her arms around the toilet bowl, feeling its coolness in her veins along the inside of her arms, as if she had injected it. "I will never drink again, I'll never," she promised, but waves of dry heaves wracked her, anyway.

In the outer room Kit asked, "Does this mean that we're friends again?" and Jack said, "When were we *not*?" Kit crawled from beneath the sheet and looked his old friend in the face. "What do you want from me?" he asked in a manner that did not invite Jack's answer. Jack stood up and seemed to make a study of the drapery fabric. Kit lit a cigarette. They both pretended not to hear the sounds of Belle's discomfort.

When she joined them, she had dressed herself in tan slacks and a plaid shirt, loafers, white socks and a red bandanna. Kit looked at her and said, "This is New York, you know, honey, not Morehead City, North Carolina. . . ."

"Oh, yeah? What's that supposed to mean?"

He gestured toward her and an ash fell on the bedspread from his cigarette.

"Well, last night it was okay for me to go around without my stockings," she reminded him.

"That was different. That was something else."

"I *know* what that was," she announced.

Jack cleared his throat and observed that such things as haberdashery were well outside the precincts of his profession. "That's only true of low life like yourself who can't make cardinal," Kit returned. Jack's color rose, and he said, "I never played at hierarchical intrigue in the Church—"

"Oh, touchy, aren't we?"

"Yes. A wee bit . . ."

"Oh, a 'wee bit' touchy this fine day—What's going on within that tortured Christian soul this morning, Jack-o? A weighty confession in the making? What'd you do—steal the joy-toy from somebody's Crackerjacks?"

Jack watched a pigeon on a window sill, across the narrow courtyard. "I wonder if you've never felt you've failed at something you were meant to do, Kit?"

"I was never 'meant to do' a thing, Jack boy, except stay angry."

"Ah, yes. Stay angry—"

"And I've accomplished that. Work at it night and day, old friend. . . ."

"As, yes, indeed. It's anger that's the *do* emotion, right, Kit? Isn't that the way you'd have it? Anger *does*: It's *love* that slakes the passions."

"You remember—"

"*What* do I remember?"

"Being young."

"Surprise me, *my* old friend," Jack said, turning toward him. "Tell me something that I *don't* remember. . . ."

Belle had no real sense of what was going on between them, except that it was something planted in them long before she'd come along. She felt the way a child feels at the dinner table when her parents are engaged in a domestic spat. She changed her clothes to make herself feel better. She changed into a dress w/ a white collar, to match Jack's, and tied her hair up in a tight knot. She wore a jacket and white gloves, and she carried an efficient handbag. She wore no make-up and tried for all the world to look like no one anyone would take the time to cross the street for.

They were still arguing about something when she walked into the room, but Kit said, "Jesus," at her getup, and they stopped. He handed her a fifty-dollar bill and told her not to let the "padre" pay for anything, especially his lunch. Jack held the door for her and said, "I wouldn't worry that I'll put you out of pocket, Kit—I've taken to not eating much these days."

"I noticed," Kit said. "I liked you better *fat*."

"I've liked you better, too, Kit," Jack agreed.

In the taxicab that took them uptown, Belle stole the chance to look Jack over in the daylight. "Have you been sick, or something?" He took her hand in his and tried to laugh. "Do I look sick to you?"

"Yeah, kinda. Pale, you know? You never know when someone looks this pale, what it could be. It could be anemia, or anything. Consumption, even."

He finally laughed. "You haven't changed a jot, lad," he assured her. "Not a jot."

"Oh, yes, I have."

"No, lad. He hasn't changed you. He only tops up the inevitable so steep, you can't surmount it if you try. . . ."

She didn't know if Jack meant God or Kit, but since he fell into a moody silence over it, she w/drew and hoped his mood would pass. It didn't. They spent the morning in the Greek and Roman wing in the Museum in a tense but not unfriendly silence. Finally, around noon, as the light shifted to the west in the Great Hall, they climbed the marble staircase to the rooms of the Old Masters and Belle found an occasion to make him laugh again when they had stopped to take a closer look at an El Greco. "Hey," she said, putting her hand lightly on his arm, "I bet you don't know the story about Tintoretto and El Greco. . . ."

"No, I . . ."

"Well, you know El Greco was a student there, in Tintoretto's atelier. . . ."

Jack raised an eyebrow at her pronunciation of "atelier." He almost broke into a smile. "Is that a fact?" he asked.

"Oh, sure," Belle told him. "Young men from all over Europe, you know, France and Spain and Italy were going there to Tintoretto's to learn the secrets, you know, of his technique. Well, the thing about Tintoretto, was he was this blow-hard, see, from day one. He was a dumb *italiano*, if you follow what I mean. Well, so in walks this really great big talent in El Greco. You know, The Greek. And he starts doing things with shadows and all, with his color, and oh yeah, he had this new line on perspective, too, and people hadn't seen things done this way, especially old Tintoretto. So Tintoretto looks at this and he's ashake his head. He's asay, 'Hey, El Greck, this asomethin' not too good. This asomethin' I can see what's gonna be. You gonna fuck it up real good this picture, and I'm agonna have to go back and unfuck it later—' "

Belle sort of doubled over at her own joke, and then she caught herself and said, "Oh, geez, I forgot and told a 'fuck' joke—"

"Believe me, lad, there are these dispensations. . . ."

"I mean, it's not the same joke without the 'fuck' in it. . . ."

"I can appreciate that—"

"Because the whole joke is the '*un*fuck' part."

"I know. I *got* it, lad. . . ."

"Oh, good. I was afraid, you know, I'd goof it. I don't tell too many jokes. I don't know too many."

"Whose was this?"

"Go on, you ought to know. . . ."

"Max's?"

"Yeah. He used to do the accent better. I didn't do the accent good at all—"

"You didn't do it badly. . . ."

"He used to do a lot of funny accents, I think, just to make me laugh. He ate a light bulb once, you know."

"He didn't!"

"Yeah—I guess he's still married to Lucy. . . ."

"He hasn't been in touch with you?"

"Naw, that's a joke."

"I wonder if he's represented here. One of his paintings . . . Shall we ask?"

"Sure, go ahead. It'll be like finding something dead up in the attic. . . ."

"Ah. Well, there's no real need then—"

"Why not? It doesn't matter. You'd be surprised at what I'm used to."

They were standing in a room w/ bright red brocade walls. Bright cheeks, more like flans than faces, glowed from the sooty depths of the old portraits. They must have drunk a great deal in those days, Jack thought. He said, "I read the book." There wasn't any question in Belle's mind which book he meant. "I wish you hadn't," she confessed.

"He sent it on to me, the galley proofs. . . ."

"I really wish you hadn't. I'd like to be around a single person any more who I could feel real sure he hadn't—"

"You know what it's about, then?"

"Yeah. Art and the Virgin Mary, right?"

"But you've read it through, lad?"

"Go on, you're kidding."

"I think you should sit down and read it."

"Go on. Would you?"

"To understand him, yes. To see what otherwise I wouldn't see. . . ."

"Like what?"

"His evil."

"Go on, don't talk that way. I don't like when people talk that way. Like everything is divided, you know, into things to do and

things you shouldn't do. There's just a whole lot you don't understand—"

"*Look* at me!" he whispered. He's angry, she realized. She'd never
seen him angry. "Do you really want to say there's something I don't
understand?"

"Yeah. Yes. Don't look at me like this. You know. There's *things*
that you don't know about. Things going on, that make a difference
between people. Like all you see is how could Kit write such a book.
You don't see the other side, the way he is, when we're together.
When we're together *that way*, you know, I feel good. Go ahead
and blush. He makes me feel good. It doesn't matter what he does
aside from that—"

"You *can't* believe that, Belle."

"You don't know what I believe! Who are you to say what I
believe? You don't know anything about the stuff we do or who we
are. You live a kind of total different way. I don't go around pretending I know stuff about the way you are. What's so wonderful
about the way you are? If everybody was like you, there wouldn't
even be kids! The world would end!"

A museum guard approached them and a woman, shielding her
little girl w/ an Altman's shopping bag, stared at them w/ shocked
opprobrium. "Papist!" she hissed toward Jack. She walked away from
them and warned her little girl, "Don't stare at the strangers, Rachel,
it's not nice. . . ." Without thinking, and responding to a prejudicial
similarity between this woman and the church women of Lake Forest
in her past, Belle shouted, "*Bitch!*" With polite force, she and Jack
were led out by the guard. At the top of the marble stairway, Jack
offered Belle his arm and she accepted it w/ formal dignity. When
they got out on Fifth Avenue, they laughed so hard they had to sit
down on the edge of the fountain and sparkling water danced on
them, and Belle leaned back and shook her hair loose.

After a while they walked south down the avenue and stopped to
buy sweet-flavored Italian ices in paper cones from a street vendor
at Seventy-eighth Street. They sat down on a wooden bench to eat
them, and watched the street traffic and the people moving by. Jack's
former dismal mood had brightened, and Belle was reminded of an
article she'd read in one of the glossy magazines about some people
who get grumpy if they don't eat breakfast. She was about to bring

the subject up when she remembered that the whole thing might have just been over Kit's writing what he had in *Hot Tickets* and she didn't want to start him up again on *that*. She patted his hand instead and said, "That was a good laugh, wasn't it?" "God, yes," he agreed. He touched the fabric of her skirt and seemed to grow more serious. "I'm sorry, lad, for what I was about to say before. . . . I hadn't taken into account how greatly you love him."

Belle blinked and looked away. "Don't worry about it, everybody says things now and then—"

"Oh, you proved that, lad! Dear God . . . I wonder what impression we managed to bestow on that poor girl—"

"Who, the bitch's daughter? Forget about it. She has weird ideas all the time already, from her mother. . . ."

"Still, I wonder sometimes how our actions enter on the lives of others—don't you?"

"Oh, you know, I'm not the one to think about stuff like that. I don't think about all that. I just go along, Jack, you know me. Just point me around so I can face the view, and that's enough to keep me happy. . . ."

"Which view is that, Belle?"

"Oh, go on, don't get too serious again. . . ."

"People? Fifth Avenue? New York City?"

"You know . . ."

"Life?"

"Go on, I don't know what I meant. It's something that was just a way of speaking. . . . I guess I meant, you know, the view outside my window. The window by our bed."

At Seventy-first Street, they entered the park and wandered through a children's playground toward the zoo. The day was bright, late-summer-New-York-golden from reflected sun. The children tied their sweaters at their waists or let them fall into the thin beige dust between the benches. Belle sat on a swing, and Jack sat on the one next to her. She doodled her tiptoes in the dust, twisting slightly in a lazy arc. The dust stayed on the bottom of Jack's black pants like pastry flour. A small brown-haired girl stood nearby in a coat the color of robins' eggs. The coat was much too large for her, either a hand-me-down or purchased in the economic necessity that she'd grow into it. Belle smiled at her. She remembered she'd had coats like that one the whole time she was growing up, even though they'd had money. Willa never bought a thing for her that fit: Belle's winter coats were always much too large the first year and worn out and small the next.

"Will you be having children anytime real soon, lad?" Jack asked, noticing the object of her gaze.

"Naww . . . I'm still a kid, myself, right?"

"Do you, ah, practice . . . you, ah, take precautions?" he inquired.

She looked at him. You'd think a priest his age could keep himself from blushing, she marveled. "Well, Kit uses, you know . . ." she admitted. "And sometimes in the middle of the month, we do different things, and all." Jack blinked and took a sudden interest in brushing the dust off his pants. "You know," she pursued, "I mean, Kit says there's a *thousand* ways we haven't done it yet—"

"I'm sure," Jack answered swiftly.

"He knows all kinds of stuff like that," Belle told him. Jack made the sort of sound that signified no further need for conversation.

They had made plans w/ Kit earlier that day to meet at Keen's English Chop House on Thirty-sixth for dinner. Kit wasn't there. "I'm glad we got here first," Belle said, sliding in across from Jack in one of Keen's high-backed booths. "He takes up with all kinds when I keep him waiting."

"Drinkers," Jack said, correcting her. "Not all kinds, lad; just the drinkers." He snapped the menu down and looked around, a little piqued.

"Well, we're early," Belle reminded him.

"Oh, Lord knows, I'm not the one to mind a little wait. It's not that, no." He seemed a little jumpy, Belle concluded, the way Kit seemed when he was waiting for a drink. "It's only that this morning Keen's seemed such a good idea, didn't it? Mixed grill. Kidney pie. How was I to know I'd be of a mind for fish this evening—a good red snapper. . . ."

"Well, there's Dover sole—"

"Dover sole. Shoe of the Fisherman. Come, lad, I mean *fish*—moist, unfatted flesh . . . lobster . . . salmon . . . abalone. . . ."

"There's finnan haddie."

"Oh, finnan haddie. I may as well be back in Indiana where the fish are eons old. . . ."

Belle was enjoying this: "There's salted cod."

"Don't tempt the devil, lad. . . . Good Christ!" He slapped the table. "Look there, lad! Does that say *shad* up on the board?" Belle twisted around and squinted at the chalk board above the bar, where specials of the day were posted. "I believe it does indeed," she mimicked him.

"With *oysters?*"

"Ah, yes, *indeed*," she mocked. She chided him, "Hey, I thought you'd stopped thinking so much about food. . . ."

"Oh, now and then its pleasures overtake me. Blake wrote, 'A dog starv'd at his master's gate, Predicts the ruin of the State.' "

A look came over Jack, and Belle knew he had spoken in a kind of code about what troubled him.

"You're not a dog at anybody's gate," she told him. "That's stupid."

"It's . . . poetry, actually."

"*I* know it's poetry, even though I don't know who Blake is. I mean it's stupid not to say right out what's bothering you. You're making yourself sick and all. It worries me."

"You're a sweet girl, lad." Tears were coming to his eyes.

"Stop it," she told him. "You're scaring me."

Jack looked away. "I'm going to Poland," he announced.

Belle wrinkled her nose. "The one that's next to Germany?"

Jack smiled. "The same."

"Why are you going to do that? I mean, I don't think I've ever heard of anybody going there. I've never heard anybody say it was any kind of place to go to, you know? Even Max. I mean, Max never said anything bad about Europe, on principle, but even he wasn't too fond of Poland. He said it's not a country, but a *zone*, like—what did he call it?—oh, yeah, like the *horse latitudes*."

"I'm not going for the climate, lad. . . ."

"He had another funny thing he used to say about Poland, too— what was it? Oh, 'Jimmy Cracow and I don't care'—the song. I mean it's not a joke or anything, he just used to think the lyrics of the song were 'Jimmy *Cracow* and I don't care, Jimmy Cracow and I don't care, Jimmy Cracow and I *don't care*, my master's gone away. . . .' " She felt embarrassed by the way Jack was looking at her. "It's a dumb song any way you sing it," she admitted.

"You talk about Max a great deal, you know."

"Well to you, sure. I have to try and be, you know, intelligent."

"You *are* intelligent."

"Some ways. Not like you. I don't read enough. It's not the way I learn. Max didn't read too much, either. He said he learned through his nose, you know, like, well, like pets, I guess. Willa, just forget it. She was stupid. She never asked a question in her life that it wasn't something or another about money—"

"Is that why they, ah . . . there was divorce?"

"I guess so. I don't know. They just never got along. Max, you know, knocked her around a little."

Jack's eyes searched Belle's face. "I didn't know. You never told me."

Belle shrugged. "I mean, she never had a broken *bone* or anything. And anyway, she deserved it."

"How can you—"

"Oh, go on. She asked for it."

"No one *asks* to be abused, child—"

"Go on, of course they do. Even *I* know that one. What the heck are all those martyrs, then?"

"The wife submitting to abuse does not exactly fall within religious context, Belle. . . ."

"Oh, blooey, Jack—"

"Yeh, Jacko. *Mlooeyjack* . . ."

An aroma of bourbon, stale ale and perspiration emanated from him. His suit, which Belle had pressed and packed in layers of blue laundry paper for the trip, was creased as if he'd slept in it. His face was blowzy, as some women are—blowzy and sad. When he sat down next to Belle she could smell his sex on him, mulled w/ a strange perfume. Her heart began to pound so hard she had to put her hand up on her chest to try to hide it.

Kit called out for a waiter and announced that they should celebrate. Jack asked, "What are you celebrating this time, Kit?"

"I thought you said you had to be at the publisher's all day long," Belle heard herself accuse him.

He closed his eyes, as she spoke, as if her voice were ugly to him. "Lesselmrate *frenshib*," he told Jack.

"Fine idea. A bottle of champagne for the lady and myself," he told the waiter. "And, ah . . . what are you drinking, Kit?"

"Murmon."

"And a, ah, bottle of bourbon for this gentleman. Do you want a glass with that, Kit?"

"Thass funny, Jack. Thass'pose be real funny."

"Let's go, Jack. Let's get him out of here. . . ."

"Youve really hadda shits ob me, huh, Jack?"

"Perhaps of everything—but you can't understand that, can you, Kit? You can't understand not being at the center of the universe. . . ."

"Waddizit? Jus I'm makn money, thassit. Righ'? Can' stan' th'fugn rich, righ'? Turn yur back on me asoons I star' makn money—"

"Right."

"Co'sucker."

"I'm agreeing with you."

"Jack, please. Let's leave. People are—"

"Shudthefugup, cun'! Who givsa shit 'bout *people*—"

"Obviously you don't, Kit. The lad and I, however—"

"Th'*lad*, oh th'*lad*. 'Ts fugn *girl*! Fugup with its sex, I beggur pardn—"

"The lad and I are going to order dinner. I fully expect we'll pass the evening in some pleasant talk and the exchange of our ideas. If you're up to that, you're welcome to join us. You remember how to exchange ideas, don't you, Kit? I'm sure you must. Somewhere in that booze-sodden brain there must be a spark of brilliance left, mustn't there?"

"Tha's righ', thass righ', come righ' out an' say it—"

"Say what?"

"You hay my guss."

"I don't hate you. You repel me. I don't hate you."

"Yeh? Well wha' 'bout ol' Kit, ol' Dzack s'pose be frens f'rever? Wha' 'bout that? Wha' 'bout 'ternal grace . . . 'Gibness . . . Symphy?"

"Sympathy, oh, yes. I do feel sorry for you. Sympathy's the one thing that I do feel in abundance. Sympathy and satiation. I've had enough of you, old friend."

"Wha' 'bout you s'pose snickeroun' gibme final amslushun, Dzack, memmer?"

"For God's sake, I'm not your ticket out of Hell, you son of a bitch! I'm a plain man. I try to be a decent one. Perhaps it's decency that stands between us, I don't know. Something does. Something refuses us equality, the likeness to be friends. You're not my friend. You haven't the quality to be a friend, not even to yourself—"

"You win'bag basnerd."

"You're not going to provoke me, so good-bye."

"Who th'fug d'you thing you are?"

"Good-bye, Kit."

"G'by, m'yass."

"*Good-bye.*"

It took Kit two tries to stand up. He fell against a table near the bar and knocked some glasses over. Belle went to him. She told a man who started to get rough w/ him that she'd take care of it, and then she helped Kit to his feet. Near the door he pushed her away, and she lost her balance. She felt her face go hot w/ shame from all the people staring at her. Outside on the street he stopped a cab and shoved her away again as he got in. She ran along beside the cab a few steps and then stood curbside in the street awhile, thinking he might circle back. When Jack found her, she was standing w/ her back against the brick building, seeming to search for him in every passing cab. "I've never seen him that way," she said. "He's never been as drunk as this."

"Spare me," he said. "I have a headache. . . ."

They walked awhile, and Belle kept saying they should make sure nothing happened to him. Jack tried to talk to her about Kit and his behavior when he was drinking in more general terms, as if Kit's individual acts were symptoms shared by others, but Belle would hear none of it. Finally, when they came across a movie house playing a movie neither one of them had seen, Jack suggested that they take it in. The movie was *It Happened One Night,* starring Clark Gable and Claudette Colbert, and near the end of it, Belle got very weepy. Later, when they stopped to take some tea at an automat, she said, "Kit could be like that. If it wasn't for him drinking, we could be like those two, Miss Colbert and Clark Gable. . . ."

"You shouldn't take that sort of thing too seriously," Jack told her. "For heaven's sake, it's just a movie—"

"Well, maybe so," Belle sniffed. "But still—it won Best Picture. . . ."

He walked her back to the hotel circuitously, walking as far west as they could go, to the Hudson River, before turning north. The

Hudson had a spell on him, he told her. He never came to New York that he didn't take a walk down by the river. He guessed, he said, of all the places he had visited he loved best towns and cities along rivers. "Is that where you're going, in Poland?"

"Yes."

"To river towns?"

"Yes."

"What river?"

"*Die Wiechsel.* The Vistula . . ."

They were standing at a corner on Twelfth Avenue under the elevated roadway of the West Side Highway, across the street from a stock pen. Ferry boats and tugs were secured along the shore, and rows of wagons full of produce, vegetables and poultry from New Jersey and shellfish from Maryland and Delaware rumbled by. A slatted stock cart, massive in the low light, was off-loaded from a barge. Three men put their shoulders to it and began to roll it down the street—Belle could see their white socks through the darkness. When the stock cart reached the corner, one of the men went around and unlatched a hasp at one end of the cart, and then a soft undulation, like a frothy channel, spilled into the avenue.

"Sheep," Jack whispered.

"Well, I'll be," Belle marveled.

A flock of sheep, fifty or sixty of them, tumbled from the cart. "Hee-*ah!*" a runner called. "Ay! Ay! Hee-ah—" The sheep, their lowing rattling through the traces of the wooden warehouses, picked their hoofs among the cobbles of West Thirty-ninth Street. Belle pulled Jack forward w/ her, so she could move among the flock. "Oh, gosh!" she called. She'd felt the sheep against her legs. "Soft, aren't they? Lookit! Can they see, or what? Their eyes are awfully far apart. . . . Hey, do they know where they're going?" she called out to a man w/ a short rope whip bringing in the rear of the flock.

"No, ma'am."

"Well, they're moving pretty fast!" She laughed.

"Oh, thems'll move more fast than this, if I should lets . . ."

"Where are you taking them?"

"Round over there," he pointed.

"For wool?"

"No, ma'am, these ones'll go for slaughter. . . ."

Belle dropped out. A tuft of wool clung to her dress, and her legs prickled a little bit. She and Jack walked back toward the Algonquin, and he drew her in along the building about a half a block before the entrance.

"Look here," he said, "if anything should happen, I want you to have these—"

"What?"

"Please. They've been mine since I was a boy—"

"Hey, what are you doing? These are your beads, for heaven's sake. . . ."

"My rosary."

"Well, what the heck am I supposed to do with someone's rosary?"

"Keep it. I want you to have it—"

"Listen, I'm not even Catholic. . . ."

"They're for praying, Belle."

"They'd make me feel real dumb, Jack. I don't pray, you know? I don't have a real idea about who's God, or anything. . . ."

"I want you to pray for me."

"Go on, you're talking crazy. You've got plenty of better people to go to for that." She pressed them on him. "Take them back," she said. "You're the one who ought to pray for me, you know?"

"I've failed you."

"Go on. You don't know what you're saying."

"No. I have."

"Hey, go on—you're just depressed."

"I want to help you, Belle."

"You have. You have already."

"I want to help you leave him."

"Well, I—"

"Even if you don't. I want to help."

"Well, sure. Don't get so serious about it."

"Telephone me tomorrow. Leave a message."

"Sure."

"I'm with Father O'Donnell at the Seaman's Institute. On Tenth Avenue. Church of the Guardian Angel. Can you remember that?"

"Yeah, sure—"

"I'll be there the next three days."

"Okay—"

"Leave a message for me, lad, if I'm not there, to say you're safe. . . ."

"Well, of course I'll be *safe*."

"Of course."

"Good-bye, Jack."

"Good night, Belle."

He shook her hand in both of his. She gave him a girlish kiss on his cheek and ran down the block. She turned and called to him near the entrance of the hotel, "Bye! See ya soon! I'll give you a call tomorrow!" But what w/ Kit being so sweet the next couple of days and their both being so busy, she didn't honestly regret it when she didn't.

The morning sickness that she'd had that day persisted through September, and after she'd missed two periods in a row she finally told him she had reason to believe that she was pregnant. "I hope you're wrong," he said. She knew she wasn't. She was sick much of the time, and there were days she couldn't rouse herself from bed. She felt distant from her body, and she lost enthusiasm for sex. Kit was drinking heavily, anyway, so they fell into a pattern of being together, while apart: when they went out to dine, they rarely spoke, except to read the menu to each other. The book was selling well, and the publisher sent them on a tour by train to different cities. Belle was expected to be looked at and to look a certain way. One evening in October, after they had gone to California, she had trouble w/ the zipper of her lamé skirt and Kit told her to take it off because she was "showing." They drove to San Jose two weeks after that for the abortion. It was quick and neat and simple—they had money. But it was illegal. She slept through the operation and woke up in a clean, bright room. They had her eat a few Ritz crackers and sip a little juice. It was a ritual she liked, because it made her think about communion.

Over the years w/ Kit, between 1936 and 1952, she had four abortions. Serial abortion, they were called—Ritz crackers, apple juice, you wash it all away. Her shame accrued. Like interest working daily in a hidden vault, biology went ticking on inside her—she came to think her body had an inside and an outside, sluiced back to back. Her babies had no faces; no dreamed, imagined lives. They were accidental griefs, like meteors that fall to earth at night and leave cold holes scored in a field.

They lived a year in California. It was a long, romantic year—

they had money, and the weather was very good. People they knew seemed swept up in the drama of the King of England's abdication, and it was commonly believed that one should sacrifice oneself for love. They went to Cuba in 1937. They were careless one night on the beach, and Belle became pregnant. Kit made jokes about her damned fertility as if she were at fault, or as if her ground needed salting, like the fields of Carthage—still, in a perverse way, he took pleasure in her impregnation, and he wrote a poem to her when she was pregnant for the second time. It was the only poem he ever wrote to her. It was about his potency.

In April 1938, they bought a house in Arizona, literally by accident. Their car had broken down on a trip to Taos to find the ghost of D. H. Lawrence, and Kit had found a bar he liked while waiting out repairs in Flagstaff. No one lived in Arizona in the thirties—no one famous, which they were; or at least, they were popularly recognized in bars and magazines. Kit was drinking steadily by then and counting words. "Five hundred words this morning," he would say. He'd begun to practice the braggadocio of sad writing men, of taking sheets of paper w/ him to saloons and giving readings from his work-in-progress. Hard drinking left its mark on him; his beauty twisted. He got fat. His eyes retreated from clear certainty to a look of glassy indecision—they seemed smaller, and his lids were puffy. He let his attire fall to disrepair—he shuffled, sockless, in loose shoes; his pants, despite his weight gain, were too loose around the seat. His shirts and vests and sweaters suffered burn holes from his cigarettes. By the time Britain declared war, it came as a reprieve to Kit's despair.

The bombing of Britain began on June 9, 1940; but by then Kit had already left Flagstaff for London. He'd put in for a posting from a magazine or journal first, but the popularity of his novelistic talents in *Hot Tickets* and his next book, *Roads*, had eclipsed his reputation for reporting, and he had to scrounge around for press credentials, finally finding some support from a Phoenix daily w/ syndication in the West and the Southwest. His first reports were gauzy, nostalgic, focusing on the kind of thing that fueled his outrage as a British national but left his American readers quizzical, confused. Through trial and error and finally from old habit, he got better. He got very good; but that was later.

In the fall of 1939 he responded to war in Britain as a chance to prove his "valor." To prove his "manhood," his "self-worth." He even said he thought he might go off the booze, and for three weeks before he left, he did. Almost at once, he lost ten pounds. His face regained its youth. His hands were steady, his work was good, his love-making was tender, almost agonizing in its sweetness, and he could make a joke, again. "Hey," he whispered very late one evening. She was crying silently, the way she cried, holding her breath so as not to sob. They were lying on their bed beside the window, watching a new moon in a navy-blue night sky. "We'll have a kid when I get back," he said to cheer her up. She couldn't speak. "We'll have a kid, and if it comes out a boy we'll call it King, and if it turns out to be a girl we'll expose her up there on the rocks the way they used to."

"That's not funny," she managed to breathe.

"I'm kidding, hey. Don't look so fucking fatal. Nothing's going to happen—"

"You don't know that for a guarantee—"

"Well, what the fuck. The roof could cave in at the White House. Eleanor could slip and break her neck in the goddam bathtub—"

"That's an ordinary thing, not war."

"Well, when you're in a war, then war is ordinary."

"What if you—"

"I'm not getting wounded, so forget it. No Kraut projectile enters this frail mantle. . . ."

"Meet someone."

" 'Someone'?"

"Another woman."

"If she looks like you, I'll fuck her brains out."

"If she doesn't look like me?"

"Then I'll pretend. . . ."

"I'll be . . . so different . . . by the time you come back. Older."

"So will I."

"But it's not the same for men—"

"Oh, come on, Belle, whoever fed you that one was a flaming asshole."

"Say you love me."

"I love you."

"No, say it like I didn't tell you to."

"Belle—"

"I've never said this about anything before, you know I never have. Every time something happens I try to make the best of it or, you know, not complain. I try to get out in one piece. But I hate it this time. I hate this idea. You don't *have* to go. You *want* to. What's in it for somebody like me? What am I supposed to do? A thing like this can come along and change my life and there's nothing anyone like me can do about it. Nothing—except to lie awake and wish it wasn't happening."

He held her tightly and let her cry. He watched the new moon, and he thought about being back in England, the old streets, the haunts, the sense of history in the making and the eloquence he hoped he had, at last, to bring to it.

On a blistering hot afternoon in August 1940, Belle drove down from the mesa to the little town of Oraibi to buy magazines. The United States was not in Britain's war, and there were men around the little square and sometimes it made her feel less lonely when she drew their stares. That afternoon there were some speeches going on in the park, and she pulled the car up in front of Sam the Trader's and walked over. Some man was going on about some local issue over "land use." Belle went to the drinking fountain, and as she leaned to take a drink of water, her eyes traveled across the street to the arcade that ran along the five-and-dime and Pedro's diner, and she gave a start because she swore the little woman walking there was her old friend from the Outer Banks, Grace Beebe. She ran across the street calling Grace's name and put her hands around the woman's shoulders when she'd finally caught up w/ her.

"Oh, Lord's sake, you know, I'm real sorry," she stammered. The woman stared at her.

"I thought you were a friend of mine," Belle said. "From over there"—she pointed toward the square—"you look just like her." It was the woman's size, Belle realized, that made her look like Grace. Her size, her stockiness, the flat planes of her face. "Say, are you an *Indian*?" Belle asked. The woman's face showed a glimmer of amusement. "Grace, that's my friend's name," Belle continued, "Grace Beebe, I knew her when I lived in North Carolina . . . she was a Cherokee. I mean, I know this is far away in Arizona and all, but I just thought since you look so much alike, if you were an Indian, then the two of you might be, you know . . . *related.*"

The woman broke into a grin, and Belle was further justified in her assumption because she, like Grace, was missing some of her front teeth. "I am Hopi woman," she said.

"My name's Belle," Belle offered.

"Bessie," the woman said.

"Bessie what?"

"Chööchökam."

"Oh, I have a strange last name, too," Belle said. "It's Benû." She smiled. "Can I drive you anyplace, Mrs. Chööchökam?"

The woman's laughter was like the crowing of a bantam rooster sent to greet the sun. . . .

Bessie lived w/ John, her son, and Ruth, her older son's widow, and Ruth's two teen-age children, in an adobe dwelling on Oraibi Reservation. The reservation was forty-seven miles from where Belle lived, but in that year before America joined the war, she drove there almost every day. Her thin form moving on the horizon, her blond hair tied up in a turquoise scarf, became a familiar sight. The children loved her; and she loved them back. She drew w/ them and brought them pencils and crayons. She discovered she could drape and sew, and Bessie eyed her hands w/ open envy as the hands of a born potter. John, it seemed, had had some trouble w/ the older men of the tribe about his education. He was very bright and wanted to study medicine. A wealthy family in Tucson for whom he'd worked one summer arranged to underwrite his education, but when his brother died the tribe expected him to support his mother and his brother's family at home on Oraibi, where Hopi men were sheep farmers. John confessed to Belle one day that the only reason he'd come back was that he'd always been in love w/ Ruth, who was his elder by nine years. He was waiting for a time, he said, when he would have enough put by to buy a place to live somewhere off the reservation, then he was going to ask her if she'd marry him. Belle was touched by this because her own hopes and dreams were always hopes and dreams along the same, uncomplicated line, and she asked how much he'd saved so far, and he said forty dollars.

Rather than joining other women selling war bonds in cities down below, Belle gave her time and energies to her neighbors on the mesa. They were the last, or nearly the last, ones served by the welfare programs. They were more or less ignored in their enfranchisement as citizens; but Philip, Bessie's grandson, Ruth's son, was among the first young men called up before the draft board in the state of Arizona. When the news came, Belle and John drove down to Flagstaff to appeal it, but they lost; and on the ride back, Belle offered John and Ruth her house. It took them all a while to quiet the few members of the tribal council who had disapproved, but in the third week of February 1942, Belle moved into Ruth's vacant room in Bessie Chööchökam's adobe house.

She was listening to the radio there and sewing one afternoon in October 1944, when Billy Póko came to the door and whispered, "*Sikángnuqa*—you here?" Belle turned down the volume of the radio and said, "Come in, Billy." They called her "*Sikángnuqa*" because it was the Hopi word for the color yellow just before the dawn. They called Billy "Póko" because "*póko*" was the Hopi word for any animal that serves a human—a pigeon messenger, a draft horse, a pet snake; it was not a kind name for a little boy. People made fun of Billy because he had the *kwána'pala*, the "eagle sickness": epilepsy.

"Tele-gram, *Siká*," he said.

Belle's breath caught in her throat. "Well, give it to me."

He handed it to her, and her hand shook.

"*Kachada*," Billy said. White man. "*Mokee*." Dead. "It say *Siká* father dead," he explained. "Whole town already know."

"Thank you, Billy."

"Sorry, *Siká*. He was good-guy?"

"Sure. Max was a real good-guy, Billy."

She read the telegram through again:

BELLE BENU CARE OF TIKHMENOV
REGRET INFORM FATHERS DEATH STOP
LETTER FOLLOWS STOP
MAJ GEN BRAMHARRIS   INTL RED CROSS   MAJDANEK ZONE FIVE   METZ
FRANCE

The wire had been forwarded from Kit's publisher in New York. Belle turned it over in her hand, read it again. Bessie came in from the yard and looked at her. "It's Max," Belle said. She shrugged and let her arms fall to her sides.

"I am full of sadness for the father of my friend," Bessie told her.

"Yeah, me, too, I guess . . ."

She frowned at Bessie. The two women, living alone in the small house, had learned to speak a lot through silence. Besides, there was no describing Max to Bessie; she could not have pictured him. But Bessie's understanding of Belle's response to Max's death was no less total for never having known him: it was the same as when a rival dies, or a blood enemy—nothing to rejoice in, nothing great to mourn; confoundedness. Belle tried that night and the next night to grieve, and couldn't. She was twenty-six years old that year and hadn't seen her father for exactly half her life. That he had died just then had a roundness to it, she thought; she was past-master at finding circles in her life, as if events—births, deaths, chance encounters—were droplets fallen from the sky on a reflecting pool.

A few days later the letter came, a sort of pouch, really, that rattled when she shook it. She didn't want to open it and have to touch her father's dog tags. She asked Bessie to do it. The contents of the package were wrapped inside the letter. When Bessie unfolded it, Belle gave a cry. Jack's rosary had fallen out. It was only then that Bessie saw the grief her little friend had been disguising.

Jack had died in a concentration camp—in a starvation cell, the Red Cross reported. Belle had difficulty understanding what that was. Reports were slow in coming out, and she at first thought camps had been established to detain prisoners of war. When the truth began to surface as the war drew to an end, her anger rivaled her grief. What had he done? Why had he done it? She'd written Kit about it as soon as she'd found out. She'd written him, anticipating solace; answers. "Dear Bazooms," he'd written back, "Got the news about ol' Jack," and that was all. A silence opened up between them, greater than before, a great maw, like Chaco Canyon. She wondered if events men caused left traces on the face of earth as clear as this geology. She wished more men climbed mesas here or mesas elsewhere, to survey. Evenings, she climbed up and looked out across the canyon and the succeeding valley and her thoughts would well up, like night bats, too swift in all their terror to fend off, or to define. She could see across Monument Valley miles and miles to the horizon w/out a single interruption. Her grief and solitude were such that she felt emptied out, a nothing. Later another letter came

that said that Philip Chööchökam—"Philip Charlie," as they had
him listed—had been killed in Italy, and Belle would stand w/ Bessie
on the rocks above the cliffs and, pointing, try to show the older
woman where that was.

III

ON THE WEDNESDAY BEFORE CHRISTMAS, 1945, Kit had
come home from the war, unannounced. The wind had been whipping across the San Francisco Peaks that day, making white eddies
of sandstone and snow and the rootless debris of the brush on the
desert. Despite the cold, there was an aroma of sage when the wind
tossed dried branches. Belle's hands turned blue from the cold,
waiting for Ruth to come out to the truck. Ruth had been having
spells of quick heat, dizziness. She hadn't been feeling well since
Philip's death, and Belle and Bessie had finally come to take her to
see the doctor, a specialist, down in Winslow. A woman's specialist,
an *obigi-wy-en*, Bessie called him. The heater in the truck was on
the fritz, and Johnnie Chööchökam fiddled w/ it; then, so they
wouldn't be late for Ruth's appointment, they took off—the three
women huddled on the seat under some blankets. Ruth's trouble
turned out to be The Change, the doctor said, and he prescribed
some medicine. Ruth held the pills in her fist on the ride back. "No
more babies," she murmured once.
   "No more," Bessie agreed. "We're old women. That's O.K. Belle
can have babies." She took Ruth's hand.
   "Are you gonna have a baby, Belle?" Ruth asked.
   "Well, not just yet." Belle laughed. She held the frigid steering
wheel w/ two tense hands. "You know, I'm kind of waiting around
for Kit. . . . Otherwise I'd have this little baby saying, 'Hello, Mama,
how are you? . . . Where's Papa, by the way?' "
   The women laughed.
   "Papa in the Sky," Ruth said.
   She was a Christian.
   When Belle got Ruth home, it was already dark. She liked coming
to this house, she always would, because she and Kit had made love
in it. John and Ruth had been living here three years, but still it

smelled to her like home—like her and Kit's home—and like cumin. She and Kit had bought the house in an estate sale from an Arab dealer. It smelled of cumin because it had been built by a Moroccan after World War I when he'd come to Arizona from the Rif to start a camel business in the Southwest. Belle and Kit had bought the house in 1938, just after the Moroccan's death. Kit called the aroma in the house the smell of antiquity. He said all Arabs smelled that way, that their sweat did. Belle didn't know, but she felt a sense of wonder when she opened the kitchen pantry and found bags the size of feed bags filled w/ cumin and pistachios. She had inherited jars of coriander . . . there was a lot she missed about this house now, especially since Kit had sent the money from New York two months ago to buy a new one. "Buy us some new land," he'd written. Flatland. Near the town. New start. I'm coming home. Belle remembered the camels, too, had died, along w/ the Moroccan. When Kit and Belle had asked the Arab dealer why the herd had perished, he said the Southwest harbors many predators, but worse, the native wind refused to speak the camel's language.

On the Wednesday before Christmas, 1945, Belle walked into her old kitchen w/ Ruth and Bessie, and there was Kit, home from the war, talking w/ Johnnie Chööchökam and sipping a beer.

"Hey, baby," he said.

He swept her up.

"God damn you," she wept.

She didn't have a bit of make-up on, nor a stitch of anything too nice. Her old plaid coat had grease stains on it from the truck, her hands were rough from the cold. . . .

"You feel real good, baby," he told her.

He ran his hands along her back. "A little skinny, huh?" he joked.

"Yeah," she acknowledged shyly.

He ran his hands under her arms. "Still have those bazooms, though." He smiled appreciatively.

"Yeah . . ." she said.

Bessie didn't say a word, but looked at Belle in a way that said: So. *This* is the man. . . .

Kit and Belle rented a house in Flagstaff for the winter, till the foundation for their new house could be dug in the spring. From the beginning, Kit was nothing if not charming and deferential toward both Ruth and Johnnie: the house up on the mesa, the Arab's house, was theirs as far as he was concerned. One night he even signed over the deed to John. "Take it," he said. John refused, but Kit was serious: he hated the high ground, unwelcoming terrain. He said he hated it—he told Belle it looked like the remains of something emptied out. Give him the desert, no high peaks, he said, no ragged interruptions. Mesa land was too unsettling—no water, no fucking plumbing and no ice. There were no fucking people out there, either; no bars, no place to go to, you were it. It was not something he needed a reminding of, this desolation in mankind. He had no need to be reminded it was coming, fucking desolation in mankind. It was coming, The End, why fuck w/ it. Why fuck w/ the point of view of the world as it had been, was meant to be, on flatland, down below, where there were wet sweaty places and strip joints. . . .

That winter Kit's war novel was published, the book he'd stayed in London and New York to write, *The Conflagration of Round-Eyed Boys*. He expected *Conflagration* to reclaim the critical acceptance that he'd compromised before the war by writing *Hot Tickets*. He told Belle this book was going to win the Pulitzer; all winter he claimed expectations for it, sometimes admitting even a Nobel was possible. The story was that of a rewritten war, w/ Japan and Germany the victors: four atomic bombs are dropped—on Boston, Baltimore, Kiev and Yalta—and the Japanese invent a gas that renders round-eyed children sterile. Critics found the story "bizarre, outlandish." They found the quality of writing "juvenile." The publisher printed a first run of two thousand copies and w/in a month of publication, the book had been forgotten.

Kit was humiliated. He drank, he stormed, he threatened to reveal conspiracies. Belle had never had a gift for soothing Kit, and everything she did to try to cheer him up made matters worse. He laughed at her; she knew he didn't mean to—it was silly to expect a fancy dessert to cheer Kit up, it *was* dumb. She was dumb. He made her feel inadequate. It seemed the only person, really, who could cheer Kit up or calm him down was Johnnie Chööchökam . . . so Belle made sure they saw a lot of Johnnie. The four of them—Ruth, Johnnie, Kit and Belle—spent almost every evening of the winter going out or coming over to each other's houses, talking, drinking. The two men seemed to do each other good—John had been depressed since Philip's death, and more depressed since Ruth had told him she could not bear children any more. Johnnie worked sometimes, but in the winter, most of the work was of a meditative kind. He fulfilled communal obligations to the tribe, but most of his time was free to spend w/ Kit, riding around, talking and hunting. Kit put John in charge of the construction for the new house, drew the plans w/ him. John hired a crew of two more men, both Hopis, and through the spring Kit spent his time w/ them outdoors, in manual labor. Other Indians would drop by the building site afternoons and help; the women brought down food. Belle was happy through that spring. In April, John brought in a man from Nevada, a Mexican named Sanchez, who wired the house for them w/out a permit. Belle found herself alone w/ him one morning in the space that would become the kitchen so she asked him, "Hey, d'you ever hear of anybody ever eating a whole light bulb? You think it could be done?" "Sure," he said. "Is easy. I'll do it for you sometime." He stripped a wire w/ his teeth and smiled at her, and Belle decided she liked Sanchez.

That spring, as work on the house progressed, Kit asked John more and more about the Hopi rituals. He drew him out. He asked John about the history, how the customs had evolved. What Johnnie didn't know, Kit made him *want* to know: the meaning of the kivas, the four sacred colors, the incantations of the Bear Clan, Snake Clan, Beaver Clan, Kachinas—the mysteries, the rites of men, the ecstasies, the drugs. There were no drugs in Hopi rites, so Kit invented them. He was possessed of an apocalyptic vision. When Johnnie introduced Kit to the old men of the tribe and when Kit had heard those old men to the end, Kit turned to other ends, the Pueblos and their mescal buttons, the crazy Zuñis. His curiosity was not the kind that honors the confessor; it knew no loyalty except to prove what it set out to prove: in 1947 Kit wrote *Tokpela: The First World.* It was the first of his "Emergence" books, based on the sacred Hopi and the ancient Anasazi doctrines. Over the years the books gained an enormous following among the young on college campuses. They promulgated a doxology of nihilism, disembodied sex and habituation to induced hallucination. In the first book, *Tokpela,* a Kachina god is consumed by his desire for a fair-haired mortal soldier, a white man named Kit—Kit Carson. In order to seduce the blond and virile Kit, the Kachina god first tortures him, then buggers him, then offers him the Spider Woman, then buggers him again, then gives him drugs that change his Form and proffer him a little Truth. Kit Carson, the character, displays an endless appetite for all this, especially the buggering; and the book was a best seller that year. The next year Kit wrote *Tokpa: The Second World*; then *The Emergence to Kuskurza, the Third World*; then *The Emergence from Kuskurza into Tuwaqachi—the Fourth World, World Complete* in 1951. By then the real Kit had betrayed Johnnie Chööchökam totally. Belle could visit Bessie on the reservation only when Johnnie wasn't there. Johnnie was ready to kill Kit. What Kit had done for the Hopis set them back two hundred years, or worse: the Navajo were moving onto Hopi land and threatening a land dispute. What good did it do Hopis to be characterized as a people who smoked *wa-wa* leaf in caves and worshiped gods who lusted after white-assed U.S. Army scouts? Belle told John no one would take the books that seriously; but Kit was asked to speak at colleges, and *The Emergence from Kuskurza into Tuwaqachi* was required reading in some Comparative Religion classes. The series was a major work for Kit—it changed his life. Sometimes he thought he *was* Kit Carson. He wore silk shirts open to the chest when he made speeches; he wore hand-tooled leather belts w/ silver inlays, smoked cheroots. He let his sideburns grow, let young girls touch him. He smoked a lot of dope, his new-found drug, and liked to walk up to a speaking lectern and announce, "Kit Carson's . . . feeling . . . *very* . . . turned on to you *all* this evening . . ." and listen to the young girls scream. . . .

The Indian community closed down to Kit and Belle. As much as Belle might argue the betrayal wasn't hers, she knew they had to think it was. A man and woman were not *two*, two things, a master and his dog. A dog could bite his master, she could not bite Kit. What Kit had done w/ John was something he had done before, would always do—he'd won a heart away, and then abandoned it. Belle felt she'd put her own heart up on the mesa, placed it there, the way the Hopis tie an eagle to the roof. They keep the eagle tied for thirty days and give it presents—little dolls, a little bow and arrow—and then they sacrifice it. They tie the eagle feathers to young willow sticks and plant the branches in the ground. At night the clouds scud off the San Francisco Peaks on wind that rakes the valley, and the eagle feathers slap and sputter in the wind—a way of praying. The prayer itself exists between the spirit of the feathers and the spirit of the wind, both good; the only thing required of the individual is to bring the two together, in the ritual: the Hopis know no sin. They do not understand the concept, they've no native word for it. Their native word for grief describes a state of psychic chasm between one's self and earth—it is the same word for the state of being not yet born. It is presumed that to be alive is to be in a state of grace, if one is Hopi.

Belle wished she could believe as they did that the ritual, the walking upright, would suffice. She sought an expiating act. She took sweet cakes in a basket tied w/ ribbons up to Bessie. She took presents to the children, tied four ears of corn, the sacred number, on her own front door. She went up when she could to help w/ washing and w/ sewing, and the Hopi men in passing trucks or cars still waved and flashed their headlights when she saw them on the road. But trust had dematerialized. Trust exists in the abstract, anyway; but when it's there, one feels it. She still felt Bessie's trust, but not as absolutely as before. She began to think she understood people who crawled to shrines on sharp stones on their knees to beg forgiveness. The Hopi people kept her at a distance, and the Anglos found her sullen.

More and more the only people that she saw were drinkers. The men and women who would come to visit them all drank. When they went out, they sat w/ other people and all drank. Belle would nurse a beer or two, and usually w/in the hour everyone would lapse away into a louder, rowdy world and leave her. These people would come and go, repeat themselves, stay overnight, get sick, get weepy, get maudlin, get violent, get fresh or get arrested. Living in the orbit of an alcoholic was an unremitting psychodrama. There was the daily pelting of emotional debris, as if one's orbit were a shuttle back and forth and back and forth between two uninhabitable places through one interminable asteroid belt. There was never a calm season. There was no such thing as spring. Kit started to bounce in and out of jail, in strange cities. He insulted neighbors and tradespeople. He was obscene toward women. He was cruel and jealous toward his fellow writers; mean to students. He left his publisher for more money at another publishing house, then left the second house for yet a third. He broke contracts. He wrote letters and made phone calls when he was drunk, declaring war on everyone. He broke things, like plate-glass windows. He was an abominable guest. He couldn't sleep. He lost his driver's license. He accepted payment in advance to make a speech and never showed. He started to undress on live television. He was outrageous and amusing in a strange bar, but at his fifty-second birthday celebration in December 1954, Belle looked around the room at all the strangers, people she had never seen before, and she realized there were only two people in Kit's life who'd known him longer than two weeks who would confess to being fond of him—herself and Sanchez.

"Someone left the radio on in the truck," she tried to explain. He wouldn't listen.

"Sanchez!" she insists. "*What happened?*"

His eyes are red, red-rimmed from crying.

"*Es el fin,*" he whispers. "I'm finished."

"What do you mean? Come on. Kit's done this before . . . what are you saying?"

"Nothing."

"*Sanchez!*"

"*De nada.*"

"Come on, get up. Get up. Help me move him from the truck. Come on."

"No."

"*Please.*"

"No. *Váyase.* Go away. *Déjeme en paz. . . .*"

"You can't . . . do this."

"It's done."

"Tomorrow, then. Tomorrow everything will—"

"No."

"What did he say to you? Did he say something? He didn't mean it. Whatever it was—you know Kit. He didn't mean it. It's the booze. It's just booze, that's all. It's not real. You know he loves you. He depends on you. Please. Come on. Did he say something? What did he say?"

Sanchez stared a long time at the wall. He was an emotional man; a small, intensely loyal man.

Belle was surprised, each time she came up to this house, how clean it was. In her mind, she confused emotional intensity w/

turmoil, but Sanchez's house was always in order. He made his bed
every day. He scrubbed his pans. He left his boots outside.

"*El es . . .* possessed. *Poseso. Monstruoso.*"

"*What happened?*"

"Nothing: the same: he's going to blow the world up, yes, O.K.?
Ka-bloom. *El final.* The atomic bomb. O.K."

"You're not making sense."

"Give it up, missus. Is over."

"What are you talking about?"

"Is done."

Sanchez rolled his head toward Belle and started to cry.

"That girl is fourteen, *valgame Dios*: a baby. *Una virgen*—"

"You don't know that—"

"*I* know it! I *heard* her! I *left* them out there—"

"You're lying, this is all a mistake, there's a reason—"

"Do you have *eyes?* Did you see her? Do you know who she is?"

"Liar!"

"Anna Paweki from Oraibi. Bessie Chööchökam's goddaugh-
ter—"

"You fucking spic!" Belle tore at him. "You fucking spic! You
fucking spic! You fucking spic! You fucking spic, you fucking spic,
you fucking spic . . ."

What did it mean to Belle to have a daughter? she thought, looking
down at baby Cathy. At first it had been very hard. Hard not to
wonder what the other babies might have looked like. Hard to nurse.
Hard to pay attention to the baby and to everything and everybody
else. She hadn't nursed. She couldn't. She'd be out somewhere and
her milk would come down and her shirt would get all wet and men
who stared at her already would stare at her more. Kit didn't want
the baby. He hadn't wanted her to have it in the first place, but she
thought a son might calm him down. The worst was how she felt
when she was pregnant, like a cow. Cow Belle. Then the baby's
head had entered her canal wrong and the doctor had to turn it w/
the forceps and the little thing looked like a monster w/ a black eye
on one side and a purple bruise behind its ear, on the other. This
is a record ugly baby, Kit observed. The kid's pudenda were all
swollen. She wouldn't sleep, the kid. Catherine the Great Mouth,
Kit had called her. She wouldn't nurse. There was an interval of

tenderness when Kit approached Belle's breasts himself—but finally
Belle had bought a plastic toy that held a bottle which she put down
next to Cathy in her playpen so she wouldn't have to hold her or
wake her up to feed her in the night. Kit liked Cathy a little bit,
Belle thought. There were times when Kit looked like he liked her
a little bit. Sometimes she thought she could almost date the trouble
from the day of Cathy's birth. Before that, everything had seemed
O.K. He hadn't flaunted his affairs w/ other women. He hadn't
wanted younger girls. He hadn't threatened her w/ leaving. Now
everything was different. Kit had left. He'd packed up the truck w/
his army blankets and his bourbon and he'd left w/ the young girl.
Belle sat there staring down at Cathy sleeping on her little bed and
wondered what it meant to her to have a baby: not a thing. She
wondered if it would do them any good to put a pillow over her and
hold it there for a couple of minutes. No. It would not do any good.
The baby's feet, she thought, reminded her of pincushions. . . .

Kit had taken the new truck, so she drove the old one to Bessie's
house up to Oraibi w/ the baby. Before she left, Bessie clutched her
wrist and said, "What are you doing?"
Belle didn't say she had the rifle in the truck.
"Where are you going?" Bessie asked.
"I know where he is," Belle said.
"Leave it. Let them be. Where is Sanchez?"
"Gone."
"Hold still, then. Leave them. Stay here for the night. . . ."
"He's capable of doing it *again*."
"You make no sense. . . ."
"To *her*, you understand?"
"No sense at all . . ."
How can two women ever make sense between them? Belle won-
dered. It's all unspoken, every bit of it. We function on our senses.
Wolves. Cats. Rabbits. Nervous, twitching senses. Does a cat say
to another, Do you understand me? She detested language, she
discovered. She was never good w/ it, the way her thoughts welled
up. Did she *love* him? Did she love him: what was that?

Belle knew what road to take out of Flagstaff—she knew where
to look for him: *Alamogordo*, the Trinity site, the site of Kit's apoc-

alypse. In recent months, Kit had become a man possessed w/ a final vision, a vision of apocalypse and rebirth. He'd honed his sanity to a bent edge, a scimitar, the sword of ultimate destructiveness. The atomic bomb was all he talked about; the replication of God's power in the splitting of an atom. The physicists had done it, cracked it open, laid it bare right there in the desert outside Alamogordo, at a place called Trinity. Couldn't she see it? he'd demanded. *God was speaking to them*. Couldn't everybody see it? For months he had been talking about having to get clearance to stand exactly on the testing site. He'd written congressmen. He'd written Oppenheimer, too, and Vannevar Bush and Edward Teller, Enrico Fermi and General Leslie Groves of the Manhattan District. They all thought he was crazy. He'd traced psychiatrists who'd been there the morning of July 16, 1945, to observe the scientists. He hounded them for their descriptions of the incandescent fire column and the trembling earth. It was his mission, he maintained, to witness it, to feel it, to be transported to the center of all power.

Belle took a road east that night toward Alamogordo—a desert road, black or blue both night and day and frequented by spectres in the guise of long-eared rabbits; *jack*rabbits, she knew. The sky seemed a playground made for mystics. The earth was flat and running, a place forgotten by man. Cactus plants, black sculptural forms, looked like hitchhikers in her headlights. The moon came out. She knew the rocks held serpents, knew the desert was a death chant, knew her flesh was no resistance to its sirens. Her reflection, where she saw it in the windshield, was composed, a good picture, she thought.

She followed Route 40 East out of Flagstaff through Walnut Canyon, onto Winslow, through the Petrified Forest. There was a back road from Winslow, across the desert to Socorro, near the Rio Grande in New Mexico, a distance of 250 miles, but the clutch was slipping in the old truck, and she was afraid to try it on a single tank of gas. Instead she took a long way through Allantown, up to Gallup. A cowhand tending gas would say later he'd sold her a tank of ethyl-extra at ten o'clock that night, and he'd testify that he remembered her. She was something to remember, he implied. Blond. Really built. She'd dipped a blue bandana in his water can, he'd say, and wiped her neck off w/ it and then she'd wiped that place between a woman's breasts that gets real hot, above their hearts. Gallup was fifteen miles east of the Arizona line, on a uranium deposit. She'd asked the cowboy the best route into Alamogordo, and he said he'd never heard of it. They looked it up together on the map, and he was going to make a move on her, but someone else drove in, and when he turned around again, she'd driven out.

By midnight she'd made it into Albuquerque and turned south on 25 where it drops down from Santa Fe along the Rio Grande. At Socorro she took the road southeast through Carrizozo, Ruidoso and Cloudcroft, toward Alamogordo. She was driving due south now, between the Pecos and Rio Grande rivers through the land called La Jornada del Muerto—The Day's Journey of a Dead Man. Pine forests loomed black in the distance to her right and left along the Sierras Oscuro and the Little Burros in the Sacramento Peaks, but straight ahead of her was nothing—desert, road, the Milky Way spilling overhead, Orion upside down near the horizon. There was no one on the road that night except her, but suddenly she had to pull the truck up on the sand along a barren stretch because her heart had started pounding. She rolled the window down and leaned against the steering wheel. She hadn't had a spell like this since she'd been a girl living in the house w/ Vern and Willa. That first night she'd started taking money that belonged to Vern, she'd wakened in a sweat just after midnight, her heart pounding, and moved the coins she'd stolen from their hiding place to what seemed like a better hiding place. She remembered how her hands had shaken in that stuffy house and how she'd hurried back to bed, afraid they'd heard her. She opened the truck door now and swung her feet onto the sand. She reached around and took the gun and turned the truck lights off. She held her breath a moment, then she walked across the sand onto the desert about thirty yards. She raised the gun and sighted toward Orion. She hadn't used it since she'd frightened off a bobcat come to drink from the *tinaja* next to their house three months ago. She squeezed the trigger and fell back a step w/ its report. She lowered it, reloaded, and then fired it again. The sound rolled from her like a fireball. She fired a third time, and then, because three is a superstitious number, the number in a trinity, she shot a fourth time, straight up overhead, into the air.

The first motor court she came to on the road between Cloudcroft and Alamogordo looked closed up and abandoned. Five miles down the road from that she passed a building marked "Otero County Sheriff's Office," and she saw there was a light on in the back. At the next motor court she saw Kit's truck parked by a cabin, and she switched the lights off and allowed her truck to drift down to a halt beyond it. She left the key in the ignition and got out and took the gun. A light was on that showed plaid curtains at the window, and she heard a radio. She hadn't thought what she would do if the door was locked, so it seemed a natural thing when it was open, and she walked right in. On the left, beside the door that went into the bathroom, the girl was sitting in a chair, eating from a bag of popcorn. She looked up at Belle when Belle walked in. On the right there was the bed, and Kit was sitting in it. A wrinkled graying sheet lay twisted on his legs and genitals.

"Hey, baby," he said. He didn't seem at all surprised. He was smoking nonchalantly, and Belle could tell how drunk he was. "If this is about money," Kit began to say, "you can just—"

Belle raised the rifle, pointed it at his chest and shot him. She saw the sheet drink up his blood. She heard the girl's high-pitched screaming—little blasts—above the radio. Nothing moved, nobody noticed, as she turned the truck around and drove back up the road to the Otero County Sheriff's Office. She walked in holding the warm rifle in one hand, and Sheriff Morgan smiled at her and stood up and fiddled w/ the waistband of his khaki pants until she said, "My name is Belle Benû. I've just killed my husband."

She was held in the Otero County Jail in Alamogordo pending a criminal complaint for a preliminary hearing by the district attorney in Las Cruces. She had confessed the murder to the sheriff, to two state policemen, to the justice of the peace, who refused her bail, and finally to the district attorney himself. Her story was consistently the same, though she became a little incoherent toward its end, after a while. There was no question of malice aforethought, the D.A. told the press, who in their turn were elevating Belle and the shooting to a status of celebrity. There was a problem, though, a minor one: The shot Belle fired punctured Kit's right lung and tore into his liver. He was alive. Given the condition of his liver from his years of drinking, he was not expected to survive. A healthy man might have pulled through. If he dies, a newspaper headline asked: "What Really Killed Him—Booze, or This Woman?"

Kit died August 4, and Belle was arraigned the next day. She was permitted some street clothes, but she said she didn't want them. She wore a prison dress and stood handcuffed to listen to the charge of first-degree murder under the Criminal Code of the State of New Mexico, Article Two, Homicide, Section 40A-2-2 ". . . when all circumstances of the killing show a wicked and malignant heart."

As soon as the judge finished reading the charge, Belle murmured, "Guilty."

No bond was permitted.

A trial date was set for the last Monday in November, after Thanksgiving.

Several defenses were offered in the interim, but Belle refused them. A rich aunt, a mystery writer from New York, sent an expensive lawyer out to see her, but she wouldn't talk to him. She wouldn't talk to anyone. Bessie came to see her once before the trial, and one time afterward. She was the only person Belle would talk to. "This lady comes for Cathy soon," she told Belle in October.

"What lady?"

"Family. Nice."

"What lady?"

"Nice. Nice lady. Henrietta."

"Not Willa?"

"No. No one named Willa."

"I don't want her left with Willa."

"No one name of Willa. Henrietta. Very nice. Your aunt, she says. She has babies, too. . . ."

"Bessie, listen. If I don't get the electric chair, I want you to bring me something."

Bessie looked down at her own knotted hands. "No," she said.

"I would for you," Belle said.

The women stared at each other through the barrier that separated them until, imperceptibly, Bessie agreed.

When she was sentenced, finally, in January, applause broke out in the press box, and she fainted. The judge reported that at a late moment during the trial the D.A. had decided to stipulate against the death penalty, and she was sentenced to life imprisonment, which in New Mexico meant she would be eligible for parole in ten years.

They moved her to the state penitentiary in Santa Fe on January 25, 1956, and ten days after that John, Ruth and Bessie Chööchökam

were let into a square green room to visit her. Belle had spent so
many hours in their company she understood at once why they had
had to come together, as a family. She understood John's nervous-
ness at having to say so much in code because of the matron stationed
at the door: "Boy, they really search you over, before they let you
in here," he said good-naturedly. He paced around. Belle nodded.
Bessie didn't say a thing.

"I brought you this," Ruth said. It was a woven blanket. "They
ripped it," she said, "right here. . . ." She pointed. "And here . . . but
you can fix it with some thread. . . ."

Belle didn't speak.

Bessie sat stock-still, not speaking either, staring at her, holding
a sad bunch of flowers that looked like Queen Anne's lace.

"Can we get you anything?" John asked. "What do you need?
How 'bout books?" A shadow crossed his face as he remembered
Kit. "Toothpaste? Anything?"

Belle shook her head.

"How about shampoo?" Ruth asked.

Belle stared at Bessie.

"Mom remembered how much you like flowers," John said. "There
wasn't much, this time of year. . . ."

"They're nice," Belle said.

"We had an awful time bringing them in," he said. "I guess not
many women in here get too many flowers. . . ."

Bessie handed them to Belle. They were tied together w/ a plait
of straw.

"Next time we'll try to bring a plant for you," Ruth said. "Do
you have a window?"

"No."

"Oh."

"Maybe a plastic plant," John said.

"Yes, that sounds good," Belle said. She touched the dried lacy
flowers w/ her fingertip. She wanted to ask them how she had to do
it, but she couldn't bring herself well enough under control.

"How . . ." she started to say. Her voice trailed off.

"Everybody's real fine," John volunteered. "Uh, we had a letter
last week from Henrietta about Cathy. She's still cutting her teeth,
how about that? I guess she's going to be a late-teething baby, you

know, some babies are like that. She still puts everything into her mouth, Aunt Henrietta writes. She tries to eat everything."

"Yes," Belle said. "I knew that."

She looked from John to Bessie. She needed to know how long it would take. She expected it would not be swift, that would be too much to ask; but she needed to have some idea how long she'd have to wait.

"I hope Cathy learns to count soon," Belle said. "Learns to tell time, I mean."

"Yes, me, too," John said.

"She could tell time from one o'clock to four o'clock last time I saw her," Belle said.

"Oh, she can probably go all the way to five or six by now, don't you think so, Ruth?" John asked.

"Five or six," Ruth said. "Six hours."

Belle looked at Bessie.

"Walter Greene says hello," John said. "He still gets awful *headaches*. . . ." He paused a moment. Ruth stared at the floor. "And remember Mary Kwani?" John went on. "Those stomach pains? An ulcer. She had an operation, and they patched it right up. . . . Boy! It gives me shivers to think where we'd be without medical science. . . ."

"Me, too," Belle agreed. She looked around at them, then stood up.

There was a moment when the matron seemed to want to take her flowers from her, and Belle felt Bessie tense across the room. She turned to her old friend a last time. Bessie held her gaze until Belle had to turn away. She smiled at Ruth and John. "Thank you all for coming," she said. "You still smell like cumin, Johnnie," was the last thing she could say.

The photographers got in next morning to record the naked body w/ the twisted hand holding the rosary. "I heard her twice during the night," the guard later said: "Jesus, you know, we hear a lot of stuff here, people cryin', but I thought I heard this groaning sound down there at her end of the corridor a couple times, so I went down there to look. She seemed O.K. Lying all curled up, sleeping like a baby, you know? She's new here, so I didn't know her habits, plus when you're new you get a lot of nightmares, right? A little after that I heard her call out for something, so I showed some light in there. She looked kinda sick, you know, her face was all white and she was sweatin' so I said, 'You feelin' sick?' She licks her lips sort of, you know, and then she says, 'I'm sorry. I guess I had a nightmare, Father.' And I said, 'What'd you call me?' And she says, 'Could I see a Father, please, I think I want to pray. . . .' And I said, 'No, lady, you can't see no *Father* in the state pen at two o'clock in the middle of the friggin' night!' You know? I mean, what was I supposed to do? You tell me. She didn't make a sound the whole rest of the night. I mean, Jesus. Here she is this morning. My wife, man, my wife is going to kill me. I mean, I used to be a Catholic, but my wife still is, you know? You watch. My wife is going to say it's like my *fault* about her *soul*, and everything. . . ."

On the cover of *Life* there is a picture of her as she was the year Kit wrote about her in *Hot Tickets*. The picture is in black and white, but still you sense the gold color of her hair. Her head is thrown back, and she's laughing. Inside, in the story, there are prints of Max's early paintings of her; photos of Max and Kit, alone; photos of Kit w/ Belle—and then there is the final photograph of her inside the cell that morning.

The autopsy showed that she'd been poisoned by *Cicuta maculata*, the water hemlock, something like the poison given Socrates. What remained of her after the autopsy was cremated: it was a ceremony nothing like the sacrifice of eagles.

April 29, 1982
Lucy Hastings Clinic
Princeton, New Jersey

⟢▬▬⟣

10

THE TRUTH ABOUT CATHY

A STORY BY ELLERY McQUEEN

IN THE HISTORY OF THE WORLD, there have been 6,853,196,427 women—not counting Cathy.

Not counting Cathy, you could take the women in the History of the World and you could lay them end to end and they would be 5,451,027 miles long; or you could lay them the whole length of the Equator and they would stack up 60 meters high, which is slightly higher than Niagara Falls. Or you could take the women in the History of the World and lay them end to end on the Equator and they would stack up sixty meters high, but counting Cathy, one of them would roll off from the top by accident, and come to grief. Or one of them would fail to comprehend the instructions in the general convocation of the Women in the History of the World and show up on a different latitude instead, and wonder why she had been stranded there, alone. The person, both times, would be Cathy, who, in a legion of the lost sex, is doubly lost. If one had to draw her, she would be a smudged stick figure made of short straight lines. If written, she would take the form bookkeepers make, jotting down a double zero when just one would do.

How can there be a quantity that equates to double zero, and where does it exist in relation to the quantity of single zero?

This is a question Cathy thinks about.

She thinks about the nature of things, their physical composition, what they would look like upside down and why they are the way they are. Because she lives alone, most of her life proceeds upon a fertile plane of active thinking. When she is at work or when she is among a lot of people or on the Number 6 bus uptown in winter, she doesn't look as if she's thinking, but she is. Certain people see she's thinking—certain people seem to sense a soul engaged in silent meditation, and these people always seem to single Cathy out on buses early in the morning or on subway platforms late in the afternoon to commend religious pamphlets to her. This is one reason she bought the roller skates to go to work—first-cause apologists do not lie in wait for people going by on roller skates. "Keep moving" is a good motto, she discovered, to avoid people who want to sell you a small bottle w/ the tears of Christ's own mother inside or who want to tell you that the proof of God's existence is w/in the fact that infinite regression of the universe could never have been possible. *Something must have come before* is the problem Cathy stumbles over when she thinks about the universe. *Time has not always existed* is another problem. New York City streets are no great places to think about such things while roller-skating, but still Cathy thinks about what, if the universe is finite, lies on the other side.

"New Jersey" is what her cousin Ellery would say.

She likes her cousin Ellery; she likes all her cousins and her aunts, but she's afraid of them. She hasn't found a way of really talking to them, the same way people haven't found a way to talk about real art. All the people Cathy works w/ think they know about real art. They think that when they talk to one another they are talking about art. It's just like women, Cathy thinks. Or like trying to keep peace between two nations using words of different histories and two different meanings. Her cousin Ellery is one woman that she's tried to talk to about this because Ellery has seen a lot of crazy people in a psychiatric clinic being talked to in the English language as if

someone believed that talking could ever be a cure. Lonely people
never get to talk; they get to think, and thinking isn't anything that
lonely people need. Lonely people get to watch and look and feel
amused unto themselves in view of tender ironies. They read a lot.
They read street signs. They find their poetry in street signs and their
evening news in eavesdropping. When they go home, there are no
special treats attending them, unless they have been robbed. Cathy
has been robbed six times.

The first time she was robbed, whoever robbed her took her television and her stereo and a plain gold ring her father had once
bought her mother. They even took the little box that it had been
in that said "Talheimer's" on it—"Richmond, Virginia." The next
time she was robbed, whoever robbed her took two Indian rugs that
had once belonged to her mother and all of Cathy's tape cassettes
and her clock radio and the Westbend Fry-Baby she liked to make
her own potato chips in.

Some people are never robbed—her cousin Ellery, for example.
Her cousin Ellery, who when she isn't in a pyschiatric clinic, lives
in an apartment on West Tenth Street, has never been robbed.
Other things have happened to her, but she's never had her apartment ransacked. The third time Cathy was robbed, her apartment
was ransacked. Even the stuffing from the pillow was pulled out,
even the Q-Tips in the Q-Tip box in the medicine cabinet in the
bathroom. The details of this third robbery confounded Cathy; they
defeated her because the destruction of her property, such as it was,
was senseless, and because whoever robbed her the third time took
her electric tea kettle, which she used each day, and all her clothes.
Cathy didn't have a lot of clothes, but she had a lot of memories of
having been places in certain clothes, and she thought of some
garments as postcards on which travel thoughts were jotted down.
More than that, some of the clothes had been her mother's and
she'd maintained them w/ great care for many years and she had
communed w/ them at times in private, silent ways. Sometimes she
almost felt a life from them and thinking where they'd gone, or to
what ragtag end, made her have bad thoughts, made her think the
worst of all society.

After the third robbery, she cut off her hair. Around that time,
someone on the street handed her a pamphlet about Saint Catherine
of Siena, who cut off all her hair and took a vow when she was

seven to remain a virgin all her life and devoted her time to prayer, fasting and other mortifications for which she was made a saint— so Cathy cut off all her hair in hopeful expiation and stopped eating for a while and thought about Saint Catherine. She thought about her mother's clothes, too, and started going to used-clothing stores hoping something of her mother's might turn up. Eventually she bought some things that looked like things that had belonged to her mother. She bought old things that had some built-in reminiscences to foreshorten time. They weren't articles she'd thought about or planned to buy—they were things she picked from need because she felt bereft of antecedents. She also bought a tea kettle to replace the one that had been stolen, but it was the kind of tea kettle she had to heat up on the stove, instead of an electric one, and she kept forgetting it was on, and one day she left it on while she was out and the plastic handle melted down all over the stove top and the tea kettle itself exploded.

This made Cathy wonder why things seem to happen to some people. Why should she have been robbed three times while her cousin Ellery, who lived just sixteen blocks away, had not been robbed? Someone suggested perhaps it was the neighborhood, but Cathy knew it was something about her. Something personal to her. Something that had to do w/ her feeling that she wasn't anyone, that she was a double zero, an invadable space, a blank territory. The two parts of her daily life did not connect in a fulfilling way. The life she lived in thinking, which she dreamed about sharing w/ someone, did not extend itself into the world in which her body lived. She was living in a big old space on Spring Street that her grandfather's estate had settled on her, and it was much too big for her to heat or to redecorate in any way and much too ramshackle and large for her ever to make secure against persons who would break in and steal things from her, but she could not afford to move. Besides, she liked the neighborhood. It was w/in walking distance of her favorite places, and on weekends when Spring and Prince and Wooster Streets filled up w/ people shopping for room-size art to match the sofas in their living rooms, Cathy walked over to the part of town she liked, among the blank warehouses near Duane Street where gray-blue painted cast-iron buildings masqueraded as real stone. There was a little park off Duane Street where she liked to sit and watch the birds and think. The park had benches and a flagpole, but no flag. On the flagpole there was a plaque that said, "This park is the last remnant of greensward of the Annetje Jans farm." Cathy liked the sense the word "greensward" imparted of sitting out in someone's field. The plaque on the flagpole also said that this triangle between Hudson, Duane and Staple streets had later belonged to Trinity Church and that the City of New York had bought it for five dollars in 1795 as a park for public use, and Cathy liked that very much. She liked to think about the men and women and birds who might have come here in the last two hundred years, and she liked to look up at the cast-iron buildings painted to resemble stone and wonder about all of history's people and their problems. It didn't help to think about history too much, because sometimes it made her feel too small and insignificant, but other times it helped, because it made her feel her problems were too small and insignificant, too. Sometimes she walked from SoHo w/ the hope that she might meet someone. When she told her cousin Ellery that sometimes she liked to walk over to the park in the hope of meeting someone, Ellery asked her, "How badly do you want to meet someone?"

"I'd like it, that's all," Cathy said.

"Well, if you'd like to, then you have to make yourself accessible. You have to go places where you'll meet the kind of person that you'd like to meet. No one in New York has ever heard of Duane Park. What sort of person do you think you're going to meet in Duane Park?"

"Someone who likes birds. I like birds," Cathy attempted to explain. "I don't know why I like birds. I guess I like them because I read that they're related to the dinosaurs. They're related to the dinosaurs even more than lizards are."

Cathy tried to tell her cousin that it was hard for her to meet people who would talk to her about birds. She tried to tell her that even though she'd changed her name to Cathy Bennett, people at the parties she was asked to always found out she was Max Benû's granddaughter, which ruined things. People asked her, "What was he really like?" and there was nothing she could say. People at work always introduced her as "Cathy Bennett, Max Benû's granddaughter," and then the people to whom she'd just been introduced were more intent on how they should react to his paintings and her relation to him than they were about how they might say a word or two that would pertain to her.

This was funny, Cathy thought, because she knew as much about Max as a canary knows about a dinosaur. Even when it came to her own father and her mother, she knew as much as a canary knows *in toto*, which—after you count how to molt and how to mourn and how to whistle—doesn't come to much. What she would have liked to say or what she tried to say always caught in her throat, and the first time she looked closely at the parakeets in the display window at the bird store on Bleecker Street at West Eleventh, she knew she had an affinity w/ birds because the parakeets have hollow bones that roll around inside their mouths through which they "speak," but that, most of the time, make them appear to be choking.

One day she was standing outside the store on Bleecker, eating a bag of chips and looking at the parakeets, and a clerk who looked a little like Elvis Costello because he wore horn-rimmed glasses came outside and said, "Come here, you really ought to hear something."

"Who, me?" asked Cathy.

When Cathy went inside, she knew something was going to happen to her. When she looked around, it looked okay, but something somewhere seemed a little funny, and she wasn't too sure what it was. Then she heard it and saw it all at once: a yellow canary w/ a touch of blue—her favorite colors, blue and yellow—singing on a little swing as if it were a piece, or the caprice, of sound itself.

"Oh, geez," Cathy said.

The canary had a little head the size of a cat's-eye marble, and its beak looked like a floribunda thorn. The canary looked at Cathy and took a side step on its little swing, as if inviting her to come and take a seat bside it.

"How much is that canary over there?" she asked the clerk.

"The one who's singing?"

"Yeah."

"Well . . . what's your name, and maybe then I'll tell you."

"Annette."

"Annette. He's sixty-five dollars, Annette. My name is Tim."

"And how much is the cage and all his stuff?"

"Oh, I think I could give you a full package, with the bird, for, let's say, a hundred and eighty dollars without tax. There's tax."

"And food and all?"

"Food and everything. And an instruction book to boot, Annette."

"And the swing."

"The swing, too. And a one-year health certificate. You live around here, don't you? I've noticed you."

Cathy smiled a thin smile at the bird-store clerk named Tim because she knew that he was going to ask her out. She didn't want to go. Not w/ him, especially, though he seemed like a nice guy; not w/ anybody. It would be nice to be at home, listening to her new canary. It would take time to learn its habits, maybe months, and even then there might be things her new canary would be doing while she was at work or while she was asleep that she would never see or learn about. If there can be a dark side of the moon, she thought, then perhaps the things we don't know in the universe exist on a dark side. Perhaps the universe itself has one side facing toward us and another side that's unrevealed. *How would this work?* she wondered: would the universe be disk-shaped or spherical or concave like a sugar bowl? She knew the clerk named Tim was just about to ask her out, and she felt alarmed and put-upon, as if he'd suddenly begun to tell her about a terminal disease or a massacre.

Evenings coming home from work she'd see smart women shopping after work, shopping for a bottle of wine w/ which to treat themselves, or shopping for berries—and the sight of these women made her stop dead on her roller skates and stare, because she didn't have the potential to be like them, a piece was missing somewhere in her, used up before she was born, her passion pirated away from her by both her parents. But now she'd have someone to talk to about birds: a real bird. Now she'd have someone that she could try to say the things to she had tried to say: *I'm a freak. I'm weird. I'm a sexual monstrosity.* The truth is she was twenty-eight years old and a virgin.

The men that Cathy had been w/ had been real slobs about the way they kept themselves; they always had a least one truly disgusting thing about themselves that Cathy couldn't get out of her mind when they brought up the idea of sexual intercourse. Somehow she always ended up w/ guys w/ scalp problems and sinusitis. Or guys w/ very hairy arms. Since her first disaster thirteen years ago w/ Tony Zambolla at Rehoboth Beach, Cathy had been telling guys that she couldn't have sexual intercourse w/ them because she was in the first two heavy bleeding days of her menstrual period. It had worked for a long time until sometime in the seventies when more guys than ever started saying, "I don't mind, if it doesn't bother *you*," and *that*, she thought, was the full influence of women's lib in her life. But then, thank God, a thing called toxic shock had come along, so Cathy said she had her period *and* she had toxic shock and might go into a coma if a foreign object, any foreign object, was inserted at this time. Most guys were so entirely stupid about the subject that they believed her.

She was lucky no one ever forced himself on her or got rough w/ her, although she thought that this had to do more w/ her attitude than w/ a thing like luck. Her attitude was to do whatever the guy wanted her to do, up to a certain point. She was an easygoing kind of person who presented no resistance except toward one thing, and the men she had been w/ hadn't found that too unusual—the men she had been w/ starting from the first disaster right on through the last had failed to notice that as a partner Cathy wasn't a participant.

Cathy would not have thought herself so unusual over the years if she'd never had it on good authority from the beginning that some women enjoy sexual intercourse w/ men—and the good authority she'd had it on was Scooter. Scooter liked sexual intercourse w/ men—Scooter had liked sexual intercourse w/ men right from the start, which is something Cathy knew firsthand because she'd been there, the next sand dune over, on the afternoon that she and Scoot had both been introduced to sexual intercourse w/ the Zambolla brothers of Rehoboth Beach and she'd heard Scooter's noises. She hadn't known enough about sexual intercourse at first to recognize the sounds she thought were sounds of torment as the sound that Scooter lent to her expression of erotic pleasures, but she'd heard the sound again from different women in movies and on disco records and she'd heard the sound approximated by enough men to know it must have been the sound of pleasure, though it didn't sound that way. Things might have taken a different turn for Cathy if she'd been allowed to grow into a state of wanting to have sexual intercourse w/ men naturally, the way things in nature grow, or things existing in the universe, instead of being led into a situation that she didn't want to be in w/ Tony Zambolla just because Scoot wanted to be in a situation w/ Tony's better-looking brother Nick.

Cathy didn't even like Tony Zambolla. He was skinny and near-sighted and asthmatic, and he didn't like the outdoors. The outdoors made him paranoid about mosquitoes and black flies, he said. The outdoors was where they were, though, w/ Scoot and Nick over on another sand dune, and as soon as Tony spread out the army blanket and got undressed he said he was especially paranoid about mosquitoes and black flies getting near his penis, so he smeared himself all over, head to toe, w/ bug repellent lotion from the army-navy store. They kissed a little while and petted, and then Tony directed Cathy's head down to his pelvis and indicated she should kiss him there and take him in her mouth, and after she had had him in her mouth for about five seconds, she got this really sour taste on all her tastebuds, and then she started to notice that her lips were tingling w/ the sour taste, and then she lost the feeling in her lips from something in the bug repellent. After that, she lost the feeling in her tongue, so she was not exactly aware of what her mouth was doing, but Tony seemed to like it a lot and it was as much relief to Cathy as to him when he ejaculated. He held her tightly and said, "Oh, darling," and Cathy pressed her chin against his chest to try to restore feeling in her lower face and wondered to herself if she'd been poisoned. Scoot was over on the next sand dune making noises, and she wondered if Scoot had been poisoned, too. On the ride back to town in Nick Zambolla's Buick, Cathy kept pulling on her lip, and when they got out of the car and waved good-bye to Tony and Nick, Cathy collapsed in the front yard of the summer house and rolled around on the stiff weeds and crabgrass, laughing. Scoot swung her arms wide open and turned around and around, and Cathy felt like hugging her because they'd done it, they'd done *everything* together, even though this latest thing was a *disaster*, but Scoot said, "Oh God! Oh God! Wasn't it *fabulous*? Wasn't it just the living *end*?"

Cathy stopped rolling around and looked at her.

"Tell me this isn't the most fabulous thing you've ever done! Oh God! I feel like a new person! Pinch me! Am I the same old Little Scoot? Oh! I'm just in heaven!"

Cathy didn't know what she should say. Scooter kept going on and on like some long flavor menu in an ice-cream store, each new taste more overstated than the last. Cathy listened, picking at her numbed lip. Finally Scoot shut up long enough for Cathy to say, "I think I better see a doctor, my lip's still numb."

"Oh, you *hot kisser!* Did he French you? Nick Frenched me. Italians are the best, I bet. I have that feeling. How many times did he give it to you? Nick gave it to me twice. He told me he's never met a girl who's good for three times, and I said, 'Well, *we'll see!'* *One* thing I refuse to do is put his you-know-what inside my mouth, though—"

"Yeah," Cathy agreed. "I think that's probably a big mistake. . . ."

She ran a fever that night, and she stayed in bed the next morning while Scoot went to the beach, and she covered for Scoot when Scoot sneaked out at night, and she listened in pained silence to Scoot's love stories when she sneaked back home again. Sometimes the past, when she was growing up w/ Scooter and they had been two equal bodies, seemed as distant as a distant galaxy, and as mysterious. When Scooter talked to her these days, her words seemed to travel over years and years and years before they ever got to Cathy, just as light takes eons traveling between the stars. Scooter had gone off like a rocket while Cathy had stayed carved in stone. Now when Scooter called her up to tell her she'd met someone special and that she thought he might be Mister Right, it took time for the inevitable to cross deep space to Cathy, and when it did, it seemed to crash-land on her surface. The occasion was a family luncheon when Scooter announced to everybody that she was getting married. As soon as Scooter actually announced it, Cathy began to cry. No one else seemed overjoyed about it, either, but no one else sat there and cried.

Millie said, "Great, kid," and Faye said, "Wonderful," and Iris stood up and went behind Scooter and hugged her, and Aunt Sydna said, "To *whom?*" and Ellery, who was an hour late by that time, was lucky to have missed it, because Cathy couldn't keep herself from crying even more when Scoot began to talk about the wedding plans. She wanted to go home and be w/ her parakeet, but she knew she couldn't stand up to the questions the family would ask if she tried to leave, so she sat there not saying anything and watched Scooter talking animatedly as though from some great distance, and she listened to her cousins complain about Ellery never showing up on time, and she drank too much champagne. She ordered something to eat, some kind of fish w/ fried potatoes, and she started to eat the fried potatoes, but Scooter, who was sitting next to her, had ordered braised Nantucket quail and when her dish came w/ the little birds' legs pointing straight up w/ paper booties on them, Cathy had to sip ice water and take deep breaths and look the other way to keep her thoughts from her bird.

"Excuse me," Cathy said and staggered back and stumbled to the ladies' room. There was a lady there dressed in black w/ a white apron. Cathy went into a booth and locked the door and sat down, and cried.

After a long while she saw the woman's shoes beneath the door of the booth and she heard the woman ask, "Does Madam need assistance?"

"No, thank you," Cathy said.

A while after that, she knew Millie had come in because she smelled gardenia, Millie's scent. She heard the sound of running water, then she heard the plink of several coins, then she heard Millie say, "Okay, what's the problem?"

"Nothing," Cathy said.

She couldn't see Millie's feet under the door of the booth, but she could imagine Millie leaning back against the mirror in a characteristic way, her arms crossed beneath her breasts and one hip cocked.

"This woman with towels out here and I would really like to know what is the problem," Millie said.

"Nothing," Cathy answered.

After a while, w/out moving, Cathy said, "Did you ever think something was wrong with you?"

Millie is the sort of person who's real good w/ kids and pets, so she immediately answered, "Yes."

The woman w/ the towels nodded in the affirmative, too.

"Do you ever think about the Universe?"

"Yes," Millie said. The woman w/ the towels sort of shrugged.

"Did you ever think the thing that might be wrong with you is maybe that you're queer?"

"Yes," Millie said. The woman w/ the towels held still.

"When we were kids . . ." Cathy started crying. "Scooter . . ."

"Scooter what?" asked Millie.

"Scooter . . ."

"Okay, that's it," Millie said. "I'm going to punch that bozo in the face right now—"

"She was nice to me," Cathy said. "She was the nicest thing . . ."
She started crying all over again.

Millie ran her hand through her hair. "Cathy, open up," she
said. "I want to see you."

"No."

"I'm asking, Cath."

"I can't."

"You know I can crawl under and come in."

"Well, don't."

"You know I will."

Cathy heard Millie move, and she could see her feet outside the
door of the booth.

"You know what I think about the most?" Cathy said rapidly. "I
think about the Universe. I can't . . . I can't think about it straight.
The thing that bothers me—you know what bothers me? The thing
that bothers me is that some people say it's always expanding, the
Universe, that it's pushing out, you know? But where's it pushing
out to, you understand? What is it pushing up against? You know
what I mean? These people, some of these people say it's finite.
That it ends. It just ends, that's it. See? Mill? What do you think?
I don't get it, see? If it just ends—then what? Get it? If this universe,
I mean the *Universe*—you know?—this *thing* so *big* we can't imagine it, if it has like a *boundary* or like a wall or something that it
just *ends* . . . then . . . what's on the other side, you know?"

"Another universe," Millie explained.

Millie helped her gather up her sweater and her string bag, and
she put Cathy in the front seat of a cab and paid the driver twenty
dollars and told him to take care of her because she'd had too much
to drink. Cathy knew she must have had too much to drink, because
while she was staring at her hands she thought her thumbs resembled
Chinese vegetables.

"Been to a party, huh?" the cab driver said.

"Yeah." She liked being in a cab going down Fifth Avenue at
this time of day. "Do you like birds?" she asked him.

"Sure, they're okay."

She liked to look at the department stores along Fifth Avenue.
She liked the mannequins in Saks and Lord & Taylor's, and she
liked B. Altman's. She liked the name "Benjamin."

"What's your name?" she asked him.

"It's on the card," he said, pointing to his license on the dashboard.

" 'Frank,' " Cathy read.

"That's me."

"Do you ever think about the Universe, Frank?"

He looked at her sidelong.

"Yeah. You drive a cab, you think about the universe." He turned and looked at her full face. "Are you retarded?"

"No."

"You ask retarded questions."

"That's your opinion."

"I'm entitled to it."

"You have nice eyes," she ventured.

"Don't everyone," he said.

"No," Cathy had to tell him, "not many people do."

When he stopped the cab in front of where she lived he said, "You want me to walk you up?"

"No, I'm okay," she said. She got out of the front seat on the passenger side and walked around back. When she reached the curb, Frank called, "You forgot your change."

"Keep it."

"You look like you need it. Are you a dancer or something?"

"Me?" Cathy asked.

"With tap shoes," Frank said.

"No."

"Dancers are skinny like you."

"I roller-skate," Cathy confessed.

"You like baseball?"

"No."

"Oh, I like baseball. You like hot dogs?"

"No."

"What do you like?"

"Potato chips."

"They sell chips at a game. You want to go to a game with me?"

"Not especially."

"Yeah, it's a crummy idea. Games are too long. You want to go to a movie?"

"No."

"How 'bout I take you to dinner?"

"It's too expensive."

"Well, what should we do?"

"What do you want to do?"

"I want to go to a game. You ever been to the Cloisters?"

"No."

"Me neither."

"I don't want to go there."

"Me neither. Hey, I know what you'd like, I went there once as a kid—the Botanical Garden. They got birds."

"They do?"

"I'm pretty sure. If not, we can go to the zoo. Once you're up there, the Bronx is the Bronx."

"Okay."

"Sunday's my day off."

"Mine, too."

"Twelve o'clock?"

"Okay."

"You won't stand me up will you?"

Cathy parted her lips and looked worried. "Stand you up?" she asked.

"Yeah."

"Who stood you up?"

"Oh, some girl." Frank squinted down at the pavement.

"I'm sorry, Frank," Cathy said.

"I'm over it now. But it hurts, you know?" He looked at her. "Has it happened to you?"

Cathy thought about this for a moment, then nodded. Frank broke into a half smile. "Hey, your name," he said. "I got carried away. First things first, right? What's your name?"

"Cathy."

"That's nice. Cathy. I like it."

"Cathy Bennett," she said. "I changed it. It used to be Cathy Benû." She watched Frank's face to see if he'd change his expression. "Well, you're entitled," he said. When he smiled all the way, he had dimples.

May 6, 1982
Lucy Hastings Clinic
Princeton, New Jersey

11

BOXING W/ PAPA

ON MAY 15, 1982—a clear, blue day, created for a coronation—
Ellery McQueen was released from the psychiatric clinic, where her
mind had held her captive for months. She was released into the
hands of a chauffeur of a limousine, especially hired by her, for
her, to drive her to Aunt Sydna's home in Darien, Connecticut.

Ellery sat alone in the back seat of the limousine and wrote as if
she were a court stenographer, taking down the utterances of sworn
witnesses. She wrote down the color and the type of upholstery
("flagstone-slate blue, in a type of artificial suede") and a description
of the flat green land they passed, which was looking extra green,
because it was the month of May. She wrote about the dogwood in
bloom inside the pine woods and a cardinal she saw in flight.

She wrote on lined paper and kept her margins wide. She wrote,
"I have stage fright. I have opening-night jitters. . . ." She wrote

against the impending moment when she would have to pay the limousine driver and step out at Sydna's porte-cochere and see the truth in Sydna's eyes that she, Ellery, was still someone who needed careful overseeing.

"This is a victory?" she wrote. She wasn't going *home*, she wrote, she was going to *Aunt Sydna's* home, to stay there for two or three weeks. Home, it had been determined, was a bad place for her to go to. Home was where she'd had the breakdown. Home was where the key tucked inside her pocket fit. Home was where some things resided that she'd rather never have to see again—and she wondered, as she sat in the slate-blue back seat of the hired limousine, if anyone had had the good sense to go in and remove those things for her. Of course, she knew, no one could ever *do* something like that for her—no one could think for her, or breathe for her, or write these things for her. She was alone.

There were things in her apartment that in the months before her breakdown had loomed up larger than they could ever have been in real life—her tape cassette, for instance. She would sometimes find her tape cassette inside the toaster-oven, and she'd put it back where it belonged, and then she'd find it inside her bureau drawer or in the closet, or—when things had started getting very, very bad— she'd climb onto a New York City bus and find her tape cassette already there, saving her a window seat. No one could see the tape cassette or hear the tape that it kept playing, except Ellery. No one could know that things in her apartment were being rearranged while she was out—rearranged the way that Mavis would have liked them.

Later she had learned, she had been brought to understand, that she alone had terrorized herself—that one part of a self, *her*self, had been in a revolt against the other. What frightened her now, what made her sit forward in the back seat of the limousine and write down every thought as it occurred to her, was the fear that her mental illness would come again, like a dive bomber out of the sun, or a vandal out of foreign hills, or a marauder on swift horseback at dawn. Whatever her illness had tried to prove to her in the first place, it might not have had the chance to prove, she feared. Whatever part of her had yielded to the illness in the first place might not be strong enough to keep her terror of herself at bay. This is why she wrote and kept on writing on lined paper w/ her margins wide.

"Writing is a mental exercise," she wrote. One cannot write, proceed to write, to set down in a logical way the details of a story from its beginning to its end, while one's mind is actively disintegrating, she believed. She believed that by writing she could gain control of a slippery existence. She believed in fairy tales and Santa Claus and that it had been necessary to invent them. She believed she had invented herself in a way that hadn't worked, a way that had broken down. Her writing, she wrote, was re-creation. "How I know who Belle was," she wrote, "is by thinking what I might have been if I'd been she." How she knows who *she* is, she wrote, is by not thinking about being like the others, *all* the others—Katharine Hepburn, Mata Hari, Harriet Tubman, Elizabeth I, Catherine of Siena, Greta Garbo, Gertrude Stein, the Virgin Mary, Saint Joan, Catherine de Médicis, Maria Theresa, Molly Pitcher, Barbara Fritchie, Betsy Ross, Clara Bow, Clara Barton, Henry James, Edith Wharton, Willa Cather, Sacajawea, Saint John the Divine, George Sand, George Eliot, George Washington, Emily Dickinson, Emily Brontë, Rasputin, Victor Hugo, Herman Melville, Hermann Hesse, Herman Wouk, Hemingway . . . Mavis.

Why was it, Ellery wondered on the day she was released, that when she wrote anything when she was younger, everybody told her to stop trying to follow in her mother's footsteps? Stories are where we need to *go*, she wrote, when we're alone and need to make the possibilities more intimate. It doesn't matter that the stories aren't true, they're our metaphors for our existence—stories about men and women, but especially stories about women, are the metaphors we use for our existence, on which we must rely, on which we must rely as much as we rely on what our mothers taught us. "What did my mother ever teach me?" Ellery wrote. "How to dress, how to be a bitch on wheels, how to be neurotic, how to order from a menu and insult the waiter. She was a mystery writer for all of her adult life, but she never wrote a word that could start to help unravel the mystery that was me. I can pretend that I am Belle and Faye and Cathy—pretend, for the sake of the story, that I can feel and think what they might feel and think (I'm an *actress*, after all). But to be Aunt Sydna, one must have been born in 1909 and gone to work for Franklin Roosevelt when one was twenty-five years old. To be Aunt Sydna, one must be steeped in liberal politics and Old World manners; one must know *exactly* who one is and one must stand

and sit and move w/ absolutely no accommodation to any higher authority. I don't know how to be like that," Ellery wrote. "The Truth about Aunt Sydna is The Person of Aunt Sydna, and the only way for me to get it down is to take it down, word for word, exactly, at its source."

Along Main Street in Darien, Connecticut, Ellery asked the driver to stop in front of an audio appliance store. There was a tape cassette recorder in the window just like the one in her apartment on West Tenth Street. She went into the store and picked it up, turned it over and looked closely at it, the way one looks at the relic of a former civilization. It didn't whisper to her, and she felt a little surge of optimism. She chose a compact, professional-looking, portable cassette-recorder w/ a shoulder strap and a long cord for the mike, and a dozen high-quality low-static blank magnetic tapes. The man in the store seemed to be amused by her. She paid w/ a credit card and owing to the dollar amount of the purchase, the credit card company would not approve the sale unless Ellery could show identification, because the card had been inactive for five months. Ellery produced her driver's license, which had her picture on it, and the man didn't mention to the credit card company that it had expired three months before. "You want some tapes?" he asked, wrapping up the items. "We got taped music. Talking Heads. The Waitresses. Men at Work. You like Men at Work?"

"Oh, no, thank you," Ellery said. "I bought this because I'm going to do an interview w/ someone."

"Oh yeah?" he said. "For radio?"

"No, I'm a writer," Ellery said. It was the first time she had called herself a writer. It sounded true.

"A writer, heh?"

"Yes."

"What kind of writing does a person do who looks like you?" he asked. "Don't tell me," he said. "You work for *Rolling Stone*."

He thought he was being very funny.

[The following transcript is an excerpt from a conversation Ellery had w/ Aunt Sydna on May 15, 1982. It was taped while they were sitting, sipping sherry at sunset, on Aunt Sydna's veranda.]

SYDNA GARRITY INGRES: No, I never went to a psychiatrist. My dear!

Freud thought all women have penis envy lodged in the unconscious—can you imagine someone as extreme as me talking with a
Freudian? Out of the question! I would be thought to have some
massive penis envy lodged back there in my unconscious like some
massive bit of *peanut* in a molar!

ELLERY McQUEEN: Did Mavis ever go to a psychiatrist?

SGI: No. I can't imagine that she would.

EMcQ: How did Mavis learn to write?

SGI: Her books? The School of Life, I would imagine—with a sop
to Oxford on the way. We were *all* overachievers, dear, all us girls.
All Lower-Class, us Garritys. Not "O.C.D." Mavis was the one of
us who tried the hardest to forget it.

EMcQ: "O.C.D."?

SGI: "Our Class, Dear." We were not "Our Class, Dear." In Pitts-
burgh, I understand, they say "N.O.S." That stands for "Not Our
Sort." We were all very *nice* girls, you understand, and certainly
very *bright*, God knows, and *educated*, but the truth is we were
never "O.C.D." Our mother, God forbid, was positively common.

EMcQ: Tell me about her.

SGI: Who, dear?

EMcQ: Grammar.

SGI: Oh, "Grammar," "Gritty," "Dy," "Tick-Tock . . ." We all
had different names for her but *c'est tout la même chose*: "The Old
Bitch." What do you want to know?

EMcQ: About her. Who she was.

SGI: Well, I don't *know* . . . Gritty. Let me see . . . Gritty: She
was a glutton. Individuals vanished around her. I understand there
is a new discovery now in planetary science called a black hole.
That's what she was, emotionally. A collapsed mass of an *enormous*
gravity. We would have easily disappeared within her, had we not
fought her off so waywardly. Well, Jahnna did disappear within her,
more or less . . . and Henrietta. Henrietta took over for us, as a
mother, after Gritty failed. I think we really have to say Henny was
the "good" daughter among us. . . . Gritty, let me see: I suppose if
she'd *any* sense of humor whatsoever she might have ended up like
Harry Truman. You remember Harry Truman, darling. No-Two-
Ways-about-It-Harry? I liked Harry because he reminded me of my

mother and everything I could never adore about her, but which I found most *vilifying* in a man. The man had the aplomb, dear, of a bull turd. *God*, I cannot fathom men. When Frank Roosevelt set me onto State in 1937 I said to him, "Look here, I think there's something you ought to know—I don't understand the first thing about what makes men tick. I can't make deals with them. I can't, for one thing, figure out why they don't understand us. . . ."

Well, this was very late at night, which is the time when Frank did most of his chatty, more interesting business. We were in his office, on the ground floor. He was smoking, and he smiled at me around that damn oral pacifier he never outgrew, and he leaned back and he said, "Why, Syd, whatever do you mean?" You know, lamb, I think I won my first posting to government because Frank Roosevelt liked to have a girl there in her twenties that he could call "Syd." *No one* will ever call me "Syd" again, my dear. I don't imagine anyone but me, though, would have dared to call Mrs. Roosevelt "Roo," either. The first time I called her that, my God, she drew herself up and said, "I beg your pardon. Why did you call me that?" "You have a face right out of A. A. Milne," I told her. Anyway, I *amused* Frank. Eleanor allowed me to believe I was of *use*; but with Frank I was a *woman*. He was pixilated toward me. . . .

EMcQ: You changed the subject, you know. You were going to tell me about Gritty—

SGI: Yes, I did. It's called negotiating.

EMcQ: What did you do in government?

SGI: I was a spy. All women are spies.

EMcQ: Gritty. Was she a spy?

SGI: Oh, my dear, she was the *ultimate* of spies. She was Orwellian.

EMcQ: Why did you measure her?

SGI: What?

EMcQ: At her funeral. Why did you take her out and measure her?

SGI: *Measure* her? My dear, who told you *that*? We wanted to make sure she was *dead*. I think it was Jahnny's idea first . . . let me remember, yes. We were all sitting around, the four of us, where were we? At the Hay-Adams, yes. We hadn't gone back to my house in Georgetown. We were sitting there in the bar—my *God*, we had fun at Gritty's funeral—we were sitting there, all four of us, and

Jahnny was wearing this most ridiculous *hat*. Jahnny had always
been very strange, walking out on airplane wings, and all of that.
Where she got this hat, I've no idea. Let me paint the picture: it
looked as if a porcelain cachepot had upended on her head, catching
a ruffled grouse beneath it, in display. In addition to which, mind
you, it had a *veil*, a *black* veil, which was redundant, darling, because
Jahnny's face always looked shady to begin with. Mavis was in a
state of blind envy with regard to this hat; need I describe to you?
Mavis was wearing some bitter-pill affair, as was Henny, of course,
who never wore hats well, owing to her squat neck. Jahnna's hat,
however, was penultimate to Jahnna's *hatpin*, which was an instrument for shish-kebabbing if there ever was one—an extraordinary
hypodermic needle with a large bejeweled kebab at one end, much
like a turkey baster. Well, we were lolling about the bar in the Hay-
Adams, feeling, I imagine, all quite orphaned, and out of the blue
Jahnny said, "I wonder if the old bitch is really dead." Well, we
tossed this off as one of those morose disputations that occur on such
occasions as a family death, and, as I recall, we went on drinking.
Soon thereafter, though, Jahnny said again, "I wonder if the old
bitch is really dead," and she reached up and extracted her skewer
and held it up before us, where it gleamed, you understand, in the
low barroom light and, well, we are not *dull*, us Garrity girls, it
does not require a river barge to nudge suggestion across our prow,
so Mavis, bless her bones, said, "Let's do it . . . if she *doesn't* bleed,
we'll know she's still alive!" Oh, God . . . I think we had to climb
in through the goddam window, and Henny, child, Henny was built
for the *commedia dell'arte*, if you recall—buffa, Henny was. Well,
what a scene. There was simply nothing diabolical about it, at all.
We stuck a hatpin in her. . . . I have to bring myself up short these
days, just thinking I'm the only one of us who's left. . . . I thought
it most particularly despicable of you, Ellery, that you didn't go to
Mavis on her deathbed,
EMcQ: I know you did.
SGI: I never inquired as to why.
EMcQ: I couldn't.
SGI: Some pressing engagement?
EMcQ: I didn't like Mavis, Aunt Sydna. I still don't.
SGI: That is very stupid of you, kitten.

EMcQ: Why? You didn't like your mother, either.

SGI: Mavis wasn't Gritty.

EMcQ: And I'm not you. You wouldn't have wanted Mavis for a mother, let me tell you—

SGI: We none of us are offered mothers we deserve. Who would you have wanted, lamb? Mother Teresa? You would have had to share her with the *poor*. . . . She never would have been at *home*. The point is, we adapt.

EMcQ: I *have* adapted. Mavis did a lot of damage, Sydna, you don't know about—

SGI: Oh, cock and shit and balls, Ellery. Mavis was a scintillating woman. A crackling intelligence . . .

EMcQ: That may be true, but—

SGI: *May* be true?

EMcQ: —she had no great gift as a mother.

SGI: So you condemn her as a *person*?

EMcQ: Who else could? I'm her only daughter—

SGI: Oh, there are plenty of others, I imagine. . . . Critics. There are always critics. Lovers. Neighbors. God knows. Mavis was my favorite sister, have I told you that? I miss her as much as I miss Betts. Betts was my life-mate, but Betts and I did not go *back*. Mavis and I went *back*, *all* the way back, all the way back to Grand Rapids, Michigan, and that farmhouse in the middle of the field. You can't understand this, I'm sure, since, as you say, you are an only daughter. . . .

EMcQ: Maybe that permits me to understand it more poignantly, Aunt Sydna.

SGI: Perhaps it does. . . .

EMcQ: Why was Mavis your favorite sister?

SGI: Oh, that goes back. That goes way back, lamb.

EMcQ: Tell me.

SGI: Well . . . I suppose I should. It's a story, actually, something that happened long ago when we were both still girls. You can add it to your trove of stories—

EMcQ: Is it true?

SGI: Of course it's true!

EMcQ: The stories that I'm writing aren't always true—I get the facts mixed up. Dates, and things—things occurring at a time when they couldn't possibly occur—I wrote this long, long story about Belle when I was in the clinic, and I needed a reason why she had to live w/ Lucy that one year—do you remember?—instead of w/ Max, so I just moved the start of the Spanish Civil War back three years.

SGI: What year was this?

EMcQ: In '33.

SGI: That might have been the year Max had that torrid love affair with that *Persian* woman—his "Islamic Calligraphy Period" . . . I believe they date that to '33. Max was always so *relevant, n'est-ce-pas?* What with everything going on in Germany in '33, he was in thrall to *Islamic Calligraphy.* . . . Were you really ignorant of when the war began in Spain?

EMcQ: Oh, no, I knew it. I just thought there was something more important.

SGI: And what was that, pray tell?

EMcQ: Belle. Her life. Who she was. What made her do the things she did—just as you asked me why I didn't go see Mavis when she was dying. Why didn't I do that? You wanted an answer. I want answers, so I write these stories—

SGI: I take it this tape recorder means you're verifying answers?

EMcQ: Yes. I have two more stories that I'm going to write. One about you, and one last one about Iris.

SGI: But not you? Not a story about Ellery? I would like to read these stories, lamb. I would like to see if they are not in actuality stories about Ellery. . . . Your mother was very dear to me, my dear. She was possessed of a quality I am going to try to explain to you, a quality that made her my favorite sister . . . but first I want to say to you—and don't fly in my face about this, chicken—you are the very *soul* of Mavis, as a daughter. I'm sure that rankles, kitten, and it shouldn't. You asked me why she was my favorite sister, and I'd like to tell you. She was—I have to say this carefully, you understand, I have to choose my words most carefully, because I *do* want you to understand—Mavis was the first person in my life to touch my heart, from her example. Do you know that feeling,

Ellery? Someone whose actions touch you, change you, by his or her example. Great men and women have it, the truly great. Frank Roosevelt had it in plus fours—"Roo" had it, Gandhi had it; Mountbatten didn't have it, neither did Picasso. I'm not suggesting my sister was by any standards a great woman—what I'm saying is that when we were both still girls way back in Michigan, she did something one night that touched my life in the way that I'm describing, by example, and I will never forget it—I mean, God knows, we may rest assured I'll never forget it at *this* advanced stage of my dotage, if I've kept the memory so bright these sixty years. It happened one night sixty-two years ago, in 1920—I know the year, because it happened the same week that Papa died.

EMcQ: Papa?

SGI: John Shaw Ellery Garrity, F.O.U.A. . . .

EMcQ: F.O.—?

SGI: "Father Of Us All," darling. Jack Shaw, he was called—or J.G. We called him Papa. He called Mavis and me "The Tail End Twins." I don't believe I ever heard him call Jahnna or Henrietta or Willy anything other than "girl": "Girl, pass the meat plate this way. . . . Watch where you're walking, girl. . . ." He was in and out of the house like a hornet—furious when roused and in a frenzied state to be set free. I believe he spoke to me six or seven times that I clearly remember. I was ten years old when he died, so you'd think I could remember if he'd spoken to me. He was taciturn. He avoided every one of us, but Mavis. She was the baby. He was a drunk, of course, you knew that. . . .

EMcQ: Yes.

SGI: Took the Cold Sleep the winter of '19 and '20. You know what the Cold Sleep is, don't you, dear?

EMcQ: It's death.

SGI: Oh, not just death, dear heart. It's when you take a bottle of your favorite whiskey with you and go walking in the woods at night in winter. It's very peaceful. No one ever knows. You drink until you pass out, just as if you've gone to sleep. And then you freeze to death. No one really knows if you were drunk or sober, sober and depressed, careless or truly suicidal. Gritty had a policy on him— well, *seven* life insurance policies on him—and only four of them panned out, owing to the circumstances. The great lament was that she hadn't found him out there in the woods herself, or else you can be sure she would have gotten rid of every trace of alcohol within a mile of his poor frozen corpse. No, Mr. Hofstaeder found him with an empty half-gallon jug of applejack beside him. Gritty always said she would have made out better if she'd killed him. I suppose she was referring to her beneficial interest in the life insurance policies, but, God knows, she could have been referring to her holy war on men and . . . oh, God! . . . her holy war on alcohol. I imagine she's turning over in her Pentecostal Heaven right now from the *whiff* of all this sherry, darling—rain or shine, in peacetime and in war, Gritty was a champion of enforced teetotalism. Bovril and barley tea were her chief stimulants, except on rare occasions when she might indulge herself a cup of cocoa—very heady stuff. To this day I cannot fathom how or why Gritty and Jack Shaw ever married. Henny compiled a genealogy once, when she was still in college— I believe I have a copy of it somewhere. Gritty's name was Clintock, and her people came from western Pennsylvania. Jack Shaw was second-generation Irish. We were never certain where they met or how—they took those ecstasies and tender moments, if there ever had been any, with them to their graves. I don't recall what Papa looked like. . . .

You'll forgive these peregrinations of an old woman's mind, El-lery—I am extremely sharp on most things to begin with, but recently I've found I can elicit very early memories with alarming vividness and detail. Betts lost it, you know—my darling Betts. Near the end I had to dress her and undress her—she had lost all knowl-edge of what clothes were for; lost all appropriateness, all sense of connection with the self. Near the end, Jahnna and Mavis drove out to visit her and we four had been chatting for a while, when Betts asked me to come with her alone into the kitchen. Well, she took me by the arm and led me practically out into the yard before she said, "Who *are* these women? Are they *family?*" Well, darling, Betts had known Jahnny and Mavis for thirty years! "Betts, dear," I said, "It's Jahnny and Mavis, our sisters—Mavis has driven all the way from New York City to see you. . . ." "Our *sisters?*" Betts said. "Really? Even the *fat* one?" Well, you know, Jahnny and Mave were never *fat*. God knows what Betts had meant to say instead of *fat*. Maybe she meant pretty, or tall, but she had lost her knowledge of the use of words. I could see words lifting from her, sometimes, like pollen, as she sat right there in that chair. I can see her quite clearly. But the bonus, at my age, is to have these memories of long ago—things that go way back—come to visit me, without my begging. They were mine, you see, from the beginning, these memories. They were always mine, God knows, they were my *life*, but now they have returned to me with a new freshness. . . .

I was upstairs yesterday in the room you're staying in—I had gone up to air the room and change the counterpane—and I suppose it was my thinking about your staying here with me and about these misfortunes that you've borne up to and about the way I always felt—will always feel, child—watching you walk out onto a stage . . . Forgive me, chicken, it's not my habit to be so sentimental—it must be the weather and the sherry, wouldn't you agree? But I would like to tell you what a *fillip* you have always been to me, what a brave little number, like your mother. I was upstairs there, turning out the counterpane, when this vision—a memory—occurred to me. We were seated in the kitchen of the farmhouse—Gritty, Willy, Jahnna, Henrietta, Mavis and myself—and Papa came in. He had that excitement clinging to him, as he always had, that turbulence of out-of-doors in wintry weather.

I could see his entrance to that room as clearly as I see you sitting here right now. I felt I could reach over and touch Willy, whom I haven't seen in sixty years. I could see the sunlight on the table, I could smell the meal we were about to eat.

I could feel the tension emanate from Gritty, the hostility, the furtive glances between my sisters. Papa had been away two weeks, on one of his bouts. Then, there he was, all of a sudden, unannounced—unwanted, really. The three oldest of us—Willa, Jahnny, Henrietta—had already come to hate these entrances of his. I was ambivalent. I was one of his "Tail End Twins," after all—the two he had created in his folly, in his *rut*. . . . Mavis *adored* him. She was the baby in the family—there were four whole years between us; we weren't "twins" at all—well, she adored him. Up jumped Mavis from the table that afternoon, and ran to him. Out went Papa's hand—it was a ritual. She positively bowled him over with her affection. Out comes Papa's hand, like this, flat up against

Mavis's forehead, holding her at reach. He couldn't say two words to her, really—he couldn't play with her, except for this ritual: "Let's see you box," he said.

Round and round the kitchen he would dodge from her, his hand like this, upon her forehead, so she couldn't reach him, and she'd box—good God, child, you should have seen your little mother throw her punches. . . . She was seven years old that year. All the rest of us sat in stony silence. But Mavis wasn't going to let him get away, even though he held her at arm's reach . . . even though he taunted her. God knows what might have happened as she grew up, between the two of them, had he not taken the Cold Sleep that year. I don't think he was a suicide. God knows. I think he was a careless drunk. I like to think he wandered out to watch a comet. . . . who knows? He died.

Mave and I were sleeping in the kitchen that year, in a bed beside the stove—after Willa left, we all changed rooms and Henrietta slept in Papa's place with Gritty. Well, the night I want to tell you about—this would have been a night that winter of 1919–20—Mave and I were sleeping in the kitchen, and I woke up to discover Mave had gotten out of bed. She had the habit—she is rolling over somewhere in her Cecil Beaton heaven, at my telling you—Mave had the habit, when she was very young, of needing to relieve her kidneys in the night; the *cold* will do that to you, don't you find? Rather than brave the cold trek to the outside loo, Mave would trundle off to Henny's side of Henny's and Jahnny's bed—Henny slept like a *log*, mind you, and would welcome any warm thing in: kittens, chickens, bed lice, goslings. . . . Mave would hitch her nightshirt up and slip in next to Henny and *relieve* herself, then trundle back down to the kitchen. *I* knew this, of course, because I've always slept as lightly as a feather and I would wake each time that nature called on Mavis—but poor Henny! *Henny* lived in shameful consternation that she suffered from a nightly problem *way* beyond control, until she moved in bed with Gritty; then it stopped. *Years* later she told me and Mavis that fear of some reprisal from the Old Bitch had finally cured a problem that she'd had in younger years over a certain *incontinence*, and Mave and I both rolled our eyes and sympathized with her. . . . Well, we were scamps. We always were. Mavis, especially.

After a while, on this one night after Papa died, when Mave hadn't come back to bed, I went up to Henny's room to look for her. Grief had not been something that we'd been allowed. We'd hardly known him, anyway, but that week that Papa died, Gritty was business-as-usual. She had a funeral to which creditors and fallen women came, and we were to cast our eyes down, but not mourn. A *pity* seemed to be the circumstance in review—but not a *tragedy*. Well, Mave was very proper. She kept looking up at us repeatedly, as if for a cue, her clue to what was happening. But nothing . . . not a word was spoken. We never talked, you know, among ourselves, unless we were *way* out in the field, or in the barn; not even there, we serfs lived in that fiefdom that was Gritty, she was everywhere. . . . So that one night Mavis had gotten out of bed I looked for her in Henny's room, in Willa's—she was nowhere to be found. There was a shed beside the house, before the barn, where Gritty kept old Peg, our cow . . . but I didn't find her there, either.

It was very dark that night, no stars, but there was snow along the ground, and God knows by then I knew my way across that paddock to that barn in any weather. I couldn't take a light, because of Gritty. I came up on the barn and slipped in through the doors. The hinges were rusted, and we girls had a way of slipping in between the barn doors sideways, without making a sound, so Gritty wouldn't know that we were in there. As soon as I was in, I heard the rustling. There was a stall along the back wall where the blacksmith worked, and where we brought our broodmares in to foal. It was a large stall, twice the size of all the others, and the bedding was kept clean. I heard a rustling noise amid the bedding, and I called out in a whisper, "Mave?" There was a lantern on a hook inside the door, and a box of matches on the shelf above it. I remember I was frightened as I felt around to light the lantern. I remember hearing the sound of straw rustling, as if something were burrowing in it . . . and I heard the sound of labored breathing—like a sheep, or like our cow with rheum. I took the lantern down and lighted it, and I could see the door of the far stall ajar. Then I saw the shadows she was making on the rafters and the walls and . . . then . . . I saw your mother boxing. She was in her nightshirt, and her hair was damp with perspiration. She was boxing, boxing . . . she was finally going to *pommel* him, don't you understand, with her next punch. I stood there, unable to speak for quite a while. Finally I said, "Who's winning, Mave?" She turned around and looked at me, and to this very day I see her face. *"He* is," she said. And then she kept on boxing, didn't she?

[The sound stops here. The tape runs on until it ends, in silence.]

12

CAT AND THE CRADLE

A STORY ABOUT IRIS AND HER DAUGHTERS
BY ELLERY MCQUEEN

AT NIGHT, one sees the family house from an approach along the state road going west, because Iris keeps the lights on in the upstairs windows. By day, one notices the house from both directions, because it sits in such a way that the house and the rolling land it is on look like a cradle.

The land is meadowland cleared from the pine forest, and it curves beneath the house as wooden staves curve underneath a rocker. Behind the house, there is another, rougher meadow, where oak seedlings start; and behind that, there are woods of oak and pine and beech and many dogwoods. When the dogwoods are in bloom in May, their ivory blossoms glimmer through the leaves like sunlight on green water. Beyond the dogwoods and the oaks and pine, across a stretch of dune, there is the ocean, where the sun and moon come up. From the house, one can hear the surf at night through the upstairs bedroom windows. In July one can hear the foghorns near the channel markers.

The house is cedar shingle on a stone foundation w/ a gabled roof of slate. It looks protecting and protected, sturdy, warm, inviting, beautiful. It is a house that, owing to the way that it was first constructed, and aided by the hands of others through the years, elicits from the passer-by a wish to stop, to pause, to transfer one's own life to there.

It was first built as a stable on a large farm on the point, but through the years the farmland changed, and after thirty years the building was converted to a dairy. The present kitchen used to be the room where cheese was made. The cheese was mostly Cheddar, but the farm was known to sell some Cheshire, too, and some pepati and Trappist types made w/ the milk from neighbors' goats. The cheese was stored in wheels on racks in what is now the furnace room. Upstairs, in what was once the hayloft, barn doors open at each end, under the gables. In the summer, there's a good cross breeze when both barn doors are open, and the bedroom drapes are redolent w/ summer fragrance from the meadows and the garden.

The house sits near the road on the front third of the meadow at the end of a curved sand-and-gravel driveway. A strip of grass grows down the center of the driveway and escaped grape hyacinths bloom there in spring. The climate is damp and cool, and one can have a flower garden of the English cottage type w/ good results. Roses like it here, and heaths. The loose, sandy soil is good for herbs, but lettuce goes to rust, and the damp and fog in midsummer are too cruel for corn. Peas do well, and kale, and all the tubers. English ivy, the small deep green variety w/ shiny leaves, grows unchecked here in natural domination over all else. There is pachysandra, too, and clematis; but it's the ivy in its full expanse on the steep side of the house that stops the passer-by. The tendrils creep through the crevices of the window sills and slip between the shingles, and the ivy spills upward, like a tide across the roof, each summer. Hap and Iris try to turn it back each spring and fall by trimming off the shoots.

The ivy covers all the ground-floor windows except in the kitchen. The kitchen windows face the road and were a late addition. All the other windows on the ground floor are the small rectangular inventions common to horse barns, placed high up in the walls, like portholes, to provide ventilation. The view through these tiny

ivy-covered windows is much the same as looking out upon the
world from a squirrel's hollow. Spiders, living in the ivy, come inside
to hibernate in the fall. In late summer, because of the dampness
held in the outside wall by the ivy, a thin fungus breeds along the
northeast wall inside the house, and the fungus, multiplied by spores,
dusts the old oak furniture and the leather shoes and all the books.
Sometimes the fog comes in the upstairs bedroom window through
the makeshift screens on the loft doors. Sometimes at night in summer Iris and Hap can see fog drifting, ghostlike, through their bedroom.

The house is cool and damp and hard to heat and no one w/out
a sense of poetry would live in it. One must bend down to get onto
the stairway going upstairs to the master bedroom in the loft. The
kitchen has a brick floor set in earth, that is always cold. The furnace
and the oil burner sit in the middle of the downstairs. There are
quirks and crannies, as there are in any house, but Hap and Iris
have been making love upstairs looking out across the meadow at
the moon for so many years that neither one would ever think of
parting from the place. Or rather, Iris wouldn't.

The kids sleep downstairs, each w/ her own room. Lise has the
smaller but the brighter room beneath the stairs that looks out on
the fenced-in English garden. Mole, or Molly, has the larger room,
next to the shed, w/out a garden window.

The kids each have their duties. Lise is twelve, and she's in charge
of waking Mole for school each morning and for keeping the downstairs bathroom clean. Lise also maintains their full supply of fresh-
squeezed orange juice and is the sole custodian of the Veg-a-Matic.
Mole feeds the cats, folds the laundry and makes custard. She makes
the best egg custard on Long Island, far better than her mother's,
and she's only five-and-a-half years old. Hap believes it is a gift that
Mole was born w/ or else it's all in separating eggs w/ chubby fingers.
Mole has very chubby fingers. Everybody else has thin, sophisticated
hands, but Mole's are fleshy. That puts Mole in charge of lending
the finger for tying bows at Christmas and for writing on the insides
of car windows when it's raining. If they lived on a flood plain,
Mole would be the one in charge of keeping tight the water wall.

The kids are expected to transfer all insects, except ticks and
mosquitoes, to the outside of the house, alive. They are expected
to shun potato chips and refined sugars. Mole is expected to wear

Lise's leftover clothes. They are expected to behave impeccably outside their home and moderately well w/in. They have been trained for nothing in particular except daily life in a moral experiment and for sustaining intimacy w/ someone who loves them but who cannot be w/ them for much of the time.

Hap works at sea. Hap's heart has these two shores.

When Hap is home, he walks Lise and Molly to their school buses in the morning and he walks out to greet them when they come home in the afternoon. He reads to them and sits w/ Lise while she does her homework. He gives Molly back rubs and tells her stories, and he comes down in the middle of the night if he thinks he's heard them cry out in their dreams. But then he's gone, and what he does while he's away and where he goes remain a mystery to his daughters. Then for three of four weeks after that he's home again. And then he's gone. And then he's home—and the rhythm of his coming and his going has gone on like this for years, like tides.

Lise hates this rhythm Hap's job has set up w/in the house.

Lise remembers a time before the Mole was born when things weren't like this—a time when she and Hap and Iris lived on Martha's Vineyard all alone. They lived in the white house w/ the red roof at the Coast Guard Light Station on West Chop, and Lise went to nursery school at the Island Children's School in the Inter-Agency Motor pool van w/ the seal of the United States Government on it. "Seal" was one of the first words she learned that had several meanings; "seal" and "light" and "deck" and "leaves"—as in *shore* leaves. There were other words that had two meanings, too, when they were spoken: "sea" and "see," and "sail" and "sale," and "plane" and "plain"—but most words Lise learned as a child were "sea" words. Her sense of how to talk about all things was formed by these "sea" words and by the acts of weather she saw effecting changes in the shore, and in one's course, and in one's balance.

When they were living on Martha's Vineyard, Lise had the bedroom in the house behind the Coast Guard Light Station, and she could see the light sweep out across the water as she lay in bed about to go to sleep, and she could hear the motor that turned the reflector lamp that guided the boats in from Woods Hole and New Bedford. She could hear the foghorn on the Nobska Light across the Sound; and Hap was home w/ her and Iris every night. He went fishing w/

her on his days off and he told her stories about the Indians who lived along the coastal waters, and he told her tales about men's great historic love for sea adventure. Then there was trouble, something about a war somewhere and about the Coast Guardsmen being called up, and it might have been because of that that she and Hap and Iris had to move to New London, Connecticut, to a garden apartment, far away from all of Lise's friends. Then they moved to Patchogue, a place that Lise had trouble spelling, to a walk-up in a bigger building; and Hap left the Coast Guard for a while to steer a tug. Then Lise remembered hearing more talk between Hap and Iris about money and buying their own house, and soon after that they moved to this old barn out on the point on Long Island, and the first year they were there there wasn't any furnace, and the next year they were there, they didn't have a car, and the year after that Mole was born and Hap came home one day wearing a Coast Guard uniform and took Lise to her room in private and talked to her and told her he'd be going out for three or four weeks at a time, this time, and that he was counting on her. He was counting on her to run a tight ship and to help her mother, Hap said. Molly couldn't be counted on at all. Lise was older; Lise was his "first mate." Molly was too young to understand. W/out her help, Molly might sink, just like an egg sinks when you try to float it on the water.

This made Lise angrier than she could ever say.

Lise had never been a crybaby, or the kind of girl who whines for things, as she knew some girls did. She'd never asked her parents for anything, not even when her heart was breaking out of want for her own pony. She'd grown up accepting things and not complaining—not like Mole, who made a fuss when she was overheated, and got cranky on long car trips. Lise had parted from best friends three times and never let her mother or her father see her cry. Now Hap was asking her to help them out again, asking her for her cooperation, and all the while exempting Mole. It made Lise angry at herself that she didn't have the way Mole had of using something in herself to get her own way. She couldn't be the way the Mole was, ever, even if somebody paid her. She felt her way was better; still, Molly had the favored position, her father's backing, so to speak, because she was the younger of the two and Hap would always think of her as being weaker. Molly was a grave intrusion on the way that Lise could be w/ both her parents. Even since the Mole was born, if Lise ever let her guard down, if she cried or threw a tantrum, her parents accused her of behavior fit for Molly. Ever since the Mole was born, Lise had lost her hegemony on childishness w/in the family. Not adult, and not the only child, she cast about between extremes and called upon a background woven of "sea" words and seeded through w/ the magic of deep waters, for her balance.

Lise believes that in the balance of all things, she had been touched by chance to exercise a special power.

The special power Lise believes she owns comes from a perfectly round, white stone that fell to her out of the sky six years ago, when she was the same age as Mole is now. The stone fell from the sky on a sunny day when she was walking near the beach w/ Hap. Hap was holding Lise's hand in his as they walked, and Lise was walking w/ her head down, because the sun was bright, and because when she walked w/ her head down, sometimes she found money. Hap said, "Look there, sweetie, that's a front off the horizon."

"A front?" Lise said, looking up.

Hap was pointing at a line of clouds, way off.

"Means rain," he said.

Lise squinted at the clouds.

"A front of what?" she asked.

"A front of weather," Hap explained.

"Weather has a *front*?" Lise asked.

"And a behind," Hap said. "And a top and bottom, too, which you have to think about if you're an airline pilot."

"*I'm* not an airline pilot," Lise protested.

"I mean, people who *are* airline pilots have to think about it."

"Oh," Lise said.

She tilted her head all the way back and squinted straight up to try to see the top of weather, but what she saw were two gulls careening through the sky above her head. Hap said, "He's got something," meaning the smaller of the two gulls, who was being hectored by the larger one.

Lise could see the smaller gull had something in its beak. "They're playing keep-away," she said.

"No, the little one's got food," Hap said.

"No, I think they're playing, Daddy," Lise advised him.

She watched the gulls soaring, the smaller the quicker of the two. It looped-the-loop and rose and swooped and seemed to stand dead still on thin air to allow the larger gull to catch it, then it opened up its beak as if to laugh, and the object of their game fell out of the sky and landed just in front of Lise.

She was so startled for a minute that she didn't run to pick it up. Then Hap said, "Let's go see what the commotion was about, shall we?"

Lise ran ahead of him and leaned over to look at it: it was a perfectly round, white stone.

"Well, I'll be," Hap said.

He leaned down next to her.

"I'll bet it's magic," he said, trying to make her smile.

Lise was always very serious.

"Really?" she said.

"I'm sure of it."

She stared at the stone, afraid to touch it. It might burn her fingers off, she thought.

"Stones like these that fall out of the sky are always magic," Hap said. "Of course, I've known of only two or three in my entire lifetime. . . . This make four."

"In your entire lifetime?" Lise said. "Wow!"

Hap pressed his lips together to keep himself from smiling. Lise was staring at the little stone as if she had been asked to make a drawing of it.

"A stone like this has special powers," Hap said.

Lise looked at him.

"A stone like this," he said, "grants wishes."

"Wishes?" Lise asked.

Hap nodded.

"Any wishes?"

"Big ones," Hap told her. "Giant ones. The kinds of wishes that are good for more than just one person."

"Not selfish wishes, then," Lise said.

"Not selfish wishes," Hap concurred.

Lise put her finger out and touched the stone. It wasn't hot at all and she closed her hand around it.

"When it rains tonight—I'm pretty sure this is a Raining Stone—hold it in your hand under your pillow and make a wish," Hap said. "But only when it's raining, Lise," he added.

It rained that night, but Lise was too afraid to use the magic stone.

She hid it inside a sock in her bottom dresser drawer and she didn't dare to take it out and put it underneath her pillow for fear some thought might leap out of her head, unwittingly, and start a wish. She thought about the stone while she was in school, and she thought about it before she went to bed and she thought about it every time she thought about how much she'd like a pony. A pony seemed the sort of thing that might be counted as a giant wish, but Lise was not that certain that a pony would be good for everyone. "Could we use a pony?" she asked Iris.

"Could we *use* one?" Iris said.

"To go to town and do our errands," Lise suggested.

"In Patchogue? That would be lovely, wouldn't it? A pony and a pony cart trailing ribbons . . . We'd have to find a place to keep him, though."

On the first night of rain after that, Lise took the magic stone out of the drawer. She held it in her fist under her pillow and she closed her eyes and wished, "Bring us a pony and a pony cart and a big farmhouse where we could live and keep him." She didn't think it was appropriate to add a "please"or "thank you." Good witches, or even bad ones for that matter, never added "please" or "thank you" in the stories that she'd read. She was concerned that Hap had not given the instructions right. She could follow the instructions, so long as someone gave them right.

Soon after Lise had made her wish, they drove out to the Point one weekend w/ a realtor and looked at houses that were up for sale, and Lise was so excited she kept standing on one foot and then the other until Iris asked her, "Do you need a bathroom?" When the realtor showed them the old barn w/ the ivy growing up one side, Lise knew her wish was coming true. "You like this place better than the others, don't you?" Hap asked her.

"Yes."

"So do I." He took her hand. Lise smiled up at him and she felt very proud that she had wished a wish that pleased her parents. But what she didn't know and what she slowly came to learn was that a secret power has such charm that it attracts unlikely possibilities— sometimes things one doesn't wish for fix themselves to one's desire. When they moved into the house she didn't get a pony after all; she got a sister.

Lise didn't use the stone again for six years. When she thought about it she thought about it as "that stupid stone." She avoided opening her bottom drawer, even though she'd pushed the stone way back and pretended to forget about it. She pretended not to miss having a pony and not to mind when Hap went back to working for the Coast Guard. Her new best friends had fathers who were home each night, and Lise pretended not to envy them. Missing Hap became an island Lise would sail to when she wanted a vacation from her daily life. If Daddy were home, she would allow herself to think, the Mole would never get away w/ all the things she does. If Hap were home, everything would be different, including Iris, who worried too much about everybody else, particularly Molly.

Three weeks ago, Lise took out the stone. She hadn't used it in six years, but this time, she determined, nothing would go wrong. She used it on a night of gentle rain, and she held it carefully between both palms in an attitude of praying and she wished Hap wouldn't come and go the way he did. She wished it right out loud. She used the words "please" and "thank you" this time and she wished, "Please make it so Daddy doesn't come and go, thank you." She knew this was a giant kind of wish, the kind that would do good for others. She was confident she'd done it right this time—but she didn't take into account the witch's joke, the reason witches laugh hornswoggled laughs. Hap left the house. He packed his bag and left two weeks ago, and each night since then Lise has heard her mother crying. Lise gets out of bed and starts upstairs but stops and sits down on the second step because she fears she knows the reason Hap has left and it's too terrible for her to talk about.

When Hap was home, he used to make a breakfast tray w/ coffee and warm milk and take it up to Iris in the morning. Lise and Molly would come up and find Hap sitting at the foot of the big bed while Iris drank her coffee, propped against the pillows. Hap used to put his hands around Iris's feet beneath the blankets and Lise and Molly would climb up on the bed and joke w/ them, and Lise liked to pretend the bed w/ just them on it was a floating raft on a big river. It was safe, when Hap was home. Now that he is gone, Lise knows her mother is unhappy, so this morning she makes up a tray to take to Iris. She puts a linen place mat on the tray. She makes a pitcher of some heated milk and puts out one of Iris's café-au-lait cups, big as soup bowls, that Iris bought in Paris sixteen years ago. She fills another pitcher w/ some coffee that she makes from adding boiling water to the coffee grounds. The coffee looks like rusty water. There are colonies of brown grounds floating in it.

"It doesn't look right," Lise says, setting the tray in front of Iris. Iris tells her it was sweet of her to go to so much trouble.

"Would you like the curtains open?" Lise asks, and Iris nods. W/ the daylight in the room, Lise sees how young and small her mother looks. Maybe it's because she hasn't seen her in the bed alone since Hap has left, Lise thinks. She thinks she'd like to sit down on the bed the way Hap used to, but she feels it's not her right.

"Is the Mole up?" Iris asks, ignoring the pot of coffee and pouring warm milk from the other pitcher into her breakfast cup. Lise takes this as a clear proof of her failure.

"Molly says she's not getting up this morning. She says she's never getting up."

"Well, I'll go down and see what I can do."

"She's being nasty," Lise submits.

"I think we need to be a little understanding—"

"Well, I don't stay in bed. She doesn't have to act the way she does. I don't want to be a little understanding."

"Obviously not. What do you want me to do about it, Lise?"

"You could talk to us."

"I do."

"Not about the thing that's most important."

"You mean about what's going to happen to us now?"

"I mean why this already happened."

"I don't know, Lise." Iris leans her head back on the pillow, and Lise can see a vein pulse in her mother's neck.

"Maybe someone wished it," Lise says.

"Do you mean me?"

"No!"

"Sometimes I think I must have wished it."

"Is that the reason why you cry?"

"You hear me?"

"Yes."

"I'm sorry." Iris turns her face away and stares at the bedside clock. Lise can see the vein pulse, and it makes her think of the hole in Molly's head when she was born. Iris said it was a soft spot and that Lise couldn't touch her sister there until it closed, but Lise was sure it was a hole in Molly's head that was unique to her. She couldn't imagine other babies being born w/ it. It worried her unreasonably. She sat and stared for hours at the pulsing soft spot on her sister's head. She couldn't believe that babies could be born both ignorant and frail. It seemed to her a great flaw in the planning.

"You hear me crying," Iris says, "because I can't sleep through the night. I keep waking up at three o'clock. It's always the same time each morning, no matter what I do." She touches the bedside clock w/ her right hand. "On our first date, Daddy tried to teach me semaphore. We were in a Chinese restaurant in New York City, and the Chinese must have thought that he was crazy. He put his arms out like this, you know, and said, 'The arms at three o'clock are Juliet. The alphabet is Alpha, Bravo, Charlie, Delta, Echo, Foxtrot, Golf, Hotel, India, Juliet, so on, so on, Victor, Whiskey, X-Ray, Yankee, Zulu. Alpha means, "I am undergoing a speed trial." ' Can you imagine telling someone this on a first date? 'Bravo means, "I am taking on and discharging dangerous goods." Charlie means, "Affirmative." But Juliet, Juliet means, "I am going to send a message now by semaphore." ' The hands at three o'clock mean, 'I am going to send a message by semaphore. . . .' Every morning when I get awake I look over at the clock and I see the hands pointing like this and then I start thinking about the first date in the Chinese restaurant. . . ."

"I wished Daddy away. It was an accident. I made him go."

"You couldn't have."

"I did. I have a magic power."

"Lisey, you're being silly."

"I have a wishing stone. Downstairs. I made the Mole be born, too, wishing for a pony. . . ."

"Lisey, stop this. Mole was born because Daddy and I planned for her, and Daddy went away because he wants to be with someone else."

The color comes real fast to Lise's face. "Who? Another lady?"

"Yes."

"You mean like sleep with?"

"Where did you learn that?"

"On TV, where do you think? Does he love her?"

"Lisey, listen—"

"Does she have kids?"

"She's no one real. She's an idea Daddy has, someone he thinks about all the time. She may even be me—"

"That's dumb." Lise turns away from Iris. She stands before the long draped windows and looks out on the meadow. "All Daddy ever thinks about is himself," she says. She strikes the windowpane.

"Stop this," Iris tells her. "You're acting like a baby."

"I am a baby!"

"No, you're not. You're twelve years old. Come on. You're running late for school." Iris glances at the clock, then quickly turns her glance away. "Thank you for the coffee," she tells Lise.

"It wasn't as good as Daddy makes," Lise says.

"No," Iris agrees. "It wasn't."

Lise takes the breakfast tray and starts downstairs.

"Don't throw the milk away," Iris reminds her.

"It's got a skin on it," Lise says.

"I know, but we can use it. I can feed it to the cats."

"*Mole's* cats," Lise says. She takes the tray downstairs and leaves the cup of warm milk and the pitcher on the counter and she pours the coffee down the drain. The coffee grounds resemble wet peat moss, she notices. Iris comes down the stairs and goes to Molly's room. Lise follows and stands in Molly's doorway and watches them. Mole is still in bed. She's pulled the sheet up to her nose so just her eyes are showing and she says she's never going to budge. When she talks, the sheet goes up and down where her mouth is hidden. "I had a dream," she says.

Iris sits down on the bed. Beneath the bedcovers Lise can see Mole wriggling her feet around. Mole is acting very serious, and there's an air of urgency in her room. "Tell Lise to get out of my room!" Mole says.

Iris looks at Lise. "Okay, I'm leaving," Lise says. She slips around the corner. When she is out of sight, Mole says, "I dreamed Domino is dead."

Iris strokes her legs beneath the sheet. "He's not, Mole, you know he goes off tomcatting awhile."

"Never this long."

"Sure he has. This is nothing. How long has it been?"

"Two weeks. Since Daddy left."

"Well, it's not unusual. He's been gone this long before."

"He's dead," Mole says. "I know he's dead. I saw him in my dream, and he was white and you could see through him and he was floating out across the meadow. Then he got big and he floated up over the house. The house was shaped like a cradle. Then he disappeared to heaven, and his paws were out like *this*. I know it was Domino, too, 'cause he had double toes."

She falls silent. The telling of the dream has agitated her.

"I know he's dead out there in the meadow. We should go out and find him."

Iris nods. "First we should go to school," she says.

"You don't care!"

"I do care. Dreams should be trusted. We'll go look for him this afternoon."

"*You* go look for him right now!" Mole's tone is nasty.

"All right, Molly," Iris answers. "No more of this. Get out of bed. Get dressed. I'll start your breakfast. After you've left for school I'll go out and look."

Iris goes to the kitchen and fills the coffeepot w/ cold tap water. The pot slips from her hand and clatters in the sink because her hands are shaking. She senses someone behind her, and she turns around and jumps. "Mole, don't sneak up on people in the kitchen," she warns.

"If you find him, wait till I get home before you bury him."

"That's fair. But I don't think I'll find him. I think he has a girl friend somewhere."

"And I don't want you waiting with me at the bus. I want to do it by myself. Everyone makes fun of me."

"I'm sorry, Mole. I didn't know."

"I can cross myself," Mole says. "I'm not a baby." She leaves as soundlessly as she came in.

When she comes back, she's dressed for school and she eats her scrambled egg in silence. Lise comes in the kitchen w/ her hair still wet from her shower. "I'll be home late," she tells Iris. "I have field hockey after school."

"Okay," Iris says absently. "Mole had a bad dream about Domino."

Mole jumps to her feet. "Don't talk about it to her!"

"See what I mean?" Lise asks Iris pointedly. Iris hands Lise's lunch bag to her. "I hope you gave me something good today," Lise adds.

"Nobody cares anything about the cats around here except me!"

"Mole, what is your *problem* this morning?"

"You make me *sick*, Lise."

"You *are* sick, Mole. You've got a *hole* in your head underneath your hair that's *this* big and spiders crawl inside your brain while you're asleep and there's nothing in there any more but spongy mess and spider babies—"

"So what! Everybody says you're ugly!"

"Oh, sure, but no one says I'm stupid—"

"I'm not stupid!"

"Oh, no, mush brains are real smart."

"Stop it, both of you!" says Iris.

"I wish I didn't have to live with you!" Mole shouts at Lise.

"Then don't! Go live at someone else's house and see if I care!" Lise shouts back.

"Stop this both of you right now and go get ready."

"I wish you were dead!" Molly yells at Lise. "I wish you would run away! I wish you'd run away instead of Daddy!"

Iris picks up the geranium pot from the window sill and hurls it on the floor. The pot shatters, and the soil spills out, and the roots lie twisted and exposed. She grabs a pot of chives and throws it on the floor. She grabs another flowerpot of herbs and tosses it and then she takes a pot for each one of her daughters to throw and she bangs one down in front of Molly and she thrusts the other one at Lise. Lise takes a backward step. When Iris leaves the room, Lise looks at Molly and begins to cry.

Lise finds Iris standing in the driveway, staring at the house, when she comes outside to catch her bus. "What are you looking at?" she asks.

"Oh, all this ivy . . . You know, I really think I better get the ladder out and start to trim it back. And while I'm at it, I think I better take the screens down and start to put the storm windows up."

"But Daddy always does that."

"Well, now we do." She looks at Lise. "You'll hold the ladder."

Soon after Lise leaves, Mole comes out. Iris says, "You're early, Mole. It's chilly. Want to wait inside?"

"I'm dressed good and warm."

"You still want to wait yourself?" Iris asks her.

"Yep."

"Okay. Well, so long."

"So long."

Iris goes inside the house and walks into the kitchen. She conceals herself behind a window and watches Mole walk down the sand-and-gravel driveway to the road. She watches Mole lean down and tie her shoe. She watches Mole stand up, look both ways, look again and dash across the road. She watches Mole stand w/ her lunch bag in one hand beneath the chestnut tree, waiting for the bus. On other mornings they'd be playing word games or just talking about news. The whole time they'd be looking at the house. The house would be there safe and solid every morning, day after day. Today it looks as if Mole is staring at the sand beneath her shoes. As Iris watches, she thinks of other chores she'll have to learn to do—the grass needs cutting one more time before the frost; an anchor line on the antenna has torn loose in a storm; the furnace should be cleaned, the windows caulked. . . . She loses sight of Mole. She sees Mole's feet move off down the road; then she can't see her. Suddenly she hears the screech of tires on the pavement. She hears the horn. She runs through the house, thinking in these fifteen years she's never had to signal him on ship-to-shore and all she's got to go on now is this strange woman's phone number scribbled on a piece of paper as an afterthought when he was leaving.

Outside, across the road, Molly calls, "Mommy, Mommy, he came back!"

She holds Domino up in both hands, and Iris sees he's lost so much weight he seems to be floating. The driver of the car calls, "Sorry, lady, he ran right out in front of me. . . ." Mole crosses the road and sets the cat down in the driveway. Her bus comes and before she climbs aboard she turns to Iris and waves. "So long, Mommy," she shouts. "I love you!"

In the driveway, Domino stops and licks himself. Iris watches the bus go down the road; then she picks up Domino and cradles him. "Hello, old friend," she says. She looks toward the house. "What would you say to a breakfast of warm milk?"

May 22, 1982
Aunt Sydna's House
Darien, Connecticut

13

TAKE THIS WOMAN

THE SUN CAME UP at Sydna's house that first Sunday in June as if it were a screen credit for a movie titled *Scooter's Wedding*.

Six women, who had been awake all night, saw the sunrise through the windows in the kitchen, and one of them, who had secretly wanted to be an astronaut, announced, "We have sunrise, we have sunrise: we are All Systems Go. . . ."

The caterer had put in an appearance three days before with his honor guard of three vans and a station wagon. While his crew set up the tables in the yellow tent out on the lawn, he took a glass of wine with Millie, Faye, Ellery and Sydna in Sydna's kitchen. The forecast for the weekend was excellent, he said, and by the way, he felt he ought to mention that he had discovered, much to his chagrin, that his original estimate was off a little, by a couple of thousand dollars.

"How many thousands?" Faye had asked.

"Two maybe. Maybe three," he had confessed.

Faye looked at Millie, who looked at Ellery, who bounced a knowing glance off Sydna.

"Well, it's recession," he submitted.

"Recession," Faye repeated. "How much has Scooter paid already?"

"Oh, a small deposit, fifteen hundred. She said there'd be a hundred and fifty people and I gave her a price of forty dollars a person without booze. The booze is going to be at least another twenty per. Champagne, you know. And then there's liquor setups and a flat rate on the tables and the place settings, and I have to pay my people and make a little something for myself. I figure I can bring it in for close to fifteen thousand. That's a hundred per guest," he said. "That's pretty cheap."

"It's highway robbery, my dear, is what it is," Sydna responded. "I suppose you think you have us by the—what is that expression that's in vogue now, Millie, the one that sounds like 'little rabbits'?"

"*Short hairs*," the caterer put in, then blushed the color of a fresh tomato aspic.

The women smiled benevolently. "I don't suppose you have the contract with you?" Sydna inquired.

"Well, ah, she didn't sign," he said.

"She didn't *sign*?" asked Sydna.

"I didn't draw one up."

"Oh, *quelle dommage*," said Millie.

"Yes, what a shame," Sydna concurred. "But that provided you your *out*, I would suppose?"

"Well, no, I never thought of it that way. . . ."

It was a simple matter, really, to negotiate from there, and in the end the women drank a toast to Sydna. Apprenticeship administering the Marshall Plan had clearly taught the woman something—Scoot would get the waiters and the tables and the rented crockery for a mere two thousand dollars, the liquor would be ordered from a discount store; and Ellery, Cathy, Millie, Faye and Sydna would do all the cooking. The wedding cake they left to Iris.

Scoot, God knows, was in a rampant state of ire. "It's *my* wedding!"

she complained. "I can't believe this! How could you do this to me? It's going to be so *tacky!* What are you going to make? There's only *three days!* What can you make? *Cathy* can't make anything! People come to someone's fancy wedding, they don't eat *potato chips!*"

"Well, *homemade,*" Cathy said.

Scoot began to gasp for air. She cried for two solid days. She stopped crying, finally, on Saturday night, because Millie told her if she didn't stop her eyes would look too puffy for the wedding pictures. It was bad enough she'd dropped six pounds in a siege of tummy upset these last two weeks. It was just her luck, too, she lamented, that she'd lost it all across the titties, a whole cup size. She'd thought she had a good half decade left within her prime, but now it seemed that all at once she'd be both married *and* flat-chested. It was a crime. Soon, no doubt, she'd get blue veins in her legs like Faye and liver spots like Sydna and stretch marks like the women in cheap porno magazines. It was depressing.

On the morning of the wedding, Scoot descended the back stairs to the kitchen in her bare feet. Her toenails were painted orange to match her freckles, and her hair was bound around a dozen plastic coils to make it bouncy. She was wearing a lime-green kimono with pink camellias painted on it, and as she sank into a kitchen chair next to an hors d'oeuvres tray, she was a riot of alarming color set around a too-pale face. She looked from tray to tray of toast rounds with shrimp paste, toast rounds with green mayonnaise and pimento, toast rounds with a Cheddar spread, and her eyes took on a look of desultory anguish. The sight of baked ham, smoked turkey, mussels vinaigrette and Belgian endive seemed to move her to despair against the superficial debris, the *de trop,* of upper-middle-class tradition— or so Ellery thought, until Scoot breathed a little sigh and said, "I think I'm going to upchuck."

"Great—that and catshit are the two things Cathy hasn't spread on toast rounds yet," said Millie.

"My toast rounds look *pretty,*" Cathy said.

"They look like Fabergé jar lids," Millie said. She looked at Ellery. "Did I say that?" she asked. Ellery smiled. Millie had been the one who had kept them awake, away from exhaustion, through the night. She'd hauled Sydna's Magnavox record player into the kitchen sometime after midnight and done some Tokyo Rose patter for them between scratchy selections from Sydna's vintage forties collection. The latest phonograph record Sydna owned was a Walter Cronkite narration of *You Are There* at the signing of the Magna Charta, which someone, maybe Ellery, had given her one year at Christmas. Millie insisted that they listen to it so they could all relive the way they learned about men in history from other men, and then, surpassing even that obnoxiousness, sometime around three o'clock in the morning when everyone showed signs of flagging, she played Frankie Laine's rendition of the song "Mule Train" eight times. Thereafter, around four-fifteen, all six of them became extremely silly, and when Millie put on a Mills Brothers record and the Mills Brothers started to sing the first verse of "Try a Little Tenderness" and they all heard the lyrics, "She may be weary / Women do get weary / Wearing the same old dress," Iris started laughing at the words, and then they all started laughing at the words, until, long after the record ended, they were so infected with delirium that all they had to do was point to some benign and passive object like *Aunt Sydna's apron* and they'd double over with renewed hilarity.

The night had passed as nights of intimacy pass, when time takes on supernal sweetness and one's senses—touch, sight, smell and intuition—are rewarded all at once, in unity . . . or so it seemed to Ellery. It seemed that she belonged no more or less to this family of women than her cousins did—she was no more or less on the outside or alone than any one of them, than any woman is, or any man, from any sense of family. She felt belonged to and she felt surprisingly assured that someone someday would find her loving and irresistible to love. She wished that she could feel assured that way for all the women in her family—for Millie and for Faye and for Iris, especially—but she couldn't. Cathy had her new beau, Frank, whose attentions seemed to make her less bizarre. But Scoot: what Scoot was doing, getting married, was not so much inscrutable fate as it was fulfillment of a loan. Scoot had a borrowed outlook on life that went from cradle to grave via the installment plan. There were probably two million Scoots just in Connecticut alone, thought Ellery. God knows how many more there were in Texas and on Long Island. God knows what one would find in California. . . .

"Can't someone pay attention?" Scoot complained.

"To what?" Millie asked.

"To *me*."

"Oh, sorry."

"I feel upchucky," Scoot repeated.

"You do look pale," Faye told her.

"Maybe she thinks if she turns white enough everyone will think she's still a virgin," Millie said, but Scoot's lips went pale and her complexion looked like tofu, so Faye went over to her and forced her head down toward her knees and told her to breathe deeply.

Sydna said, "Just nerves," and Iris ran a towel under cold water and placed it on Scoot's neck. "Don't get my hair too wet," Scoot cautioned her.

"I think you ought to have some breakfast," Faye suggested. She knelt down in front of Scoot and looked at her. "Would you let me make you a little breakfast?" she asked.

Scoot hesitated. "Like what?" she asked.

Cathy said, "Have some toast, there's plenty."

"How 'bout shirred eggs?" Faye offered. "Some nice shirred eggs with cream and a dry English muffin . . ."

"Well," Scoot said.

Faye took her by the arm and led her toward the living room. "You just lie down in here and let us pamper you," she said, and Millie threw a Spanish olive at her.

"I have to talk to Sydna," Scooter said.

"When you've had breakfast," Faye insisted.

"But I have to talk to Sydna, it's important—"

"Later," Faye said, and led her out.

When the door closed, Sydna said, "Remind me, chickens—" holding up a firm tomato she was trimming to resemble a red rose— "remind me *not* to wonder what we're thinking."

"I'm not thinking anything," Cathy assured her.

"Please, God," Iris started praying, "if there is a God . . ."

"Scoot's dumb, but she's not that dumb," Ellery submitted.

"Putz," Millie said, "I'll lay you odds she is, right, Syd?"

Sydna turned toward Millie and her hand froze in the action she was making, and it seemed to Ellery that with the yellow morning light around her she looked very young. Ellery remembered Sydna telling her that no one but Frank Roosevelt had ever called her Syd. She remembered, too, how Sydna looked when she had told her that—the way she'd thrust her chin out and thrown her head back slightly with some pride. Now Sydna looked at Millie, toward whom she'd never expressed much fondness, and she said with what Ellery understood to be amusement, "Right as ever, Milicent." Then she looked at Ellery and smiled.

Sydna had been briefing for the role of "Father of the Bride" for five days in advance, and she had said to Ellery at least a half a dozen times during this last week, "Well, just thank God for William Powell." She was not a giddy woman, but she became quite giddy trying to decide how she should walk, how she should crook her arm exactly, in the fulfillment of a role traditionally held by a man. Ellery had never known Sydna to be so girlish, or so vain. "I think I should simply walk beside her, what do you think?" she asked Ellery. "I think my offering my arm would be in poor taste, don't you? The two of us should never touch, exactly. I mean, God knows, I hardly know the child, although I must say I'm very pleased. Not about Raymond, of course. I'm very pleased about just giving her away. Perhaps we should have done it earlier, when she was three or four. . . ."

Scooter had dictated the design of all their dresses, but Sydna had held forth for a distinguished pearl-gray floor-length dress that she already owned. Scooter suggested Sydna wear a man's white linen suit, and Sydna had said that in the first place, she had never worn men's clothes, and in the second place, that if that's what Scooter wanted, she should find someone like Sydney Greenstreet for the ceremony. Sydna said she'd rather walk Scoot down the aisle with a parrot on her shoulder than dress up in men's clothing, but Scoot said that was weird. Scoot had never heard of any people who had included birds in their wedding ceremonies except people who got married in places where there were pigeons outside churches as soon as everybody threw rice, and other people, mostly Italians, who put live doves inside a wedding cake. "Who would want to eat a cake that had live doves living in it?" she asked. And anyway: what if you cut into the cake and found out the birds had died? That would ruin a marriage right there, in her opinion. Besides, Raymond was allergic to bird feathers and had to sleep on foam-rubber pillows and wear parkas that were fiber-filled. So parrots were definitely out of the question, she told Sydna; but by the time she'd made the point about the parrot, Sydna had forgotten how or why she'd mentioned it in the first place. She told Ellery that the only reason she could tolerate even a casual exchange with Scooter was that she'd once been very fond of Gracie Allen. To really get on Sydna's nerves, Ellery had asked, "Who's Gracie Allen?"

By ten o'clock on the morning of the wedding, a group of people that Scooter called "the music people" had arrived to set up amps and mikes, and speakers in the willow trees; "the flower people" had come with garlands of honeysuckle and tea roses for the tent and buckets of lily of the valley and French lilac for the tables. Mr. Rick, "the hairdo person," came to braid the bride's and bridesmaids' hair with violets and baby's breath, and when, twisting her hair into a plaited chignon, he accidentally touched the nape of Ellery's neck, she had to force herself to think of something as dumb and stolid as a hairbrush or a Wednesday to keep herself from thinking about human touch and tenderness and weddings. Two women in pink smocks who worked for Mr. Rick did their make-up and made everyone look gorgeous and made up, except Millie, whom no one except herself knew how to make up without making her look slatternly. Both Lise and Molly watched the women being made up with wide, attentive eyes, even though Lise pretended an indifference and Molly knocked a box of facial powder on the floor.

Scoot was dressed by noon, an hour before the wedding march was expected to start, and she sent word from her room along an upstairs corridor that she would like to have a word with Sydna alone before the wedding. When Sydna entered the room, she was struck, despite herself, by Scooter's fresh loveliness. Perhaps all brides look lovely, Sydna thought. She said, "Am I to make a ritualistic speech?"

"I'm sorry?" Scooter asked. She was standing very still, so the flowers in her headdress wouldn't wilt. She was trying not to breathe or sweat.

"About your honeymoon?" Sydna prompted. "Surely you're not ignorant of sex. . . ."

"Me?" Scooter asked.

"We *are* alone?" Sydna tried to verify.

"Well, actually," Scoot said.

She looked at Sydna and tried to be persuasive without moving. This wasn't easy, because Scoot does not possess a stimulative mind. "I want to try to get them back together. So does he," she said.

Sydna placed a passive hand on a pearl button on her pearl-gray dress and drew a breath. Speaking to Scooter, she considered, was much facilitated by grasping onto something. A walking stick, if offered at this moment, she thought, would seem a special boon.

"What are we trying to discuss, exactly?" she asked Scooter.

"Hap. And Iris. You know," Scooter said.

"I *know*?" Sydna reiterated.

Scooter sort of turned, the way a marionette might turn, and called, "You can come out now!" as if this were a game. And then to underscore the sense that Sydna felt that this was hide-and-seek, Hap stepped from the bathroom dressed ridiculously, Sydna thought, like a virgin admiral, in a uniform whiter than the bride's dress. Sydna saluted him, and Hap, clearly embarrassed, removed his cap. He mumbled something like, "It's good to see you, Sydna."

"You've caused my niece and grandnieces some unnecessary pain, I understand," Sydna accosted him.

"I have," he said.

"What are your intentions?"

Hap looked at her. "To be a husband and a lover to my wife," he said. "To be a father and a teacher to my daughters."

"Pigeonshit," said Sydna.

She looked around. It occurred to her that the last person she'd put up for the night in this particular bedroom in her house had been a friend of Betts's, a nun, who had later been killed in El Salvador. "I know something about love," she said.

"I know you do," Hap said, but not too quickly. "I think we always liked each other because we knew how much the other knew."

"You think that, do you?"

"Yes."

"Well, I don't care too much for your kind right now," she admitted.

"What kind do you figure is my kind right now, Aunt Sydna?" Hap asked.

She assessed him. "The current kind," she said. She looked at Scooter. "Does Iris know?"

"No."

"Who knows?"

"Us three. And Raymond."

Only then did Sydna understand what Scooter had in mind, and she smiled and shook her head and said, "I trust it's not because I wouldn't wear the linen suit?"

"It's not," Scoot said. She didn't smile, because she couldn't take the chance she might get lipstick on her teeth, but she nearly fell over backwards anyway when Sydna said, "Amazing child," and walked right up and kissed her.

At one o'clock the organ broke into a minor march by Richard Wagner and Molly started down the aisle, throwing rose petals directly at invited guests. She sort of slung the petals out like someone feeding slop to hogs. Lise, behind her, clenched her teeth and wished to God that she were dead, or that most people wouldn't know Mole was her sister. Cathy came down the aisle after Lise, and her bridesmaid's dress kept falling off one shoulder. Ellery came next, then Millie and Faye, and then Iris in a different kind of dress to identify her as matron of honor. The next thing that happened was that Faye whispered, "Sydna," and Millie and Ellery saw Aunt Sydna slide into the aisle seat in the bride's first row. Iris didn't notice because she was trying to make Molly look at her to get the Mole to stop swinging her flower basket around in rhythm to the music. Then, unaccountably, the Mole did stop and broke into a grin. The organist played the first four notes of the wedding march from *Lohengrin*, and Mole brought her gloved hand up in front of her face and wiggled her fingers in a wave and moved her eyebrows up and down and called, "Hi, Daddy!"

Iris turned around and saw her sister, resplendent as a bride, escorted down the aisle by her own husband. Hap was in his summer whites with all his braid, and he looked as young and beautiful as that first summer when she'd met him. Iris heard Millie whisper, "Holy Christ," beside her and she took hold of Millie's hand and squeezed it while she bit her lip and tried to keep herself from buckling. When Scoot drew near her, she looked at Iris and smiled real wide and said "Hi!" as if she were home from a long vacation. Faye and Ellery and Millie, watching this a few steps away, were mesmerized. Cathy, standing next to Lise, expressed everyone's stupidity when she said, "Hey, Lisey, it's your Dad."

Hap stood next to Raymond as best man, and through the ceremony all the women watched as Iris and Hap began to exchange silent glances, silent vows. Ellery has no specific memory of the ceremony until Raymond lifted Scooter's veil and kissed her. The music started playing very loudly, but beneath its sound Ellery heard Millie say to Faye, "Well, I came fourteen times, how 'bout yourself?" After Raymond kissed her, Scooter turned around and kissed Iris. Then Scoot went up the aisle with Raymond, and Iris went up the aisle with Hap, and Millie went up the aisle with some friend of Raymond's who sells packaging for TV shows, and Ellery found herself hanging on the arm of a guy she was supposed to know, but didn't, who said, "What was *that* about?" Ellery smiled and whispered, "*Family.*"

Hours later she was standing by herself under the tree of heaven on a grassy knoll behind the house beyond the yellow wedding tent. The guests were seated and the wedding cake was being readied in the kitchen and the speeches were about to begin and the dinner had proceeded perfectly and everything had been splendiferous and she had walked up here alone to get her breath. She saw Cathy come out of the house and catch sight of her, and she watched as she came up the hill. "What's up?" Cathy asked.

"Not much," Ellery said.

"What are you doing?"

"Looking." Ellery motioned toward the yellow tent.

Cathy looked at all the tables with all the people and the one big table along one side where all the family sat, with Scoot and Raymond in the middle.

"Why?" Cathy asked.

"I want to make a picture of it in my mind."

"Why?"

"I want to keep it."

Cathy squinted down the grassy slope at all the bright colors and the people laughing and talking and having a good time.

"What are you going to do now, Ellery?" she asked.

"I don't know. What are you going to do now, Cath?"

"I don't know. I guess I'll stay at the museum. I'd like to quit, but I don't think I can. I mean, the pay is good for someone like me, but I can't stand the people."

"Yeah, people are a hazard," Ellery agreed. "I guess if I were going to choose a job just on the basis of the kind of people it attracts, the only place to be would be the circus."

She smiled at Cathy and took her hand, and they started down the short grassy hill together. Cathy had left her shoes somewhere, and Ellery noticed for the first time that she was barefoot. Suddenly, in one of those shifts in the explicable, Ellery became aware of the aroma of the grass, of the intense colors in the sunlight and the sounds of voices, and she felt palpably frightened that it was all about to end, the way she felt the final night of a performance. She put her arm around Cathy's shoulders as if she needed to hold on to her a little longer, and then, in lieu of masking her emotion, she said, "You've put on some weight, kiddo."

Cathy shrugged and said, "Frank's got me eating better. We go to games a lot, and I eat hot dogs and a lot of peanuts."

In the tent, the dinner service had been cleared and Hap was going to make a speech honoring the newlyweds. Ellery sat down between Faye and Millie and put an arm around each one of them. She felt as if they were about to say good-bye, which was ridiculous. She heard someone down the table tell Sydna what a perfect spot this was on the lawn for a wedding reception, and she heard Sydna say, "Thank you—it is lush, isn't it? We're right over the septic tank." Ellery felt as if she should say "Thank you for being so funny" or "I love you" or "You helped me through my mourning"; but instead, when the bottles of champagne arrived in preparation for Hap's toast, Ellery said, "I think we deserve the first toast, what do you say?" She poured champagne for Sydna, Iris, Cathy, Faye and Millie and herself and said, "To us—" Before they had a chance to raise their glasses, there was the sound of someone tapping a spoon against a drinking glass and standing up and calling, "Yoo-hoo!"

Ellery saw Scooter smooth her veil back and announce, "I know this is out of order, but before Hap starts the speeches and we all get too carried away, Raymond and I have a little announcement we want to make. . . ."

Ellery looked at Millie, and they raised their glasses to each other, and they didn't drink but held each other's gaze awhile. Ellery thought to herself that the lessons in such moments are the things that mothers need to tell their daughters, but then she sat back and heard Scooter say, "We want you all to know that we didn't plan it this way, but, well, here goes. Do you want to tell them, Raymond? No? Oh, well. Guess what? *I'm pregnant, everybody!*"

The author wishes to acknowledge the following individuals who, by dint of being, were the inspirations of these stories:

Carol Carrick and Gay Nelson	"Separate Checks"
Allan G. Levine	"Millie and Hesh"
Carl Anderson	"Desk"
Carl Anderson	"Going Off Booze"
John Frederick Wiggins	"Boxing w/ Papa"
Lara Courtney Porzak	"Cat and the Cradle"

For anecdotal bits and pieces borrowed from real life, the author owes a debt to Lisa Detlefs, Darren Lobdell, Jim Higgins, Gisela Soldovieri, Elaine Markson and Cristofer Sitwell.

For legal advice on the trial of Belle Benû, thanks to Jay F. Rosenthal, Chief Deputy District Attorney of the Twelfth Judicial District, Otero County, New Mexico.

A special debt of gratitude to Mark S. Lender.